The Great Anti-American Novel

Daniel Della

H.H.B. Publishing, LLC

Paperback ISBN: 978-1-937648-15-2
EPUB ISBN: 978-1-937648-16-9
Kindle ISBN: 978-1-937648-17-6
PDF ISBN: 978-1-937648-18-3

This book is a work of fiction; all characters and events contained herein—even those based on real people and real events—are entirely fictional.

Published by H.H.B. Publishing, LLC
Henderson, Nevada

Manufactured in the United States of America

www.hhbpublishing.com

The
Great
Anti-
American
Novel

Ecce Homo—
"Behold The Man"

Iuventutis veho fortunas.—
"I bear the fortunes of my youth."

I don't mind, usually.

Inside of me are the remains of billions of super-novas from trillions of years ago.

Same with *them,* though.

Same with all of us, I guess.

Those thermonuclear supernova-sparkles in our blood and bones make us all special, I suppose. Or all not because whatever is all cannot be special, right? I admit that I feel special, at least.

They've got guns, though, so right now they're definitely specialer than I am, because bullets are made out of concentrated supernovas, and I'm largely just supernova goo.

Not only the bullets but also the iron bars and the grey cement floors and walls are concentrated, and the stainless-steel fences and barbed wire, and the streaking and hovering drones and the big missiles and tubes they've got.

There's some goo in the towers, but they're also specialer—they've got guns, too.

I've just got my goo.

1

Saint Fuck-All knows why the warden or the guards have decided to let me Write. Perhaps it's a chance for them to take my time while I tie my own noose? A prison manuscript, a confiscation, a backroom edit—maintaining my brainvoice but changing the don'ts into dos and the wouldn'ts into dids—then revealing it all to the New American goo, who would declare me kill-worthy, lending a supposedly democratic fulcrum to the evil machinations the corrupt Old Government goldbricks were aiming for all along—those nauseating, noxious parasites.

There are no books here! I know I deserve punishment, but I consider it cruel and unusual to be deprived, in my vast empty life, of all the great rivers of literature I could readily be indulging (or re-indulging) in to fill my vast empty present and future, but ages ago, in Old America, the Attorney-General stated that "Both 'cruel' and 'unusual' are merely a matter of perspective," and nobody who mattered made a peep, so there that went and stayed. Of course the few Muslim assholes still here at least got to keep their goddam *Koran*s—Arabic is a hideous language whether written in blades and hooks or hocked in my face—and yet I, the godless bibliophile, am not allowed to turn a single page except, evidently, these endlessly blank ones beneath my one good hand.

To quote a dead poet: "Small welcome to the days that lengthen life."

I suppose I'm fortunate now to even have this plump white stack sitting here rather perfectly representing the nothingness of my current purposeless existence. (In fact, was that the point, O Silent Facility Guard With The Nameplate "FRANKS," He Who Delivers Pencils And Paper Overnight? Well then here I am, Officer Metaphor, avidly stomping your hilarious burning bags of dogshit.)

Maybe I'm dead. Maybe I died at the conference and this is the afterlife I deserve—the existential

2

miscegenation of a denial of the freedom of action eternally coupled with a boundless freedom of thought: the mind always free, the body in offshore federal detention.

Have I been sent to my room to think about what I've done?

Very well, then; why not?

As long as I have this opportunity, and as long as the events keep surging through my mind like some sort of beloved, powerful drug anyway, I shall write down the notes, the ideas—the whole fucker—as best as I can.

And you might be able to say that I could include an entire bloated generation of humans in this growingly painted stack's list of *dramatis personae.*

Before I ended up here, my tremendous sister and I were two of the world's foremost information-gatherers and amateur assassins, so nearly every word of my story is based on the information she and I gathered in the years before I found myself here, feeling like poor Meursault on this hot, desolate, sandy, sun-glaring, Arab-filled island. Nevertheless, there are certain things she and I were not able to discover or verify, and those places—those missing shades of blue, you'll notice, Mr. Hume—have been colored in by me, myself, this guy, using an idea of everybody's trajectories as I understood them to serve as anchors for my necessary imagination-bridges. To that end, I draw an argument in my favor regarding such matters from Vietnam-veteran author Tim O'Brien, who masterfully showed us all that there's no such thing as a true war story, anyway. And if that's not enough, one of my heroes used to quote one of his heroes:

"Sometimes fiction is truer than the truth."

Finally, I never had the opportunity to speak at my "trial," during which I was heavily medicated. In fact, I don't remember the trial at all, but I've been repeatedly reassured that it happened, and seeing as how I never had any say, I say here's as good a place as any to state the truth of things as I understand them.

I don't doubt my guilt—I'm a monster—but I'm not the total monster most of the nation thinks I am.

PART ONE

De Oppresso Liber—
"Free From Having
Been Oppressed"

Contemptus Saeculi—
"Scorn For The Times"

Dennis Robert Justin was a mean son of a bitch who hated America.

When those around him laughed, he frowned, and *vice versa*—and to lonely young Mr. Justin it did not feel like contrarian enlightenment but despairing estrangement, made him feel angry sometimes and sad sometimes, but never content, never invested.

One chilly October morning, after a short, long life of toil on the family farm, at the enraged age of twenty-one, Mr. Justin honked the car horn twice, waited for the family to emerge at the front door, shot two middle fingers (an American cultural custom signifying the phrase "Go fuck yourselves") to his psychologically abusive mother, his physically abusive father, and his bullying, condescending, vicious older brothers, and he drove away in the piece of crap his father was always complaining about.

When he reached the Blunt River and the far town of Sweet Bend, a trading outpost on the edge of the forests of the Titan Mountains, he sold the car to the first stranger who could produce the meager asking price. As a rigorously moral young man he reasoned that he had worked on the family farm his entire life and had never been paid or given anything but scraps of food and entrees of grief, so he took a small severance package in the form of a car that was barely worth anything and loaded up on all the survival gear he could afford from its sale.

He piloted a small fishing boat upriver until he couldn't see any signs of civilization, until he found the natural bank where he grounded the boat and set out to live or die.

Comparable to how the Chinese word for "crisis" is also the Chinese word for "opportunity" (I don't know that for a fact, however, as I don't know Chinese; it's just something I heard once and liked), Mr. Justin's run into the wild could signify both "suicide attempt" and "life-starting attempt"—if he couldn't make a life alone work, there was no type of life for him at all, he figured.

Mr. Justin always minded, was his biggest problem. But it was the sort of problem that helped him a lot, too.

He had to learn how to survive on his own because he always minded so much what other people were about—he was always disappointed by their weaknesses, their cowardly decisions, and let them know it, and they didn't like being told that kind of truth.

Nobody likes being told that kind of truth except Mr. Justin, was Mr. Justin's problem. So he had to go because they weren't going anywhere.

He'd learned to fish when he was young, from another boy's father. Additionally, he'd just acquired a brand-new tent to keep the bugs out, and he'd also purchased nearly all the tools he'd been informed were essential if he were really serious about what he seemed to be serious about. Finally, he had two more must-haves: a stack of books on hunting and survival, and the deeply human need to learn and apply the information he read in those pages, in that tent, while the raindrops plopped on the taut fabric inches from his stuffy head.

The fed-up, desperate autodidact entered the forest.

A Parable
by Søren Kierkegaard

Let us imagine a pilot, and assume that he had passed every examination with distinction, but that he had not yet been at sea. Imagine him in a storm; he knows everything he ought to do, but he has not known before how terror grips the seafarer when the stars are lost in the blackness of night; he has not known the sense of impotence that comes when the pilot sees the wheel in his hand become a plaything for the waves; he has not known how the blood rushes to the head when one tries to make calculations at such a moment; in short, he has had no conception of the change that takes place in the knower when he has to apply his knowledge.

In the first year of Dennis Robert Justin's new life, he lost almost forty pounds—down to a feral, rib-counting, disturbing weight—and grew seven inches of tangled beard. He overcame two illnesses that nearly drove him back to the boat, downriver, to a hospital, but his immune system had fought them off, barely. And by the end of the first year, he knew he'd done it—he'd survived four seasons, and now all that was left was for him to survive more and grow better at it.

Eventually, though, he ran out of books to read and re-read, and that's when he discovered something important: He could more or less survive alone physically, but he needed new ideas to think about or he'd lose his sanity—he needed other people!

At first he tried to stubbornly muscle through it: no heading back on the boat, no matter what. But he eventually took his little aluminum tub back to Sweet Bend the day he found himself laughing at a joke that he believed had been told to him by a squirrel. (Squirrel: "Hey, D, you know how I know it's almost winter?" Mr. Justin: "I don't know—how do you know?" Squirrel holds up two acorns: "'Cause my nuts are *freezing!*")

He had to go back.

Once he made the decision, the agony abated, at least momentarily. He dug into the deepest pocket of his rucksack and pulled out what little money he had left over from selling the family's dirty shit. As he held it, he thought about how he had envisioned himself perhaps one day desperately using the paper money as tinder to start an emergent fire. And he chuckled to himself when he realized that indeed that's what he was going to use it for, kind of.

He dragged the boat to the Blunt, fitted the teeth of the rotor into the body of the river, and slowly plied those dark brown waters back to his leaping point, back to *it*.

His wild appearance clearly disturbed everyone in Sweet Bend who saw him, and they made their way across to the other side of the street, or they gawked as they drove by and described him to the people they were talking to on the other end of the line. A year of beard, and the gaze of a man who lived in the wild, literally Western-homeless, but not begging, and in fact putting on the air of a man who owned his feet and thus owned every inch of ground they found—the sight of such a woolly, dirty, unusual man would drive nearly anyone to the other side of the street, or into pedestrian-endangering, narrative description, Mr. Justin figured.

Unfortunately it wasn't only to be silent judgment, because a police cruiser pulled up and slowed down.

Mr. Justin gritted his teeth and kept walking.

"Can I help you, son?" the cop asked.

"Sure," Mr. Justin said and looked in the officer's beady eyes. "You can keep driving."

Mr. Justin had never met or seen a police officer he didn't consider a moron, a bully, and a coward.

The car stopped, and the cruiser's door opened and closed, and Mr. Justin heard the fat cop say, "Hey, you, stop!"

Mr. Justin stopped and turned.

"Something wrong, officer?"

"What're you doing on my streets, son? Ain't never seen your gnarled face 'round here before."

Mr. Justin shrugged indifferently and then looked at the cop curiously. "Am I under arrest or something?"

"Not yet."

Mr. Justin turned and walked away.

From behind, the cop called out, "You keep up

that attitude . . . you keep up the way things seem to be going for you, son, and you'll find yourself under worse than arrest—I guar'ntee it."

Mr. Justin said over his shoulder, "Same to you, officer."

The frustrated cop followed him in his cruiser—from a passive-aggressive distance—and watched while other Sweet Benders made their way across the street, revolted by the sight of the living dregs of American desperation and rugged individualism.

The woman at the book store might've been the most appalled of all. Just a moment after the door shut behind Mr. Justin with the second clanging of a bell, she was already speaking up.

"Jesus God!" she said. "Do you realize what you smell like?"

Mr. Justin, always the offended, never feeling himself to be the offender, shrank into himself when he self-consciously realized how truly disturbing he must be to the woman. "I'm very sorry, ma'am," he said. "I only intend to be here for a few minutes, and then I and my smell will go back to where I'm sure we'll further compound ourselves."

The offended, Miss Emily Thompson, owner of the bookstore Biblio-Files, expected the strange man to say almost anything but that.

"Who are you?" she asked, still disturbed but not as bad as at first.

"Dennis Justin," he said. "You sold me some books on survival and the outdoors a little more than a year ago."

Miss Thompson scanned her memory and gasped when her mind finally connected and compared the man she remembered from a year ago to the man she was seeing and pitying and *smelling* now. "Yes, I remember you—what happened?"

"I survived."

Miss Thompson looked at Mr. Justin for a long,

thoughtful moment. After the moment passed, she responded. "You're going to have to give me more than that, sir."

Mr. Justin chuckled. "The books you sold me worked, but now I need the opposite kind of books. I can survive out there, but my mind . . . ."

"Wait, so you really . . . live out there?" Miss Thompson asked. "Why? People don't do that anymore—unless they're crazy. And the way I see it, even if you have survived on your own, that means you must have plenty of skills that could be—"

"I don't like America, but I don't like anywhere else, either," he said. "I like me, and I like being alive, so I went out there, to somewhere else I like."

"But you came back here."

"For ten minutes."

A change seemed to come over Miss Thompson—an understanding—and she asked with earnestness, "So we've got a Shrugger, do we? Why don't you love America anymore, Atlas?"

Mr. Justin had no idea what she meant, so he cut to the seed of it: "I don't want to ruin your day, ma'am. I just want to live alone, and I need some books so I can make it bearable."

She could not say why the tear arrived in the corner of her eye, but it did, and he saw it.

"Exactly what kind of books were you thinking?" she asked, recovering, driven by a natural desire to want to help.

"Blow my mind, ma'am."

Miss Thompson smirked—what an interesting man!

"Mr. Justin, I own the apartment above here; please go upstairs and use my shower to clean your-self—and for God's sake take your time. Meanwhile, I shall put together a little galaxy for your able mind, an *American* galaxy."

"Thank you, miss," Mr. Justin said, and he headed

towards the stairs. Over his shoulder, he added, "And frankly it doesn't matter to me where good ideas come from, but most of the time it bothers me greatly where bad ideas end up."

I'm afraid there are going to be a few breaks like this in the telling, to tell about the telling as it's being told, which is potentially relevant. You see, I am only permitted to Write during a certain period of the day. Most of the rest of my day is spent minding my the fuck own, with my back against the corner of a wall or fence, or sitting and facing the ocean, but always ready for volcanic eruptions of violence from my fellow prisoners or random psychological torture from the fuckotronic goo with all the guns and Tasers and keys around here. Outside, on the sand, by my palm tree, anyone comes at me, they better be conversational, or—well, I suppose a way of specifying the consequences of coming at me with anything other than Socratic intent would be to say that I am very rarely approached anymore, but when I am it is always conversational.

Mr. Justin didn't call me Big Boy for nothing.

I'm sure some of the others recognize me from the news, too, and the rest have probably learned from the word around.

There is one hour of light before lights-out, and that's when I Write, under this nauseating fluorescence, flickering, droning, urging me onward with the telling, like a pushy Jew (just kidding, my wonderful Jewish friends).

Outside my concrete cube, FRANKS, the eternally reticent guard, got himself some new boots—I can hear it as they thud on the grate—good for him, asshole.

Let's resume.

16

After a year in the wild, taking a shower isn't just taking a shower: It is *being loved and embraced by pure sparkling streams of blissfully hot water while you stand there and feel its richness with a physical sensation that almost makes you want to cry from joy and gratitude.* But you don't cry simply because it feels so fucking *good;* the hot water, the internal and external hug of the steam . . . the core temperature for once not having to completely fend for itself.

Mr. Justin took his time.

When the water was starting to cool, he turned it off and stepped out of the shower, cleaned the tub, and dressed in his dirty laundry. He emerged in the apartment and saw a small pile of Miss Thompson's father's old clothes lying in a tight stack in front of the door, clearly placed there for him.

He picked them up and went back into the bathroom.

"Breezes From Yesterday" by Six Grandfathers was playing on the radio in the bookstore, which was a song Mr. Justin had never heard before, and he liked it—what an enjoyably undermining little beat.

"Is this a bookstore, a bed and breakfast, or a stationary parade?" Mr. Justin asked Miss Thompson as he walked down the stairs and saw her two-arm-unloading another stack of books on the counter.

She looked up and was comforted to see him in the clothes she'd given him.

"Is that 'stationary' or 'stationery'—'e' or 'a'?"

The pleasantly outwitted Mr. Justin—who was finally comfortable with himself around her because he was no longer actively offensive—really *looked* at the woman who'd been so kind to and forwardly helpful with him: She was six inches taller than most women and two inches taller than Mr. J himself. She had very long, straight, brown hair, the vertical effect of which made her appear even taller than she was—a height-effect which was even further accentuated by her genetic skinniness. As for her face, one might look at her and see plainness, or one might look at her and see the perfection, or perhaps standard, of humanity. Perhaps a passive beauty that could be metamorphosed into an intoxicating allure if she wanted you to feel it?

Intoxicated, Mr. Justin made his way over to the counter and saw six fat stacks of books standing tall there, too.

"Um—"

"Yeah, it's a lot," she said, "but I have an idea."

His open mouth closed as he waited curiously for her terms.

"You live off fish and berries out there, right?"

Before this highly refined woman, the truth seemed too . . . unrefined . . . for Mr. Justin to admit aloud, so he merely nodded his head.

"So you're good at fishing?"

"Sometimes."

Miss Thompson tittered.

She recovered, cleared her throat, and said, "OK, what I meant is, you don't have enough money for all of these books, but I don't like spending my money on the stinking-foul fish at the market, so I'll trade you: fresh fish filets for books."

"At what rate?"

"Well, let's see: There are, what, forty books here, and the rate is that whenever you have two extra fish, you filet them and bring them to me here, and I'll inspect you and make sure you're still OK, and that'll be the deal. So I'd say you owe me eighty fish over forty inspections at whatever interval you like."

Mr. Justin thought about it.

"It might be a while," he said. What he said through inflection and body language was, "Are you planning on leaving anytime soon? Because I would like to know you are here when I'm back out there." As they say, the majority of communication is nonverbal.

Miss Thompson topped the last stack and gave the stack a playful pat, and she said, "Mr. Justin, you'll be out there, and I'll be here, 'cause everybody else here likes me and my stationary-stationery parade just as much as you do."

The droplet of truth in her observation hit Mr. Justin's brain, and the ripples curled up the corner of his mouth, and he said, "OK—fair. Any particular kinds of filets?"

"Blow my mouth, sir."

Mr. Justin gave an unintentional double-take, and Miss Thompson clasped her hands over her face in mortified horror and said, "Oh, my God! I was just making—Oh, my God."

Mr. Justin chuckled. He waved his hand in such a way as to indicate that he was moving past the part-intentionally, part-unintentionally funny line.

"Dennis," he said, not just being polite, but dropping a further seed of intimacy into their strangely distant-yet-intimate interaction. "Now that we are friends, you could say, 'Blow my mouth, Dennis.'"

She could feel that intimacy where it counted, and she liked it—made her vibrate inside and feel nervous.

"Well, friend, if you're Dennis, then I'm Emily," she said and blushed beautifully.

They shook hands for the first time, even though he'd already used her soap and shampoo.

"Do you have bags for these books? I can take care of 'em once they're on the boat—"

"You have a boat?"

19

Mr. Justin wasn't the sort of person who answered questions like that, after he'd already just said it.

Miss Thompson realized he wasn't going to answer and also realized, "But of course you do—I suppose I asked because I'm rather curious to see it."

"It's a small fishing boat—not worth a huff or a puff."

He was embarrassed by what he perceived as its shabbiness—a man, even a caveman, wants to impress a beautiful woman.

Miss Thompson saw her opportunity to use silence as a response to Mr. Justin, like he'd done, and he caught it and eventually said, "But if you'd like to help me carry these down to the docks, I suppose you could see it there."

Just before she closed and locked the door behind them, on the way out, she flipped a sign on the door that said, "Out To Lunch!" and which featured a drawing of a little duckling that was passed-out drunk.

Mr. Justin still had a year of beard, but because he was freshly bathed and wearing clean new-old clothes he wasn't quite the sight he'd been, but he became a sight all the more because he was walking next to Miss Thompson, and the people who saw the two shook their heads and thought *One of these days Emily Thompson is going to get herself into real trouble,* and she saw them thinking it, but Miss Thompson, a proudly independent woman who loved to keep things interesting, could be described with an American phrasing: She didn't give a good goddam shit what they thought about her decisions.

The two of them walked together the short distance to the docks, where at the end of the last pier Mr.

Justin's fishing boat waited. The sun was warm, but the wind was blowing crisply, with flavors of autumn in the nose and on the tongue.

"It's been getting colder every day," Miss Thompson said rhetorically, worrying about this man already.

Mr. Justin picked up on the empathy in her statement and appreciated the psychological stroke therein.

"You'd be surprised how you eventually get used to it—once you go feral," he said, but Miss Thompson didn't laugh and still looked worried about him, so he added another seedling of intimacy. "But I know where to come now when I need some warmth."

Miss Thompson smiled and felt the sun dazzle on her skin, and she said, "Keep it in your pants, big boy."

Mr. Justin chuckled, and they found themselves at the end of the pier, where the boat was sloppily dancing on the water, tethered to the dock.

"This is it, huh?" Miss Thompson visually inspected the vessel that would bring her fresh fish. "I declare it seaworthy, sir."

Mr. Justin set his double-armload of books on the pier, and Miss Thompson did the same, and he turned to her when she stood, and he held out his hand.

"Thank you, Emily—good luck," he said, not really being any good at this.

Miss Thompson shook his hand confidently and said, "Good luck to me? I'm not the one who's about to go back into the *jungle.*"

Mr. Justin was like a movie character sometimes. He looked around at the small town of Sweet Bend and then at her. "Sure you are," he said. "The jungle's deep in the skyscrapers, too—it's just invisible there."

He stepped into the boat and started stacking the books on the bottom like ballast. When he was finished, he fitted the teeth of the rotor back into the body of the water, and before he yanked the engine to life, he said to Miss Thompson, "I'll probably be back—" and he gazed into his own thoughts for an approximation of when he

21

honestly felt he would return, and he discovered that the answer was: "—soon."

The fishing boat didn't go very fast—it was, after all, a lake/river fishing tub—but for most of his motorized trip away from the docks, Mr. Justin refused to turn back to see if she were still there watching him. Finally he felt he'd gone far beyond curiosity, into cruelty, and he turned, and the tall woman on the pier waved back with joy, and what a warm rush that was for Mr. Justin, and Miss Thompson also enjoyed the way it felt when Mr. Justin waved back with his left hand—his right hand manning the tiller, Mr. Justin getting smaller and smaller away.

Back in his tent, Mr. Justin was suddenly unable to control himself. So many thoughts of the hauntingly tempting Miss Emily Thompson filled his mind and refused to leave that he couldn't help himself: He took his matter into his own hands and let his mind fill with imagined passions and lustily handled himself with vigor and authority. He'd never met or known another woman like that in his whole goddam life (he'd had too much else on his mind the truly first time they'd met, more than a year ago, when she'd sold him the entire Biblio-Files "Survival" section at his distracted, hurried request), and now that he was alone and sorting out his thoughts after his sortie back into civilization, a year of neglected, cast-aside, deeply rooted lusts all found their footing in the name of Emily Thompson and marched forward and grew louder and larger in the internal conversation.

But Mr. Justin was hard in more than just the sexual way, and soon, after several deeply pent-up rounds of personal vigor and authority, he eventually started to hear Miss Thompson's voice in his head not as a luscious memory but as a Siren's Song, calling him back into the trappings *(le mot juste!)* of civilization. His Thompsonian lusts had indeed found their footing, but a philosophical dogma soon washed them to the bottom again. The sexual urge is perfectly natural, but to Mr. Justin there was nothing natural or enjoyable about his abandoned American culture—those swine. That woman, yes, but those people, that corollary evil?

My tent, my books, and, when necessary, my memories of that seraphim, that cloud-tall statue.

He was not hungry, and he spent the rest of the day weatherproofing a storage unit for all his new books except the two he would keep in his tent, and he read from the first book, using his new dictionary when necessary, until the sun set, and then he drifted to sleep thinking about two fish out there swimming in the river, which he would offer to her.

Can you believe marijuana is still illegal? Is it still? I don't know what's happened in the outside world. Even if it's legal, my outrage, the Khans' outrage, our outrage is still valid: How long did it take for America to remember what America was?

"It's not a War on Drugs; it's a War on Personal Freedom."

(RIP, Mr. Hicks.)

Mr. Justin had the answers. He should have been happy, but the Boomers drove him crazy, and they weren't even happy themselves.

It wasn't all 'cause of marijuana (Mr. Justin didn't even smoke marijuana): It was what marijuana represented to Mr. Justin.

Things meant something to Mr. Justin.

Sometimes, on a misty morning near a fat river running lazily and glassily, an adult rainbow trout will come to the surface and circle for a brief rapid moment with its expert fishy movements, and that quick sigh of aquatics will be all it takes to drag a man from deep within the sleep of his own mind and into the wakefulness of looking at the roof of a cold dewy tent glowing a gloomy blue glow—another day to be faced and survived, called forth into hungry movement by the hungry movements of his own breakfast.

It had been a week, and Mr. Justin did not want to give the impression that he was any sort of a flake on payments, so he overfilled the basket, gutted the fish on the bank, and boated downstream, back to Sweet Bend, to have a ravenous breakfast at Biblio-Files.

Miss Thompson was no trophy behind a glass case, to be admired but inhuman. She was human as hell (God knows pretty much the entire world would eventually get to witness the undeniable profundity of her truly deep sexuality), and it turned out that as Mr. Justin was plying the Blunt River back to Sweet Bend, to see her, with some particularly human thoughts on his mind, Miss Thompson was getting plowed by her lover from town.

The man was dressed and walking out whistling when Mr. Justin arrived at Biblio-Files, and immediately Mr. Justin could see from the goofy looks on both of their faces that Miss Thompson had just received a proper plowing, and that knowledge hurt Mr. Justin where it counted. A long week of desirous thought crashed into the rock wall of brutal reality, and Mr. Justin just wanted this to be over with now.

"Dennis!" Miss Thompson said, still floating. "So wonderful to see you."

Mr. Justin felt sick.

"Here's fish. I'm fine. See you in a while."

He turned to leave.

"Wait, Dennis, don't you—?"

The bell clanged twice as the door opened and closed.

On the walk back to the boat, and on the long ride home, Mr. Justin thought about how you just can't have it both ways.

Cucullus non facit monachum.—
"The hood does not make the monk."

The Lost Angels Orphanage was founded by a pedophile named Fr. Michael Peter Kenton—a Catholic priest and missionary, born in '53, a Boomer.

After abortion was recriminalized, a whole bunch of bastard babies went up for adoption, and there weren't nearly enough orphanages to handle the overflow, and Fr. Michael saw the social development unfolding like gold appearing in the sky and dropping down into his overstuffed pockets.

Fr. Michael built Lost Angels deep in the woods,

because almost anyone who spent enough time around Fr. Michael knew that there was something fundamentally *wrong* with the man, but as sometimes happens with the ferociously disturbed, in order to survive he'd developed the ability to disguise his true identity for long enough to earn the trust of the crying mothers who came to him out of spiritual and practical helplessness. If they wanted a compassionate Catholic priest, that was exactly what he'd be for them.

But he alone wasn't enough, and Lost Angels' mother-convincing clincher, who always arrived a little late to the meeting, toweling off her rearing-busy hands, was Sister Anne Marie McClusky, who was a goddam innocent fool, but who always carried herself as a woman of tender trustworthiness, to mask her vast stupidity. Her smile was all heart, and unfortunately so was her brain.

Obviously Fr. Michael was never really a proper Christian (I agree with historian Will Durant: The last Christian was Spinoza)—and sister Anne was too stupid to ever figure out what he really was before she died—but it seems that when desperate outsiders give that much trust and belief to an organization (or even just its name), the wrong people can see gold popping into the air, and they can sodomize dozens of children before one of those children does something gruesome about it.

Fr. Michael's wheelhouse was kids, both sexes, aged seven to twelve. He took 'em in from all ages, but seven to twelve was Hell on Earth at Lost Angels. That's important to remember, at least until you can forget it.

Mr. Justin, out hunting one time, had come across the Lost Angels Orphanage. He'd scouted the place out and saw it for what Fr. Michael wanted people to see it for: an out-of-the-way, Catholic orphanage. So Mr. Justin, who didn't want to draw any attention to himself, had just moved on.

What happens when a kid turns twelve? Well, generally around that time, he or she has the sexual voice significantly step up in the internal conversation, and the first days of adulthood begin.

Fr. Michael liked it when the kids didn't know exactly what he was doing but they were large enough for him to fit right; nevertheless, for whatever psychological reasons, after they were old enough to *understand* what was going on, he was done with them.

He didn't even have to stray that far from Catholic dogma to justify his actions to his unfortunate wards: All people, after all, had souls blackened with Original Sin (the orphans' sins made doubly obvious by their having been abandoned by their parents), and after all the path to righteousness is not an easy one. But he would show them the way.

Of course, certain sacrifices would have to be made.

And then when his victims were too old for him, Father Michael told the other children that the pubescent boy or girl had suddenly found a family to go live with—the story was always very pleasant.

Mr. Justin didn't know any of this until it was too late, but there's still a little bit more to get to before Mr. Justin smells smoke.

FRANKS, the guard, the paperboy, had new soles put on his old boots—he didn't get new boots, after all. Fuck him.

It's worth noting that just now I found momentary relief from the nauseating fluoro-flicker: I frustratedly slammed the fat of my fist against the wall, and the shockwaves of my strength must have jiggered the connection a bit, and now that vomitous tube above me is beaming bright and silent. No more flickering and buzzing, at least for—

And yes, the flicker is back, and my poundings have done nothing but draw the ugly glare of FRANKS, whose boots aren't new.

"You know a cobbler, FRANKS?" I ask, but he just spits on me like he always does.

"Do you yourself cobble?" I ask, but each echoing thick-soled bootstep is quieter than the last.

Fortune favored Mr. Justin on his next, snowy return to Biblio-Files. As things stood, Miss Thompson's former lover had been increasingly scorning Miss Thompson, who unconsciously had been becoming increasingly distant with a man she'd realized was her former lover.

So when Mr. Justin walked in hopelessly, merely living up to his end of the bargain and begging The Fates to not see the beautiful woman doped on cock again, Miss Thompson saw the strange-looking man she had secretly been hoping to see.

Miss Thompson's entire being seemed to beam into a welcoming smile, and with every long stride towards him, Mr. Justin's confidence and hopefulness grew, and she opened her arms and said, "I'm not letting you get away so quickly this time, Dennis." She hugged him deeply, and Mr. Justin felt the depth of her affection for him (for all people?), and he was warmed by it. In his head he realized she had done it again!

They unlocked and looked admiringly at each other, and Mr. Justin spoke up.

"All those books were American except one, and I can't figure out what the *Tao Te Ching* has to do with the rest. Do you find that old man's ideas to be in harmony with American culture? Because I've never seen anything Lao-Tsu ever talked about—except you."

Mr. Justin had a way of just getting right at it.

Miss Thompson brought her hands together in front of her chest, as if to clasp her joy and hold it to her heart. "My star pupil! Is it possible that you've finished all those books and found the core of my riddle already?"

"Maybe?"

Miss Thompson giggled the giggle of the curiously smitten.

"The *Tao* was a prequel to your next assignments, of course—into History, Biography, and Philosophy. Now run and catch a shower whilst I prep the ages."

"I've been washing with what you gave me; I still—?" he shyly asked.

"No, you don't," she said and she unconsciously opened her arms to him again, because she could feel that he needed some humanity, and he happily shared the space and contact with her, and she smelled like everything he ever wanted. Eventually, however, she said, "OK, yes, you do," and as they laughed she noticed that their torsos bounced with the same rhythm.

While Mr. Justin was in the shower, Miss Thompson said to herself, "I must be crazy!" But when the sound of the shower disappeared, Biblio-Files was closed—the drunken duckling facing the world—and Miss Thompson let herself into her bathroom intentionally early, saying, "I found some extra—" and then finding what they both wanted: the bathroom door opening, and a freshly cleaned Mr. Justin standing naked, looking at her dubiously and then understanding what her staged, "accidental" early entry into the bathroom meant.

This time they were his strides, and he came to her and grabbed her by the waist and met her face to face, and they kissed. Their bodies came together, and he quickly grabbed her dress by the hem and handed her the handful and then yanked her underwear down while she pulled her dress the rest of the way off. He pulled her to him again and briefly rubbed himself up and down the outside and then entered her savagely, to the hilt, and her eyes bulged briefly and beautifully as she entirely quaked with pleasure. They kissed again moments later, fully inside, when their faces met, their mouths joined, and they spoke to each other in the wordless ancient language of made love. Then he took a handful of hair from the back of her head and used the sweet pain to convince her to flip over, where he put her face to the counter and entered her again, this time *more ferarum*—"in the manner of wild beasts," rapidly pounding the length of himself into her while she moaned at first and eventually screamed the best way there is. Then he took her by the neck and pulled her face to his, and their mouths met awkwardly yet passionately and locked and he thrust as hard and fast as he could while she seemed to enter some sort of new biological state, and soon the depths of their passion yielded to simultaneous orgasms so explosive that their mouths were pushed away from each other, so that their hip-thrusting bodies could properly shed and express the joy they'd just drilled so deep to discover within each other.

Mr. Justin spent the night—with the full implication of spending the night being accomplished seven times before and after any sleeping took place.

The next morning, Miss Thompson made Mr. Justin a hot mountain of breakfast, and after they ate, Mr. Justin returned to the woods.

Miss Thompson cried after he left. Her sadness was eventually alleviated a bit by her acknowledgement of the inherent bind her predilections had put her in: She couldn't permanently have the man she loved because the man she loved couldn't permanently be had. But there was love. Oh, God, there was love—they both loved and cried over how much love there was.

They lived together and apart like that for six months, until something happened.

Do you know how long it's been since I've seen a naked woman?—a woman at all?

I have lost all track of time. There are only two

days in prison, and there is only one day in this prison. How many months or years has it been? Nobody will tell me a goddam fuck. Maybe it doesn't matter.

I'm bringing this up because some of the stuff that happens from this point on gets pretty extremely sexual and violent, and I think I might plumb the depths of my impulse to overindulge in those sexual descriptions, like I already have, because it's been an excruciatingly long time since I had a woman (and only once was that), since I felt a woman giggle and wriggle on my lap and more importantly on my big ol' me, and short of shivving my wrist and using the spurting blood to draw a big ol' pair of bongos on the wall, this is all I have left.

I bring it up as a fair warning to the reader—*please forgive the mutant for his hideous invisible hump*—but I also bring it up merely to distract myself for a moment, because the next part isn't sexy at all.

George Donald Humphrey was placed in the care of Lost Angels when he was two days old. His sexual abuse began on his seventh birthday and continued into his eleventh year, per the Father's proclivities.

But George was a strange boy in this way: Sometimes there are nine-year-old boys whose pituitary anomaly throws them into being in a position where by ten years old they're already fully conscious of the sexual side of life. Although the Father did not notice it in George, that's what happened to the boy, and consequently that understanding meant that George suffered more than most of the other confusedly abused, and as the Buddha might've said, (I heard it attributed to him once), "Without pain, there would be no need to create."

George's catastrophically traumatic pain led to a similarly overdeveloped need to create, or more accurately destroy, and early one morning he sneaked into the Father's bedroom, raised a butcher's knife over the abusive tyrant, and stabbed down with a violent series of convulsions—sending the tip of the knife into the Father's mouth and down to the spinal bones at the back of the neck, over and over until the priest was lying paralyzed and choking on his own gushing blood and eviscerated tongue.

Killing someone is a sort of point of no return, and some people can't handle it. George, twelve years old and the child of a hellish amount of abuse, couldn't handle the full implications of what he'd done. After he heard the Father's ugly gurgling finally come to a stop, he panicked. He knew he'd done something wrong, but he didn't know what to do about it now, and even the one thing in the world he thought would make things all right, that would turn the lights back on . . . it hadn't worked. The priest was dead, but the world was still rotten and dark.

"Everyone here is ruined; everything here . . . ."

The matches for the candles on the altar were in a drawer near the sink in the sacristy.

"We're all ruined," George said. "There's no hope." Striking matches and throwing them and letting them catch whatever they caught. As the fires grew, the sound behind him was like distant bacon fat on a pan, and eventually the whole room was like that.

One of the children, a nine-year-old boy, smelled the smoke and came running, but George knew the boy, Henry, had been ruined by the Father, too, and he balled his fist and punched Henry's nose bloody, and Henry ran off, and George went to set more fires. Everyone who came running to George, he did the same or worse—George had the strength of the insane.

There were two adults and fourteen children living at the orphanage, and within a half-hour everyone there would be dead except two boys and a little girl.

Mr. Justin smelled smoke, and this wasn't the usual kind of smoke: It was more than just firewood that was burning. Immediately recognizing that something emergent may be happening, he scurried out of the tent and dressed in the ample moonlight. The night was freezing; given the season, the surprisingly cold winds were a bitter reminder of the long past winter. The winds brought more acrid air, and Mr. Justin, when fully dressed, headed into it, towards the source of the smoke.

By the time Mr. Justin arrived at Lost Angels, the entire complex was on fire, and the bearded man could hear two distinct kinds of yelling: one crazed voice, and several scared voices.

He headed towards the scared voices, running along the outside of the building, looking for the kids and a usable door, looking in all the dark windows.

Having entirely circled the building, he found the main entrance to be the only one that wasn't in danger of imminent collapse, and he hyper-oxygenated himself and dashed through the door, into the inferno.

What I remember of the fire was me on my bed while

most of the other kids were running around scared and calling out to Father Michael and Sister Anne for help, and when they started falling down from the smoke I knew I had to do something besides what they were doing. I looked around, and there was only one other kid, a little girl, who wasn't running around. She was looking at me, just staring at me and breathing scared. We then both realized the same thing at the same time, which is crazy 'cause she was only two, (I was only five,) but anyway with the way nobody was yelling anymore and nothing but the sound of hissing and bacon and popcorn all over the place, I got out of bed, but my legs were so scared I dropped to the floor awkwardly, and immediately I noticed the air was a little cooler and fresher near the ground, and I had to tell that to the little girl—now that I knew—and my legs came to life.

I monkey-shuffled under the cots, right to her, in the good air, and I pulled her to the ground with me, and she flopped down awkwardly, too, and it must've hurt but she didn't wince or anything, and I said, "The air's better down here," but I realized she wasn't really old enough to say anything much, and she started crying.

She knew at least two words, and she said them to me: "*I . . . scared!*"

It was all she'd say, and she sobbed and screamed and cried, and I held her with me near the cooler ground, so she wouldn't fall down like the other kids.

But I was scared, too, and I didn't have a plan, and I couldn't move anymore.

Igne natura renovatur integra.—

"Through fire nature is reborn whole."

Mr. Justin burst through the front door and into the glowing, smoldering skeleton of what was once a mediocre church. At the far end of the room, near the gilded tabernacle, was young raving George—still muttering to himself and striking matches and throwing them into already burning pyres.

When Mr. Justin saw the spluttering George for a moment between huge black dancing ghosts of smoke, the bearded man could see flashes of something in the boy's eyes that said George was a rabid dog and no longer a human being in any of the right ways, and the wise man worked his way around the outside of the church, under the cover of the smoke, in the direction of the helpless voices he'd heard before, trying not to draw the murderous George's attention.

A conflict inevitably was inevitable, and just before Mr. Justin reached a promising door he heard George's crazed voice cry out, *"Hey! Who are you? Are you with him?"*

Civilized men might not have done so, but Mr. Justin was no longer a part of civilization, so he did: He balled his fist and hammered little George in the face, knocking the pyro-psycho-freakout unconscious. Then he threw George's unconsciousness over his shoulder and tromped through the rectory until he found the children's sleeping quarters, where he located the only two other conscious children thanks to the voluminous blasts of the shrieking two-year-old girl being held on the ground by me—a scared-paralyzed five-year-old boy.

Mr. Justin lifted me, and with me came the girl, and Mr. Justin hoisted our tiny bundle over his other shoulder, but when he went to leave, we could hear a terrible structural collapse in the main area of the church. The only option left was one of the windows, which had blown out and was jagged all around, so he set us down in the corner farthest from the fire, picked up the cot closest to the windowpane (coincidentally George's), and chucked it through—everything going out with the cot: the window now a big hole in the wall.

By that point, however, he'd inhaled a dangerous amount of smoke. He dropped to his hands and knees to try to find some breathable air, and he crawled towards us on the ground and made it halfway before he passed out.

Because there had been an adult to lead the way, the little girl was no longer crying, and I relaxed my grip on her. I could hear George's unconscious gargling breath behind me, and then I heard George mutter something, perhaps coming out of unconsciousness. In my continuing panic, I let go of the little girl and scooted away from George, and that's when I heard the little girl pitch into the worst wail yet.

I turned from George, to her, and through the smoke I could faintly see the outline of the man on the ground. Panic, sadly, again begat paralysis.

The little girl was in the part of adolescence between being a baby, when crying is your only method of getting anything done, and being a human capable of logic and reason. In that ambulatory and stressed-out state, her only option left, seeing as how crying was not solving anything, and maybe even making things worse, was action.

She didn't like the man's big ugly beard at all, and she kicked it because she didn't know what else to do, and she blamed him for the whole burning, scary night. But she wasn't very coordinated, and her third kick landed square on Mr. Justin's nose, breaking it, and the pain from the break must've brought him back to us, because he shook his head, coughed, snorted, groaned, and then became rigid with life when he recognized the context he'd awoken back into.

Within the next thirty seconds, George had been safely defenestrated, and soon thereafter Mr. Justin, with me and the little girl clutching his shoulders and neck, safely defenestrated himself and us, his cargo.

When we were outside, he carried us and dragged George a safe distance away, and when George started waking up, Mr. Justin bashed him to sleep again. Then he started heading back into the inferno, to try to save some of the kids who'd fallen down, but the little girl and I cried and wailed so savagely from our fear of losing him and being alone again that he paused for a moment, between the children alive outside and the children possibly alive inside, and that's when the majority of the rest of the structure collapsed on itself, sending a million sparks in every direction—a fireworks show and a funeral at once.

The decision was made by fire—everyone inside was now dead.

The bearded man, who'd leapt to the ground under the rain of sparks, crawled over to and held us frightened children. We sat, and Mr. Justin waited for some authorities to arrive, for surely the inferno had been or would be noticed by someone else.

But what Mr. Justin and we kids would not find out for quite a while was that no authorities were coming.

Mr. Justin didn't want to keep knocking the rabid George unconscious, so he improvised a set of handcuffs out of one of his bootlaces and tied George to a tree. Then Mr. Justin sat down, and the little girl and I snuggled up against his bigger warmness, and we continued to wait while we watched the Lost Angels structure throw off incredible amounts of light and heat as it burned to its foundation in the otherwise black forest.

We all fell asleep that way, waiting.

"Where's the orphanage?" George asked, which woke everyone else up.

It was before dawn, the sky between the leaves a lightening grey, the once-roiling orphanage nothing now but some glowing dust.

Mr. Justin, the little girl, and I—everyone shivering—opened our eyes and looked at each other with an already familiar chemistry, with the look of each asking the other, "Is this kid kidding?"

Seeing that George was still tied up tight, I built up the courage to say, "You burned it down, George—last night."

There was a moment where we three could see the old George going over the events from yesterday, and then his memory reached the point where the break happened, and he broke again—all emotion and human connection faded from his face, fell away like a tide, only the tide never returned: George went catatonic, not rabid, this time.

Three new friends simply shivered in the lighter grey and watched the catatonic George.

The little girl and I turned to Mr. Justin with looks of mounting hopelessness.

The bearded man looked around as the day grew brighter and felt his own sort of hopelessness: "Where the hell is anybody?"

Sometimes it's too much, being in here. I've been in

real or virtual prisons nearly all my life, and the only time I was out, they sent me back. In a free society, it's in the interest of whatever powers that be that the free people don't actually exercise any of their freedoms or powers—or at least that's the situation I've faced. I know I went too far, but nobody in America took the Muslims seriously until they gave us a pair of explosive middle fingers in New York City—and seemingly forever after that all the politicians and news organizations ever talked about were men with Muslim names. I know I didn't spread my message in the best way, but the best way wasn't available anymore, and a wise man changes his sail to match the change in the winds.

Sometimes I'm fine with being in here. When you care about something that much, sometimes it's a relief when they take the job out of your hands and put you in a detention facility. Life was already miserable—now it can be miserable and I don't have to feel my shoulder on the wheel.

I just miss Candy and Mr. Justin and Miss T and Dr. James.

I miss words and the world.

Miss Emily Thompson's uterus developed a cancerous cyst when she was nineteen years old, and within three months her uterus had been surgically removed and she'd been told that she would never be able to give birth to her own biological children.

Miss Thompson had never even really had the chance to think about whether she wanted to have children someday or not, and then life had held her down and aborted that thought before it could ever be born. Consequently the news and the surgical procedure were understandably traumatic for her, and she spent the next few years throwing herself fuck-first into life—in the bedroom, in the car, in the movie theater, wherever it was, she went well past where other women wouldn't go. But ultimately she found that the emptiness inside of herself was never adequately filled by her hedonistic indulgences, and she eventually began to regard the overdoses of her physical passions as merely a palliative. She needed to find a real meaning.

Lust has low tides; rivers are unapologetically dependent; she wanted to be a lake.

She found a love and a constancy of meaning in ideas—in books and wisdom. She could not give birth to children, but she could still give birth to those things that most make us human: thoughts and ideas. If life were only about the propagation of the species, there would never be a need for consciousness. There was more to life than that, and she would fill it with as much as she could.

Consequently, in the American culture of her time, that made her significantly different from most other people.

Mr. Justin was just as hungry as we kids were, and everybody's bellies were groaning—even wordless George's belly was bellowing.

"I'm *hungry*," I whined for the third time in a row to the bearded man who was still thinking about and processing everything that had happened and was happening. Finally, he reached a stepping-stone of a conclusion, and he said it aloud to himself: "Emily will know what to do."

"Who's—?"

Before I could ask the question, Mr. Justin said,

"You kids ever eaten fish?"

George didn't move; the little girl and I shook our heads no.

"You even know what a fish is?"

George, stoic as ever. Meanwhile, I wasn't exactly sure, so I shrugged, and the little girl saw me and gave her best attempt at a shrug, too.

"Jesus," Mr. Justin said to the ether, and this time George responded, but it was just a turn of his head—a twitch.

Mr. Justin stood and looked down at his three musketeers, and two of us looked up at him starvo-hopefully.

"Follow me," he said.

We stood and followed. Except for George. When Mr. Justin approached, George snarled and snapped at him, but Mr. Justin was much bigger and stronger than George, and he folded George's feet under George's bound wrists and carried him like a snarling bag, with the exhausted little girl eventually in his other arm, all three miles back to Mr. Justin's camp by the river.

Marching proudly into camp while the panting Mr. Justin double-hand carried George, the little girl showed off another word from her small vocabulary with a darling frustration—in fact, a demand.

"Food!"

Mr. Justin set George down away from the firepit and chuckled at the little girl's hungry instruction.

He said to us, "Break up those sticks over there and put them in the middle of that circle of rocks."

I walked, and the little girl waddled, to the branches, and we did what we were told, for The Beard was still quite terrifying even in the daylight—terrifying and therefore in control, but not like Fr. Michael: That was sinister-terror; this was good ol' intimidation-terror, very effective with traumatized children, or at least it was proving to be this time, with the exception of the exceptionally traumatized George.

Mr. Justin didn't feel like today was the day to put us kids through the grim paces of gutting a fish, so instead, after we watched him light the fire, he cooked up some kwehju—a local edible root that, when grilled, would soften and glaze itself deliciously—and everyone ate ravenously, except George, who spent all of breakfast absently staring at the fire.

"You kids got names?" Mr. Justin asked well into the communal gorging.

With our hunger impulse headed towards satiety, we felt like we could relax enough to begin processing the trauma of the previous night, as well as our uncertain and half-terrifying, bearded present circumstances.

"Hey!" Mr. Justin said, which snapped us out of it. "What's your name, big boy?" Mr. Justin asked the younger boy, me. In that moment, for whatever reason, I liked the way that sounded, like that name was as good as any—better than the boring Old Testament name they used to call me at Lost Angels—and it was what my heroic rescuer had just called me, named me, so that's what I wanted my new name to be. I said, "Big Boy!"

Mr. Justin wasn't sure if I were being rebellious or cheeky or what, but he was the kind of guy who could roll with things if they didn't offend him.

"All right, Big Boy," he said with a grin. "What about this little one, then?" Mr. Justin was indicating the two-year-old girl, who looked to me for support—Mr. Justin's nose was still broken, and in the light he looked halfway demonic.

I looked at the little girl, who was looking at me, and then I said, "The Father used to call her Jezebel."

The little girl recognized her name, but with the

sound of her name came the connotation of the past, and her mouth shriveled into an unmistakable frown.

Trying to help both Mr. Justin and the girl, I said, "Abraham, one of the boys that lived with us, he used to call her Candy Baby 'cause he said she was so sweet. Then we all called her that after that."

Mr. Justin cut another slice of kwehju for the little girl, and she took it from him and licked the caramelized outside and scrunched her face from the sugar rush and seemed to have a little epileptic seizure of energy and enjoyment, and Mr. Justin said, "OK, what the hell—Big Boy and Candy Baby work for me."

Mr. Justin, who always minded, didn't mind this time. He rather agreed with the kids. What's so great about the name Dennis?

"What about him?" Mr. Justin asked, indicating the thousand-yard-staring George.

"He's George," I said. "He—"

At the time I didn't know how to say what I wanted to say about George and Lost Angels—I had heard stories, but, being five, I didn't know what to say because I didn't know what was true and what wasn't, at the time, and it took an hour of careful interviewing before Mr. Justin could piece together what had happened to precipitate the events he now found himself a part of.

After breakfast, he had me and Candy Baby help him clean up the camp while he put out the fire and prepared everyone for the boat ride to Sweet Bend.

The four of us in the boat had been awake since 0530, and it was nearing 0700 when we reached the docks. The whole time it looked like it was going to rain, and over the course of our travel from Mr. Justin's camp to

Sweet Bend, Candy and I said very little to each other, and nothing to Mr. Justin. Instead, we watched the morning break in overcast silver on the brown river while Mr. Justin anxiously wondered what would happen when we reached Miss Thompson in Sweet Bend.

Little did Mr. Justin know but Miss Thompson was about to tell him more than he was about to tell her.

The streets of Sweet Bend were completely empty.

Mr. Justin had pictured a hardworking morning commuter spotting him and his obviously kidnapped children, and then he pictured the hardworker calling that fat police officer, who would arrive with his brothers in blue *en adipal masse* and have Mr. Justin sent to the kind of federal prison where men catch hepatitis C via their large intestines.

Candy and I were just kind of trauma-blasted, and we followed the scary man who'd saved us while the scary man who'd saved us guided the scary George towards the store.

But instead of any of the things Mr. Justin had pictured, the streets were only populated by the light grey mist of the morning, and on the darker side of the street, unnoticed, Mr. Justin marched with his squad of desperate ducklings all the way to Biblio-Files, where a newly awakened Miss Thompson met the grizzled group at the knocked-upon door.

Hannibal ad portas.—

"Hannibal is at the gates."

"Goodness, Dennis!—what kind of surprises should I expect next? Have you got Hannibal and some elephants out there with you, too? And look at your face!"

Miss Thompson reached towards Mr. Justin with affection but held herself back at the ugly sight of his broken nose.

"Three fish," Mr. Justin said and looked at her for her response. "Wasn't even fishing when I caught them."

Miss Thompson was incredulous. She might have stood there shocked for minutes or hours, rather than moments, but moments later the threat of rain became an accelerating drizzle, and while Miss Thompson anxiously and pensively gazed up into the dreary rainclouds that had followed us, Mr. Justin led us kids into the warm, glowing store.

There is a break in the story here, but I have nothing good to say presently about my status as your captive narrator. My spirits are downwind and under attack from the beast that rules this island. It's happened a few times since they sent me here. But so then *why* am I here (not the off-coast American detention facility but the consciousness-detention facility of this bittersweet bodily existence)? To be happy?

Big Boy, happiness is a goal and a reward, but it is not your only purpose, you beast.

Speak, memory!

Tell the story!

"Don't be a coward, James; damn the risks!" Miss Thompson said with such vocal stresses as indicating the end of the argument, and when she hung up, she returned to the four she'd left sitting at her kitchen table and poured us children some juice and tried to find a few threads with which to sew her mind back together.

"Dennis, who are your new friends?"

Mr. Justin and the kids (one of the kids, at least— I) then told Miss Thompson the story of how we all ended up there. When our story had us on the river where the day broke in grey mist, Miss Thompson was able to piece the rest together from there and was about to bring up the first of her many concerns when all of us were startled by a loud banging on the side, more personal, door of the apartment.

Miss Thompson, with Mr. Justin following her, walked over and let in the inexhaustibly tall Dr. James Thompson. The two towering siblings—Emily and James—looked so similar and regarded each other so casually that Mr. Justin didn't need to inquire as to their personal status. The introductions went like this: "James, this is the man I was telling you about," and Dr. James said, "OK, a pleasure—if you don't mind I'll get to that nose in a bit, but let's take care of them first."

The three adults turned their attention to us juicers at the table, and two of us were watching them all avidly.

"Children, this is Dr. James," Miss Thompson said. "Do you know what a doctor is?"

George stared at the wall, I had no idea, and Candy Baby looked at me and then wagged her head no like I was doing.

"I help make people feel better," Dr. James said.

George stared at his own thoughts. I liked the way those words came together, and I was reassured, and thus Candy Baby, too, relaxed a bit, and everyone else relaxed because two of the children had relaxed.

Over the next half-hour, Dr. James medically checked out us kids (he didn't get much from George), and in retrospect his bedside manner was the perfect combination of science and reassurance. After that, he adjusted Mr. Justin's broken nose into a more nose-looking shape and tried to probe the depths of George's mental stability.

While all of that was happening, Miss Thompson prepared a place for us children to sleep while the adults figured out what the fuck.

"Dennis, the firefighters never arrived," Dr. James said, "because there are no firefighters anymore—not like there used to be."

"What—?" Mr. Justin asked rising with a loudness that might awaken the children—I was awake already and was watching and listening from our dark corner across the big room—and Miss T cut Mr. J's loudness down with a shush.

"Something else happened, Dennis—something big," she said and put her hand on his forearm, and that stroke of contact was also a communication to her brother, stating wordlessly how close she and this wild-bearded, broken-nosed weirdo, who might've been lying to his sister the whole goddam time, actually were.

Mr. Justin sat back down slowly and with even more intensity than usual, and he said, as calmly as he could, "Enlighten me, Emily."

"It turns out you may have been right when you left us," Miss Thompson said. A great tension within her was seemingly about to burst.

48

Dr. James's eyes went wide from her revelation: *Left us?*

Miss Thompson continued: "The fact is that America—oh, Dennis, I've been trying to avoid talking about it with you because I know how upset it makes you, but I can't avoid it anymore, because God, it's the whole world now—it's . . . . It's as bad as . . . and the problems are so big that even the best minds can only seem to point at them awkwardly or profit from them usuriously, but nobody is *improving* anything. Most people who are doing anything are just joining different groups and blaming all the other groups who don't agree or the individuals who aren't on board with their group. The American economy, oh Hell, Dennis, America itself . . . it's just completely broken down, and it's destabilized everything, and all around the world it's like this—it's tied up a Gordian Knot, only there doesn't seem to be a brain or a blade or a single man who could wield one! Dennis, in the past week alone we've had two different Presidents assassinated! The whole continent, every group, every nation in the world, it's suddenly all just a lot of hands pulling ropes from every direction!"

Miss Thompson sometimes got poetically carried away when she was stressed out, but in reality her attempt at an explanation was fundamentally hopeless given the fact that the raw details of the world's economic and political collapse were still unknown even to the government historians and sociologists at that farce of a peace conference I attended. Given all the layers of blacked-out NSA/DHS secrecy, as well as the Federal Reserve records that were destroyed outright, I, the narrator of these events, have no useful way of filling in the exact details Miss Thompson seemed to be poetically glossing over in her bewildered rant: Almost nobody in the world knows the details of what really happened, which has only served as a catalyst for the continuing devolution that sprouted from the decay.

I don't know what happened, but I know enough to know that the official records and accounts are pure propaganda bullshit that I won't even bother repeating, and evidently the private memories of the triggering agents themselves have so far proven to be too shameful and scandalous to ever be admitted publicly.

The fact is that Americans were deep in the dark well before the lights went out.

Mr. Justin, in a warm glowing room under the roof-patter of rainfall, was swept up in Miss T's despairing speech, but he was not following her logic—he, too, wanted more details. Dr. James could see the confusion in the bearded man's face, and he spoke of the issues a bit more clearly.

"America's fallen into such a politico-economic death-spiral that all of our firefighters and police officers have been militarized and called to serve in America's several military fronts. Firefighting has been left to the locals, and Lost Angels had no locals besides you and that out-of-state billionaire who owns all that property."

Mr. Justin said, still confused, "All right, if it's as bad as you say, why aren't you yourself on a fighting front, then, heeding the cries for medics?"

"It doesn't quite work like that, anymore, I'm afraid," Dr. James said. "The fact is, Dennis, that right now we don't even know if America technically exists, and do you know where all the fighting fronts are? They're right here—right here, amongst us, on this land, where America used to be."

"It's a civil war, Dennis," Miss Thompson said, staring at the almost-black pane of her cup of coffee. "They're not calling it that yet, but that's what it is. And you left—how did you know?"

Outside, the rain hammered on the town and half the former nation; inside, Mr. Justin and the other adults sat in silence, thinking. It felt like lifetimes.

Finally Mr. Justin shrugged, smirked, and said,

"Well, you know what happens next, right?"

Mr. Justin had been through four rounds of chosen books with Miss Thompson (Outdoor Survival, American Storytellers, World Philosophy, The Encyclopedia), and that night she put together the next giant batch, which included the most informative volumes she could find on firearms, combat, war tactics, woodworking, glass-making, plumbing, engineering, and, strangely as usual, a biography of the parenthetically aforementioned Baruch Spinoza.

While Mr. Justin built two cabins in the woods and prepared a place for everyone to flee to in the event of Sweet Bend turning into a domestic war front, Dr. James pulled some old bureaucratic strings and forged two birth certificates for the two remaining children—the catatonic George having been sent away one morning, without much fanfare, to Candy's and my great relief.

Miss Thompson insisted on giving me and Candy contemporary names on our "birth certificates" (Dante Marcus Thompson for me, Sylvia Alice Thompson for Her Candiness), noting that putting "Big Boy" and "Candy Baby" on forged birth certificates would call undue attention to the forgery, and her argument won out. But Mr. Justin and we kids had formed a deep bond with our nicknames. Thus, Miss Thompson won the *de jure* battle, but the names Big Boy and Candy Baby won the *de facto* war.

There were plenty of guns around.

Before they were dubiously declared illegal, there had been a boom of gun manufacturing and purchases— the people of Old America had seen something dark coming and were girding themselves appropriately— so even though firearms were made illicit, they were ubiquitous.

There was, after all, a war on.

Mr. Justin assembled a small arsenal (that is, a handgun and a rifle) with the help of the adult Thompsons, and he trained with the weapons until they were his tools, until he knew them and their capabilities and could use them as a reasonable means of defense against the roving, violent gangs of the new America, which could show up in Sweet Bend at any time.

Candy and I were closely tended to, even if our adoptive parents' complete-opposite existences within the context of a continent at a sort of hundred-years' war with itself made for a much more challenging and tooth-clattering youth than it seems like most other American children have to endure.

But honestly for the rest of my penitentiary life I could think about my memories from that decade and soak within my gratitude over having the unique experience of growing up loved in a world falling down hated.

In fact, on this tooth-clatteringly cold night in my wall-weeping cell, I think I'd like to skip the heavy stone of this narrative over the waters of those times and show you the splashes that jump into the moonlight.

There's much more to get to on the far shore.

Eheu fugaces labuntur anni.—

"Alas the fleeting years slip by."

There were tons of tears and tantrums from both of us children the first year. In the first skip-splash tossed up by this flat-spun memory-stone, I just see myself and Candy wailing and red over one thing or another, from being constantly uprooted, back and forth between Sweet Bend and Mr. Justin's camp. Candy's potty training backslid (pun intended), and when I wasn't miserably enraged I was quiet and sad, kind of like George had been but not as bad. In response to our unraveling, Mr. Justin and Miss Thompson simply swaddled us in strength and love. Whenever we burst into flames, we were smothered with affection and restored to room temperature through comforting logic and affection. Miss Thompson was much better at it.

Candy Baby and I were not to make a sound—were to read and read only—while Miss Thompson, downstairs, tended to a couple of customers. I, who loved Miss Thompson so much my heart hurt sometimes, happily indulged in the pursuit of the end of the tale in front of me, but Candy Baby just wasn't at a point in her life that reading had any appeal whatsoever, at least to her. Reading, to her, *smelled.* She sighed in a way that she didn't mean for Miss Thompson to pick up on, but Miss Thompson, who had come upstairs to check on us kids, did. Candy looked at the book, at the pretty, colorful, shiny cover, and then she opened it, and there were still some pictures, but the pages were mostly white and full of words that looked *boring as heck.* Then a blank piece of paper floated onto Candy's desk, and Miss Thompson The Tall was standing over her, handing her a box of colored pencils, saying, "Candy, these don't have to be the pictures in this book, you know. You know what I'd like to see? I'd like to see you read the words and draw the illustrations you would draw if it were your own book." And Candy Baby thought that was a very good idea—she'd show Miss Thompson what an *entertaining* book would look like.

"Gutting a fish," Mr. Justin said to us, "ain't no picnic." His grizzled hands were always so graceful, especially when handling anything dangerous. "But fortunately I've found that almost anything you do in life can start to feel ordinary if you do it enough." There were three fish swim-flopping in confused circles in a threaded basket in the river off to Mr. Justin's right a few adult strides from one of the cleaning tables he'd built next to the river, where some just-placed gutting instruments gleamed meanly. "But I've gutted enough by now that it's past ordinary and into tedious." Candy Baby's little eyebrows furrowed in confusion, and she raised her hand, and Mr. Justin said, "It means I'm sick of it." Little Me, who'd seen Mr. Justin gut a fish before, said, "I don't want to gut any fish, Mr. Justin." "Why not?" "Because it's gross." "You know what else is gross, Big Boy?" "What?" "A lot of shit. Get used to it."

I was crying. I had just returned from another week with Mr. Justin, and once again I'd perhaps allowed myself to be rattled by his gruffness in order to be soaked in love from a breast-to-holding, tear-kissing, back-stroking Miss Thompson. "Why's he so *mean,* Miss T?" I asked, my voice quivering with my melodrama. Candy Baby walked over and joined Miss Thompson in stroking my back, and she said, "I don't think he's mean, Big—he's just always so sewious." After hearing that, I stopped crying so desperately, and eventually Miss Thompson was able to rock me to a sleepy calm. After Miss T put me to bed, she went downstairs and found Candy Baby coloring pictures at the desk of the closed shop, and Miss Thompson said, "Candy, that was a really bright thing you said to Big Boy up there: I'm very proud of you for being so perceptive." Candy Baby kept coloring as if Miss Thompson hadn't said anything. "Candy?" Candy must've been playing one of her games again, Miss Thompson figured. "Candy?" Miss Thompson tapped Candy's shoulder, but Candy just kept coloring. "Can'?" The tap stayed on the shoulder and rounded down to under the armpit—a devilishly ticklish spot for Candy Baby, who Miss Thompson could see was biting her cheek to keep from revealing her tickly delight, but when Miss Thompson got her fingertips under the other armpit, it was over: Candy Baby burst into laughter and gleefully squirmed away from the tickling fingers, and upstairs the comforting sound of Candy laughing helped me drift to sleep.

A night so freezing cold even the trees looked like they were shivering to the shivering Candy Baby, and the whole world was howling. The black leaves above were not only being slapped by sheets of rain but whole trees were being tossed—black-green cathedrals waving helplessly—from side to side by the force of the huge winds. Barely capable of being heard over the storm, Mr. Justin shouted, *"You're probably not going to like this, kids!"* We were all huddled on the floor of the forest, miles from our shelters, on purpose, because Mr. Justin had his own extreme ways sometimes. *"But you're going to be able to look back on this for the rest of your lives—"* A cloud-to-cloud lightning strike, remarkably close to the ground, threw off a roar of thunder that sent a wave of spasms down the spines of us kids as we and Mr. Justin all clung together in the freezing, forest-bottom dread. *"And you're going to be able to say, 'I was out there when it was the worst! I was out there! I was afraid, I was a child, and here I am alive and stronger than you now!'"* This time, the lightning was cloud-to-tree, a hundred yards away, and the explosion of sound was a blast of heart-freezing fright. The man was utterly insane. *"If we survive!"* I screamed out in terror and rage. *"Isn't this exciting?!"* Mr. Justin shouted in response. Candy Baby breathed deeply and watched the trees wave and shiver as she shivered. The black and electric-white storm continued to howl and strike.

In the map in my head, the stream we were high-knee stepping across was called Black Bear Stream, because I once saw a black bear there and shot it. This was the first time Candy Baby had come out shooting with me, and she was "as nervous as a purse in prison." It was always one thing with Mr. Justin there, big as God and twice as powerful, but when it was just her twig arms and clumsy me, who was only three years older, she realized how deeply complex it was, where we lived. The forests and the fields never seemed to stop, and there could be anything in them. She'd been warned by Mr. and Miss both: First sign of something strange, something besides the animals she'd been sent out there to shoot, she was repeatedly and much-stressingly instructed to beat the fastest path back that her Candy Baby legs could carry her, right back to Mr. Justin's camp. Both of us children had those marching/running orders. The first orders, however, started with Miss Thompson, who'd given us the cameras we were holding high above the chuckling waters of Black Bear Stream as we crossed. "Big, why do you think Mr. Justin is makin' us creep up and take pictures of animals?" "Let's just get through this, Candy—you know I don't know."

Non scholae, sed vitae discimus.—
"We learn not for school, but for life."

Candy Baby burped, I laughed, and Dr. James swallowed his frustration. "No, Candy, a belch is not the answer. Would you like to try again?" It looked like Candy Baby was trying to force herself to fart, and Dr. James said, "No!" and Candy Baby laughed with delight now that she'd gotten a rise out of him. "It's five," I said, trying to get the lesson back on track. "No, it's not," Candy Baby said, "it's seven!" Dr. James slumped his shoulders and said to himself, "Both incorrect—I'm not a very good teacher, am I?" "Nope!" Candy Baby said. It was warm in the upstairs of the boarded-up Biblio-Files, and outside everything was voidishly quiet.

Mr. Justin said to me, "What is this—impatience? A fish is a fish for its own sake all its life; you wish for it to be a fish for your sake in an instant?"

It was so early in the morning even the foliage was yawning. A light-silver mist rose into the rapidly heating summer air. The sun was not yet day-yellow, was in the transition from sunrise-red-pink-orange-yellow into the brief orange-yellow of acute evening and morning, getting hotter by the breath. At the other end of the plowed field, at the top of the smallish column of carrots—on the border of a personal garden he had cleared out back in the second year of his reclusion—Mr. Justin was hunched down and weeding just like us children and Miss Thompson at the bottom of the column. Everyone's marching orders had come from Mr. Justin: "If it doesn't look like these"—the above-ground, telltale sprouts of carrots, kwehju, and potatoes—"then pinch it by its stem and worm out the roots." Worming out: taking the stem and carefully sliding it back and forth, worm-style, until the roots lost their footing and the weed came out fully intact, to be thrown into the big pile off to the side. A breeze arrived and pushed everyone's hair around and cooled the sweat sprouting out of our scalps. Kneeling painfully, with my big legs and arms and hands, I hated weeding, was just no good at it, and many times I impatiently/accidentally snapped the weed off at the base and looked around embarrassed and kicked the dirt where the roots were still intact. Behind me, Candy Baby seemed to delight in the worming, and each time she pulled out a full weed, she held it aloft and exclaimed triumphantly, "Ah-*HA!*"

The first time Candy Baby pulled a trigger, age ten, her shot (almost miraculously) exploded the bottle she was aiming at, and though her arms and shoulders were able to absorb the shock, her sense of balance didn't absorb it, and she would've fallen straight on her butt had not Mr. Justin seen it coming and caught her before she fell. I burst out laughing in a cruel/uncruel way, and Candy Baby looked at the ground embarrassed. "Sorry, Mr. Justin," she said. But Mr. Justin had been proud that Candy Baby, who loathed guns, was willing to pull the trigger. "Candy, you're a natural—you just needed to experience it once so now you can master it. And I'm not sure why you're laughing so hard, Big Boy—from what I remember, you and Candy handled your first shot about the same, except I don't see any piss in her pants."

(Thinking back on it, I've realized that a controlled fire, a glowing firepit, was the first form of entertainment. Before plays, books, radio, television, computers, OmniViewers . . . there were people sitting around staring stupidly and appreciatively into the brilliant magic of fire.) It was night, and we were all watching the logs and tongues: Mr. Justin and Miss Thompson huddled together warmly, listening to the snaps and gazing contentedly into the glow, Candy Baby slightly turned away from the light, using it to read by—she had entered one hell of a reading kick—and me, my freshly cleaned and unloaded rifle across my lap, the flickering firelight reflecting off the long gleaming barrel and my stupidly slack, appreciative eyes as I gazed into the breathing fire. An animal snapped a twig nearby, and Candy Baby looked up from her book, saw nothing in the blackness, and continued her gaze up through the canopy to the tiny dots of light hanging in the air trillions of miles away. The firelight and the starlight both flickered.

Late fall, a cold rain pecking at the ground, something didn't feel right, or maybe smell right, in the air. A day has a song and sound and rhythm that can be broken by human voices and activities. If those human signatures are expected from long familiarity, they become a part of the song of the day, but if they are foreign, it can have the effect of the proverbial needle scratching the proverbial record. Around midmorning the song came to a stop, and the sounds of humans and horses filled the air. Two each. Candy Baby was already inside the kids' cabin when I came flying in, throwing the door closed but slowing it down right at the last moment so as not to call attention to our location with a slam. "I already *told*—" "*Shhh!—strangers.*" I moved the desk and chair into position, and Candy Baby, closer, grabbed our hunting rifles with quivering hands—she'd still never shot anything living yet, only cans, bottles, and disappointing books—and to reassure her as I took my rifle I said quietly, "If anything happens, I got it—just hang onto yours in case I miss." When the two men with their two heavily packed horses came walking into camp—eight hooves and four feet squishing wet leaves—they also came upon a seriously grizzled man pointing a high-caliber rifle at them, who seemed to appear out of nowhere. "STOP! Who goes?" "Jesus! Apologies, sir—we didn't see anyone here." The men's guns were close at hand, but the bearded man had the jump on them. "WHO GOES?" "Larry and Jason Gilmore, sir—travelers and traders, trying to survive." "Brothers." Larry Gilmore tried to step forward to offer his hand, but Mr. Justin took a compensatory step back and kept the barrel fixed on them. "What sort of trading?" "As he said, sir, we're just trying to survive—commerce trading." "We trade what we have to trade with." "You can ride those things; they can be ridden?" "The horses?" Mr. Justin didn't answer obvious questions. They looked at their horses and then back at Mr. Justin. "Yes, we can ride them." A long moment of silent thought. "I've got stockpiles of food hidden in these woods—teach me and my kids to ride and I'll feed you during their tutelage and provide you with a week of provisions when you leave." To Larry and Jason, that sounded like a fine deal. "One rule: You touch either of those kids in a way that's improper, or you try to pull something over on me—" "Let me guess, you'll think it's hysterical and clap our backs with praise and good humor, right? Listen, fella, we're just two guys trying to figure out what's next in a world full of what happened, and even if we were a threat, look at us, we wouldn't be much. We think your deal is a fine one, and we'll teach you and your kids how to horse, no problem." Mr. Justin appreciated the brothers' candor. He whistled loudly, and Candy and I came out from our cabin timidly, scared of both the strangers and the staggering size of the pack-laden beasts they'd brought.

Candy Baby hadn't been able to sleep lately. There was something curious deep down in the bottom of her mind—there was something down there that she couldn't see clearly and couldn't successfully seem to suss out. She couldn't even see the edges, to see what generally it might be, since specificity certainly wasn't rushing towards her. She lighted a candle and dug back into "L" (*Children's Classic Encyclopedia,* Volume L—that month's assignment from Miss T) while it was still blackest night outside the cabin, even after the bugs had gone to sleep themselves. The sound of the pop of the match awakened me up in my loft, and I opened my eyes and saw the softly glowing tides of candlelight running up and down the wall by the door, by the furs. "Can't sleep, Can'?" The placement of a bookmark, the closing of a book. "Can't stop thinking. But what's weird is I don't even know what I'm thinking about." Nothing from me in the loft. Then, from the loft: "Um . . . Hmm." "I know; you don't know—it's fine." But I was still curious. "When did you start thinking about it?—whatever you don't know you're thinking about." "That's the thing: Part of the thing I keep thinking is about how I feel like I've been thinking about this for a long time and not knowing it, and I think that's why it's so gnawy now." A sleepy, bemused snort from the loft. "Gnawy?" "It's gnawing at me." "For how long?" "Kind of for as long as I can remember." Nothing from the loft or the room below. "Maybe you're thinking about George." "What?" "The boy who set the fire." "The boy who set what fire?" "The fire Mr. Justin saved us from—do you really not remember, Can', or is this one of your things?" "Big, I was *two,* for crying out loud." "OK, jeez. George was an older boy who got possessed or something one night and set the whole orphanage on fire—I saw him running around screaming and punching old Abraham flat before I ran back to the bedroom. For some reason, Mr. Justin saved crazy George along with us—you have to remember that,

62

at least." "Yeah, I kind of—I think." Nothing from the loft. From the room below: "You know what? I think I might be thinking about whoever George was." I could anticipate her next question. "Mr. Justin and Dr. James got him adopted within a few days of gettin' to Sweet Bend." For a moment that was somehow pleasant to hear, but then it kind of didn't make sense to Candy Baby. "Who'd want to adopt a crazy kid who set fire to an orphanage and killed a priest?" The truth was that I had been so glad to be rid of that creepy lump, who used to be a big bully, that I'd immediately believed the guardians who'd told me of the adoption. "Good question, Candy." Candy blew out the candle and said, "We'll have to ask Mr. Justin about it sometime."

We were out on a hunt, and in many places when you are hunting you are also being hunted. Three months previously, on a fine, early-summer evening, Candy Baby had shot a rabbit—her first successful hunt. In reviewing the day of work, she'd found that she loved the hunt and hated the kill. Unfortunately, the crumbling American infrastructure of the time meant that the timely deliveries of stocks of food and resources (via Sweet Bend, via Miss Thompson, who stuffed us children but good thanks to a maternal instinct to Feed as well as her own revolted reaction to Mr. Justin's ascetic woodland diet) was growing more and more uncertain, and the first war after peace breaks down is against the undomesticated animals: Humans gotta eat. To Candy Baby, traps were even more fun than hunting, but then she had to kill with her own hands or a knife—right up close. Nevertheless, though she hunted and trapped, make no mistake: Candy Baby, like many human females, loved animals like they were angels.

But more than animals she loved Mr. Justin, and Mr. Justin said he needed her and my help, gruesome help sometimes, if we were all going to survive while the world tried to catch its breath and fix its hair in the mirror. Thus, she had her rifle, and I had mine, and Mr. Justin had his, and we all had our knives tucked away safely yet readily. Perhaps the most ridiculous hunting party ever assembled: a (remarkably strong for being so small but still just a) twelve-year-old little girl, a fifteen-year-old large boy whose feet looked like skis and who had a similarly ski-footed, stumbling gait, and a wildly bearded thirty-three-year-old, slightly hunched man who was half-feral and half-philosopher and who almost never said a word at all. "I smell bear," he said, and we kids, who'd been dreading this whole hunt since Mr. Justin told us about it the previous night, went pale with fear. Mr. Justin looked back and saw he was losing his troops at the most critical time, so he snapped his fingers between our heads, gathering our attention to him: "It's OK to be afraid, but it's not OK to let the fear be the only hand at the wheel—just let it give you its energy; it's a gift." Candy and I both tried to get our internal motors to convert anxiety into intensity. It was kind of working, or at least, for now, possibly having a placebo effect. We looked up at him as if awaiting further instructions. "OK, now if—" but he was interrupted by a terribly frightening sound: foliage being crushed heavily, heading directly towards the hunting party, and the low chuff and growl of an attacking grizzly bear. Evidently, these were the bear's tactics: The little one was too small to be a threat, and the middle one could be dealt with later, but the biggest one had to go first. Knocking the middle one— me—aside with a forehand swipe that gashed my right arm, the grizzly went up on two legs, over ten feet tall, and came down on Mr. Justin, who dropped himself to the ground as the bear came down, and the bear's swipes and bites missed, and Mr. Justin continued rolling back, onto his back, and thrust his legs up with adrenaline force, effectively resulting in a boot-first, full-body's-worth-of-upperkick to the lower jaw of the starving, powerful animal. Mr. Justin continued rolling back over his head and ended up sitting on his feet momentarily while he reassessed the situation: I kept switching from looking at my wounds to looking at the scene, from crying to incredulity, and Candy Baby was bawling and reaching helplessly towards the strangely Buddhist seated figure that Mr. Justin had ended up in. The bear was weaving dizzily and trying to remount a charge after a big unexpected blow and turned its attention to me, for I was the only one bleeding, and a bear can smell blood like pizza. "Candy!" Mr. Justin shouted, already standing and having shouldered his rifle to the It's Business Time angle. Candy saw him. "THE NECK! NOW!" Mr. Justin fired his first shot, which ripped into the bear's neck, but this barely seemed to register with the desperate behemoth. The bear was within arm's reach, smelling like death, but it was looking at Mr. Justin now, who'd just shot it. I was of no help at all—was in fact on my side, pale as a possum, breathing but staring at nothing, in shock. Candy Baby knew what she needed to do. Mr. Justin was rapidly chambering another rifle shell, and now the bear was interested in Candy, was headed towards her, the easiest prey. "THE HEAD, THE NECK—DO IT, CANDY!" Mr. Justin put another round into the area of the neck where he thought/hoped there was a major artery, near his first bullet. The bear had been slowed by this second shot, but Candy Baby was in the unfortunate position of being the thing the dying bear was going to spend the last remnants of its energy rage-killing. But Candy Baby spoke up on behalf of her own destiny and fired a bullet through the upturned mouth of the roaring bear, and five of its jagged teeth were blown out into the forest, and the bear had had enough, tried to make a fatal, diagonal, almost piteous escape, and slumped to the ground, where we all watched the beast's heartbeat die along with the cannonshots of blood spurting from the holes in its neck.

Ducunt volentem fata nolentem trahunt.— "The fates lead the willing and drag the unwilling."

The skipping pebble has reached the far ten-year shore.

Despite the fact that Candy and I had been put up for adoption and almost died in an orphanage fire and later in a grizzly attack, we had been lucky—or at least luckier than the other children in the orphanage, and the bear. But in late summer of the extraordinary year I turned fifteen and Candy Baby turned twelve, just after the bear attack, our little bit of luck shrank to almost nothing.

The technically successful but rather unsuccessful bear-hunt ended with those pulsing cannonshots of blood around midday, and five hours later we were all back in Sweet Bend, with Mr. Justin holding one of his shirts against my four open claw wounds, pretty much carrying me like that, with his big arm wrapped tight around my shoulders. I cried the whole way, and Candy Baby was an absolutely nervous wreck, especially after Mr. Justin had said, "There might be others, Candy, so watch our backs on the way back." And no two backs were ever so thoroughly watched as those that were watched on the dreadful hike back to camp by an adrenaline-charged twelve-year-old Sylvia Thompson.

Back at the camp, Mr. Justin pulled the shirt away from my wounds, and for a moment the cuts were clean and pink, and then they began filling with and streaming red tears.

I screamed louder than anything Candy'd ever heard when Mr. Justin splashed pure rubbing alcohol on the wounds, as an anti-infection stopgap until Dr. James could get at the arm. After my painful shriek, I went back to moaning and weeping, and Mr. Justin, who'd never cottoned a single tear from us kids, just let me go on with it, reasoning to me later that if he'd been hurt like that he would've probably been crying himself.

It used to be that Candy Baby would get nauseous when she saw open flesh, but living half your life where the wild things are can have a way of curbing the disgust. It's like Mr. Justin said about anything becoming ordinary. And now that she was getting old enough to harbor her own ideas, she shared one with Mr. Justin as he tended to my wounds.

"We should get Dr. James to help us."

Mr. Justin was the type of person who could say this sort of thing and not make it sound offensive: "No shit, Candy."

Candy Baby was a little embarrassed, and she clarified. "Sorry, Mr. Justin; what I meant is maybe he could teach us some medicine stuff, if it isn't too hard to learn."

Times were dangerous, indeed; whether in the mild of the protracted civil war or in the wild that is always at war, medical knowledge would help us kids survive in our times' general disarray.

"I apologize, Candy," Mr. Justin said. "You're right."

Back in Sweet Bend, Miss Thompson nearly fainted from the sight of me all bandaged up and scared like that, and it felt like forever before Dr. James, who was the only capable doctor in the area, arrived back in town and was able to tend to my dreadful-looking arm and shoulder.

That night it was arranged that Candy and I would also begin receiving basic lessons in health, anatomy, and chemistry from Dr. James, who received nothing in return except the feeling of making a contribution to the tattered lives of good people in piteous circumstances.

Unfortunately, no good deed goes unpunished.

The morning after the bear attack, back in the woods, Candy Baby, who'd been correct in seeking Dr. James' tutelage, once again brought up something else she'd been thinking about.

"Why do we live in the woods, Mr. Justin?"

Candy Baby and Miss Thompson had asked the question before (I was always too afraid to), but Mr. J had always just laughed it off by saying something like "That's a funny question for someone with a big ugly green thing stuck in her teeth like that," and the ladies would usually clutch at their faces and look at him angrily when he started chuckling. But that morning, under the shadow of the attack, my arm still weeping blood between the stitches, the question was justified to the point that Mr. Justin not only wasn't laughing it off but was finally taking it seriously. Candy Baby was internally thrilled to have finally asked the question that broke him.

"Because to me this is life, Candy, so this is where I live and where you sometimes live with me."

"Why don't you like it in town?" I asked now that the horse was doing backflips out of the barn. "Don't you like Miss Thompson?"

"Like a family?" Candy added. We children had been thinking about this a lot, Mr. Justin could especially tell, because I, doped on painkillers, hadn't said much all day—had just followed the conversations with my eyes, with a dopey smirk of opiate sunshine on my otherwise cloudy face.

"'Our ways were two ways—one each—and each one went one, and not the other,'" Mr. Justin said quoting a line of poetry he'd once read. "Your mother is alive in her store—she can take it there."

"Take what?"

Mr. Justin, when he was really thinking about something hard, would trace the line of his jaw with his thumb and index finger, meeting under the chin, where he'd pinch the beard hair for a moment and start over. He often did this when trying to frame his answers in a way we kids might understand.

"You children haven't been very much exposed to it, and I suppose on your medical runs with Dr. James it'll be inevitable, but the American country that you read about in your books is really out there, but nothing in those books has translated it properly that I've ever seen. There's a culture out there—and from what Emily and James tell me, it's only gotten worse—but yeah there's a culture out there that can kill you dead and keep you alive the whole time. A culture where everyone you know is dead but still walking around."

"I don't understand," Candy Baby said, and she sounded spooked. In my glazed confusion I agreed with Candy Baby on both counts.

"Think of it this way: When one person acts a certain way, that's his or her personality, and when you look at all of those personalities and behaviors all together, that's a culture—it's everything people do and celebrate and value. Kids, you two couldn't be further from the norm of that culture, and I'm not happy you're headed out into it, but our ways are three ways, one each, and you'll need to know what's around you before you can figure out where you want to go with your lives. I ended up in the woods, but our brains have unique fingerprints, brainprints, and you might find the feeling of sunshine on your shoulders somewhere else. But we live in the woods because I live in the woods, and I live in the woods because I had nothing in common with anyone in my culture—even people like me, I don't like people like me. I like you kids, and I like Emily, and James is a good man, but when I thought of living with Emily, I thought of all those people she and James know, all those artificial hierarchies of social power, and I guess they can take all that. But I can't take almost anyone or anything. My brainprint—"

"What's wrong with all the people's behaviors?"

"Tell you what, Candy, when you head out with Dr. James and meet the people out there, you tell me what you think. Maybe I'm wrong about them. All I really know is I'm right about me. Even if I die out here, I feel like I'll have been more alive for a lot longer than anyone around here for miles."

Candy Baby and I both grew even more nervous about our coming travels with Dr. James.

"Yeah, but, so, it's like, but, what do you say when we have a problem around here?" Candy Baby asked, nervously willing to see how far she could put her finger in Mr. Justin's psychic wound. "'Fix it,' right? So how come you didn't fix it if there's something wrong with it?"

"'Cause I'm not Atlas, Candy—the world doesn't turn on my shoulders. I'm just a man who didn't see a solution and wanted out of the problem. If you kids see the same things I saw, maybe you'll figure it out. I used to have some answers, but they were unpopular. Now my answer is this, here—*awayness.* It's not much of an answer, but it's been a rewarding solution. If it makes you unhappy—"

"It doesn't, Mr. Justin," Candy said. She was lying, but the lie contained truth, too, because she'd go anywhere in the world to be with her big heroic bearded father whose occasional approval seemed to keep her spine straight.

Children, even the opiate-doped, are aware when real love is given to them, and both of us had always felt the warmth of that love and loved Mr. Justin back.

Candy Baby, who was starting to get too old to do much lap-sitting anymore, walked over and sat on Mr. Justin's lap and put her arms around his neck and hugged him.

"I'm so sorry about yesterday," he said to us, fighting off his tears. "I'm just so worried about making you both strong, I—" He didn't want to say it out loud. In his haste to grow us up he'd almost led us to our deaths, maybe also his own. He asked himself why he constantly felt like he was in such a hurry, and he was earnestly striving towards that idea when we first heard the surreal jingling.

Individually they were invisible; in sum they were a glimmering mist of invisibility with rounded, rainbow edges—billions of transparent bubbles moving like a swarm that rose and fell, probed and recoiled. The swarm was made visible only by the way the round outsides of each drone in the swarm bent the light and color of the objects behind it. The jingling, the sound produced by contact between individual nanobots within the pulsing cluster, was eerie in an abstract way: Normally the jingling of metal, the tiny chiming of little bells, is associated with something holy and cherished and celebrated; but the aural signature of the drone-swarm took, in the human brain, an innocent sound and put it in a completely foreign context.

The first sight of a nano-swarm often drove people to the ground with nausea—although humans had seen flocks of birds and insects before, the sight of a flock of R&R nanobots was so foreign to the mind and body that the two often complemented each other in response: The body tried to purge whatever had gone wrong through diarrhea and vomit, and the mind went into the familiar confines of nausea and dread. After a few more moments of exposure, the mind and body gave up rejecting the sight of the surreal swarm, and a sort of awareness or acceptance broke through.

Mr. Justin and we kids, fresh off our life-threatening battle with the bear, merely regarded and accepted the swarm: We were able to skip the part where we shit and puked all over ourselves like most people—at the time our brains were just too fried to fry.

But although Mr. Justin didn't have to endure the usual rigors of acceptance, he immediately knew, with heavy dread, that our old life was gone—the bloody gashes on my arm, which would eventually scar impressively, would be a sort of tattoo, a symbol of something gone that was worth remembering, that had cut deep.

Candy and I watched the swarm in a quiet awe, but Mr. Justin knew his forest bubble had finally and irrevocably been burst, and after the swarm became a mist and penetrated every nano-space in the camp (and even it felt like our bodies), it became a swarm again and jingled off deeper into the forest.

Mr. Justin began wondering where we could possibly go next.

Secretary of the Department of Homeland Security Milton W. Blank, born in '49, a Motherfucking Boomer, had authorized the release of the first swarm of R&R drones on the North American continent three years earlier. Today, his desk was piled with Action Plans and Data Reports concerning the sixty-eight percent of the North American continent that the swarms had so far investigated. Despite the piles of waiting work, he was saying the same thing he was always saying, this time to Secretary of State Patricia Donahue, '47, Boomer.

"Whole damn country—" Blank said and was clarified by Donahue.

"World."

"Whole damn *world's* unraveled like diarrhea out of time's butthole, and the President, this President— *for now*—wants a whole heap of Action Plans—"

"We still have some might," Donahue said irono-bemusedly. "We might as well use it."

Blank mumbled a sarcastic reply, mocking the cliché, but also possibly fearing its truth: "The Leviathan will not go down without a fight, eh, Patty?"

Mrs. Donahue, like Mr. Blank doing her damnedest to fight the good fight for America's failing life, saw an opportunity to emerge from Blank's doldrums and get some work done. "Speaking of which," she said, "I'm here to make some notes on those, if they're ready."

Blank's hand immediately and subconsciously reached out to and landed on top of the day's queue of Action Plans. He had not yet gone through them, as, truth be told, he spent most of his days staring out the window, at the horizon, searching for the answer to an impossible question: How could he get the genie back into the bottle? It certainly wasn't going to happen by poring through the weak-witted Action Plans sent up by his subordinates. For now, he had no answer, and he had to buy some time.

"They're not ready."

"All right—so what am I doing here?"

"Do you think this is working? This whole process? Is this how we're going to do it?"

These kinds of shifts in Milton's mind gave him a certain perspectival wisdom, in the lawyerly sense, which isn't saying much. He was the type of person who could vacillate on whether he liked the sun. He could divide himself endlessly, and just as easily, he could combine seemingly unrelated ideas as well. Ultimately he was one of history's most capable bureaucrats, which isn't saying much.

"Christ, Milton, grow a pair. We have to do something, and you're not the President yet, so just do your job, you ninny."

She left Blank's office with disgust.

Patricia Donahue was quickly rising in the line of succession to the Presidency, and Blank knew that she'd grown short with him mainly because lately the line of succession was essentially a countdown to her death—in the ten years since the federal collapse, she'd attended more than her share of (former) state funerals, and she was starting to see her own ahead, possibly.

Milton Blank slumped back in his chair, shrugged further, sat back up, and picked up the top Action Plan, titled: "PROBABLE LOCATION FOR PEACE CONFERENCE SITE LOCATED, DEPLOYMENT READY."

Finally an interesting report—a ray of light, something to keep that string-pulling Savage off his back! He set it on his lap and gave himself a cheat-peek at the Action Plan below that one, the next in the pile, as a way of gauging how the rest of his morning would go. The next Action Plan was titled: "T.S. PROJECT VELVET WAVES READY FOR FINAL TEST, LOCATION/SUBJECTS TBD."

"Finally, indeed!" he said and a broke into a half-grim smile.

Master Sergeant Saxon Rhysdale, the pilot of PRGN-5-5571—a common predator drone generally known as a Peregrine—was one of the finest drone pilots in human existence in the period after the collapse. His sortie-effects were as dependable as it got in what was formerly America.

And the formerly American military, fighting for its life and funded by the two deep-coffered political parties and the AARBB, was getting more and more desperate by the dying day.

The Master Sergeant lived on base and walked to work. Once he was settled at his desk, he looked at the day's list of Actuated Action Plans and found only one—a cleansing run near the mouth of the Blunt River in the Titan Mountains (a cleansing run being the quick deployment of a mist of R&R bots that, in being atomized and spread out, invisibly researched and reconnaissance'd an area before a squad of troops would hike in). M. Sgt. Rhysdale could finish a sortie like that drunk while asleep with his hands tied behind his back, so he was looking forward to another easy day of using his bird's billion eyes to search for nude sunbathers and outdoor survivalist fornicators.

The National Guard, by order of an Action Plan from President Conrad, deployed a squad of ten soldiers to locate and arrest a Mr. Dennis Robert Justin for housing and possibly having kidnapped two children not recognized in the national database of citizens after the area's R&R-tube nanodata had been adequately sifted.

The squad was led by First Sergeant Frank Herman Kenderdragen. The nine privates at his heel were unknown to him, but he was lucky anyone had shown up at all—he'd once been ordered to quell a riot at a federal building, and the only soldiers who'd reported for duty were himself and a coked-up hermaphrodite named Kennedina (one hell of a shot by the way). The National Guard just couldn't keep up with the scale of the social decay, and its own ranks shrank and grew seemingly at random.

Now he was in the woods? With all these guys?

Ours is but to hike in pines he thought to himself and listened to the men wheeze behind him. He had stopped them so they could catch some air.

"It's good to stop here—we're almost there."

"Shit, even if we are, what are we doing out here, Sergeant?"

"Don't you read your A.P.'s, Private? Possible terrorist or kidnapper in these woods—wanted thief, unregistered survivalist with two unrelated, only regionally registered children—and we've been tasked with assessing and suppressing the threat."

"Ten of us, Sergeant?"

Kenderdragen wasn't alone then. "That is strange, isn't it? But the A.P. said this guy had a good amount of guns and ammunition, so maybe they're just being cautious."

"That sound like The Wolf to you, Sergeant?"

The other men laughed.

"But orders are orders; right, Sarge?"

Kenderdragen shuddered briefly and stood more erectly, assuming the posture of a man who was ready to again take on a more literal leadership role. "Silence from here in—and no firing unless fired at: Intelligence and PR want these people alive."

A few of the less encouraging younger punks were disappointed this wasn't an authorized wet mission, and they grumbled at the back of the ranks. Kender-dragen would have to keep an eye on them.

By the time Sgt. Kenderdragen and the National Guard squad arrived at Mr. Justin's camp, the camp was deserted, but Mr. Justin and Candy and I, as I said, had run short on luck, and the same time the soldiers were arriving was the same time we had finally loaded up both boats (the new one—a gift from Miss Thompson—and Mr. Justin's old one) with all our best stuff from camp, to be moved to Sweet Bend and possibly beyond.

Moments after Kenderdragen and his men began searching our abandoned camp, they were drawn to the river, to the sound of Mr. Justin cord-yanking his old fishing boat's outboard motor's engine to life—and the soldiers all ran to the shore, where they saw Mr. Justin and us kids scrambling into the boats.

They shouldered their rifles.

Candy and I jumped on top of the older boat, which Mr. Justin had brought to life, and which Candy manned and pointed downriver. As we escaped we both desperately yelled for Mr. Justin to hurry, and Mr. Justin was hurrying, but his new engine wasn't catching—he'd put the older fuel in the newer engine.

Kenderdragen said something to Mr. Justin, and Mr. Justin stopped trying to start the motor, even though we were screaming for him to get away from all those scary soldiers.

Rhysdale's Peregrine streaked overhead.

M. Sgt. Saxon Rhysdale, expecting to see nothing on the river or in the woods where he was ordered to release the R&Rs, instead saw ten members of the National Guard pointing rifles at a man who was trying to join two smaller people in escape. Because he'd done it a thousand times before, when his system began its countdown to launching the tube Rhysdale began and executed the process for a perfectly timed chuck of his technological spear.

Something was wrong, however, and with furrowed eyebrows of confusion he turned the drone around and watched what happened next.

Above us, the drone released a tube the size of Mr. Justin, and the tube tumbled through the air and then popped open fifty feet above the ground into a puff of fog that softly descended onto the river and its banks.

M. Sgt. Rhysdale's confusion was further compounded by whatever the hell that mist was, which was obviously not a tube of R&Rs. Perhaps a defective tube? He'd never seen one before, but it might happen—he was no nanoscientist.

He kept watching.

Top Secret Project Velvet Waves was the result of an

early Action Plan authored by Milton W. Blank himself.

Blank's only son was a recovering drug addict who'd become an aggressive, condescending, self-righteous asshole since going clean, and Blank was darkly laughing at his own misfortune—having a son who was either a massive jerk or an aloof addict—when suddenly he realized maybe he could backwards-engineer a solution to the cancer within the American culture: Perhaps it was the drugs themselves that quelled his son's typical short-tempered, intolerant temperament; in which case perhaps the boys in lab coats could possibly come up with a safe drug that the former federal government could spread across the continent in order to quell the nation's growingly violent nature. Perhaps if people could experience a sustained relief from the simmering belligerence of late, they could begin to look for answers with an eye towards peace.

Three months later, the lab coats had a beta mist and some very promising rat results.

Already with an eye on a peace conference, the mere possibility of which he hoped would plant the seed of nonviolence (the former federal government had not announced it yet, as Frank Savage, the shadowy man behind the plan, was still in the early stages of assembling all the elements he would need to enact his full plan for peace), Blank figured what more perfect test for this new peace-creating drug could there be than at the very site where the peace conference would be held!

Blank was warned, and he eschewed the warnings: "They should have read the paperwork when they signed up; we didn't violate a single letter of their contracts," he told, in his mind, the theoretical defenders of the National Guard soldiers. "If they were completely innocent, they would've been on the national database of citizens," he told, in his mind, the theoretical defenders of Mr. Justin and his wards.

The DHS needed to see what Velvet Waves would do to children anyway.

He eagerly looked forward to the Data Report from his much-anticipated Action Plan.

A DHS scientist named Melissa Montague authored the chemical combination that was eventually given the code name Velvet Waves. I do not have a more precise technical writer's gift for making hyper-details interesting, so I'll stick to my broad strokes and say that later in the story we'll hear more about its chemical composition, and for now it's just important to note that it was aimed at the brains of physiologically male adults. And as has been noted, the adult lab rats seemed to love it.

The Peregrine circled the fog above the river and the forest, and M. Sgt. Rhysdale cycled through the views from his bird's many cameras and lenses in order to see what was happening. At the same time, he was reading the file he'd pulled up for the Action Plan the National Guard was actuating in that same mist, and in a nauseous awe he watched what happened next.

Hic sunt dracones.—
"Here there are dragons."

Nobody—not Mr. Justin nor Sgt. Kenderdragen nor we kids nor any of the other National Guardsmen—was encouraged to see the air filling with the tube-puffed mist, but just as suddenly as all the men's anxiety began to rise over what could be happening, what was happening started to happen, and their anxiety shrank like Alice and fell down a rabbit hole and disappeared completely: Sweet merciful Christ! How could they all have never noticed how much *love* there is between all people and all living things in existence? In fact 'love' is an ugly *grunt* for what really that word is supposed to represent; the soldiers and Mr. Justin knew that now because they'd finally truly felt what it was to love in a way so complete it made the whole world and all of life simple—there was love, and we have it, and it's the only thing we want now!

All the world is constantly making love to me, and I am constantly making love to all the world.

The men began to take their clothes off, all of them.

What are these uniforms? What are these layers between us? They are barriers for the love we hide from each other, which no longer can stand to be hidden. What a delight! Feel the fresh air of this world on the full truth of what you really are. Feel the full truth of you yourself, as I feel you! As we all feel each other and nibble and kiss and drag our lips across each other's beloved bodies! Oh, all of life is connection, and all connection is affection; the spirit animal begs to be petted and played with and acknowledged and longs to be let free—that which connects with and affects me shall receive double the connection and affection from myself to you, and if you love me as I love you, our love will become a perpetually growing emotional bliss!

The men began to love each other, and were loved by each other, and it perpetually grew in intensity.

In the boat still slowly motoring towards Sweet Bend, Candy and I watched, unable to look away but desperately wishing to—loving Mr. Justin too much to turn away from him even now.

All of the drugged soldiers and Mr. Justin stripped themselves naked and hugged and became aroused and loved each other, and their love and lust kept growing and doubling as promised by the powerful psycho-physiological machinations of Velvet Waves, and they thrust and grunted and gagged harder and harder to express the perfect mental and physical love they'd suddenly been blessed to discover, and the love they felt was so perfect that they didn't even notice that the feeling of *not being able to breathe* had become a literal danger—everything felt too good to ever stop; they could only go forward and down into the dynamic source of that love, within themselves and each other.

Mr. Justin was the second-last man to suffocate to death. He'd been pinned down and love-suffocated by Frank Kenderdragen, and then the giant Kenderdragen, having nobody else around to love, but still loving so much, began to writhe blissfully on the dead pile of naked men, alternately tipping himself back and trying to love himself, and finally tipping himself back too extremely and breaking his own neck.

Then I heard the Peregrine above, and I looked up, wanting something to feel pain for what I'd just seen. I lined up a shot with my rifle and narrowly missed hitting the fucking thing as it circled above us and watched.

M. Sgt. Rhysdale used the drone's cameras and homing

systems and discovered that the larger person in the boat's rifle slug had missed the Peregrine by a little more than an inch. Not wanting to risk the drone again, and not wanting to launch a missile at two children in a fishing boat, Rhysdale quickly pulsed at and copied two body-signatures of the kids on the river so he could subsequently follow what happened to them, us, and piloted the drone away from the Titan Mountains and back to its base. And then he looked away from his optics and into the room he sat in, and he leaned back and wondered what he should do about what he'd just seen.

Iuventuti nil arduum.—
"To the young nothing is difficult."

As we slowly motored, Hellshocked, to Sweet Bend, I was filled with psychic rage, and I wanted to go back and butcher all the men who'd hurt Mr. Justin, but a screaming and crying Candy Baby wouldn't let me. CB needed to see and hug Miss Thompson as soon as possible, and she was able to curb my rage and get me to let her just drive us to Sweet Bend by swinging an oar at my head when I started reaching for the tiller. She crunched me in the shoulder, the good shoulder, and that drove the message, and she drove us, home, to Miss T—yes, I finally realized and agreed, Miss T must be hugged and cried to immediately.

Candy's rage at me had quelled her weeping, and then both Candy Baby and I went quiet—the only sound we heard was the hum of the outboard motor.

Both of us were more or less dead inside by the time we arrived at the pier. Like clockwork oranges we tied up the boat and didn't even consider the idea of one of us staying behind to protect our remaining belongings—we just trudged into town, me clutching my rifle to my chest, Candy Baby following, frowning, staring at the ground, her fingers interlaced, holding her own hand, rifle shoulder-slung and sagging.

When Biblio-Files was in view, the recognition renewed our spirits enough that we both wordlessly broke into a run and pepper-stepped up the side stairs, to the more intimate door, and began pounding on it and yelling for Miss Thompson, who at the time was preparing some lunch, and she opened the door and was bumrushed by two children who dove into her grasp, tackled her to the floor, and Candy and I let ourselves go—*bawling.*

Immediately Miss Thompson knew that Mr. Justin was dead. That was the only explanation. After a chilling wave of nausea rippled through her body, which only lasted a moment—I could feel it happen—she put her arms around us and stared out the open door, at the largely boarded-up buildings of the town of Sweet Bend.

What earthly force could have possibly killed that man?

Candy and I cried and wept and wailed into Miss Thompson's breast, but eventually Miss Thompson emerged from her incredulity, felt a deep and terrible gash rend her soul, and the emotion that flowed to the top was not sadness but anger.

"Now STOP IT, kids!"

Miss Thompson had literally never yelled at us like that before, and we were so surprised by it that we both stopped crying, but a moment later she could feel all four hands clutching her dress beginning to tighten from emotion again, and she said, "Don't *indulge* in it; there's nothing to be gained—trust me—and you might lose your balance."

"But—" Candy Baby said.

"But what, Candy?" Miss Thompson asked, not in an aggressive way but in a way that indicated Miss Thompson was capable of listening to and logically defeating any counterargument Candy might provide.

"But you didn't see it!" I screamed, and because I was fifteen years old and hormonally a mess and traumatized for the umpteenth time in my fucking miserable life, I was so distraught by every nightmarish image flickering and gyrating through my head that I began slamming that head into the linoleum floor with all the energy I could put into it—I tried to dubiously bash the memories out of myself—and Miss Thompson caught and embraced my head after the first revolting-sounding slam.

"Tell me, Dante," she said, her voice quivering. "Tell me what happened—no matter how bad it is, I promise it will help you feel better if you both just tell me what happened."

These silent, scratched pages already know, and we children did an adequate enough description of it to the point that Miss Thompson eventually put the back of her right hand to her forehead—so heavy her feeling of anguish—and joined us in weeping in an agonizing mourning over the bizarrely horrible death of a man who filled his time and place as honorably as any man has ever done.

Secretary of the Department of Homeland Security Milton W. Blank was called into the office of the

President of the United States of America (former federal), who'd been serving under that role for nearly two months. His name was Jonathan Abraham Conrad, born in '50, Boomer, and before Blank sat down Conrad was screaming at him about the incident in the Titan Mountains.

The drone footage had been leaked to the *RothReport,* and now the terribly embarrassing and disturbing video was all over the place—with renewed arguments to step down being shouted from both sides of the aisle.

"Mr. President, in my defense, Project Velvet Waves was—"

President Conrad didn't have time for Blank's backpedaling.

"A tragedy? An embarrassment? Or I should say another! Christ, Milton, we're America!"

"Yes, sir, the b—"

"Did you not think about what would happen if your experiment were caught on camera by the firing drone or any of the dozen or so birds and satellites that could have recorded the incident without even intending to?"

The truth was that Blank had been thrilled it would be recorded; he had, after all, hoped it would be the moment the cure for the escalating decay had been found.

Also in the Oval Office was Secretary of State Patty Donahue, who spoke up on her own behalf by speaking up on Blank's.

"Sir, Milton sought my counsel on the matter, and I knew there was a risk, and I told him he had my full support. He's new at his job; let me take credit for the incident, and I'll resign, with your permission."

"Who knew being in the line of succession to the Presidency would ever be such a horrible threat?" President Conrad asked with a grim humor. The Secretary of State went pale; the Secretary of the Department of

Homeland Security chuckled sardonically at the truth of the rhetorical question. "No dice, Patty. Now what do you assholes propose we do about this?"

"Mr. President," said Blank, "besides the . . . incident . . . everything else went perfectly, and the contractors are already over at the forest beginning construction on the conference center—so rest assured that the grounds for peace are being built."

"Great," the President said. "We have a place to hold peace and no peace to hold."

"Sir," said the Secretary of State, "I'm completely willing to be the fall-woman for this, honestly."

The rough sound of the little boat's bottom rubbing against the sand and rocks of the riverbank announced the return of Miss Thompson and Candy Baby to Mr. Justin's camp. Miss T and Candy dragged the boat ashore approximately ten yards from the gross naked pile of dead men.

The previous night, everyone agreed that we had to return, to give Mr. Justin a proper burial, before any other government agents arrived and took what was left of him away from us. Miss T, however, would not allow me to return to the scene, after a night full of screaming nightmares. She wanted me to rest, and Dr. James stayed with me at Biblio-Files while the ladies returned for the corpse of their man.

The sound of the flowing river, the sough of the wind rustling the colored leaves, whistling and skirling in the treetops, the soft crunch of long-dead leaves underfoot, and the whining cries of the flies buzzing around the mouths, eyes, and anuses of the dead.

The first thing that happened was Miss Thompson fell to her knees and wept again when she saw the circumstantially horrible and bewildering proof that Mr. Justin really had been chemically induced into fatal lusting homosexual suffocation. Her heart figuratively burst when all the horrible truths began to rain upon her: such a great man and such a pawnish death; such good children and such a baffling and revolting final image of their devoted father-figure—surely there would be devastating psychological repercussions in her poor children, who'd already been through enough; such anguish would she feel in her chest, in the heart of every one of her seventy-five-trillion cells, for the rest of her life.

Eventually, Candy Baby, the quick study, tapped Miss Thompson on the shoulder and said, "Don't indulge in it, Miss T."

Miss Thompson stopped shuddering, put her hand on Candy Baby's hand, stood, and breathed life back into herself.

Rigor mortis works in stages, waxes and wanes, and fortunately for the ladies both Mr. Justin's and Mr. Kenderdragen's corpses—the two on top—were on the wane and malleable. The women (Candy Baby, twelve years old at that point, had seen and done enough in her troubled life to be called an honorary woman, despite the fact that she was still eight months away from the completion of her first menstrual cycle) worked silently as they dressed and dragged, as honorably as they could, Mr. Justin over to the landed vessel, where they draped the body into the center section between the two seats and covered it with a tarp from Mr. Justin's still-loaded and -anchored boat.

Afterwards, Miss Thompson piloted the boat with the body, and Candy Baby eventually started and drove Mr. Justin's, and they returned to Sweet Bend, where Dr. James and I met them at the dock with the home-made casket we'd built while the women were gone.

Dr. James and Miss T transferred the body to the casket, and we all carried the casket to the Sweet Bend

Cemetery. The cemetery was now owned by no one (formerly owned by the federal government, formerly owned by a Sweet Bender named Ramses James Huntington) and tended by the same. In silence we let ourselves in and met no resistance.

We found an open spot under a tall willow, and beneath a metallic-grey summer sky we drove the teeth of our shovels into the ground and pitched mouthfuls of dirt into the pile behind us, until the size and depth were enough that we had a grave, and using ropes we carefully lowered the casket into the dark earth and looked down onto the pale pine length of the box, spattered with grains and clumps of dirt from the descent, and an unsolicited moment of silence passed as we honored and contemplated the saintly deceased.

Dr. James eventually cleared his throat and asked, "Emily, do you or the kids have anything you want to say?"

Bitterly, Miss Thompson eventually responded, *"What's there to say?"*

Candy Baby didn't say anything. She had the same question.

I was the host of a storm of emotions, and the brightest flashes of lightning leapt from my rage.

"We'll probably be saying it for the rest of our lives, whatever the hell it is we're supposed to be saying now," I said, and I pitched a fistful of dirt at the casket and walked away.

Candy Baby put her hand in Miss Thompson's hand, which seemed to bolster them both in a much-needed way.

"Here lies Mr. Dennis Robert Justin," Dr. James said. "May he rest in peace." He began shoveling the soil back into the ground, on top of the casket.

Candy Baby and Miss T left together and walked back to the boarded-up Biblio-Files, both of them armed, because things were only getting worse in the world around them, but both of them were so dead to the world they might not have even noticed it even if trouble had introduced itself.

Well after the ladies were gone, I returned from an unsuccessful head-clearing walk through the cemetery and helped Dr. James finish the job. The whole time in my mind I just repeated vile heresies to myself, to God, the worst shit I could think of, to assuage the pain.

Upon returning and helping Dr. James, the exertion of the burial (and the continued internal heresy) was somewhat reining my psychic fury, and I kept working harder and harder at the job, but Dr. James could tell I was starting to get extremely emotional about the act of burying Mr. Justin, losing the reins again, and Dr. J didn't know what to do about it, so when the job was almost done the good doctor slunk off and waited by the entrance of the cemetery. At the gravesite, I heaved giant shovelfuls of dirt into the pit and let the basic needs of the job burn the excess energy off my jangled voltage, but again the emotional reaction began perpetuating and expanding itself until finally, when the ground was packed flat, I completely lost control and pitched myself on the dirt and began pounding on the ground with the face of the shovel and repeatedly howling, *"FUCK! YOU! GOD!"*

Eventually my strength gave out, and I fell prone on the bald gravesite, breathing heavily from my petulant fit, and stayed down there and watched as my breath and the wind pushed and pulled all the little grains of dirt on the ground right in front of my face, unable to think about anything more complicated than that.

When I emerged at the gates of the cemetery, Dr. James said I was back to looking like myself, rather than the George-like state I'd briefly entered during the shoveling, but he said I did look very tired. We walked back a little after a dark-grey noon, carrying our rifles silently and listening to the wind in the trees and the distant deep booms of thunder or bombs—at that point, who knew or cared?

After he'd finally been forced to give up his medical practice, Dr. James purchased a huge used van and painted it white and added a big brown cross on both sides, along with two white flags hanging from the back, also brown-crossed. Traveling in a conventional vehicle was an invitation to freeway robbery, kidnapping, and murder, Dr. James had discovered. But only a small percentage of desperate lowlifes are so anti-human that they could look at a medicine van and see a mark—and even if they did, it would only be to flag the doctor down, force him or her to perform medical procedures, and steal all the money and supplies; but they almost always were willing to let doctors live, Dr. James had discovered.

Miss Thompson and Dr. James thought it would be best for all of us to travel as a family on Dr. James' medical rounds—to distract ourselves from our mourning and worries, to begin introducing me and Candy to the world outside of the woods and Sweet Bend, and in the process Dr. James could begin to lay the pedagogical foundation of his accumulated medical knowledge so that we kids would always have the safe harbor of the brown cross to give us a fighting chance at survival in the new, ancient world.

After the first trip, which had taken five days—an uneventful visit to a quiet village and a town that appeared to have been deserted—we returned to Biblio-Files and were awakened the next morning by loud knocking at both doors, followed immediately by broken windows and flash-bang grenades, followed by a storm of National Guard soldiers. They grabbed all of us, but when the soldiers grabbed me, I put up a hell of a fight briefly until one of the soldiers clacked his rifle's butt into the back of my head, and I went back to black. They physically carried all four of us out of the building, where I was laid out flat and Candy was instructed to kneel in the mud with her hands behind her head, and the adults were kicked and shoved into the same position as Candy. Dr. James tried to explain that he and his sister were now the regionally recognized legal guardians of the children. All they knew of Dennis Robert Justin was that he was the man who had saved the children from the fire at Lost Angels. No, they did not know what happened to the man—in fact, they were more than relieved to hear that the creepy woodsman was being sought by the authorities; they suspected he might've liked little Sylvia a little too much, if they were being honest. The children weren't on the national registry of citizens because Dr. James thought the orphanage had taken care of that—a simple lack of vigilance, hastily overlooked considering the unique circumstances of the adoption.

Dr. James had played his part perfectly—he'd had interactions with black-uniformed soldiers before.

Miss Thompson unfortunately broke under questioning. She loved Mr. Justin too much to lie about him being a possible pedophile, about feeling relieved that he was missing or dead or wanted. She was devastated, and she wanted them to know that what they had done was a soul-poisoning injustice. But looking into their thoughtlessly condescending, power-drunk-yet-scared faces, she knew that the old cliché is a lie: A pen is only mightier than the sword when words are capable of registering, when there's a listener.

She finally broke when I moaned loudly, starting to come out of the fog.

"That's it—" she said, standing.

"Shut up, Emily!" Dr. James said desperately.

Miss Thompson never flinched, just kept staring

into the eyes of Capt. HILLOCK.

She said to the soldier, "You make me sad, and I no longer recognize your authority over me, which doesn't even really exist anyway."

She stood and began walking towards my sprawled helplessness—I don't remember any of this, just what everyone told me later—and Candy and Dr. J's faces filled with more horror as a nameless soldier stepped forward and knocked Miss Thompson in the back of her head with the butt of his rifle—it was apparently a prized move of theirs, the fucking bullying cowardly asshole fucks—and Miss T fell to the ground woozy, and two of the soldiers arrested her and carried her to one of their trucks.

Candy was too frightened to do anything but follow Dr. James' lead, because Dr. James hadn't been smashed in the head. Candy usually just followed my lead and seemed to transfer that responsibility to Dr. J, who himself was sadly coming to the understanding that he couldn't help his sister any longer, at least at the moment, but he could still help the children by not giving the soldiers an excuse to detain us all, especially after my and my mother's outbursts.

HILLOCK's shoulder had a tiny speaker attached to it, and the speaker chirped to life for the first time: "TEN-FOUR-FOUR IN DREARY PLAINS—DIAMONDCUTTERS, YOU'RE UP."

HILLOCK clicked the button and said into the speaker, "That's affirm—we're a go."

The leader scowled at the muddy Thompsons and then joined his comrades getting back into the armored trucks. Before he left, though, he said to us, "Whether or not you recognize our authority doesn't matter: It's ours. America can't have that authority questioned if it's ever going to get back to what it was."

The trucks' back tires threw up spumes of dirt, and the engines roared, and a foul wind was kicked up, and Dr. James and Candy remained kneeling with their hands behind their heads while watching the trucks speed up the hill, out of town, towards Dreary Plains, where some unfortunate people were certainly about to receive similarly miserable treatment.

When the trucks were gone, Dr. James stood, and Candy stood, too, and Dr. James said to himself, to the spot on the horizon where the last truck disappeared, "Christ, Emily . . . ."

He looked at Candy and then at me as I was sitting up on my knees and rubbing my temples with my palms, clearing the fog and trying to figure out what had happened, and he looked up at the clear sky, drew a deep breath, accepted his fate, turned back to me and Candy, and, trying to reassure us, said, "You know what happens next, right?"

M. Sgt. Saxon Rhysdale waited outside the office of the Secretary of the Department of Homeland Security, by the Secretary's secretary, a large male somehow named Therese. Rhysdale drummed his fingers on his dress cap, which sat in his lap, and he wondered whether he were about to be promoted or hanged—each seemed equally possible—while Therese vacillated at intervals between typing into a computer and openly staring at Rhysdale, but Rhysdale couldn't read from the stare whether it were a normal tic or the curiosity of one who wishes to look at a dead man waiting, or something.

A desktop buzzer sounded, and the tiny speaker announced, *"OK."*

Therese came out of his slack stare and nodded in the direction of the door. As Rhysdale was putting his hand on the doorknob, Therese said, "He'll see you now."

The timing of the statement—way too late—

threw Rhysdale off. Was that intentional or just part of the inscrutably David Lynchish procedures inherent in any (former) federal building? Rhysdale could never tell where the military's psy-ops ended and their blunderings began. But then such would almost seem inevitable in the most highly funded and lethal government bureaucracy in the world. Nevertheless, Rhysdale's conscience was clear, so he was not ultimately rattled, if a rattling were even intended.

Milton W. Blank was standing by his office's large window, with his back to the door, looking out over squat Washington, D.C., when Rhysdale walked in.

"Close the door, Saxon."

At the click of the door, Blank turned and observed as the Master Sergeant walked over and stopped next to the two brown leather chairs facing the large highly polished wooden desk. Rhysdale was so normal-looking it almost made Blank weep: *Has it come to this? Here is our enemy? The average American?*

Rhysdale couldn't read the immortal bureaucrat's face for the life of him.

"I'll skip the bull and get right to the beef," Blank said as he sat down in the leather throne behind the glimmering desk and invited Rhysdale to join him in sitting, which the five-eight, brown-haired man nervously did. "The Titan Mountains."

Rhysdale feigned dubiousness and chose his words carefully.

"What about them, sir?"

"You know damn well what about them, Master Sergeant!"

Rhysdale made a show of furrowing his brows in utter confusion. "I'm afraid I don't, sir—I mean, I had a sortie there two days ago, but I don't know what distinguishes that mission from any others I've flown recently, is all, sir. I mean I do have a complaint about that mission, but I was using the normal channels for it, but there might also be something I know but don't realize you need to know."

"That's exactly why I've called you here, Rhysdale: There's something you know and which I need to know. But first tell me about this complaint."

"Well, sir, my mission was to pop a quick RRC, easy as breezy cheese, but the tube was a dud or something, and it sprayed everything with a white mist that didn't collect a thing, as well as the fact that I launched my tube right as the N.G. squad was arriving, and that was way after protocol, but I know I flew my sortie on the right schedule zulu, and the National Guard's A.P. said they were on track, too."

Blank carefully investigated Rhysdale's face and demeanor, searching for the truth of whether the M. Sgt. were being deceitful in any way.

Rhysdale waited. He was already hanging, and he wasn't going to give Blank any more rope to add to the noose.

Blank blinked first. "Nothing in your Action Plan mentioned filming the results or pulsing the kids in the boat, is my concern."

"Filming the results? Sir, I circled for a bit as I tried to figure out what had happened: I'm pretty proud of my reputation as an aviator, and that was my first ever unsuccessful sortie, and I wanted to know how my mission had gone so godd—had gone so FUBAR, sir. While I was trying to figure it out, one of the kids on the raft took a shot at my girl, so I pulsed them as S.O.P. and also because I wanted to follow up and see if anything happened to them vis-à-vis that aberrant tube. The data would have been useful for my official report of complaint."

Blank felt comfortable enough to ask perhaps

the most important question of their meeting. "So you didn't see the arrest that was made on the river?"

Saxon Rhysdale was in the conversation-fight of his life: Could he convince this master bureaucrat of these crucial lies and truth-evasions? If he couldn't, he would be executed at best.

"Sir, when that tube popped wrong I got so pissed that I immediately started studying it—I've launched all sorts of different ordnance from my drone, and I was trying to figure out what I'd launched by looking at the way it reacted in the winds after atomization. All I saw of down below was the N.G. squad talking to someone in the fog. Between you and me, sir, the whole situation, top to bottom, seemed *off* somehow, but no offense, that's sort of normal these days, as you probably know."

Blank was impressed by the set of balls on a young man who could so casually bite the hand that fed him. But was the kid wrong? No. But the kid was a problem: Blank didn't believe him. But he didn't *disbelieve* him, either. The problem was that they still couldn't figure out how the footage had been released, so Blank had no upper hand besides the vastness of his authority, but that authority didn't seem to have much sway over the impassive Rhysdale, who was internally relieved to find that Blank somehow hadn't found out about his tracing of the kids to an Emily Thompson of Sweet Bend, who was currently in federal custody.

In the end, Blank decided on a compromise: Rhysdale would not be hanged as a traitor to his (former) country, but he would be dishonorably discharged and stripped of his citizenship—without explanation: a brief, inglorious, hollowing affair—and sent to live at the camp at Rushmore with the other No Longer Americans.

Terra Nullius—
"Land Of None"
("Land Not Under Any Political Sovereignty")

The Rushmore Concentration Camp and the South Dakota Freedom Zone were the exact same thing, but it was named differently depending on the reason you were there. Saxon Rhysdale and Miss Thompson had been sent to the concentration camp for threatening/ not recognizing the (former) federal government's authority, whereas others had moved there intentionally, to live in a so-called Freedom Zone.

The RCCSDFZ had been erected as a response to the growing "dispatriotism" (to borrow a word coined by leading political columnist Fitzgerald Concubine) in the post-collapse American culture. The nation-state paradigm, which had been undermining itself since its very conception, was starting to lose its grip on the hearts and minds of American citizens. Nearly every segment of the (former) federal government had served either the international businesses that exploited the American infrastructure or the political representatives themselves who represented the international businesses but who were supposed to be representing the exploited citizenry. So, some Americans began to express the idea that they no longer wished to be Americans at all, and would rather simply be citizens of the world, like the major businesses were. But those international businesses required the fulcrum of the nation-state to accomplish their nation-state-deteriorating, highly personally profitable ends, so when the perpetually aggrieved citizens finally started to threaten the idea, the powers that be flexed their plastic powers, and the nation-states fought back. The Supreme Court, nevertheless, a combined age of seven-hundred-forty-five years old, could find nothing in the Constitution that criminalized individuals who no longer wished to pay homage to any single nation-state, and out of their nearly incomprehensible ruling the newly written legislation resulted in the quick construction of a large concentration camp and Freedom Zone: a massive acreage of land that was surrounded by armed (former) federal soldiers in watchtowers. Above the watchtowers, a murder of drones, fully armed, crisscrossed the sky and kept all but God's eye on the noncitizens.

Everyday life in the RCCSDFZ was surprisingly boring. Although the media from both sides of the aisle had played up the idea of scads of normal Americans "turning NLA" (to borrow another Concubinism), the truth was that most Americans were content to ride out the revolution from the deeply cushioned sofas in their warm homes, and they only revoluted when the eye of the revolution was focused on the particular hill they'd be willing to die on (usually near the bottom of the rights barrel: the issue of gun-ownership), which, the revoluting, was still rare but not so rare that the revolution ever stopped. Consequently, there weren't many people who'd actually philosophically shed the nation-state paradigm, and thus in the beginning the majority of the people in the RCCSDFZ were homeless schizophrenics who'd been sent there by local legislators looking to clear their streets of the unsightly. In the beginning, it was a lot of land and a few people.

And as a consequence of that, the former M. Sgt. Rhysdale was rather easily able to locate Miss Thompson the very first day he arrived at the camp (which was a euphemism they all used for the RCCSDFZ). She was the tallest woman at the camp by far, and she looked positively statuesque as she leaned against a tree and gazed up at Mount Rushmore in the early evening, with her whole frame outlined golden by the lazy western sun.

"Emily Thompson?" he asked, and the woman—he once described her as "taller than the Industrial Age"—gracefully turned to him, looked him over, and smiled the smile of someone who was abstractly curious about what fresh nightmare was about to introduce itself.

"You already know my name, so tell me what you're here to tell me."

He suddenly realized that he wasn't exactly sure what he wanted to say.

"I'm a friend. Kind of. I mean, I saw what happened . . . on the river . . . and . . . I think I can help . . . reunite you . . . with your kids."

Miss Thompson's eyebrows crossed impatiently.

"What is this? What do you know about them? Who are you?"

She looked like she was preparing to strike Rhysdale down and drink his blood through her hollowed-out fingertips, or something.

"Like I said, I'm a friend, or at least I'm trying to be," Rhysdale said, backing up, intimidated by the woman's sudden belligerence. After she was taken off edge by his reply, he regretted being so callous about broaching the subject of the weird hope he was so happy to be able to offer her: He'd already known so much about her, but he'd forgotten that she had no idea who he was. He blushed at his error in judgment, and the blush only served to make Miss Thompson more confused.

"You were there? On the river?" she asked, now needing to know.

"No—but I saw what happened, and I was discharged from the military for asking about it."

The day was ending, and she knew it was best for everyone to be back in their tents or shelters before the last of the evening's light—the not-schizophrenic-but-rather-criminal elements had taken back the night—so she began heading back to the shelter she'd constructed, indicating with her body language, however, that she wanted Rhysdale to join her on the way.

"Young man," she said, "tell me everything you've ever known."

You could call it the oldest trick in the book because it probably was, but only because it preyed upon a common link through billions of years of evolution: the reproductive drive.

Rhysdale and Miss T had scouted each of the eight watchtowers, which were staffed by three soldiers each—a sniper and a drone pilot in the tower and a heavily armed guardsman at the base—and the two NLA investigators eventually settled on the southernmost tower, where the sniper had paid particular interest to the sensually ambling Miss Thompson, and who'd said to the drone pilot, if Rhysdale'd overheard him correctly from below, "I'd like to chop her down with my cock." (The drone pilot, MARTINEZ, had reportedly responded, "Been sending files to my personal address since she got here, bro.")

The southernmost tower gave them their best chance, so one morning Miss Thompson took a stroll to the fields before the tower, carrying a book and a blanket. When she reached a spot where she knew the sniper could see her, and where she could see the sniper, she laid out the blanket. For a moment she gazed up into the tower for long enough that the sniper knew it meant something, and as she straightened out the blanket she took her time in the bending, really *smooooooothing* out the edges while still up on all fours, and then eventually she lowered her hips to the ground and her torso onto her bosom, propping her head on one hand, and began to read.

The sniper watched.

Miss Thompson may have been the bookish owner of a bookstore, and may not have been nearly as OV-literate as many others in her culture, but she was a woman with a libido and a healthy curiosity, and at the bottom of her investigations into the pools of pornography from all kinds of different media she had nearly always seen certain congruities in the faces and comportments of all those mostly unfortunate women: a look and effect that a woman puts on when she's proverbially *just begging for it.*

Miss Thompson enjoyed all forms of writing, even so-called "cliterature," and she'd fortunately and rather predictably found a few old titles in a bin of goods sent to help those estranged in the RCCSDFZ. It would be a good help, indeed; as she read, and as the sniper watched, she rolled over on her back and lifted the book over her head and used it to shield her face from the sun while she continued, and while she continued, her now-free hand began tracing along the lines of her body, and she started pulling her dress up, but then she stopped and looked around.

"Oh, do it, honey," the sniper said. (Rhysdale, flat on the ground and hidden in the tall grass twenty feet from the tower, could hear the sniper clearly this time.)

And indeed she did. She stood and pulled the dress off, and the sunlight gleamed first upon her thin legs, smooth thighs, NO UNDERWEAR! COY VAGINA!, flat stomach!, pendulous breasts!, alluring shoulders!, and then upon her white-golden entirety!, the sunlight finally finding something truly worth illuminating for the universe to see, its reverie!

"Jesus Christ!" the drone pilot said.

Miss Thompson lay back supine on the blanket and picked the book up and let her free hand go truly free without any layers of fabric to dull the frottage of a personal, imagination-foreign touch, and the sun shined on her skin, and both the sniper and the drone pilot could see that she was glistening where you want a woman to glisten, and then that free hand started heading towards that glistening treasure, and two fingers stalked the perimeter for a little while before—

"Dude!"

"Dude!"

"Bro!"

Miss Thompson, her hips catching a rhythm, lifted her head and looked up into the guard tower while she rocked and wriggled on the blanket.

"She wants us to go down there, dude!"

"No way!"

"Why's she looking up here like that, then?"

Silence. During the silence, the sniper and drone pilot hastily scanned the area for possible threats.

The clattering of men stowing their equipment, the dull ringing of boots tromping down metal stairs, and then the sniper and drone pilot emerging at a sprint. In an ecstatic hurry, they ran past the guard at the door, who yelled out, "What the hell's going on up there, guys?" The two running men said nothing, and half-scared, half-curious, the guardsman followed them up the hill into the field, unsure of the heaven that was in store for him.

The men slowed to a cocky stride when they were close enough, and Miss Thompson was so faux-going-to-town on herself that she pretended she hadn't noticed they'd arrived.

The sniper said, "Everything OK, ma'am?"

At first she acted shocked—tossed the book down and covered herself with her blanket. All three men went red with embarrassment, and the hook was set, which was when Rhysdale ran through the ajar door of the tower and up the stairs as quietly as he could and took over the controls of—he saw the name on the desk and assumed it was his—MARTINEZ's Peregrine.

Taking it out of autopilot and putting all of its engines into overdrive, he simultaneously ran the children's pulses he'd copied to his nonmilitary files and found me and my sister in the foothills of the Titan Mountains still, but traveling west between Vectorville and Cornish at sixty miles per hour.

As the Rushmore Peregrine sliced through the upper atmosphere on the way to the Titans, Miss Thompson addressed the three tantalized soldiers.

"What are you doing here?" she asked in a way that indicated she knew what they were doing there but that her modesty forced her to ask.

"You looked like you needed some help," the sniper said.

"Oh, I did, did I? I looked like I needed some help?"

She let the blanket drop a little, revealing a bare shoulder. "What kind of help?"

"The kind help you're gettin' at."

"Oh?"

"The kin' a help yer gonna get."

"Oh, so you've *all* come here to help?"

"Oh yeah," MARTINEZ said.

And the guardsman added, "You bet yer tits, miss."

When you have nothing to lose, some of the worst shit in the world suddenly isn't so bad, is how Miss Thompson probably saw it.

"Well then, if you insist," she said, laying out the

blanket again, and as she bent over in that pursuit, the men came over and took over, and Miss Thompson closed her eyes and imagined the three best lovers of her life, and it wasn't so bad, except none of those lovers had ever fucked her like they were getting away with a crime—which she found disturbingly hot.

Former M. Sgt. Saxon Rhysdale had taken a chance, and sometimes fortune really does favor the bold (such as three bold soldiers who took the porno-cliché chance and were fucktorious), and for Rhysdale fortune favored his boldness by his having guessed correctly what kind of drones were piloted from the watchtowers, and this more advanced Peregrine was capable of both weightless hovering and supersonic speeds, so it only took ten minutes (the longest ten of Rhysdale's life, during which he looked down and saw Miss Thompson more than living up to her end of the nasty bargain) before his drone was following above and behind a white van with a brown cross, which evidently the kids were riding in. Immediately, though he hadn't been able to research enough to know about Dr. James, he recognized the man driving as Emily Thompson's brother, and he recognized the girl next to him, riding shotgun, as Sylvia. It was them, us, all right. Rhysdale looked to see how things were down below in the field, and it was all pale muscular limbs and torsos with poor Miss Thompson somewhere inside there. He went back to the drone optics and brought the Peregrine down to the van's level, and then right alongside the van. And so good was Rhysdale at piloting it that nobody in the van had even noticed that the drone was flying along right next to us, so the talented Rhysdale deftly used the drone's van-most wing to tap the driver's-side window—tap tap tap—and when Dr. James and Candy Baby turned, they both screamed from surprise and fear, but Rhysdale kept flying right alongside them and matched whatever pace Dr. James sped or slowed the van to. When Dr. James returned to driving normally, having understood that the drone was there meaningfully and with a human intelligence behind its behaviors, the drone added more meaning to its enigmatic actions by rolling ninety degrees so that the stunned-stupid people in the white van could see the words RUSHMORE CONCENTRATION CAMP emblazoned on the bottom. Then Rhysdale straightened the drone, tapped the window again, presented the name again, zoomed forward a little bit, let the van catch up, nodded its nose up and down, and then rocketed back into the upper atmosphere, supersonic back to the camp.

Rhysdale again looked down and saw that the guardsman was having an orgasm somewhere in the middle of the foursome. A few minutes later (thank Whatever), the two others finished also, and Miss Thompson got exceptionally post-coitally clingy, to buy Saxon some time. Meanwhile, Rhysdale's heart was a metal-press in his chest, but the heroic Miss Thompson clung like a pro for long enough that the drone arrived back in the airspace above South Dakota, and Rhysdale set it back into its autopilot orbit and was evidencelessly out of the watchtower by the time the soldiers were finished helping Miss Thompson wipe the warm glacial lakes of sperm off her face and breasts with her thoroughly soiled government-issued blanket.

Fortune favored the bold in more ways than one: Three

hours after the successful Thompson Temptation/ Rhysdale Redemption, video of the outdoor foursome filmed by another Rushmore drone was leaked online— like Velvet Waves, once again to the *RothReport,* whose editor was a self-proclaimed "news cockroach" who'd publish anything as long as it was true. People tend to love the truth when they can get it, and the *RothReport* was, at the time (things are always changing, so I don't know anymore), *the* place to go to find the truths that some organizations didn't want known, which was usually the best and juiciest truth, and a few days after the posting of the video of a beautiful woman being gangbanged by three soldiers in the RCCSDFZ, the first converted school bus arrived, and security at the camp doubled overnight. The sight of the both aberrant and politically charged scene in the viral sex video had become a sort of inadvertent mating call, an unintentional trumpeting cry to all the freaks, the not exactly politically minded but still inherently revolutionary, and they began to arrive.

In the spirit of the old days of the Burning Man festival, before large outdoor gatherings like that were "proven" to be illegal, the naturally contrarian (and even, sadly, the most wretched of all, the trendily contrarian) started to appear on the horizon in psychedelic school buses and spiky-looking dune buggies, and a real scene unfolded. The world outside the camp had begun to see the Freedom Zone, with its noncitizen inhabitants, as a sort of collection of the exact kind of element where the most life-celebratingly humanistic times could be had, in the best Wild West left in the grey world, where the existential party was held along the dangerous edge of a drug-chopping razor.

What had once been a shantytown full of displaced hobos and intentionally placed politically dangerous noncitizens soon became an even more truly human scene, where nearly all races and genders and ages came together, united not by compunction but a philosophy that demanded they rebel against almost anything that was accepted except the value of human life, which all could agree was a beautiful thing that should be celebrated and lived all the way in, to the Henry Miller hilt—balls deep.

If any ten of these volitional NLA immigrants were asked what their ideas were for the political stabilization of North America, they would offer ten vastly different answers—the philosophy that united them was not easily expressed, and because it was not easily expressed it avoided being easily dismissed besides into the gutters of abstract hogwash, but even the people who ridiculed the freaks were mildly put off because they suspected that not all abstract hogwash was equal, and even deeper inside they also knew that their beloved simple and easily digestible sound bites had incrementally and wisdomlessly navigated the nation and world over a socio-politico-economic cliff.

Beneath the immortal gazes of Washington, Jefferson, Roosevelt, and Lincoln, an artificial pen of the unwanted became an international party that escalated as the word spread and the world's systems remained stagnant and hopelessly corrupt. Tents were erected; cars and trucks also became shelters. In response to the onrush, the soldiers tried to erect a border fence, but the crowds outside were always tunneling or bridging, breaching, and anyway the zone was not intended as a prison or concentration camp in the traditional sense of the words—at least, not at first.

At the beginning of the program, an NLA with an international visa expressing NLA-ness could still visit the United States, like a visitor from a foreign country, but just like those foreign visitors the U.S. laws still applied to them. (NLAs like Miss Thompson and Saxon Rhysdale, however—sent there by the former federal government—were implanted with small chips in their ankles, chips that promised a quick IncaTubing if they tried to leave.) Essentially, the RCCSDFZ had been created mainly because an unsurprisingly high rate of offended, patriotic police officers had delighted in heaping any number of charges against every NLA within his or her jurisdiction, and because the laws in America had been so ambiguously written and interpreted, the charges added up quickly, and the former feds, thanks to several painstaking lawsuits, had been begrudgingly forced by the dusty Supreme Court to section off the RCCSDFZ in order to give the NLAs somewhere they could go without being actively persecuted. Thus, the fence idea was dropped, and the crowds swelled further, and the eight guard towers and fully loaded matrix of drones watched from above as the poor and huddled let their technicolor freak-flags fly.

In response to the onrush of NLA emigration, the rules from above changed: NLAs soon only had permission to *enter* the Freedom Zone—the guards were instructed not to let any of the NLAs leave.

In response, the next wave of people who arrived did so with the intent of trying to live there permanently, as long as they were away from what America had become.

M. Sgt. Rhysdale, figuring what the hell, had made a move on Miss Thompson a few days after her . . . sacrifice . . . but she wasn't into him like that, and when all the new NLAs started to arrive, he ended up moving into the back of a fogged-up SUV with a pair of sexually adventurous Japanese sisters.

Meanwhile, Miss Thompson had built her own shelter away from the tent city, and there she lived with a fourteen-year-old runaway she had met shortly after returning from the Temptation, finding the girl asleep in the shelter Miss Thompson had constructed, looking to sleep herself. When the girl awoke, she went wide-eyed, but she did not speak, and Miss Thompson soon saw that the girl would not speak at all, and through gestures they developed a living arrangement, at the end of which the little girl, who reminded Miss Thompson of her dear Candy Baby, had put her arms around Miss Thompson's neck and squeezed tight, clutching her close and eventually issuing a low moan, proof of vocal capability if not refined ability, and Miss Thompson recognized it as a moan of despair, just as she also noticed that the poor dear's whole body was trembling.

Over the course of the time it took for us and Dr. James to make our way north, to the camp, the scene at the cutting edge of civilization kept growing.

M. Sgt. Rhysdale and Miss Thompson, through their daily arriving guests, found ways of spending the long hours in their time in the *terra nullius*. With each new arrival came new stocks of as much food as possible—to more adequately supplement the brick-hard black bread the military was being forced to provide to the prisoners like Miss Thompson after closing the outgoing borders—but as the crowds grew, there was less food, fewer bricks of nutritionless bread to go around, and certain human needs repeat themselves and can undermine all hope for civilization if they're not met sustainably.

We left Sweet Bend the day after Miss Thompson was taken away; Dr. James had figured there was no sense in stewing in our depression in Sweet Bend, which was a sort of corpse itself. The good doctor knew enough about what had happened with Miss Thompson to know that we might never see her again—long legal precedents had established a hopelessness when it came to trying to find out which Freedom Zone/Concentration Camp/ Prison/Federal Detention Facility a family member had been sent to—and like many people in this story so far, he just had to get on with what came next, because more was always coming, and getting on with things would certainly help the scared-stupid children.

With the legal kidnapping of Emily Thompson, Sweet Bend unofficially lost its last real resident, and Dr. James decided to hit the road full-time as a traveling doctor—kind of like we'd previously planned, but without Miss Thompson—to do his medical rounds in the nearby still-populated communities and try to keep us kids alive into adulthood.

It was the only realistic option left to any of us, and our first stop was a small but important town called Vectorville.

We numbly and unceremoniously departed Sweet Bend around 1000 and arrived in Vectorville around 1200, and we arrived to quite the clusterfuck.

A miraculous, unlabeled supply of food and aid had been airdropped into the town square the day before, and the struggling townspeople had thrown a hell of a party in celebration, eating the food and then guzzling their own homemade liquor afterwards. (Several Vectorvillians had complained that the mysterious airdroppers "didn't send any goddam liquor!") As the party lasted later into the night, more home-brewed alcohol was consumed, and eventually a vicious fistfight broke out over the remaining provisions, and just when it looked like Sam Cornbone was the last man standing, the town was loudly beset by a gang on dirt bikes and motorcycles, who had witnessed the airdrop and waited until everyone was passed out or unconscious, who took what was left of the water purifiers and food, loaded it into their bikes' saddles and sidecars, and roared off.

Besides our previous one brief and largely uneventful trip, Candy and I had never been exposed to the outside world beyond the usually quiet streets of Sweet Bend. It was less the war than the times that had had such a devastating effect on the town, and now Candy and I were nervously headed out into what was left of America.

Here it came.

Dr. James kept a pretty dependable schedule, and consequently many of the Vectorvillains never left the town square at all—just waited for the arrival of the medicine man's white van.

There were about a hundred citizens in the town square when the pale van arrived, and immediately Dr. James could see that nearly all of them were in a surly state of agitation, and he honestly considered skipping the town altogether, for fear of the safety of us kids, but when he saw Benny Gorman's dangling, broken arm, he continued into the square, through the crowd, and stopped right near Gorman.

The crowd rushed around the van and thundered upon it with demands for treatment. Dr. James repeatedly honked the horn, to clear them away, but the thundering and pounding continued. He rolled down his window, stuck his head out, revved the engine, and shouted.

"HEY! BACK OFF OR I'M GONE!"

Throughout the crowd a few people started yelling things like, *"Y' cain't talk a' me like 'at!"* And through the windshield we kids could see that the offended people who were saying it were indeed frighteningly offended and angry. Nevertheless, the crowds receded enough that the pounding on the van stopped, and Candy and I relaxed a bit, and Dr. James yelled to the crowd, "Send in Gorman, and start a line. I'm sending out my two assistants to help with triage; if you give them a hard time, we're leaving."

He rolled up his window and turned back to us. "Sorry to do this to you, kids. I was hoping this was going to be a milk run, but obviously something's happened, and I need your help. I need you to go out there and look everyone over, and bring me whoever has the worst injuries."

Completely overwhelmed by the prospect, I asked, "How the heck are we supposed to know?"

Candy no longer imitated me, but her face was filled with the same question.

Dr. James held up one finger. "Severe bleeding." He held up a second finger. "Real bad chest, belly, or head pain. After that, I trust your judgment to know who needs treatment more urgently."

The side door of the van swung open, and Benny Gorman, clearly comfortable enough with Dr. James to enter the van as casually as his broken arm permitted, was surprised to see that the doctor's assistants were a twelve-year-old cutie pie and the largest teenager he'd ever seen. "Hey, Doc, Jesus it's—WHOA, hey, uh, hello."

"Benny, these are my sister's children—Dante and Sylvia. Kids, this is Benny Gorman, mayor of Vector-ville."

We both said, "Hi."

"Pleasure."

"Before I send them out there," Dr. James said to Mayor Benny, "I need you to tell me what happened while I show the kids how to set that arm."

"Right, all right, but this thing is a cold chainsaw, doc; any chance you picked up some painkillers out there?"

Dr. James did the smirking equivalent of a frown. "Not in at least a year, I'm afraid."

"Still being hoarded in the goddam 'burbs, huh?"

"At best," Dr. James said. He didn't want to talk about it.

Mayor Gorman shrugged with resignation and told us his general understanding of the riot, including how a biker had broken Benny's arm with a chain, while, as tenderly as he could, Dr. James set the broken arm in question. At the same time, Dr. James introduced me and CB to the general goals for setting the different bones to heal throughout the body, how to make a plaster cast, how to know when the limb is really in trouble (when it's time to break out the hacksaw and a stick for biting), and how long it takes for certain bones and bone-sizes to heal. Eventually, the plaster cast around Mayor Gorman's forearm dried stiff.

"So you didn't see who actually started the riot?" Dr. James asked.

"Liquor," Benny said, shaking his head. "Goddam liquor started it like always. And greed. Fear, too. Ah, hell, what'd that guy say? 'Human history repeats itself because human circumstances repeat themselves.'"

Dr. James smirked and turned to me and Candy and said, "OK, kids, I need you to be top-shelf safe out there, and like I said pretty much bring me whoever makes you feel the sickest."

As we were exiting the back of the van, backing into the crowd, Benny Gorman said to Dr. James,

"You're really sending them out there?"

The last thing Candy Baby and I heard from inside the van, before we slammed the doors, was Dr. James say, "Are you kidding? Those kids are wolverines—the crowd should be nervous."

By far the largest gathering of people my sister or I had ever been around, and not only that, but we were the MCs, the center of everyone's agitated attention—the nervous nuclei at the heart of a swollen mass of sneers and furrowed brows, blood, broken limbs, and as the mayor had said, an almost aromatic fear.

"What the goddam hell is this?" "What the fucking shit are these two 'shots gonna do?" "Look at that big goofy one!" "Doc Thompson must be outside his brainpan!" "Or a fuckin' ped'!" "Hey, you! You kids! C'm'ere, little girl!" "Naw, come here!" "Over here, kids!" "I'm hurt bad!" "He ain't hurt!"

I tried to speak up. "Um, well—"

My uncertainty stoked the moment's chaotic fires, and the yelling became that frightening wall of sound produced by a crowd of individuals yelling to be heard over the sound of the sum. In the center of that aural tidal wave, Candy and I started to blank out, panicking in the alien-human nightmare we'd been all but shoved into. And just like the crowd had bumrushed the van, they also started advancing towards us, and Candy Baby SCREECHED. You know how little girls can screech and seemingly rip the air apart like lightning? The sound was probably heard by dogs in what used to be Japan, and the Vectorvillian crowd definitely was shocked into a stunned silence.

I coughed to break the silence. Clearly all these people needed our help, whether they liked it or not.

"Like my sister said," I stated more clearly, "you're starting to freak us out, and what's going to happen is that I'm going to point at you, and you're going to say what's wrong, and then my sister and I will decide who sees Dr. James next while everyone else waits patiently."

"Why the hell should I listen to a couple of kids—" someone started yelling, piqued.

"Then LEAVE, asshole!" someone else yelled, also piqued.

The asshole didn't have a good comeback for that, and we waited like Mr. Justin and Miss Thompson had always silently waited while we were being rambunctious during a lesson. Eventually, the crowd was shamed back to silence, and I pointed at a quiet woman.

"You, ma'am; what's wrong?"

Fear sometimes cripples me, but it also makes me brave sometimes—I wish I understood it myself. I turned out to be an efficient-enough bureaucrat, pacing an effective triage, and Candy Baby was a world-class empathite—seemingly personally feeling the pain of all the patients, and through that connection alleviating the sense of isolation that can result from extraordinary discomfort, to the point that she was often escorting patients who were remarkably calm and focused by the time she knocked on the van's side door. "Oh, my goodness!" she would often say when she spoke to the next patient. "I'd be crying like a baby if I had that kind of hurt! But don't worry," she'd state with complete credulity, "Dr. James could've fixed Humpty Dumpty!"

More than anything else, Candy charmed the crowd, was how we got through it.

The Vectorville mayor had worked out a deal with Dr. James around a year ago: If the doctor came by every other week to perform medical consultations and procedures, the town of Vectorville would keep Dr. James in their best and most stabilized gasoline for the van's largely electric motor, which, the great gas, was Vectorville's primary resource, which they defended much more rigorously than they'd defended the mysterious food drop, as Vectorville had been the home of a regional storage hub for an oil company that now no longer existed but whose millions of gallons of stored oil still did.

In addition to the van's topped tank and the two spare brim-filled tub-cans tied to the roof of the van, we Thompsons were also given a free night's stay at Vectorville's only hotel, which was where many citizens lived, rent free, everyone just trying to survive now that the banks and real-estate sharks that still existed owned most people's homes and sat on their fortunes while waiting for the world's economies to spark back to life.

The hotel room had two beds, and Dr. James almost immediately fell asleep on one of them (the van was parked just outside the window and had an alarm that could've awoken Jesus Christ on the *second* day).

Candy Baby looked so tired it appeared as though she could've slept standing up in the middle of an earthquake if it came to that, whereas I was much too wired from the day's events to sleep, so I wordlessly ushered Candy over to the other bed, untucked the sheets, helped her up, and tucked her in. She was asleep before she ever even said goodnight like she always did. Then I sat on the windowsill, feeling the coolness of the night on my back, and I pulled my feet up, put my arms around my legs, and thought about all those crazed people, their blood and broken bones, bruises, gnarly scars and temperaments, and in the background of those crazy, clustered, fresh memories I could hear a soothing voice in the choir, a voice that seemed to be singing about how lucky I'd always been despite how unlucky I'd always felt.

In the morning I woke up shivering on the ground by the sweaty cold window.

Without fanfare, the white van pulled out of town just as the sun was a golden fingernail over the dark horizon.

Early on the long drive from Vectorville to the suburb of Cornish, Saxon Rhysdale's Rushmore drone descended from the sky and held its vehicular conversation with our van. Dr. James and Candy were shocked and screamed, and I came forward to see what was happening, and I just watched uncomprehendingly as the scene unfolded, and then the drone shot back into the vibrant blue.

After it was gone I suddenly felt nervously sick and said, "OK, that really just happened, right? Am I having an aneurysm or something?"

"Maybe we all are!" Candy Baby said.

"It happened," Dr. James said. "I was here, too, and I was the one who slowed and sped and nearly wet myself."

We rode along in a ruminative silence for a while. Finally, Dr. James pulled the string: "So let's treat it like it really happened. I've given it some thought, and to me it seems pretty clear."

"That they're onto us?" Candy asked.

"Onto what?" I asked.

"For burying Mr. Justin maybe, or for you shooting at the drone!" Candy said.

"Think about this, though," Dr. James said. "That was a Peregrine, right?, and Peregrines are loaded with incredible firepower and incapacitation-power. So I think if they really wanted us, we'd either be a crisp or paralyzed right now."

"Yeah but, then, so, but, then how do we know that it won't come back and—?"

118

I was following Dr. James' thinking, and I said, "Candy, that drone just *danced* with this van. Have you ever seen or heard of anything in a government dancing like that, trying to communicate like that?"

"No, but I'm only—"

"Candy?" Dr. James said.

"Yeah?"

"Do you think instead of a trap maybe it means Emily found a way to get someone friendly to tell us where she was taken?"

I was already there, but young scared Candy thought about it for a second, replayed the whole scene in her head, and became for thirty seconds perhaps the most edified and excited little girl who ever lived.

Before we reached Cornish we encountered a caravan of serious trucks on the road. Dr. James slowed, offering aid if needed, but the head of the convoy's wife, or road whore, put her arm out the window, made a flat back and forth movement with her hand, indicating "no services necessary," and then waved. Dr. James and we kids waved back, but only the first vehicle in the convoy communicated. All the other drivers and passengers just looked at our van as they went by, and Dr. James noticed several rifles pointed at us, ever cautious. Once the convoy was past us, we didn't see anybody else on the road and reached the suburban town by midafternoon, arriving to the opposite of the scene we'd found the day before.

The van came to a stop in the parking lot of a closed-down shopping mall. There was still a sun-stain on the biggest wall, in the shape of the words "WEST-SIDE MALL." On the parking lot's black asphalt Dr. James had spraypainted his simple white flag with the brown cross.

"It takes a while sometimes," he said to us when the van stopped. Even though the parking lot was empty, Candy and I were almost flinching after what had happened last time. "Like I said, this place isn't as combustible as Vectorville, so we're just going to sit here and see if anyone shows up."

"Could we check out that building?" Candy Baby asked, whose general curiosity was growing by the day, feeling like nothing bad could ever happen now that she knew that we were going to be heading to Miss T.

"Not today, Can'. I saw a pretty scary-looking character come out of there once. Most of the patients around here trickle in through those trees." The trees he pointed to comprised a rather spotty forest at the far edge of the parking lot.

"Why?"

"They live in the houses up that hill, but not all of them up there are Boomers—"

As CB and I leaned in for more details, there was a knocking on the driver's-side window, and we both startle-jumped.

Dr. James rolled down the window.

"You are doctor?" the swarthy brunette woman said, looking around nervously, definitely an immigrant.

"Yes, ma'am."

"I need . . ." she said and looked down at her stomach, "help."

Dr. James immediately understood, stepped out, and escorted her over to the side door with his most delicate vanside manner.

When she was inside and acquainted and comfortable with the doctor and the kids, she explained.

"I am pregnant, but I no want. You have wand?"

"Of course," Dr. James said. He sat back and cleared his throat. "Kids, do me a favor and step out and run security for us, please."

"Why?" Candy Baby asked, wanting to learn more medicine.

"I'll tell you out there," I said opening the door and letting in a chilly gust of cool air, which we headed into outside.

Candy Baby, perturbed by what she felt like was her being treated like nothing but a kid, slammed the door closed behind her and said to me, *"Well?"*

With the exceptions of Sister Anne and Fr. Michael, none of our guardians had ever much beaten around the bush, so I didn't even think to—Candy was too smart for euphemisms anyway.

"We wouldn't be learning any survival medicine in there."

"Why not?"

"Do you know anything about sex?"

"What do you mean?" Candy asked, embarrassed. "Maybe."

I broke it down to Candy Baby as understandably as I could, which was more clinical than subjective given my complete lack of experience beyond what I'd read in my more advanced encyclopedia than hers. The fact of the matter is that even at fifteen I was still more boy than man, which was evidenced by my not becoming a part of the glistening pile of men during the mist attack—frankly it turns out one of the ways I've been lucky in my life is that I was lucky to be a late bloomer when that mist hit the river. Candy Baby felt no real effect from the mist, and I, who barely had any of the adult hormones the drugs in the mist targeted, evidently, was rather made to feel categorically *weird* by it—spawning a few rare, uniquely violent neuroses—but that's it.

So rhetorically moving from the sexual act to conception, I then delved into the matter of what abortion was and the various thoughts on its morality. (Though I was only fifteen, I was an informational sponge, and I was spitting out quotations remembered verbatim.)

I said to Candy, quoting something I'd read but passing it off as my own thought, "Whether it's moral or not essentially depends on when exactly you believe human life begins: at conception, heartbeat, or birth."

"They have heartbeats when they're in there?" Candy said looking at her own stomach.

"Yep—eventually, I guess."

She kept looking. "Wow." After a while, she asked, "Do you think that lady in there is being immortal?"

I laughed, "'Immoral,' Can'."

"Do you?"

"I think it's not my call to make."

"But *do you?*" Candy Baby wanted to know where her brother stood, as a sort of anchor she could use to safely navigate the waters of the big question herself.

"I think . . . the only way I could answer that would be if men could get pregnant, and then— Would I . . . ? Yes, if I could get pregnant, and I could die from giving birth, I'd think it's moral to get rid of a fetus if I didn't feel right about it. After all, like I said before, a woman's body can unconsciously get rid of the pregnancy if it doesn't feel right about it, via a miscarriage, so to me it seems to come down to whether she's allowed to have a choice in the matter. So I guess I don't think that lady is being immoral. You?"

When Candy Baby didn't answer, it usually meant, "I'm going to have to think about this for a while."

Inside the van, the woman told Dr. James the sad tale of her bizarre rape.

"I no want baby, I want you Miracle," she said. The "Miracle" she kept referring to was a specially designed medical tool called a MedicaMiraco. In short, the tool could be tuned to produce unique pulses of electromagnetic waves that had the initially intended therapeutic effect of healing muscle injuries faster through advanced electromagnetic stimulation, but which also turned out to produce what grim old OGBYNs used to sardonically refer to as, "the perfect miscarriage."

"Well, Carmen, here's the thing: As an independent doctor, my stance on that procedure is that you have to tell me the context, I have to believe you, and only if I agree with your decision will I do it—deal? And remember," he quoted an obscure old movie, "'I can smell a lie like a fart in a car.'"

The woman was disturbed by both the frankness and the message of the doctor's response, but after her shock she resigned herself to replying, "Fine, I will tell." She was quiet for a while, but eventually she said. "You know I work nurse up for the old in houses?"

Dr. James nodded, knowing about the hives of Baby Boomers living in many of America's suburbs and how they had many immigrant workers tending to their daily needs.

"In one house the old man he is always so lonely and grabbing me and making me touch him, and I always say no but he keeps grabbing and I say nothing because they fire me and I need money for my family my house already full. But the old man he's grabbing me all the time and I tell him no but he get me fired or he says he has gun. So one day I am working like normal and he is doing something but I cannot see and I am staying away because I am glad, but then he say, 'I tell you to come here!' and he grab me and put . . . he put his hand up my dress . . . under panty . . . and I feel his hand down there is wet but I am not wet and I know. I get sick in the morning and I know. Why does he do it? I cannot stop him, and I need the money my house already full."

She was crying, and Dr. James let her cry into his shoulder.

He believed her—maybe not the actual story she'd told, but that she'd been raped. He looked into the tangle of trees outside the suburban homes, and he gritted his teeth.

"Before we begin, I'm going to need to do a

medical history."

Eventually the patient emerged from the van, and Dr. James was right behind her, with the MedicaMiraco in a kit-bag in his hand, and he shouted to us, "Kids—van, coverage."

Dr. James and the woman took a walk into the woods, away from the electronics in the van, while we made sure nobody bumrushed them and stole the expensive MM.

Within six hours the sad patient would have her perfect miscarriage, and within no time we were all regrouped near the van.

"Mrs. Renata, I don't charge people for my services, but—"

From the relief on her face I could tell the woman was profoundly grateful that the doctor had shown up as she'd been told he would, and in the rumors about the off-the-grid doctor, the only one these workers could afford, she'd heard that the great traveling doctor, like most medical professionals, was direly low on painkillers, which had surprised her because the medicine cabinets of her clients' shelves were filled almost exclusively with a galaxy of opioid medications. Before her "appointment," she'd stolen the first bottle of pills she'd seen that included the words "For pain."

"I have pay," she said, and she reached into her purse and pulled out the bottle of painkillers. "You take."

It was a half-filled bottle of Temogen—a strong painkiller prescribed to a Mr. Harold Pemulis, for "post-operative discomfort."

"This is great, Mrs. Renata—thank you." But Dr. James was curious. "Is this Pemulis the man who—?"

The woman refused to say anything other than, "Thank you, doctor. I tell people you are good doctor, and good man."

She left nervously, just as she'd arrived, but also slightly, sadly relieved.

After we all piled back into the van, without even planning it, Candy Baby and I simultaneously asked Dr. James, "So what happened?"

Nobody else ever arrived that day, and in the evening Dr. James drove the van right up to the edge of the woods, and he and we kids camouflaged and securitized the van as best as we could, trying not to draw any attention from whatever subculture had taken over the abandoned mall.

The night passed without incident—we each pulled three hours of night-watch, and during my watch I shivered and listened to nothing and saw the sun rise—and we slept otherwise soundly to the insect symphony of the forest beside us when we weren't shivering, armed, and awake.

In the morning, Dr. James drove straight out of the camouflage, into the parking lot, and back onto the road, north, towards four Presidential countenances carved into an ancient mountainside.

Feeding off Dr. James, we went tense when we saw him go tense, and he went tense when he looked in his mirrors and saw a swarm of motorcycles behind us, coming up much faster than the van was capable of going.

"What do we do?" Candy Baby asked when she heard the roar and saw the bikes.

"Candy, all we can do is have faith right now, because if those people want to kill us, there's nothing we can do to stop them. I'm just going to keep heading towards Emily, and if they do anything funny, I'll try to take out as many of them as I can, deal?"

"Can we help?" I asked.

He looked in the mirrors—the bikes were closer.

"Fuck it—grab your rifles. They're going to be all around us, so just shoot through the van's walls, but DO NOT FIRE UNTIL I SAY SO."

Candy and I—hunters of bears with crazy old Mr. Justin—knew how to cover someone, but never like this.

The roar of the motorcycles was soon thunderous and bone-rattlingly ubiquitous as the hundred or more chopped and heavily saddlebagged bikes were all around the van as it raced north as steadily as it could.

More than anything else, it was the bearing of the other motorcycle riders that indicated to Dr. James which of them was the leader, and pretty soon that independent leader was riding along next to Dr. James, who continued driving and then casually inclined his head towards the leader, acknowledging the leader's presence and gesturing through body language a communication of, "You see that I am a traveling medicine man, and I wish you no harm, and if any of your riders need my assistance, I would be more than obliged to offer such assistance respectfully in the hopes that you would choose not to quite easily kill me and steal all of my relatively expensive medical equipment for an easy profit but a, you must acknowledge, perhaps heavier cost to humanity than the usual murder-robbery."

Or at least that's what Dr. James hoped to communicate with his inclination, nod, parting of his

126

hands in plea, and then returning of his hands and continuing northward while awaiting a reply.

The leader, a large, square-headed man wearing a red bandana, with a scar down the side of his face, kept his eyes trained on the doc, possibly watching him for signs of weakness, for an excuse to kill.

Eventually, the leader nodded slightly, turned his head back towards the northward road, and roared off, with the rest of his gang following suit, until soon all the roaring was gone, and it was back to the normal sound of the van on the road.

Nobody in the van's pulse went below one-twenty for several minutes. Finally, Candy Baby broke the silence by asking, "Dr. James, was it always like this?"

Dr. James laughed dryly and said, "You know what? Kind of. It's just worse now."

About an hour later, the day's grey skies gave way to a rain that drummed on the metal roof of the van. There was plenty of fuel, so Dr. James just kept going despite the fact that the rain wasn't letting up, and the exhausted man at the wheel was beginning to almost feel hypnotized by the synchro-dancing windshield wipers. While he drove, Candy and I read: Dr. James certainly wasn't going to suspend Miss Thompson's educational plans just because she wasn't around right now to enforce them. So while we were reading and he was going wiper-crazy, he was thinking about pulling over for a little bit when he saw a reason to: a broken-down truck waving a big flag that said "JESUS!"

"Why are we slowing down?" Candy Baby asked nervously when she felt the van begin to decelerate.

"Broken-down car, looks like a missionary," Dr. James said. "Might need help."

Candy and I looked at each other and then up to the front.

"How do we know it's not a trap?" Candy asked, having been warned, by the very man she was asking, about road traps by thugs and thieves.

"We don't, but if we were broken down, wouldn't you want help from people like us?"

She didn't have a reply for that, but Dr. James could probably still feel our anxiety. And our anxiety doubled when he finally brought the van to a complete stop behind the brokenfooted truck with its rain-soaked flag.

"Tell you what: I'm heading out there, but you two cover me from here. If this guy does anything violent, fire off a few shots and see if he runs, OK?"

Candy finally had a comeback: "We wouldn't *need* our help."

But Dr. James could see that she and I were mentally preparing ourselves for the covering operation.

"Candy, you stay here in the van, and I'll climb underneath so we have two different angles," I said.

"Sounds like a plan," Dr. James said, giving us a few moments to further mentally prepare ourselves before he stepped out of the van and slammed the driver's-side door at the same moment I stepped out one of the back doors and slammed that one. While Dr. James walked over, with both hands open, to show he wasn't holding any weapons, towards the dead truck, I got on my belly on the wet cement—the rain was down to a light drizzle—and crawled underneath the huge white behemoth, slightly ashamed of the fact that I'd chosen this cover spot not because of superior tactics but because I somehow felt safer down there, under the giant machine, given the situation, than inside it. Superior cowardice.

Candy and I watched in silence from our hiding places while Dr. James reached the truck. The door opened, and a man only a few inches shorter than the tall Dr. James emerged, wearing all black, with the customary white collar of a man of the cloth. The missionary and the doctor talked for a bit: The missionary repeatedly gestured towards the *Holy Bible* in his hands, and then motioned all around. Dr. James motioned towards the van and made a similar all-around motion. The missionary chuckled and made a "one moment, please" gesture, fished around the back of the cab of his truck for something, and then emerged as Dr. James was looking back at his own van, possibly hoping to calm us kids through his display of cool confidence. But to my and Candy's horror we could see that the missionary had emerged from his truck with a metal pipe. He stepped up and cracked Dr. James in the back of the head, and Dr. James went down like he was dead.

Instead of firing, Candy Baby yelped from shock and fear, giving away her position, and the missionary ran towards the van. Meanwhile, I, under the van, was once again frozen in fright and hugging my rifle—I had been trying to put the reins on my anxiety, but this was mortal, billion-year-old, crippling terror. Once again I simply (or extremely complicatedly, or genetically) couldn't move. Everything was happening too quickly. Dr. James was dead? Candy Baby was next? Then what? Would I just panic and die right there? Would I be murdered? Would my heart explode?

The missionary reached the van, pulled the door open, ripped the rifle from little Candy Baby's shaking hands, and she screamed, "NO! ST—!" He used the butt of the rifle to knock her out. Soon her body and cleared rifle were tossed out of the van, and I could hear the missionary rummaging around inside.

On the ground and seeing both Dr. James and Candy Baby unconscious in the mud, I went into full panic mode and unintentionally let out a groan of utter desperation, which caused the rummaging above to go silent. I heard the man say, *"What the hell?"* There was a little more rummaging, and then the missionary was back outside the van, circling around it while I watched with big afraid eyes, my chest rising and falling to match the high tempo of my panic.

My eyes went even wider when the knees bent and the missionary looked under the van, where he saw me frightened and clutching a rifle like a toddler clutching a blanket to fend off the bogeyman.

"Get out here!" the missionary yelled at the large cowardly body under the van. But I couldn't move, even from a command from a scary man.

The robber-missionary saw that I was, as they say, paralyzed with fear, so he reached under the van and began pulling me out.

But there was a problem, which the missionary couldn't have possibly known about, with that plan.

The post-traumatic fact of the matter was that I hadn't let anyone besides Miss Thompson and Candy touch me, and most goddam especially not a man, since I'd seen Mr. Justin's death that day on the banks of the Blunt. In fact, the only other time I'd been touched by a man since then was on the morning Miss Thompson was arrested, when I'd briefly tried to kill the National Guard soldiers who'd grabbed me out of my bed, before they bashed my head in. After everything that happened that morning on the river, the whole nature of normal intimacy and physical contact was ruinously shredded to pieces by the harrowing, hollowing, haunting experience of seeing my beloved father become a perverse murderer and then be perversely murdered, so when the vile man grabbed my arm, a catalyst was triggered—I fucking snapped. As I was pulled from under the van, I felt the man's strong hands on my arm, my shoulder, back, neck . . . my fear started to turn into a psychologically, exponentially multiplied rage, which grew further and greater as I began to become animated through the perfect confidence of that blistering core of hate.

The missionary had planned on stomping on my head once my cumbersome giantness was halfway out from under the van, but by the halfway point my fission-like rage had already twice doubled, and I shifted from being pulled out from under the van to racing out from under it, putting my shoulder into the missionary's stomach and knocking the angled pile of flesh to the ground. We wrestled savagely in the mud—me out of my goddam mind, the missionary now fighting for his own life—but I had the physical advantage of size and the mental advantage of PTSD, combined with my survival instinct, while the missionary only had a relatively defeated form of his own size and survival instinct. When I had him pinned down, I took the butt of my rifle, still slung around my shoulder, and repeatedly smashed down at his head with it until it wasn't a head anymore and I howled violently like the physical damage wasn't enough, like my volcanic wail could damn to the depths of Hell the very metaphysics of the fleshy smithereens.

Defeated, indeed. By the time the fight was over, the dead missionary's formerly normal-looking, symmetrical, perhaps even attractive face had been turned into a lumpy pile of red and pink and white and yellow. The man's head was no longer anything but chunks—supernova chunks once again being reintroduced to the second law of thermodynamics.

When I became truly cognizant of the fake missionary's ghastly head-pile of flesh, I fell back on my knees and abstractly stared instead at the legs of the corpse, for some reason—a body that I almost seemed to discover for the first time as I kneeled there. At the time, all I could remember was Dr. James slowing the van down, and then my memories started up again as I looked at the fake missionary's thermodynamic head chunks.

When I saw the blood and grey matter on the butt of the rifle slung over my shoulder, I puked myself empty and collapsed and probably would have gone unconscious or insane from the weight of everything that happened if it weren't for one thing: Out of the corner of my eye I could see Candy's lifeless body on the ground, then I also saw Dr. James' sprawled helplessness, and although I was filled with loathing for my life, there was also a deep love in there for the two people I was able to worry about once I got over the solipsistic persuasion of my murderous emotions and could see that I and my despair were not in fact the entirety of the miserable universe.

Automatically and without thinking, I knew where the smelling salts were in the van, and I used them to bring Dr. James back to consciousness, who sprang back to the world as confused as I've ever seen anyone: "What happened? Where am I? What happened? Holy *cookies* my head hurts . . . ."

Dr. James clutched at the back of his head and looked around and remembered stopping the van to help the man in the truck, and then he woke up on the road. Something bad must've happened, and finally he asked me the questions with an understanding of what he actually meant when he said, "What happened? Where's Candy?"

I didn't answer the first question; I helped the doctor stand up and said with a broken voice, "The van."

Dr. James saw the gooey missionary on his way to the van, where he used the smelling salts to revive the knocked-out little girl on the ground, who awoke with the world's longest and loudest inhalation of surprise at awakening where and when she did, with two grim aspects hovering over her face, before realizing she was fine. The effect was almost comical and helped to lighten the aptly grim mood.

When Candy was up and drinking some water, Dr. James turned to me for the third time and asked, "What happened, Dante?"

I had been staring at my empty thoughts, like I do a lot, and I returned to the here and now to address the doctor's question.

"I'm trying to remember."

Candy said, "The man hit you with a pipe!"

That triggered it, and most of my memories returned.

I spoke up: "Yeah. Candy yelped loud 'cause she was afraid, and I was too afraid to help, and he came over and let himself in and knocked her out, too, and threw her out, and—" My speech was interrupted by the painful recollection of everything that was appearing in my memory, and I literally choked for a moment on my still-swollen throat. The sound that came out of my mouth when it happened was almost subhuman. But I had to confess it all.

"He found me, too," I said, and as I remembered, the rage from before once again rose to the surface, but in a way I could control this time but which I could not keep out of my voice. "He started *grabbing* me, Dr. James—pulling me out! I didn't want him to *do* that; I couldn't *move!* I was *scared,* but when he started . . . I didn't like him *touching* me like that! I got so mad . . . I wasn't even *scared* anymore; I just—"

I subconsciously balled my fists, and Dr. James watched my face as I once again relived the memory of having gone blind with fury, the rage building until the memory completed and my eyes went wide with another spike in the knowledge of the objectively done deed and its eternal ramifications, whether justified or not, and from my pregnant silence Dr. James and the ruminative Candy Baby inferred what had happened.

"You were defending yourself, Dante," said Dr. James as supportively as he could while still being troubled. "You did nothing wrong."

Dr. James had an instinct as human as anyone's, and he knew that people who did what I just did need some human contact, and he very consciously showed that he wanted to hug me, but I blanched. Not only did he have instinct, but he also had keen perception and diagnostic skill, and Dr. James quickly deduced that probably the grisly, chemically-induced, homocidal sight of Mr. Justin's death had given me—had churned up—quite a bit of permanent psychological damage.

Candy Baby, possibly the mentally quickest of us all, saw the rebuffed attempt at care and announced, "'Nothing wrong'? Dante, YOU SAVED OUR LIVES!"

All of God's armies couldn't have stopped Candy Baby from launching herself at me, and she hugged me until the frickin' love just *radiated* into this crumbling mountain of a young man. And I did not blanch or recoil from my loving sister's affection: At first I went rigid simply from the shock, but she really was a world-class empathite, and I could feel so many negative emotions pouring out of myself and into the vessel of the incredible Candy Baby, whose inner lightness simply nullified them like garbage launched into the sun.

We quickly looted the missionary's truck of its food and fuel and then Dr. James loaded the bandit's grisly dead body into the driver's seat of the broken-footed truck.

We left the scene almost like we'd found it.

All three of us miserable fucks had terrible headaches—Dr. James couldn't remember and never would remember anything between stepping out of the van and being awakened—and we didn't make any medical stops that day, opting instead to hide the van like we'd done in Cornish while Dr. James monitored his and Candy Baby's mental acuity after their brain injuries.

When the van was suitably hidden and we had all eaten, I set up my hammock and fell asleep almost immediately, even though the sun hadn't even fully set yet. Dr. James knew that he and Candy shouldn't go to sleep for at least another few hours due to their probable concussions, so he asked her to join him on a short hike through the woods.

In the dark woods, on the sodden ground, they hiked for a bit until they found a grove with an opening in the middle, where a firepit was already set up from someone else's old camp. There were hacked stumps set up around the pit for chairs, and Candy sat while Dr. James quickly kindled a small fire. When it was aflame, he sat down and they both stared into it.

"How much longer until we can go to sleep? Can you take first watch? I'm so tired," said Candy, whose brain felt like it was rattling around loose inside.

Dr. James checked the time: "We've got a while before we can sleep, and we'll figure out first watch in a second. But first I want to talk to you about your brother."

They weren't far from a pond in the forest, and the frogs were having a frat party.

Dr. James cleared his throat and said, "Candy, I think we both know that something must have happened to Dante when . . . Mr. Justin . . . happened."

Candy Baby was too tired and fuzzy-headed to give much of a reaction at all, but she'd also seen what was left of the fake missionary's face, and she eventually said, "Yeah—it affected me too, Dr. James . . . but not like that."

"Thing is, I don't know what to do about that kind of hurt—I do body healing, and that's mind healing, and I don't know how to do that."

"Does anyone?"

Dr. James stared at the fire.

"Dr. J?"

"I don't know. I mean, I'm sure there are mental

135

therapists who could give it a good try, but I've never known any good ones, myself."

Candy Baby was growing impatient with the old man. "Then why are we talking about it?"

The good doctor looked over the fire at Candy Baby, whose eyes had returned to the fire after they'd so scornfully looked at her guardian. "Because you seem to be the only thing in the world that can keep his emotional outbursts under control, Sylvia. And I . . . we . . . I'll include Emily in this, and even Dante himself, we need you to look out for him, for all our sakes. He's a good boy, but he's . . . combustible."

"What could I do? He's as big as a house!"

"Even big elephants get spooked by tiny mice, Candy—just be yourself."

She'd never heard that expression before. "How do I be myself?"

Dr. James laughed.

"Welcome to the world."

On the brief hike back to the van they edged past the pond, which was now weirdly quiet, but every now and then Candy heard the pleasant plop of some nocturnal frog leaping from the shore into the black pane of water, with the moonlight and ripples bearing proof of movement.

This was our sleeping arrangement during those travels: In the van I strung a hammock lengthwise, and Candy Baby strung a hammock diagano-widthwise, and Dr. James strung a hammock in the trees outside, both for security and to give us kids a feeling of at least temporarily/nightly having our own space. Then we all bundled ourselves with layered, heat-trapping fabrics and zonked out, sleep-deprived from the previous night, while one of us ran security. We found our body-clocks worked best where nervous Candy took first shift, Dr. James, the light sleeper, took second shift, and I crashed for as long and hard as possible before having to awaken in the bitch-chill of black morning to tap Dr. James's shoulder and secure us into daylight.

"At least our mothers had the guts not to be our mothers," Candy mumbled as she was awakening. It was a subconscious, dream-based utterance that entered the real world and brought both herself and Dr. James to wakefulness, but with neither of them remembering at the time what had been said. Dr. James, who realized he was at that level of awake that doesn't promise a return to sleep, having heard a sort of distressing muffle from the van, let himself down from the trees and landed feet-first in some dry leaves below.

He shook out his boots, put them on, crunched over to me in the foxhole, and said, "Good morning, Dante. How are you feeling?"

I had been watching the sunlight change the pale wall of a distant abandoned building into every shade of yellow I might ever see, moment by moment.

"Please just treat me like it's normal, Dr. J."

"OK," said Dr. James. "You have eye- and nose-mucus all over your face, Dante."

The first members of the Emily/James/Dante/Sylvia Thompson family line had settled in a town called Curly in the American Midwest, coincidentally and conveniently a short drive from Rushmore, and from there the family had spread in all directions, but seemingly all Thompson children had always been told that long ago their family's American history had begun in a town called Curly. Dr. James, the leader of our pack, decided to head to Curly before we reached the controversial camp at Rushmore, having always been interested in actually seeing the fabled town of his American roots and pragmatically not wanting to arrive at the RCCSDFZ at night.

On the drive from Blamrock to Curly, which took around eight hours, we encountered more fellow travelers than we'd seen the whole previous trip, nearly all of them in overloaded jalopies headed in the same direction as we. Many of the jalopies traveled in packs and included gunships (mounted machine-gun turrets on top and rifle barrels pointing out all of the windows). There were also more motorcycle packs and people stranded on the side of the road and waving for help, and receiving help, and everyone kept smoothly moving towards the receptive horizon.

Dr. James eventually pulled off the highway and onto the state road that would take us into Curly. We were the only vehicle in the giant convoy to do so, and soon it was back to the oblivion of our earlier travels.

The last vestige of small-town America . . . was dead. The beautiful, picturesque, perhaps even once gorgeous town of Curly was empty—had been evacuated. On all the houses and buildings was an official proclamation: "CLOSED DUE TO CONG. EMER. A.P. #308971-A.b2—ANY INDIVDUAL [sic] CAUGHT ON **CURLY** TOWN PREMISES WILL BE DETAINED IN-DEFINITELY."

"What's that Cong Emer AR stuff?" I asked.

"One of many incredible laws that led to where we are today: Congressional Emergency Action Plan Blah Blah Blah. This one said that any community that refused to comply with federal search-and-seizure laws was tacitly admitting to traitorous activity, and thus all property and governance rights were subject to federal eminent domain.

"I bet some of those jalopies we saw today were like the people from this town," Dr. James said. "And if that's the case, then I honestly don't know what we're about to head into tomorrow. Lots of outcasts out there these days—could be a real agitation of people."

Nobody said anything for a while, until Candy Baby said, "I just hope one of them is Mommy."

I knew Candy better than Dr. James, but even Dr. James knew that Candy almost never called Miss Thompson "Mommy" anymore unless even Candy's seemingly inexhaustible existential infrastructure were crumbling, and I said something to try to make her feel better: "Candy, I bet right now she wishes all of them were you."

It somewhat worked. And Candy must have over-heard when I had said to Dr. J that I just wanted to be treated like normal: She showed her appreciation by saying, "Shut up!" and affectionately punching me in the arm with a fair amount of force, which made me laugh.

"Well, I was thinking," Dr. James said, but he was interrupted by a sound that broke the windy quiet of the abandoned town—a barking dog.

The first bark had been an oddly muffled sound, and we all turned our heads in that direction, for clarification.

We saw nothing unusual, but then we heard another, clearer bark, and all of a sudden a blurry, furry mutt flew by, barking at us again but continuing on its unbelievably quick pace up the street. Then the dog had an idea, stopped, turned, came back, and started barking animatedly at the three humans who were just staring at it. The dog woofed and ran between us and then shot back into the direction it had come from, and that's when we all saw the six coy-wolves tearing down the street, directly towards us and the barking-scared canine.

A relatively new breed of animal, the coy-wolves were a mix of coyote and wolf—two species whose interbreeding produced a dangerous menace in North America during the decay. Somewhere in size between its parents, it was dangerous because it had the cunning and pack-hunting abilities of wolves, but unlike wolves it took on a dangerous trait from its coyote parent: a lack of fear of humans and human environments. Thus, as America's neighborhoods and infrastructure crumbled from corruption, neglect, and economic stagnation, the coy-wolf population swelled, and currently six of them were hungrily chasing down a wind-quick mutt.

Looking into the faces of those six coy-wolves, I could see the eyes of animals that not only were devoid of fear but were filled with the solitary and tremendous determination of rapid murder.

The coy-wolves raced down the street, fanning across lawns and driveways.

"Here we go again, kids," Dr. James said, leveling his rifle. We raised ours. "Two each—Candy Left, I'm Middle, Big Right."

If you practice something enough, it starts to feel ordinary, even if it's coy-wolves bearing down. If you do it enough, they're not trying to kill you—you're just calmly hitting spots in spacetime. Mr. Justin and we kids not only practiced a lot, but when we did practice we had to practice perfectly—Mr. Justin and Miss Thompson had been able to afford only so much ammunition (a good amount, but not an infinite supply like in the Old Government's military), especially after the federal government recognized their ability to create an ammunition choke-point.

Candy Baby and I took down our wolves with one bullet per heart—four empty shells and four dead coys—while Dr. James, who had not been raised by Mr. Justin, wildly missed both his targets.

Candy and I didn't even say anything—just eyed the two charging coy-wolves.

Five. Six.

The dog, which had been barking at the coys—below the rifles' barrels during the first volley—was so shocked by the explosion from the guns that it had darted far away from both the humans and the wolves, but after the last two wolves took awkward face-dives from being rifleshot lengthwise, the dog ran over to their six bleeding bodies—lying on their sides, breathing their last breaths—and barked at them triumphantly.

Dr. James lowered his rifle barrel and turned to us children and somewhat bashfully said, "Thanks, kids."

The dog ran over to us, and with its inborn amazing athletic ability it leapt six feet off the ground, into Dr. James' chest. It was a loving leap, and Dr. James' arms wrapped around the dog as the surprised man was brought to the ground by the dog's heavy momentum. On the way to the ground, Dr. James' arms sought to protect the dog during the fall while the dog itself smilingly started licking Dr. James in the face and neck.

Literally never before in our lives had either Candy or I heard Dr. James make the sounds he was making while the jovial mutt licked his face. Was he . . . was that . . . giggling?

Dr. James was so starting to lose himself in the giggle-fits that he had to block the dog's licking with his forearm while he emerged from the giggles to pleasantly-desperately say, "Get off me, dog!"

The dog did get off him, and it immediately leap-tackled Candy Baby to the ground, who also started giggling uncontrollably and also had to say, but never could say, but sort of laugh-said, *"S-s-s-s-s . . . (laughter) toppit! (laughter)."*

And then finally the dog tried to bring me down, but I had seen its tricks and braced myself for the leap, which came, and I, caught up in the moment, caught the dog with a triumphant, Candy Baby–like, "Ah-*HA!"* But the dog was less than impressed and started barking straight up into the air, displeased but still playing along, and I looked up to see what the dog was barking at, and while my head was up I realized the dog was trying to convince me into falling back, and to Candy Baby's delight and Dr. James' amusement and the dog's satisfaction, I slowly, intentionally took a controlled fall backwards until, safely on the ground, the dog exercised what I considered an overwhelming sophistication in the canine art of tickle-licking.

The dog's tag said TYGER. It was a she, or a her. A bitch. There was also an "If Found" address, which indicated a house we located after walking around for a little bit, with the dog weaving between us and looking up at us as if she absolutely could not possibly ever have been happier than to be in the company of these three fine, noble, indeed *spiritually significant* humans. The people kind of smelled like the Old World for the dog, and that was a most welcome smell, indeed; the New World had shown the now-happy mutt much stress, hunger, and persecution by various humans, bears, dogs, wolves, coyotes, and coy-wolves.

The house was dark and boarded up like the rest. We could tell Tyger was reacting differently to it, that she knew she was from there, but we could also tell that the dog knew that her old family, her Old World, was not there anymore, and she seemed more interested in what else was out there than where she was from, so we headed back.

Dr. James had an idea: We harvested the pelts of the coys—two pelts each, and an awful lot of offal—while the dog feasted on the scraps. By the time we were done and had chucked down some barbecued coy-wolf ourselves, the sun was dark gold, drowsy, and dipping towards the horizon.

We hucked the pelts back to the van and started setting up our respective hammocks. Tyger must have sensed that we were settling in for the night, and, realizing that the cramped van was where we were to live, barked to life with a better idea.

Bark! Bark! Bark! Bark!

Having summoned everyone's attention, she darted away, came back, darted away, and came back.

Bark! Bark! Bark!

"I believe the dog intends—" Dr. James started saying, but he was interrupted by Candy, who clapped me on the shoulder and said, "Let's follow her!"

The dog led us back to the address on her tag, to the backyard, and doubled her barking. The backyard, like all the rest of the lawns, was overgrown in some places and dead in others, and Tyger was barking at a boulder in one of the dead sections. Barking like crazy, and then nipping at Dr. James' ankle.

"I believe Tyger intends for—"

"Check under that boulder!" Candy Baby squealed excitedly. Next to her, I had the look of someone whose tiredness had been temporarily offset by a genuine curiosity.

When the boulder was moved, Candy's and my view was obstructed by Dr. James, who turned to Tyger with amazement.

"What is it?" I couldn't help myself asking. Candy Baby addressed the tall man with a tone of friendly scorn, as if he were cruelly keeping an important secret from us: "Dr. *Jaaames!*"

Dr. James moved aside, and we saw a circular opening in the ground. The top of the circle was capped with a circular door with a circular handle. "It's a bomb shelter," he said. "Tyger, what manner of genius-beast be thee?"

"What's a bomb shelter?" Candy asked at the same moment I asked, "Do you think anyone's in there?"

As an answer to both questions, Dr. James started unscrewing the locking mechanism on the circular door.

"Wait!" Candy Baby said, but only because she was overwhelmingly excited.

Dr. James kept unscrewing, and then there was a click, and the door started to open on its own, but at the pace of an automatic old piston, not of a bellicose dweller.

When the door was fully open, everyone looked below, but it was completely dark—the late evening light did not penetrate to the bottom.

"Wow," Candy said. I chuckled because although I understood what she meant, we were in fact simply looking into a black hole, which was hardly wow-worthy.

Dr. James called down into the hole: "Anyone in there?"

Nothing.

"What do you think?" Dr. James asked us. We kids, in reply, were as silent as the hole.

"I'll go," I finally said. "If there's anything bad, I'm the one we want down there, right? I'm violent and expendable."

It was hard not to regard us adopted Thompsons as more adult than most adults, and it was because Dr. James felt that kind of respect for me that he didn't contradict my equal-parts grim and accurate appraisal of things. But Dr. James did offer me an out.

"You're sure?"

"This is anxiety from excitement, not fear—I love this shit, Dr. J."

Dr. James furrowed his brows in confusion and tried to hide it, but Candy Baby kind of understood what I meant. Even though I could become overwhelmed and paralyzed in some really bad spots, I was also a fearless adventurer when we would go for hikes back when we lived with Mr. Justin. Candy, usually the bold, at those times when we were in uncharted (by us) territory, became overly cautious, and I, who could be so cowardly in the face of immediate danger, almost felt like I was finally in the right mechanism for the kind of cog my life had given me.

I wish things were a little less complicated.

Dr. James, if anything, always preferred to abide, and he certainly didn't feel like climbing down into that dark pit. "Go south, young man."

We all looked down into the hole again, and I began to position myself over the rungs of a ladder built into the concrete tunnel as the darkness below me continuously exhaled spookily. When I was in position, an important fact quickly dawned on me.

"Candy, can you bring me my headlamp?"

Candy ran to the van and returned with my headlamp, which we used when we would camp with Mr. Justin: a guiding source of light shooting from the veritable third eye on my forehead.

"Here's mine, too—you're going to need all the light you can get down there."

When the headlamps were both kinds of on, I received some reassuring thumbs-up from the wincing (from the light) Dr. James and Candy and an impatient bark from Tyger. I then turned and looked down the concrete tunnel, to prepare for the descent, and Candy, above me, said, *"Oooh! It's carpeted!"*

I saw the crimson carpet, too, and, somehow reassured by it, began descending.

The metal rungs ended at the ceiling, which was approximately nine feet off the ground. I dangled from the bottom rung only momentarily before letting go and landing easily on the soft, still-plushy carpet.

James and Candy heard the landing from above, and Candy asked, "You OK?"

But I, when I landed, became, or at least imagined I'd temporarily transformed into, a superhero, and from my easy landing I put myself into a fighting position and spun around quickly, ready to unleash evil pain on anything that moved towards me—living person or flailing ghost—whatever might be stupid enough to step up and try its bad luck. My whole attention was on the dynamic balance between offense and defense necessary for physical combat, and thus I did not hear Candy Baby's question. I spun and clenched my fists and was ready to roar when I completed my spin and was completely certain there was nobody else down there: The spider of my senses detected no foreign movements in the web of perception.

Dr. James, becoming as worried as Candy from my lack of reply, called down with his booming voice, "Everything OK down there?"

There was still no sound for a few more moments, and then there was a click, and a bright flood of light emerged from below.

"*Sweet!*" I said. The sound rebounded off itself up the walls of the tunnel.

Candy Baby started letting herself down, got to the bottom rung, dangled, and dropped light as anything, landing with monkey-grace and looking around.

"*Wow!*" she said, a sound that rebounded off itself up walls of the tunnel, and this time it was a full wow.

Dr. James started letting himself down, said to Tyger, "We'll be right back," and dipped out of sight. The dog started barking down at us. When he got to the bottom rung, his feet were inches from the ground, and he too landed and looked around, like me and

Candy, while Tyger barked above.

The carpet was thick and new (but slightly, just slightly used, I could see). The furniture was large and soft and also new. the walls were packed: cabinets, open arrays of tools, rifles, ammunition, storage containers, a gigantic OmniViewer, several ordinary doors, one large, safe-like door, a stainless-steel sink and counter, an oven, a washer/dryer, a workbench, and one section of one wall was completely lined with what looked like thousands of old musical records.

No expense had been spared: Everything from the ammunition to the furniture to the stainless-steel heater-oven was a top-of-the-line purchase.

Meanwhile, Tyger above was still barking at us, and it got to the point that Candy Baby went down below the hole in the ceiling and called up, "Hey, Tyger! You doing OK, pup? What are—? *WHOA!*"

I had been investigating the wall of records when Candy's yell caught my attention, and I watched as she, while looking up in horror, braced herself and then caught the dog that had evidently jumped down the tunnel. The mutt squirmed through her arms and then, standing happily on her own four legs, barked twice at Candy Baby and then immediately began sniffing around all over the place, happily engaging in her dog responsibilities.

I laughed, and Dr. James emerged from one of the ordinary doorways to see what had happened, and when he saw the dog sniffing and Candy Baby looking at it with relieved affection, he put it together and chuckled. "You OK, Can'?"

"That dog is CRAZY," she said.

"Yeah," I said.

"It's really cool," she said.

Dr. James chuckled again.

There were two bedrooms, one with a large bed and one with a bunkbed (on each bedroom's small nightstand was a personal OV), and there was also a huge pantry that had tons of stored food and a fully loaded powder-printer. There was a gigantic bathroom that had a tub, a shower, a washer/dryer, a toilet, two sinks, a full-length mirror, and a linen closet, and the only door we couldn't get open was the safe-like door, which required a key that we hadn't found yet.

When the overall investigation was complete, we gathered in the living room, and Candy Baby threw herself atop one of the big couches and was seemingly swallowed entirely by its softness. From the depths of the cushions she said, "We are definitely sleeping here tonight."

"What do you think, Dr. James?" I asked hopefully. I, too, was eager to get a full night's sleep somewhere flat, soft, and warm.

"I think I feel bad that the person or family who put all this together never got to use it for anything other than what looks like a little recreation or something."

To that point, to me and Candy, the shelter had been this thing that had always existed, which we were lucky to have found, but when Dr. James put it like that, I pictured some hopeful guy like Mr. Justin or some thoughtful woman like Miss T putting in all the effort to build it and stock it, and I started to feel guilty. Candy Baby squirmed uncomfortably.

"Should we go?" she asked.

"Of course not," Dr. James said with a wry grin. "The dog invited us."

While Candy and I prepped for bed—I got the top bunk; Candy Baby got the bottom bunk and the freshly cleaned dog—Dr. James climbed up the ladder and parked/hid the van in the garage (fortunately it just barely fit), and as he walked back to the concrete hole in the ground, it was late evening, and he listened to the empty town of Curly, which was night-quiet.

I awoke to the sound of Tyger scratching at the door, and Candy Baby awoke a few moments later after the dog half-barked.

Still partially asleep, Candy Baby said, *"Wasss-sup, dog?"*

"I think she has to piss," I said from above, "at least."

Candy Baby moaned sleepily. A moment later I heard and felt her rise out of bed. I dropped my head back down to the pillow and tried to go back to sleep, but I soon felt something fishy in the air, and suddenly Tyger, tossed up by Candy Baby, landed on my stomach, and Candy said, "Go ahead, girl! Pee on him!" But the dog simply sniffed my face and neck and licked both a little bit while I laughed at Candy's antic. She must have been as excited to see Miss Thompson as I suddenly was.

We got Tyger outside by putting her in my backpack. Dr. James evidently wasn't awake yet because he never came out of the master bedroom. First I lifted Candy up to the lowest rung, and she climbed out, and then I leapt up and pulled myself out, being careful with the bagged dog on my back. Tyger, to her credit, seemed to understand the situation and did not protest being put in the bag and carried around.

Outside, the air was pale with light and was still wet with the chilly breath of early morning. We watched Tyger run out of the bag, sniff around briefly, and quickly seemingly deflate herself via urination and defecation.

"Wow!" Candy Baby said once again, and I literally laughed out loud at the vast size of the puddle and pile left behind.

"Guess I'm lucky she didn't do that on the bed," I said.

Tyger sniffed at her laid pile of feces and looked like she was about to take a bite of it, which was going to gross out Candy, so she yelled, *"Tyger!"* The dog snapped her head towards Candy, and she beckoned the dog forward, away from the pile, into her arms, and the mutt was happy to oblige.

"Let's get you fed, girl."

Sure enough, down below, on one of the bottom shelves in the huge pantry, there were two gigantic barrels of dog food. And as Candy Baby, after filling a small dish with chow, was closing the top of the barrel, she noticed that along the rim of the barrel it said TYGER. Out of curiosity, she looked at the rim of the second barrel, and it said RAVEN.

"There was another dog?"

Inter arma enim silent leges.—
"In a time of war the law falls silent."

The metamorpho-militarization of America's domestic police happened incrementally, but once it started it never stopped or slowed down. What were once brave servants of the public increasingly were called upon to serve more as tactical fighting units in America's dubious wars on Drugs, Terrorism, Poverty, and Crime. The metaphorical blue shield was replaced by a literal black one, and midnight raids went from highly publicized, major events to ordinary procedures. Sometimes—many more times than the police officials or the politicians who encouraged them would ever admit—mistakes were made, and one night a man named Harold William Kramer and his two young dogs were awakened by six police officers in full military, bulletproof apparel, who tossed in three flash-bang grenades and then stormed the premises, spooking the sweet holy glory out of Kramer's beloved dogs. The owner himself, stumbling out of bed, unsure if he were dreaming or awake, was quickly tackled by two officers, who beat him about the head and back until he went completely limp. While that was happening, the officer at the back of the house was spooked by the sudden emergence, through the doggie-door, of a blurry-fast dog, which shot between the officer's legs and into the night. The first dog was followed by a second, larger, slower dog, which the officer had enough time to react to, be scared of, and shoot twice.

Raven, a black Labrador, was dead.

Upstairs Kramer heard the gunshots, and he knew. He'd heard about the escalation of police raids. He knew they figured any dog on the premises of a possible "drug den" was a possible "guard dog" that was a threat to officers and therefore legally permissible to kill on sight. He knew at least one of his dogs was dead, and he completely lost his mind with rage.

His wife, in their divorce, had taken the children. He had "rescued" the dogs at the local shelter because seeing his kids once every two weeks wasn't enough to replace the fullness of what he'd lost, and he'd gone to the pound and gotten two puppies and named them and trained them and became friends with them in his loneliness. And then a cowardly cop killed Raven for being hugely spooked by unnecessary flash-bang grenades during a no-knock raid on the *wrong address*.

The sound of the two gunshots had the effect of turning Kramer—lying on the ground and in the process of being put into handcuffs—into Dr. Frankenstein's monster. Suddenly the man's mind and body flared with life, and he went on such an attacking rampage against the two officers in the room that one of them required six surgeries on his wrist, and the other took such a beating that he'd literally urinated himself in fear. Eventually, when the rest of the SWAT team cleared the other rooms, they came in and found all of Kramer in a rage and put him in a pain cage.

Kramer didn't receive any corrective surgeries—he received indefinite detention.

Almost the entire town of Curly grew outraged by what happened, and the Old Government shut down the town entirely. The powers that be couldn't risk any more fulminating hotbeds.

Tyger, the mutt that'd survived for two years on her own before stumbling upon the rifle-shouldered Thompsons, *certainly deserved a nice warm blanket on the floor of the van while we all traveled to Rushmore*, Candy Baby figured, and she opened a compartment in the van where she thought she remembered seeing one of Mr. Justin's old blankets, and bingo, she found it and pulled it out.

The preparations for leaving were almost complete. I was already packed and ready and was spending some idle time meditating behind the garage, and Dr. James was down in the bomb shelter cleaning up the post-breakfast mess, returning the place to like it had been before our arrival, while Candy Baby was all set except for getting a spot ready for the panting Tyger.

The old wool blanket, which smelled like Mr. Justin, she noticed wistfully, would be perfect for the dog—soft and warm. The way it was folded up was just too small even for the twenty-pound dog, so she set out to unfolding it but stopped halfway through the first unfurl because something clattered to the ground. It was a notebook, and it almost hit Tyger. The dog was immediately interested in chewing it to pieces, and she snapped up the notebook in her teeth and started running away, but Candy Baby was quite quick herself, and she snatched it from young Tyger.

"That isn't yours, Tyger!" she said and turned the notebook over and saw what was written on the front:

DENNIS ROBERT JUSTIN— CAPUAN YEAR 12

It wasn't hers, either. But she became so interested in it that she unintentionally dropped the blanket to the ground and stared at the cover of the journal, and Tyger, enraptured by the blanket, bounded into and out of it and cutely wrestled with it, which Candy would have adored had she not been so shocked by what she'd read. It was only because the dog, in its bounding, landed on her foot that she pulled her mind away from her memories of her father-figure, and she tucked the notebook under her arm, picked up the blanket, went to the van, carefully tucked the journal in her backpack, and spread out Mr. Justin's blanket on the ground in the corner by where she liked to read.

When Candy was finished, Tyger jumped into the van, clattered over to the blanket, sniffed it, circled around two-dozen times, and settled comfortably with a yawn.

"Looking good, Tyger!" Candy said to the dog,

which stood back up on all four legs and barked twice, as if to announce she was pleased with her travel accommodations and was ready for departure.

I watched the whole scene after returning from behind the garage, and while Candy was busy with the dog I sneaked up behind her.

"HEY!" I said loudly in her ear, and she screamed. In immediate response to Candy's scream, Tyger barked, and Dr. James, who was just emerging from the tunnel, also said, for completely different reasons, as a stern guardian, "HEY!"

By humorous coincidence, in rapid succession it went: "HEY!" "AHH!" "BARK!" "HEY!"

Candy and I laughed.

Dr. James hurried to the van and hissed, "Kids, we need to be a lot quieter than this. We don't know who's here or not, and if we get picked up and taken anywhere besides Rushmore, we'll probably never see Emily or each other again. Does that all make sense to you?"

"Yes, sir," I said back quietly, and Candy nodded and pretend-zipped her mouth shut, held up the invisible key for us to see, and then looked around in pretend-amazement when the key popped out of her hand and the air completely. It was one of the awesome stupid things she always did.

"Well, all right," Dr. James said, coming out of his moment of sternness and sounding almost like a different person he was so well rested from the night before. "It's about four or so hours to Rushmore, and we don't even know what we're going to find there, so get ready for anything, OK?"

It's funny that Dr. James had chosen those words: All Mr. Justin and Miss Thompson had ever done in their rearing of us kids was to try to do just that— prepare us poor fuckers for anything we might face in our brutal lives.

The one who'd taught me and Candy the most

about what love was, and what it was to love, was awaiting us at the end of our day's journey, and Dr. James could see in our faces, and he felt it in his own being, that all of us needed to reconnect with the fountainhead of that loving knowledge—to be under the care of a kind, noble, intelligent, loving woman—because while the body is fed with food, the soul is nourished by love, which even Mr. Justin had begrudgingly learned and accepted. And while there was love between oafish brother and empathic sister and sober uncle, all of us were still clumsy with our giving and receiving of it, and we looked forward to learning more from the heaven-tall woman waiting for us in an NLA concentration camp.

"Let's go," Dr. James said.

The sun wasn't far from the down horizon—the drive was taking *much* longer than anticipated—and Dr. James was piloting the van carefully in the intermittently dense and open traffic. Candy Baby was in the back of the van, nestled in her deep corner, reading, sharing the blanket on the ground with Tyger—the dog's warm head in her lap, Candy's hand on T's head and her other hand holding up the open notebook, which she was reading. Dr. James and I were scanning the road and the horizon for any signs of danger. Again there was more traffic than earlier in the trip, mostly headed in the same direction, but not with the exact same intentions as those in the white van with the brown crosses. Those of us up front, however, had to keep our eyes peeled, because after what had happened earlier in the trip, we knew not to trust any other vehicles on the road unless completely necessary.

It was usually necessary, and thus we up front

kept extra vigilant whenever we could.

As the dog in her lap sighed, a riveted Candy Baby turned the page, and Dr. James, feeling safe enough on the road to ask, spoke up.

"Whatcha been up to back there, Candy?"

I turned around and saw Candy and the dog in fine detail through the light streaming in from the windows up front: Tyger had lifted her head and was looking at Dr. James, and Candy Baby had taken ahold of her collar.

"Reading," I said.

"Reading what?" Dr. James asked the back of the van.

"Looks like a notebook," I said.

"Dante, keep watch," Dr. James said to me as sternly and yet delicately as he could. To the back of the van he said, "Whatcha readin', Can'?"

"Looks like a notebook," Candy said in a snooty tone, mocking me.

Dr. James looked at me long enough that I knew he was upset with me for again not letting Candy Baby speak for herself. Given the anticipation we all felt to be reunited as a family, Dr. James wasn't surprised by such behaviors, but that didn't excuse the rudeness.

I was offended by the look Dr. James had given me because I didn't feel like I'd done anything wrong, and I crossly whispered to him, "I was only trying to help."

Dr. James whispered back, "Dante, when you speak up for someone who's willing to speak up for herself, you're being the kind of person nobody likes."

I had been shamed again, and in that shame I also noticed that sometimes Dr. James almost enjoyed when he took me down a peg—I could tell. In Dr. James' mind, Mr. Justin had been correct: Vigilance is one thing, but oversensitivity is evidence of a childish ego—all the world so egotastically sifted through the prism of ME. Perhaps that's why Dr. James quietly delighted in shaming me, the big emotional clod, especially because we were headed into God knew what, when I would need as much skepticism and caution and manners as I could get.

(I know something else, though: I'm sensitive like Mr. Justin was sensitive. But oversensitive? I defer such judgments to my Creator, and if I have no Creator, it looks like the judgment and the struggle are mine to wrestle with until it all goes black.)

Despite not wanting to, Candy Baby heard both whispered comments. She'd been disturbed from her reading, was all—she wasn't eavesdropping.

"What sort of notebook?" Dr. James asked.

"It's Mr. Justin's diary, if you must know," she said. After a pause, she added, "It's OK to read someone's diary if they're not alive anymore, right?"

Simultaneously Dr. James and I incredulously asked, *"What?"*

Candy Baby sighed the sigh of twelve-year-old girls who are already accustomed to the shocking news that's been revealed, and she singsong-said, "I *found* it this *morning.*"

Before anything else could be said, everyone's attention was grabbed by the blinking horizon.

Blue, red, and white flashing lights leaped from the roofs of government vehicles on the outermost border of the Freedom Zone—federal trucks and local police. Helicopters hovered and thumped. The former tent village Dr. James had seen on the OV was now a tent city, all everything everywhere. With no governing body, people just settled as logically and lazily as they could, and before long it was impossible to penetrate farther into the grounds, and the white van stopped at the periphery of the tent city, which was swarming with activity and commotion.

"How will we ever find her?" Candy asked, looking at the rock concert out the window.

Dr. James replied, "I've been thinking about that, and Emily and I used to have a code word when we were kids. We both loved this cartoon *Squawky Talker—*" The name was silly enough, but the fact that the seemingly humorless Dr. James had ever watched cartoons compounded the silliness, and despite our circumstances Candy Baby, who'd never heard of the show, couldn't help but giggle, which unleashed my laugh. Dr. James smirked and cleared his throat. "Anyway, whenever we wanted to make each other laugh, we'd pause for a moment and then do our impression of Squawky's catchphrase."

Dr. James's face, usually so emotionally impassive, filled with a reddish-pinkish embarrassment. This sea change in Dr. James's demeanor further ignited our interest, and I asked, "What was the catchphrase?"

Dr. James shook his head as he laughed at the stupidity, and then he did an impossibly good impression of old Squawky. "He'd go"—he cleared his throat—"*'Cuh-CAW! Cuh-CAW!'*"

Candy and I laughed—more at Dr. James than with him—and we were immediately skeptical of the plan, and Dr. James could probably feel that skepticism in the air.

"Trust me," he said. "Almost nobody else in the world ever watched or heard of that show: It's very personal to us—she'll know it as soon as she hears it."

We looked at him blankly.

"Trust me!"

"People are going to think we're crazy," I said.

"And?"

" . . . "

Dr. James explained his confidence. "Kids, it's

going to be a human circus out there—nobody is going to notice us, and even if they do they're just going to think we're crazy, which is fine because most folks don't hassle crazy people, and we don't want to be hassled; we just need to find Emily and figure out what's next. And hey, I'm all ears if you have a better plan."

Candy and I would need to see it to believe it, but neither of us had a better idea, so we prepared ourselves to look stupid: The end, after all—being reunited with the most valued wellspring of love we had left—was well worth the embarrassing and dangerous means, we figured.

"OK," Dr. James said, reassured by our reluctant acceptance of the plan. "I have one more bit of bad news: We're going to have to look particularly stupid, because I'm going to need us all to hold hands as we walk through the crowd."

"Why?" I asked. I was a teenager.

"Because I could get kidnapped or something," Candy Baby said. "Right?"

Dr. James's answer yes came in the form of the way he looked at Candy wondering how she could have deduced the thing he didn't want to say, and she interpreted that look as well and said, "Penelope Fairyweather got kidnapped at a big circus in one of my *Kelly Four-Eyes* books."

Fifteen books in the series about a bookish little problem-solver: Candy had already wolfed them all down four times over.

"To be perfectly honest, kids, it's because human free will plus the lawlessness of these gathered masses equals the possibility of almost anything happening, including any number of really horrible things, so let's all join hands and squawk our butts off until we find Emily, all right?"

We slung our rifles over our shoulders, cracked the windows so Tyger could breathe while we were gone, said our goodbyes to that fine young bitch, deputizing her with full rights to protect the van from possible looters while we were gone, stepped outside into the roar of the lawless human assembly, joined hands— Dr. James holding Candy's hand, Candy holding Dr. James' and mine, and me holding Candy's—and started walking towards the center of the masses.

"*Cuh-CAW! Cuh-CAW!*" "*Cuh-CAW! Cuh-CAW!*"

It was a survivalist tailgate party: people cooking out of their cars, sleeping in the backseats, milling around and sharing jerky and black bread, barbecued meat, iodine water, and AZN-Paste, etc., with so many layers of music coming from so many different stereos they all overlapped and created a loud static it was hard to *Cuh-CAW* over; nevertheless, we were still able to pierce the static with our weird squawks. But we also listened, or at least we kids listened, to hear what the people there were saying, straining to hear anything that even resembled the word "Emily." Between the *Cuh-CAW*s, we heard snippets of the conversations we passed as we headed farther towards the heart of the chaotic conglomeration.

"IncaTube strikes the dude like a bolt of lightning! He just . . . I didn't tell the old bag of shit nothing she never heard before . . . Well, I thought there were supposed to be crazy hot chicks here, but mostly it's just . . . Jesus the Risen Christ would be *throwing over every table in Washington if he were alive today!* . . . If anybody is even paying attention to what's happening

160

here, I mean *look* . . . Are these people homeless? Are we homeless now? . . . I mean, dude, there are some things you just can't fucking *un-smell* . . . That used to be, used to be so, but it ain't anymore . . . Hey, Brody, where do people shit around here? . . . Listen, folks, I got WEED if you got some extra FOOD and WATER . . . Oh, my Gawd, LOOK at those FUH-REAKS over there; Tricia, you said this was going to . . . Like, what is this place anyway? That video made it fuckin' look . . . Apples? APPLES?! Are you telling me that stupid . . . Dude! I haven't heard any Velvet Underground in frickin' decades, man! My older brother started a . . . Have you guys seen that woman who got slammed by those soldiers yet? She was fuckin' HOT! MILF! . . . The doctor said she's not due for another month . . . He's dead now, but that's what he said . . . But instead of their lottery we'd stone you to death for the innermost secrets that we'd infer when all your OV searches were made public . . . Is there anybody here who knows what in the WORLD is going on out here? . . . Hey, is that weird family droppin' some *Squawky Talker?* How fuckin' cool is that, bro? That's some retro . . . Back when the Old Government hit the wall like the rest of the world, but they're still trying to get the band back together, so this should just be . . . God, I'd KILL for an apple right now . . . That little girl's got a rifle over her shoulder! All three of 'em do! . . . Those people are fuckin' crazy, but I guess here's the place to do it . . . I saw a Libertarian tent somewhere over there, and some Green people farther out, but it's . . . Jim Morrison is what happens when attractive people actually . . . One neighbor helps another; got to these days . . . Look at that fat dude alone over there; let's go rob that bitch . . . Mommy, who are these people? . . . You think you know me, but you only know who I give you . . . We're pretty much dead here; it's just a matter of time . . . You ever heard of a guy named Stephen Stone? Some dude over there was just saying

161

. . . The *Elvira*-looking chick at the Rage tent has cigarettes if you're feeling lucky . . . There's a pack of teenagers somewhere around here, freaky looking bunch of kids, so pale they *glowed* . . . You might be seeing something; you might be seeing something beautiful that is not there . . . Man invented beer out of necessity—to make it through his wife's stories! . . . Order us here at gunpoint! Our property is not our property anymore! Whatever they . . . Blew up all the bridges surrounding Tremblay Island, and I hear people there are starving to . . . What do you think them folks over there is building? The folks around them look like . . . This whole, this thing, you guys, it's just . . . Where's the party, anyway? This place . . . ."

Hope was already dying in us Thompson squawkers. We saw no sign of Miss T, nor any sign of any sort of difference or noteworthy anchor in the wild hive of the estranged which we could use to orient ourselves, and the dirty cars and people continued *ad nauseam.* As mentioned, the reason Dr. James had wanted us to all join hands was because the scene in Vectorville was nothing compared to the free-will 3D human symphony now all around. We kids had known the social solitude of the forest and the look-after-each-other goodness and conversational pockets of small-town life in Sweet Bend in the early years of the decay; alternatively, we had never been in any situation like the concentration camp except maybe Vectorville and the thunderstorm that one night with Mr. Justin, just by the sheer overwhelming amount of sensation we were suddenly exposed to and seeking to survive.

Despite everything but hope, we marched, hand-in-hand, through the scads and scabs of people gathered or imprisoned in the camp, and we squawked with a determined vigor, suddenly becoming so over-whelmed by the situation, Dr. James included, that a sort of thoughtless intransigence kicked in—the feeling that if we were to stop we would consequently and instantaneously die.

The masses received us and let us pass through, and we kept listening like deer while Dr. James nearly choked on the anxiety that something had happened to his sister after all these other people arrived. He also wondered how he, who no longer had any orientation with where we were, could serve as a guardian for the two children in his protection. (He later told us that the only thing that kept him from completely unraveling in that infinite-ring circus of people was his faith in the idea that if he were to have a nervous breakdown right there, Candy and I had already been so hardened by our lives that he thought we would be more or less fine without him.)

Sometimes it's just crutches leaning against other crutches.

Anyway, yes, the masses let our squawking family pass through.

"How about we go find some then? Anything's legal here, right? ... I don't even see how the government can keep us here if the government doesn't even exist anymore ... The *people* still exist, though, and they're still trying ... Some old guy's got a bunch of liquor over there, and he'll let you ... All we've done is make sacrifices, and on what altar? *Whose altar?* What are ... Adam, I can't say it any more clearly, *flurglebuglr gmehgthsem* ... One sec, gotta drain the wang vein ... *The best minds of my generation destroyed by shitheads, strafing,*

163

rhetorical, flaky . . . Maggie, beautiful, do you think there was ever a moment . . . What's going to happen when this place bursts, you know? We might as well . . . I just hope one of those drones doesn't accidentally launch our death at us 'cause of a glitch or somethin' . . . My taxes paid for those guns and those towers . . . Well, back when I had income my taxes paid for 'em . . . *Luk, Mummy, dare's anuddah heckacoppah!* . . . Bro, bro, bro, bro, don't even, bro . . . Even in this hopelessness, under the stone-dead stare of those crumbling faces, you'll notice there is peace here . . . I smell weed; you smell that? . . . Ladies and gentlemen, it's time for you to take center stage in your own life's performance! . . . Oh, Mary! Oh, Mary, what joy! You . . . Sullivan, Arthur P.; Tanner, William R.; Tenderdrine, Maxwell S.; Tenzing . . . Stars and stripes? More like bombs and bars, bro . . . And yet here we are *loafing* on the shoulders of giants . . . Pete, nobody fuckin' here wants to play soccer, OK? God gave us two . . . Fella over there says it's s'posed'ta rain tomorrow, so you be sure'n' get the catchment ready the moment . . . Even though this is bad, it's still better than, well, we came from Cleveland . . . If you don't mind, I'd like to try out an ability of mine . . . Now look at us, they call this liberty? We about as free as . . . So, like, is this it? Is this our life now? . . . This is fuckin' awesome, man; the wave of civilization is rolling back! Here comes the low tide of humanity! . . . Stephen Stone? Never heard of him, sounds like an asshole . . . Ha, ain't nobody fuckin' with those rifle-slingin', quackin' weirdos; just let them through, creepin' me out . . . There's a dead body about a mile that way; nobody knows what to do with it . . . Girl, I bet you e'r'body tells you that you beautiful, and they ain't lyin', but I bet ain't nobody else but me knows what makes . . . Intentions aren't enough! People forget it, but even that fuckwit Hitler had both science—the now-disproven-but-at-the-time-completely-valid theory of eugenics—and intentions—the betterment of the human race—in his . . . Steve, have you seen Mitch and Nick yet? They were supposed to be . . . There's, like, no old people here; isn't that weird? . . . What do you expect? Octogenarians roughing it for The Resistance? . . . Mommy? Mommy? Mommy? Mom! Mom! . . . So completely FUCKED, just, like, SHIT! . . . Civilization was privacy until civilization overruled privacy, and now we're back in the wild . . . I think I heard there's a river about three miles . . . *Cuh-CAW! Cuh-CAW!"*

Dr. James knew it as soon as he heard it. Though his rasping voice was flagging after our long journey through the haphazard camps at the camp, he shouted louder than he ever had before in his life: *"EMILY!"*

"JAMES!"

Everyone was now looking at us, but only one person in the crowd was coming towards us—a towering woman with long brown hair, bounding through gawking camps and leaping over blankets and children and passed-out NLAs with her lifelong grace, her face shining from light and firelight and glistening with streaking tears of happiness—and suddenly we were all smashed together in a hug, the whole family bawling with joy. Together again! The reassurance of each other's love and reality and feel! Our family, momentarily, became communally solipsistic—the only truly existent beings in the cradle of our own universe.

Dr. James stepped aside and let Miss Thompson shower us with love. She started with me, raining on my face with kisses while I in turn tried to hug all of my love into her heart, to use my strength to tell the story of my happiness at seeing her again, until she coughed and I laughed and let her have her moment with Candy

Baby. Both women's lips curled when they regarded each other, and then they both re-burst into tears and hugged each other in that way women have where they can become mirrors of reassuring emotion.

A photographer from the Associated Press named Simon Winchester, covering the goings-on at the camp, was one of the many people whose attention was captured by the cries of James and Emily, and when he saw the reunion of our desperate, broken family, he photographed the big embrace from where he was kneeling (he had been on his knees taking pictures of a laughing toddler at a different family's camp), and the iconic picture that resulted was the first of the five he took of the reunion: He was still on his knees, and our family embraced each other in tears through the dancing arms of fire flickering from within the laughing toddler's family's firepit. The symbolism was so obvious it was perfect: In a world on fire, humanity finds its flagging purpose in each other's love. Nevertheless, although no news agencies ended up using it, instead preferring the flames picture, Simon Winchester's favorite of the five he shot was the last one: The Thompson family—with eyes full of tears but smiles on our faces—started heading hopefully towards an uncertain future, together.

The flames photograph came to be an iconic image in the news for a few days—no doubt aided by the fact that the woman in the picture was *the woman from the Rushmore Sex Video*—and spread across the world's news agencies, and brought to light the plight of America's growing lost generations.

The people who put two and two together had to ask themselves what the hell was going on in their (former) country.

Simon Winchester received James and Emily Thompson's permission to use the photograph, and he remembered the request not only because of the photograph's eventual success but also because of the answer he was given to his query before Emily Thompson signed the permission contract.

"That was a beautiful moment, ma'am, and I'm a photographer for the Associated Press. I took a few pictures of you guys, and I'd like your permission to use them."

"Young man," Miss Thompson said, wanting to be rid of the man and be with her family as quickly as possible, "I don't think I have any legal rights anymore, so, sure."

That quotation was used in the story that was written about what was happening at Mount Rushmore.

When Mr. Winchester was done with us, we Thompsons took each other's hands and double-timed it back to the van, which we found just as the last of the set sun's light was purpling the sky, and which we found (the van) partly by luck and largely because Candy Baby had one of the world's foremost internal compasses.

At the oversized van we were greeted by Tyger barking at us from the driver's-side window, and the dog happily nosed everyone hello and then began sniffing at and investigating Miss Thompson, who scooped up the mutt and nuzzled her face and called her darling. And then finally, when everyone was reacquainted and the stress began to subside, we found ourselves all exhausted, like we could finally rest now, but even as the stress drained out of us in our togetherness, we did not get sleepy so much as finally relax. Anyway, it was still too early, and we were much too wired to sleep.

A hundred yards to the west and fanning all the way to the south was a dense woodland that went beyond where Dr. James's eyes could go, and he saw people streaming into and out of the forest—emptyhanded those entering, firewood-loaded those emerging—and while Miss Thompson and we kids caught up on what each other had been up to since her arrest and our departing Sweet Bend, Dr. James went to the woods to do as he'd seen done by others, but better. He didn't want us going into the woods with strangers out there when it was dark, so he went with himself and his rifle and of course the quite-eager Tyger, who'd been a very good girl while we were gone. Consequently, it not having been his first rodeo, Dr. J tugged the little sled Candy Baby had lazily invented (she'd stolen the idea from a family of Inuits she'd read about), to make carting larger quantities of firewood easier, dislodging the hard plastic door for the storage compartment on top of the van and dragging it behind her with some rope.

Dr. James dragged his little Candy Baby sled contentedly. The air—flavored with woodsmoke—was cooling. As the color of the day seemed to bleed into the night, so too bled out the warmth from the air. Dr. James picked up his pace to stoke his heart and warm up his body, and the little dog ran around sniffing and returning and leaping into and out of the sled Dr. James pulled, as if it were a game they were playing together.

The woods were lovely—dark and deep—and now that he had deposited the children and they were with their mother again, Dr. James no longer had any promises to keep, and he took his time, relaxing in a long-sought seclusion (a talented doctor does not reach the age of thirty-five without a wife unless he is the sort of man whose personality ultimately longs for isolation when the day's most important work is done—The Introvert), his own headlamp ablaze as he and Tyger tromped through the undergrowth that crackled beneath their feet and paws. Dr. James took his time in gathering the necessary ingredients—fluffy tinder, what he called "transitional sticks," and finally what he termed "the log-burners." He worked his way over to a great pile of deadfall and stacked his favorite choices in the sled while the dog raced through the woods chasing smells and sounds, returning every so often to the headlamp, which had continuously scanned the woods for firewood from side to side and worked for the dog almost like a lighthouse.

"Tyger—*hyup!*" Dr. James called into black woods when he was finished, and he could hear the sound of a dog racing through the dry undergrowth of the forest and emerging right at his side with a look like, "What's up now? Things cool here?"

Dr. James stooped and petted the grateful dog, which burrowed her head into Dr. James' chest and made little doggy sounds of recognition-appreciation, and as he petted the dog Dr. James also removed the burrs and forest detritus that had accumulated during her romp.

Breathing heavily, Tyger kept alternately looking at Dr. James and nuzzling her head into his torso. The whole time, Dr. James kept repeating, "That's a good girl, Tyger," but clearly he was thinking about something else. He kept saying it, but the fear and trepidation kept building, the source of which he was mentally, internally seeking—it is not only women who receive intuitions.

But he didn't indulge in it, and eventually, when the dog was acceptably free of the woods' dandruff, Dr. James and Tyger stood and started heading back towards the white van, and as they marched away from the woods, back into the human hoard, some of his worry was chased away by a movingly beautiful sight:

Ahead of him, at the camp itself, there were hundreds of little campfires ablaze, with people gathered around them, warming themselves and sharing each other's lives. It was an overcast night, so everything was black on every horizon, and then there was color, little pockets of glowing dark orange, the flames flickering, a warm pointillist polka-dot blanket in the inky black.

Candy and I immediately recognized the duet of sounds coming from Tyger's collar and the rhythmic crunchy groans of the firewood sled, and we all emerged from the van—the inside of which was glowing chemlight green—and we each had a comment for Dr. James.

"*There* you are," I said—I had started to worry.

"Did everything go OK?" Candy Baby asked, who definitely had been worried.

"*Well that took long enough,*" Miss Thompson said sarcastically and beamed at her brother because she knew him well enough to know that he'd been reveling in his momentary solitude. He caught the understanding and felt better that she understood, so he made a joke, or at least tried to.

"That's what she said."

At the time, neither Candy nor I got the joke—of course that's what she said; she just said it!—but Miss Thompson got it and chuckled.

Using the sledded kindling, Candy and I quickly built a fire, and soon we were all gathered around it like the hundreds or maybe even thousands of families and groups Dr. James had seen from the edge of the forest—which he told us about.

Miss Thompson and Candy Baby were snuggled up together, sitting on the floor of the van—the side doors wide open, facing the nearby fire—and Dr. James and I sat on our own QuickChairs across the way. As the night persisted, the air kept getting cooler and colder, and we leaned and scooted closer to the fire and warmed ourselves with it.

While Dr. James had been gone, Candy and I had sentence-fragmentedly caught up Miss Thompson on our adventures, and we had been so eager to tell her everything about them (everything except the story about the dead fake missionary; I didn't want her to know, and I didn't want to talk about it) that it dawned on Candy Baby, now that Dr. James was back, to finally ask what Miss Thompson had been doing that whole time. Which, of course, given certain actions she'd performed, made Miss Thompson slightly uncomfortable.

"Well, Candy, I was put in a truck, and I was brought to an airplane where there were others. We landed near here and were put on another bus and brought to the easternmost tower, over there. On the buses and plane nobody said much, but there was one woman who just moaned, scared, and when we got here, they implanted our chips"—she showed us the tiny scar—"and a man at the tower told us when we could pick up our daily bread ration. At the time it wasn't nearly as crowded as it is now—something serious must have happened in the past week—but I tried to leave anyway because I told myself that I at least had to try, but the guards quickly tracked me down and said people like me were only allowed in, not out. Then I made friends with another NLA, and he helped me contact you three, to tell you I was here."

"Your friend was a drone pilot?" Dr. James asked, and Miss Thompson nodded yes.

"How'd he take over the drone?" I asked, looking at the nearest tower and not seeing an easy way in.

"I distracted the guards," Miss Thompson said coyly.

"And the pilot?" Dr. James asked.

"I made quite a scene."

Without being able to say precisely why—perhaps because he understood his sister's occasionally amoral derring-do so well—Dr. James suddenly felt sick, and meanwhile Candy and I were innocently trying to imagine how she could have distracted the guards. *Did Miss Thompson know magic tricks?*

"How?" Candy Baby asked.

"Candy, if I gave away all my secrets, you'd suddenly find me boring."

"Miss *Teee-eeee!*" Candy Baby whined pleadingly.

"Emily?"

The voice came from outside the family circle. Miss Thompson recognized it immediately.

"Saxon!" Miss Thompson said with clear delight (there were no hard feelings on either person's part after his rejected advance). She patted Candy's hand, stood, and walked over to Rhysdale in greeting, and they hugged warmly but platonically.

"I recognized the van—so your family found you?!" Rhysdale asked excitedly.

"Yes—the plan worked!" Miss Thompson said. "You must meet them!"

Miss Thompson introduced Rhysdale to her brother and her children. Dr. James was brought out of his sister-mortification when he realized he was meeting a man with the kind of balls it took to do what Rhysdale had done in contacting them using the Rushmore Peregrine. I studied Rhysdale closely and found him to be a rather thoroughly consistent character: He did not appear to be putting on any sort of act—I had already seen and met quite a few "acts" in my short life away from Mr. Justin and Miss

Thompson's little earnest bubbles, especially already in the Freedom Zone. I felt like I could see why Miss Thompson would work together with the man. And Candy Baby also liked Rhysdale—he was courteous and handsome and gave her an innocently flirtatious wink when he announced he was "pleased to make [her] acquaintance." Although sexual thoughts and such start kicking in as early as like five years old, they are largely just a big part of the overall sensation of life, and it is only around twelve, as previously mentioned, that they start to take on a bigger role in a person's personality, and Candy Baby, at that time in her life, was in an early phase somewhere between both worlds: Her sexual personality still had not taken a solid shape, but it was certainly starting to grow and become differentiated from the other pleasurable sensations of life. Thus, all she knew was that she really friggin' enjoyed it when the handsome former soldier winked at her.

We were all kindly inclined towards him—even Tyger, whom Rhysdale stooped and petted for a while, seemed to regard him in that way dogs have, where they, even though they are dogs, behave in such a way as to let it be known that they accept you as "one of us"—and it seemed like Rhysdale had been equally impressed by us as well: the brave doctor who looked so much like Emily that Rhysdale no longer had a crush on her, as can sometimes happen when one sees the eerily same-looking-but-other-sex siblings of the objects of our desire; the giant, intense teenager, me, who, when I got through puberty, was going to be a powerful force of nature—or at least Rhysdale said as much to me and Miss Thompson; and then the cutie-pie blonde little squirt with a handshake like a bear trap.

"I love you all!" Rhysdale said in a jovial manner that was really the expression of something like *I find you all to be amazing people,* and it was taken as such and met with our warmest smiles in the firelight.

"Join us for dinner, Saxon?" Dr. James asked,

opening a cooler that was brimming with refrigerated, hunted meat.

"Where are you living now?" Miss Thompson asked, effectively trumping Dr. James' question.

"Uh, well, I was living with these, uh, sisters," Rhysdale said. His memories of the raw sexual adventures he'd had with them flashed through his mind, and he blushed, but then the memories continued, and so did he. "And it started off as a lot of fun, but to be frank, their, uh, 'noncarnal' personalities were alternately, like, either superficial or belligerent, you know, back and forth, and after a few days of . . . adventure . . . I headed for the proverbial hills, and just yesterday I won a spare tent off a decent man in a game of poker, so now I'm out here in the unwanted suburbs, just like ten yards away that way—maroon tent. And anyway no, I can't join you for dinner—I was actually just coming back from a big barbecue, ready to pass out I'm so stuffed, but then I thought I heard your voice and came over here to see if you were my friend."

"So you've made other friends? Whose barbecue?" Miss Thompson asked with earnest curiosity—we were all in need of as many allies as anybody.

"Well, I was, uh, 'fox-hunting'"—he winked and smiled generally—"out in the crowds, and I heard some music I liked. The way I see it, I don't know why I like the things I like, but I tend to like the people who also like those things, so I followed the sound of Six Grandfathers to what I hoped would turn out to be a fox's lair, but instead it was a husband and wife. They looked cool enough anyway, so I introduced myself as a fellow fan, and now we're friends—good people. College professors. Sent here from a protest camp out West. I'll have to bring them by now that I know you're here—if we don't all get firebombed or something before then."

Rhysdale's joke deflated the mood rather than produced any levity, and he mentally scrambled to make things right again before he left. "That is . . . you know . . . kids . . . it's . . . ."

Candy Baby had read Mr. Justin's journal several times, and Rhysdale's statement produced an idea for her.

"It's OK; it's been like that since the end of World War Two."

Everyone around the fire, not just Saxon, gawked at Candy Baby stupidly. "You know," she said defensively, "with nukes."

We kept looking at her, and she said to Rhysdale, "We just need to accept it and live big anyway!"

Did Saxon Rhysdale just take a sparring point against a twelve-year-old girl? He did!

"Sylvia," Rhysdale said—Candy and I had been introduced with our "legal" names—"that's the smartest thing I've heard anyone say in months."

"Thanks!" Candy said, and then her face took on its trademark honest, eyebrow-pleading admission, and she said, "But my Daddy said it."

Rhysdale suddenly put together that the kids in front of him—Candy and I—really were the kids on that river, and like a bolt of lightning he felt stunned by the reality of everything that had happened, and his heart swelled, but he was the sort of person who could have all that happen to him in a moment and have the self-discipline to, in the next moment, keep himself in check without anyone catching on to his sudden internal shock—the military had actually trained him for that sort of thing—and consequently he more than amply knew not to inquire about this Daddy, and instead he said, to make Sylvia feel even better, "Well, he sounds like the smartest guy I've ever heard of."

And by that sentiment Rhysdale remembered the other big news he'd been meaning to share, and he was glad of it, to clear his emotional palette of the past and consider the future. He shared it with the family while Candy felt a rush of pride in her Daddy based on what the good man had said about him.

"Oh! I also meant to ask you, Emily—have you ever heard anything about anybody named Stephen Stone?"

Miss Thompson shook her head. "I'm sorry, no—why?"

But before Rhysdale could answer, my face brightened with sharable knowledge, and I announced, "I heard a few different groups of people talking about that name when we were looking for Miss T."

"Me, too!" said Candy, and suddenly I, the protective older brother, felt bad that Candy had also overheard many of the crass things we'd heard on our search. Dr. James had a similar revelation, which was why his agreement was flat: "Me, too."

"It's getting around, then—good," Rhysdale said.

"Who is he?" Miss Thompson asked.

"That's the thing—I don't know," Rhysdale said. "There's a drone here that's knocking out all OV transmissions, but, uh, my"—Rhysdale looked around cautiously—"college professor friends are hobbyists, and they built a tiny drone of their own. We launched it the other night. Got it outside the jammer drone's range, but then a security drone shot it out of the air and traced the transmission back to the spot in the field where we'd buried the computer. But before it got shot down, we were able to download most of the day's top headline, which said: 'Enigmatic Businessman Stephen Stone Steps Forward On Issue Of Rushmore—Heading To Controversial Camp To.'"

"To what?" I asked.

"That was all we got before the screen went blank," Rhysdale said. "Anyway, just wanted to see if you'd heard the word."

"We heard nothing besides what we heard in the crowd," Dr. James said. "We drove up from the Titans, and none of the media ever mentioned the man, but we weren't checking very closely."

"I haven't heard anything, either," Miss Thompson said.

"I guess let's just hope it's hopeful news, eh?" Rhysdale said.

Everyone agreed, but there was a tiredness leaking into our voices.

"Well, I'm off to hit it," Rhysdale said stretching in that pre-sleep way. "Wow, it's chilly away from the fire; you folks got any extra sleeping bags? Tent just came with itself."

Not having any extra sleeping bags now that Miss T was with us, Dr. James instead gave the former M. Sgt. two of the coy-wolf pelts—with my and Candy's permission—and Rhysdale held them up, one in each hand, in appraisal, and said, "Oh, yeah—these'll do. You people are crazy, but yeah, these are great. Thank you."

Rhysdale said goodnight to everyone and walked away muttering to himself, "And then they hand me coy-wolf pelts out of the back of their giant medi-van . . . ."

Tyger followed him to the tent, sniffed around, urinated near one of the tent's stakes, and came back to the Thompson fire to the sleepy maneuverings of setting-up-for-bedtime. Her blanketed corner was already Candy-fluffed, and she, not wanting to be in the way, went up to the blanket, briefly circled around a few dozen times, laid down, and curled up. But every time I looked over in that corner, her drowsy eyes were open, somehow watching her family both tenderly and tiredly.

The morning broke with a shotgun blast.

Startled by the sudden explosion of sound, the

four suddenly awakened Thompsons' hammocks all swayed, and Saxon Rhysdale, who'd already been awake in his tent, snapped his head in the direction of the blast.

"WAKE UP, EVER'BODY! IT'S A NEW DAY!" a man's voice boomed, and from the general direction of it, it was the same souse who'd pulled the trigger.

"FUCK YOU!" yelled another man's voice from pretty far away.

"YEAH!" a half-dozen people all around yelled sleepily as a chorus.

"EHH, FUCK YOU ALL!" the bloated shotgunner thunderously mumbled, and Dr. James and Miss T, who were still swaying outside the van, could hear the sound of the shotgunner foomping open a bottle of bathtub gin and helping himself to a spirited second breakfast.

Getting along to get along, Dr. J and Miss T rolled out of their hammocks, onto their feet, and started stretching into the day, and when the shotgunner— medium height, square-headed, barrel-shaped, curled mouth chomping a cigar—turned in their direction, they waved good morning, and the shotgunner said, with the cigar still clenched in this teeth, *"Hiya."*

The Thompson adults put together a plan for the day that would get everyone away from that *bona fide* creep, and when she opened the van, Tyger greeted her at the door, I turned away from the sunlight, and Candy Baby looked at her from over a book propped on her chest in the reading position.

"Good morning, beautifuls," she said. "Breakfast soon."

"Mornin', M'm," said Candy, but I said nothing.

"Dante?"

I didn't answer; I could barely understand what she'd said. Overnight I had fallen victim to a powerful influenza. Checking for a fever, Miss Thompson felt my forehead, and evidently it was white-hot. Suddenly her hand was gone, and there was more light, and outside the van I heard a woman's voice, and then a man's voice.

I had a fever—"probably the flu."

Miss Thompson wasn't very happy about it, but she talked it over with her brother and me, and we all decided I would spend the day resting in the van (unfortunately near the shotgunning drunk) while she and Candy went back to Miss Thompson's old shelter and Dr. James took Tyger for a long walk in search of opportunities to trade Dr. J's medical aid for useful goods.

After they'd all eaten and gone to the woods and boiled me some water and otherwise prepared for the day, the pairs left, and I was already drifting back to sleep when Dr. James locked and slammed the door shut and knocked twice on the side as a goodbye.

I slept most of the morning—it was the energy-draining, fevery, sore-throat kind of flu, not the vomit kind—but I did awaken for a few different thirty-second, frazzled moments of consciousness.

I would find myself eyes-closed awake, though I'd been asleep only a moment before. I would open my eyes, look at the way the light through the windows illumined the inside of the van, listened to the eclectic sounds of the scattered and scared people living at the camp, and exhausted even from that mere movement, my head would fall back to the hammock, which would gently sway, and I'd be asleep again.

One occasion, though, required a bit more effort.

A little before noon, 1200, at least by the position of the sun in the sky, I came to. There was something pulling on one of the lines of the spiderweb of my perception, and I opened my eyes to investigate. There was a man's face in the passenger-side window—the face fat and square, browned and greyed by weeks of stubble, mouth sneering, two cold blue eyes looking in, then the whole face darkened by two hands put up to shield the light so the man could see better inside—and I, weighted by too much malaise to be startled, simply looked at the stranger. But then the stranger tried the door handle, and I immediately decided upon a lazy way to scare him off: I grabbed the rifle lying right below me, much heavier than usual, and, as hard as I could—letting gravity do most of the work—slammed the butt of the rifle onto the floor of the van, which produced a tangible sound and quake throughout, and immediately the face was gone from the window, and I leaned the rifle against the side door, for easier access, and listened for a moment before heavily melting back to sleep.

It was around 1600 or 1700 in the afternoon, judging by the slightly oranging light, when I awoke to the sound and feeling of three casually paced knocks on the side door of the van.

"Anyone home?"

I recognized the voice.

"It's Rhysdale," the voice said, and my memory confirmed it, and I reached over, unlocked the door, and pulled the handle. The door was barely ajar for a few seconds, and then Rhysdale pulled it the rest of the way open and looked in.

"Ah, it's yo*ooouuuuuu*—wow, you look terrible, big guy; should I come back another time?"

I felt the best and most awake I'd felt all day, and I was glad to have someone else around after the earlier face in the window, so I turned my head no and gestured for his company. Rhysdale climbed in, sat on the floor, and left the door open, which resulted in a breeze that I found quite agreeable to cool the accumulated sweat from my fevery sleep.

"You sick?" Rhysdale asked, and I nodded yes.

"Flu? Throat?" Rhysdale guessed, based on my silence. "Or at least that's the hope right now?"

I nodded yes.

"Well, actually, that—" Rhysdale said but stopped. "Good . . . well, ha, not, like, *good* . . . but—"

I furrowed my eyebrows in confusion while Rhysdale's eyes were everywhere in thought.

"You know, Dante, I've tried to distract myself," Rhysdale spluttered, without intending to say it.

Half-lidded on the hammock, I raised my head in curiosity.

"I thought I could keep acting normally," Rhysdale said, a comment connected to the previous one in his own mind, but another *non sequitur* to me. "And everything would be fine, because, maybe what I did . . . but . . . ."

"*'Sup, Saxon?*" I rasped weakly.

Rhysdale cleared his throat, sat up, and took a deep breath—a man attempting to clean his emotional palette and talk before the emotions began again.

"Dante, I need to ask you something. Something important. Do you have enough strength for a little thought-experiment?"

I turned my head no and let my tongue loll out of my mouth as if I were dying, but Rhysdale was so entrenched in his horror that he didn't catch it; instead, he began speaking, to try, once again, to sort

181

it out himself: "Dante, if you trained all your life to shoot a bow and arrow, and you made your living that way, every day shooting arrows masterfully, and one day they ordered you to shoot your arrows where they said they needed to be shot . . . what would you do if what you thought would be a normal arrow turned out to have a poison on it that killed everyone on the battlefield—good guys and bad guys—what would you do?"

"I didn't know . . . the arrow . . . ?" I asked softly.

"You just thought it was an arrow."

"Who?" I asked; meaning, Who poisoned it?

"There's an armory that packs all the quivers; you just took the one you were handed, so you don't know— someone way up the unbreakable chain of command."

"Why?" I asked, and Rhysdale correctly guessed I meant Why was the arrow poisoned in the first place?

"They were running a live test with a secret new weapon—wanted to see how it worked, and they knew you wouldn't . . . shoot it . . . if you knew."

The van was quiet for quite a while; the vehicle and the hammock were both mildly rocking from Rhysdale's nervous foot. Then I asked, with my break- ing voice, *"Poison . . . like a mist?"*

At first Rhysdale didn't answer, and I finally looked up for his reaction: The man's eyes were closed, and his whole body was shaking: He was the sort of man who wept silently, eventually sucking in a huge inhalation. He balled his fists and raised them to his temples and curled into a fetal position on the floor. "Please, Dante . . . I'm so *sor*— . . . I just can't forgive . . . I can't for— . . . Oh, God, *Jeeeees*— . . . Everything that happened . . . Dante, you were so close; how are you two still . . . And I mean who *deserves*—?" To try to vent some of his overwhelming emotions, he made a fist of his hand and cathartically drove its fatty butt into the floor of the van, which produced a loud re- sounding sound and quake throughout, and said, "I am *crushed,* crushed!, by guilt! . . . by a guilt I may or may not have earned but which I feel as though it has sunk my soul to some hopeless depth."

There was another short conversational silence while Rhysdale and I wept like men.

"Had your . . . they . . . ever done anything like that before?"

Rhysdale at first didn't hear me, and then repeated it in his own head and thought about it.

". . . Yes."

"And you . . . still joined?"

Rhysdale had killed himself with these questions so many times, and he had a reply for that one: It was the only thing that kept him sane.

"Have you ever heard of a book called *Les Misérables?"*

"Yes . . ." I said, and because I didn't have a worthy rejoinder, as Rhysdale's allusion was a valid response, I said, *"I've read it."*

Neither person said anything. With the door open, the sounds of man and nature outside were no longer muffled. There were tears still on Rhysdale's face; on my face there were wet tracks. Rhysdale's right metacarpal knuckle was swollen; I was running a temperature three degrees into dangerous, and my breath felt and tasted wretched.

"Thank you for your apology," I said as well as I could. *"But if you didn't . . . pack the quiver . . . then . . . Actus me invito . . . factus non est meus actus."*

"What?" Rhysdale asked. "Was that the fever talking?"

I smirked through my malaise.

"Latin," I said. *"'The act done by me . . . against my will . . . is not my act.'"*

" . . . "

"It means," I said, *"you're not . . . the person . . . who's going to die."*

Rhysdale, weighted by remorse, suddenly felt

183

a chill—as we have seen, men sometimes have intuitions, too, and in this case Rhysdale felt a chill upon hearing of the homicidal revenge aspirations of a fevered, emotional, combustible teenage fuck-it-all like me. What sort of life could that lead to but further sadness and devastation? But could Rhysdale blame me? Would he have behaved any differently with the same prologue of the damned?

"Dante," Rhysdale said, still lying on the ground in the fetal position. "There's a man, he's retired now, a man named Milton W. Blank. . . . He lives in a highly securitized suburb called Swanson Falls. If we ever get out of here, ask him about the quiver. He knows more about what happened than I do. He sent me there to shoot that arrow, and he sent me here, and for all I know he packed the poison, too."

His gaze fell from me to the floor of the van, and I nodded my understanding and laid my head back and looked at the roof in mourning and thought. Rhysdale's eyes settled on the thoroughly cleaned butt of the rifle on the ground, and we both rested there silently—me awake and thinking, Rhysdale drifting off to sleep, having so completely unburdened the caravans of guilt and grief that had been trampling the fields of his heart.

Miss Thompson and Candy Baby were already on their way to Miss Thompson's former camp when they heard Dr. James knock on the side of the van twice as a goodbye; it was the last sound they heard that came from their camp before they were back in the shiftless crowds, working and wending their way north, towards the largest tree on the edge of the forest just before the trees gave way to the gravel of the mountainside.

In their previous lives, Mr. Justin had taught Miss Thompson how to set up a stable shelter out of whatever was available, and she'd set up her shelter against the toes of that largest tree.

She figured Leni would still be there because Leni never left; she just tried to help out when she could, and otherwise she sat in her corner and watched Miss Thompson. The only conclusion that Miss Thompson could draw from the circumstances was that one governor or another (or several) in the (former) United States had decided to unload the overflow at his or her state's mental institutions into the Freedom Zone.

Now that America had a stateside rug, things could be swept under it.

Leni was Miss Thompson's new silent ward, and Miss Thompson was correct in her inductive reasoning: "Leni," whose name will remain Leni in this telling—because that's who she was to us—was actually named Elizabeth Marie Franklin, which Candy eventually exhaustively found out via pencil, paper, and a hard-fought, temporary victory over Leni's truly crippling fear of the past, whose muteness was caused by severe PTSD with an unknown cause. Despite Candy's best efforts, the only people who ever knew what really happened were Leni and the parents who placed her in the institution and who never returned. In short, Leni was mute before and after she got off the bus to camp.

Miss Thompson had named her Leni for two primary reasons: one, Miss Thompson didn't have Candy's strong tendency to joyfully investigate other people's selfmost selves, so Miss Thompson's new silent ward needed a new name for practical purposes, and two, Miss Thompson, a sometimes dark humorist, feeling as though she were living in a story by Steinbeck, thinking about how her own best laid plans had never involved guardianship and caretaking, named her new adventure's companion after ol' George Milton's developmentally disabled sidekick.

Candy Baby and Miss Thompson made their way towards the tallest tree as quickly as they could, not even looking towards or responding to the occasional catcalls that were hollered out to them by the few standing drunken NLAs of the golden morning. Miss Thompson didn't make Candy Baby hold her hand, but she kept looking back just the same, and Candy kept trying to reassure her that she didn't need to because Candy was well aware of the fact that they were on their own out there: Candy could feel it. She didn't admit, however, that the scary feeling made her excited, and maybe she was maturing or something but she was starting to see what her brother liked about adventures. In fact, the look in Candy's eyes made Miss Thompson uncomfortable, but she couldn't blame the child, given everything Candy had been through already.

And perhaps it was that. Perhaps it was that sisterhood of shock and stress and nightmares that so quickly—instantaneously, a Gladwellian blink— created a bond between Candy Baby and Leni.

The two ladies reached Miss Thompson's camp after walking generally as the crow flies for about two hours of intense edging around the borders of the other NLA camps, and when they arrived at Miss T's camp it appeared just as Miss Thompson had left it, which she found encouraging.

Before they left the vansite, while breakfast was cooking, Miss Thompson had first told Candy Baby about Leni, whom Miss Thompson had completely and eventually sorrowfully forgotten about the moment she heard James and us kids hollering *Cuh-CAW!* Candy, who'd never really had a friend her own age, was quite eager to meet this girl who was only two years older.

"Is she nice?" Candy had asked. And, "So she doesn't say anything?" And, "Nothing at all?" And, "Did you think we weren't gonna come?" And, "Is that why you took her in, because you thought we wouldn't come for you?"

Miss Thompson had answered all of Candy's questions with her trademark grace, and now, at the entrance of the camp, with the flap of fabric hanging over the squared opening, Candy had one more: "Do you think she'll like me?"

Miss Thompson put her hand on Candy Baby's shoulder and looked tenderly into her worried face. Treating the premise of the question as unanswerably false, she said instead, "Let me go in first, and I'll talk to her and let her know you're here, and then I'll call you in, OK?"

Candy was so OK with it she was proactive—she turned away from the shelter and said, "Good—until then, I'll watch our backs."

Miss Thompson didn't say anything; instead, Candy felt Miss T's long arms wrap around her in a motherly hug, and Miss Thompson laid a big loud smooch on Candy's soft cheek.

Then Miss Thompson was gone, and Candy heard her voice, lower, murmuring, inside the shelter. There was a long moment of silence, which seemed to last half of Candy's life at least, and then Miss T said, "C'mon in, Candy."

It was dark in the shelter, but a few beams of light succeeded past the layers of branches and illumined the ground and the air in golden shafts. Across those shafts, after Candy's eyes adjusted to the darkness of the shelter, she saw Miss Thompson and Leni sitting cross-legged near a small firepit glowing warmly via a stick-crackling fire. There was also sunlight, Candy suddenly noticed, coming in from a small opening at the top of the shelter, which was acting as a flue for the smoke.

She only had the impression of shapes: Miss Thompson's and Leni's—since her eyes were adjusting she didn't get a good look at either, but even in that moment, just by the way the stranger was sitting by the fire, Candy sat closer to Leni than to Miss Thompson. Candy just felt pulled to that figure, and wanted to befriend it, like it were a wounded little animal she knew she could help and protect while it healed.

When Candy was seated and seeing clearly, she looked over the fire at her mother and smiled reassuringly and then turned to the figure next to her and said, "Hi, I'm Candy."

Whoa.

Candy looked in Leni's face, and it was like she saw beauty for the first time: That face is beautiful! Those eyes are galaxies! That mouth is the complete alphabet for every perfect human expression! Even her nose is the nose they illustrated in her first dictionary!

But what was that look on Leni's face? In what way did she regard Candy? Miss Thompson saw that Leni had started off in the picturesque posture of being "closed off": one leg hooked under her on the ground, the other bent up to the chest, like a shield, and both of her arms, two more shields, layers of defense, wrapped around the stabilizing tower of leg, her head in the pocket between her knee and her arms, angled towards Miss Thompson. But then the head lifted, turned towards Candy for appraisal, and subconsciously answered Candy's last question from outside. Would she like Candy? Within moments, all three shields were down, and Leni was instead holding her own hand in her lap, seated Indian-style, and she suddenly, bashfully turned her face away from Candy and looked into the fire.

Candy recognized most of what Miss Thompson recognized, and she wanted to say something to make Leni feel even more welcome in her life, so she paid her a compliment.

"Leni," Candy said, "Miss T told me you don't talk, and I thought that was kind of weird at first, because I sure like to talk when I can, when I have something to say, you know?, but now I think it's kind of cool you don't talk—you're, like, so pretty you don't even *need to.*"

Leni's hands parted, and she placed them on the ground, and Miss Thompson watched in wonder as Leni scooched herself closer to Candy, and Candy did the same, until they were shoulder and hip to shoulder and hip and staring into the fire in the same posture, the instant spark of friendship glowing likewise between them.

"So here's the situation, girls," the pleased Miss Thompson said. "We've now got two different camps, and I'd like to keep them both and try to bring the van around here. What do you think?"

"But if we leave here to get the van, someone might come in and take this shelter."

"Indeed," Miss Thompson said. "That's why I was thinking maybe you two could stay here and protect it while I go find James and try to figure out how we're going to pull it off. Can you handle that?"

Candy felt Leni stiffen with anxiety, and Candy explained, "James is Emily's brother, and my big brother Dante is sick today in our van." The anxiety lessened, but it was not gone, and Candy saw that Leni was looking at the front flap of the tent nervously.

Candy grabbed her rifle from where she'd leaned it against a wall of the shelter, held it up, and said, "Leni, my brother and I grew up in the forest, and I swear to God I've killed a *bear.*"

The anxiety lessened a little more, but it was still there, and that was OK because Candy was nervous, too.

"So you'll be fine?"

"Miss *Teeee,* I'm almost *thirteen.*"

Miss Thompson was one of the soberest women

in the world, and while normally that sort of statement would have been cause for a bemused grin in a woman with such an aged perspective as hers, she knew Candy had already lived lifetimes in her almost thirteen years. And anyway they had no other choice: In a Freedom Zone, possession is the whole law.

It wasn't difficult to find Dr. James: She set out towards the biggest gatherings of people, knowing that her brother would be at the center of one of them.

The first gathering whose periphery she entered was circled around and actively encouraging an ongoing fistfight between two grizzled white men, and in discovering what was at the center of that human galaxy she set off for the next. At the center of the second galaxy was an ongoing one-on-one mortal combat (more than a fistfight) between two black women. The third was some delicious-smelling barbecued meat "curdasee uh some ol' NLAs from the great state uh Texas, y'all!" The fourth was a man who was reciting news headlines, but to Miss Thompson, who admitted she could be wrong, they sounded like he was making them up for the attention.

Finally she heard the words she was listening for, snatching a bit of conversation from a female passerby who'd said, ". . . *doctor* over there . . . ."

Miss Thompson headed in the direction of the woman's inclined head, excusing herself to pass the woman and her friend—all three women headed towards the doctor, but only one of them in that kind of hurry, with those long strides.

Eventually the crowd was so densely packed around the doctor that she had to begin elbowing her way forward, explaining to the affronted that she was not there for treatment, was in the doctor's family. And then she reached the front of the masses, where there was a very distinct line carved in a big circle around the doctor and the gloriously crotch-sniffing, petting-receiving Tyger. The doctor was sitting on a boulder, which was located next to another boulder, where a man was sitting and showing Dr. James his right foot, which was pale in the late-morning sunlight.

Miss Thompson approached her brother and put her hand on his shoulder, startling him, and he shouted, "I TOLD YOU PEOPLE TO STAY—" He was cocking his fist back, but then he recognized his sister, and, relieved, his agitation deflated.

"James, we need to go."

Before Dr. James could answer, the man being treated said, *"Excuse me?"*

Miss Thompson said to him, "Please accept my apologies; the doctor here is my brother, and we have a family situation, which I'm sure you can understand."

The man with the pale foot said, "Yeah, whatever, I guess, but when you're done you gotta help me, doc; frickin' thing is *murder.*"

Miss Thompson could see that these frightened, ailing people all wanted to speak with the doctor, so she helped her brother as best as she could until she noticed how late it was getting, and then they left with apologies and promises to see tomorrow those who didn't get seen today.

They had a patient of their own to check on.

Rhysdale shot awake to the sound of two burly men arguing loudly. He looked up: I was not in my hammock. He made an awakening-stretching sound like, *"G'muuh!"* and then he rolled over and sat up on the step of the van, his boots on the dirt, shielding his eyes from the bright dark blue of the late-afternoon sky. The air was cooling, and he felt the warm embrace of sunlight on his legs, and his eyes adjusted to the day and saw me half reclined, half sitting on the ground, leaning against a sittin'-log, still feeling sick but soaking sunrays and sucking in fresh drags of air.

"How long was I out?"

I held up one finger.

"That's it? Felt like days—feels good."

The two men yelled again. The man who'd shotgun-blasted everyone awake was yelling at what was either his brother or his doppelgänger, and the brother or doppelgänger interrupted him, yelling back. What they were yelling was drunkenly and Southernly incomprehensible.

"What's going on there?"

I weakly shrugged. Rhysdale noticed that my rifle was reclined next to me, the barrel pointed in the direction of the argument, just in case. I had grabbed the rifle once I recognized one of the drunken doppelgängers as the man in the window from before and also remembered the day's shotgun sunrise.

"You feeling any better?"

But there our moment of friendship, or whatever it was, was broken by the immediately recognizable murmur of the two tall adult Thompsons, and Rhysdale, who'd looked so unburdened just a moment ago, was once again uniquely uncomfortable around the people whose lives he had unintentionally devastated, and he left quickly, saying, "Nice to see you both again; I was just leaving—hope to see you soon."

Before he left, he tried to give me a meaningful look, but I was flat ill and not on top of my perceptive game, and I just rested there in fevered misery.

"That was odd," Miss Thompson said of Saxon's sudden departure as she felt my forehead and prepared me some tea they'd received during their day of doctor-bartering. "Everything OK between you two?"

I nodded yes.

"He . . . confessed."

Miss Thompson looked curious. "To what?"

"To me," I rasped with a faint smile.

Miss Thompson was not smiling. "What did he confess to you?"

"He told me . . . what he needed to say."

Miss Thompson didn't like the sound of that at all. She had always harbored some suspicions about Rhysdale that she always felt bad about feeling, which pretty much turned out to be true.

"Such as?"

"Mom," I said. *"It was a confession . . . Mr. Justin used to say that . . . everybody needs to tell somebody."*

"OK, Dante," Miss Thompson said, peeved but unable to do anything about it really. "Should any of us be worried, at least?"

I slowly shook my head no. Sleepily, I mumbled, *"Les Misérables."*

Dr. James and Miss T helped me back to my hammock, and I ended up sleeping through quite a commotion, although I do remember one particular sound reaching me through the malaise.

Just after Miss Thompson closed the side door of the van, to let me sleep in my metal cocoon, she and Dr. James hurriedly cleaned up the camp, and they were moving with purpose because the argument between the disputatious drunks was only escalating, only there were no cops to call, and nobody wanted to get involved because both men had fire in their blood and firearms in their hands.

Things continued to escalate. A finger to the

chest begat a push, which begat a shove, which begat a punch, which begat two shouldered shotguns and two men screaming at each other in complete incoherence.

A whiskey standoff.

It ended quickly: One of the doppelgängers pulled the trigger, the shotgun gave its one-word reply, and the other man flew backwards while his torso fountained blood—he never felt his back hit the ground. Then the shooter looked at the corpse stupidly, uncomprehendingly, and as the dreadful moments passed, his comprehension sprouted and grew, and Miss Thompson saw a look come over the shooter: The mounting reality of the unimaginable moral debt he'd just accrued revealed its devastating final tally. While the drunkenly emotional murderer's suddenly remorseful self-loathing accumulated, the nearby camps emptied, and an agitated, armed crowd gathered around the shooter, who was falling to his knees and was preparing to shotgun-blast his own brains into the sky when Miss Thompson scooped up Tyger and yelled to her brother, "Get in the van and drive!"

Two doors opened and slammed, and the huge white van crashed through the camps that had settled behind us since we'd arrived, and Dr. James headed down a road towards the woods, and he followed it through the woods until it arrived at one of the guard towers, and he turned right down the road that encircled the entire camp, which he followed all the way to the tower nearest the tallest tree in the northernmost woods.

He and Miss T followed the van's headlights all the way to Camp Candy Baby, parked in a small grove in the woods just outside the shelter, and announced their presence to Candy and Leni by stepping out of the van and yelling, *"Cuh-CAW! Cuh-CAW!"*

"YOU'RE ALIVE!" Candy bellowed as she sprinted out of the shelter and launched herself into Miss T's strong arms. "We were SO WORRIED! Is everything OK!?"

That was late summer.
Stephen Stone didn't arrive until the fall.

Auribus teneo lupum.—
"I hold a wolf by the ears."

The late Sen. Charles "Buster" Tramp, in the paranoia of the Communist Red Scare, had affixed a little-known provision into a Senate bill in 1946 that legislated the creation of a secondary, contingency government in the case of an unforeseen strategic, federal-government-destroying attack by America's enemies (Russia)—that way, America would have a chance to organize itself against its aggressors and drive them out before the foreign power (Russia) established dominance and rule. Nevertheless, Sen. Tramp was also concerned about a foreign (Communist) takeover of the federal government from within, and the contingency govern-ment was to be initiated by either of two situations: one, a strategic, federal-government-destroying out-side attack; and two, under any suspicion that the fed-eral government may have been responsible for the deaths of anyone born in America and thus infiltrated by a foreign agenda.

In the devastating and far-reaching aftermath of the attacks on 9/11, there was a vitally important repercussion that changed the course of history: Americans lost nearly all sense or perspective of what a free society actually was, and eventually the President of the United States found himself in a position to authorize the first non-trial, drone-launched death of a United States–based, domestic "NLA Terrorist"—a man born and living in the (former) USA. And things continued to devolve so rapidly in America after the economic collapse that eventually (unelected) President Aaron Wells did just that—authorized revolution-fomenter Neal Houston Smith's death—and Sen. Buster Tramp's emergency bill was automatically put into effect without anyone in power—neither the all-powerful Executive nor the Congressional/ Senatorial parasitical cowards—knowing about it.

Five letters were sent out.

One of the recipients took it seriously.

Dear Sir or Madam,

My name is Sen. Charles Tramp, and I am an American legislator writing to you from the Year of Our Lord, 1946, where, if you check the legislative record (carbon copy enclosed), I have just authored a bill establishing the creation of a small but powerful backup government in the event that our beloved America is overtaken or infiltrated by a foreign influence. Whether you are receiving this letter because the ravaging hordes have destroyed what we once were, or because there has been a treasonous suspicion, I cannot know, but you who received this letter will know by the following instructions.

(Second Half of Letter: TREASON)

There is a criteria-meeting reason to suspect a

treasonous influence has infiltrated the federal agenda, and, by the mailing of this letter, you are hereby deputized into an instantaneously created offshoot of the Executive branch of our government, unknown even to the President himself.

You were chosen at random, as it is my whole-hearted belief that any man can rise to the occasion if he truly desires justice: After all, the vastness of human intellect is not a vastness of the moral knowledge required to govern—that difficult knowledge is borne by the individual. Trusted citizen, you might have the weight of the nation upon your shoulders, and you may be a free America's last hope.

In Washington you will conduct a series of investigations detailed in a packet you will receive at the U.S. Treasury, and my bill assures you the full powers necessary for the specified investigations. When people ask how you were given such a high-security clearance, you will say, and this is all you will be required to say, "I wish I could tell you." After a period of between one and five years, your investigations should be complete. If there is evidence of treason, you must alert the nation; if there is no evidence, you might look like a fool stepping forward to announce that all is well, so you can decide what you want to do with your information, but at the very least you have the profound personal gratitude of a man who deeply loved his beloved country. God be with you, and Godspeed to you.

Most sincerely,

Sen. Buster Tramp

Imperium In Imperio—
"A State Within A State"

Four years after he received the letter, Stephen Stone, a divorced, childless restaurateur from Orlando, Florida, told the man he was talking to at the bar, who happened to be a reporter, that he was headed to the RCCSDFZ to make a grim announcement, and Stone's hard face looked like dread. When Stone saw how curious the reporter appeared, he realized he'd said too much, and he went home and finished preparing for his trip. But the reporter started looking into it, and that's how the legend of Stephen Stone had started to spread.

In late October, a little more than four years after Stone received the letter, he arrived at Rushmore escorted by all the major media left in America. Stone drove himself, and the rest arrived in trucks and helicopters, and the sky above the camp became even more hectic than before, but not as hectic as on the ground, where the lack of law and hope and direction had fostered a roiling cauldron of untethered humanity, which, once we were "settled," we Thompsons tried to both live in and protect ourselves from.

Just like a riot of dogs will all turn their heads simultaneously in the direction of a nearby gunshot, so too was everyone's attention drawn to the buzzing and flashing and whumping arrival of Stephen Stone and the extant national media. The curiosity of the spectacle became a sudden distraction from the bleakness of our fenced, penned, NLA lives, and we all headed towards the commotion while the commotion headed towards us.

We Thompsons headed towards the lights and people like everyone else, with the exception of Tyger, who was on a long tether and providing a marginal security at camp.

Stone, who had not thought his plan all the way through, began to look around for some sort of P.A. system he could use to address everyone—he'd been so worried about his message that he'd forgotten about how exactly he was going to deliver it to the people who needed to hear it most: the NLAs in the Freedom Zone. But he was a quick-thinking guy, and he saw a large truck that had some gigantic speakers set up outside of it—known informally as the Rage camp, not far from the easternmost tower.

The media—those reporters and cameramen who came with their (former) American passports, to show the soldiers at the gate—followed him.

The confused, expectant crowd gathered around the man in the clean suit, following and preceding him as he headed towards the Rage camp, where Zach, the unofficial alpha of the Ragers, noticed his interest, and said, "What's up, guy?"

Stephen Stone addressed the long-haired, bearded NLA with respect: "Hello, young man; I was wondering if those speakers had a microphone."

"Might—what of it?"

"I've been sent here by the federal government—" Stone started to explain, but he was interrupted by laughter and jeers from the crowd.

"Ain't no federal government anymore, friend," the Rage camper said. "Just assholes with guns."

"Part of my speech will speak to that," Stone said. "I am from a part of the government that never existed before. I just need a mic and a few minutes."

The curious crowd sided with Stone, and Zach could feel it.

"Hey, put on a show, bro," the Rage camper said and then dug into the back of a box of electronics in the bed of his truck and emerged with a microphone, which he soon married to the sound system, and one of those piercing electric hawk-cries squealed into the afternoon air, and then a very loud version of Stephen

Stone's voice said, "IT'S ON?"

The crowd chuckled nervously. They weren't half as nervous as Stone, who looked at the speech he'd written by hand and saw nothing but gibberish. Suddenly a woman's voice from the crowd shouted, *"Wooo!"* and Stone was back in the moment, and he looked at the dirty faces of the NLAs, and he saw that what he had to do was what was necessary, which made it easier.

"Hello, my name is Stephen Stone. Four years ago I was rather arbitrarily commissioned with the duty of observing our federal government, out of the fear that a treasonous influence had infiltrated American governance. Today I am reporting my findings. I will cut to it and say that it's rather fitting there is no formal federal government anymore, after the collapse more than a decade ago, because it would be incorrect to say that they were a government, for they no longer served the citizens of America. My investigations found the benefit of American legislative action landing on nearly every side of every cause in the world with the exception of the actual citizens of actual America. In short, it's entirely fitting they're not the government anymore, because they weren't really governing.

"One of my responsibilities involved running a gamut of tests looking for evidence of corruption. Ladies and gentlemen, let it resound: *Corruption. Was. Rampant.*

"Another duty was to test for the quality of written laws, whether they could benefit our enemies and harm our citizens: All I can say is yes, that's exactly what they did.

"Another was to test America's real readiness response via various hostile means: *All* of my attacks would have been successful.

"Another duty was to look for fiscal accountability: We all know how that story ended more than ten years ago, and the sequel has been worse.

"These miscarriages of legislation point to the infiltration of a foreign influence, and yet I ask you the question that has been pounding in my head for the past several years of my investigation: What foreign influence? Our politicians were and are not Communist nor Islamo-Fascist. They were not Japanese, Chinese, nor German nationalists. What mysterious interest could so effectively weaken America?

"I still don't have an answer; I just have all this proof that something died.

"My evidence for everything I've just claimed is in this binder in my hands, and the digital files will be sent to all the media cowards out there. The man who tasked me with these duties was an Ohio senator named Buster Tramp, and he told me in a letter that when I had the evidence of treason I should bring it forward in order to discredit the existing, or formerly existing, authority of that federal government, in order to establish a new one, and I believe that if there's anywhere in the world a new America should be born, it's here amongst those who rejected and were rejected by our treasonous former federal government.

"So here today, on this 'Free' land, I hereby establish the New Government of America."

Rather than thunderous applause, or even general applause, there was a long silence. The crowd digested what it was told, and murmurs rolled through the gathering and sounded like nervous brookwater.

"I don't believe you," someone said loudly. The crowd harumphed in agreement.

Stone spoke gravely into the microphone. "Believe me or not—I assure you this is a free America's last hope."

With the files they received, and the speech they recorded, the media emerged from the OV blackout wrought by the jammers and filed a most extraordinary story that set the nation on fire and pitted brother against father: A combustible catalyst had been added to the smoldering American skirmish—America had a new dichotomy.

New v. Old.

And lo, not long after Stone had returned to his car and erected his tent alongside his fellow NLAs, people in the camp came forward and investigated the evidence and the plan for moving forward. The ideas were spread and discussed, and the rest of the day was spent in small circles of great debate.

Seeing a threat to their unchecked wretchedness in the possible birth of law and order in the Freedom Zone, the criminal elements among the NLAs doubled down on their efforts that night, while the getting was good, and by morning there was a huge crowd gathered around Stephen Stone, who began the process of building a government that would oversee the creation of the brand-new nation of New America, which consisted of the ten-thousand acres of the Rushmore Concentration Camp and South Dakota Freedom Zone.

The process of governing Rushmore began with Buster Tramp's deep faith in general human competence, and anyone who wished to hold a temporary governing position was asked to submit a basic application, and then applications were drawn at random, and after an interview with Mr. Stone the man or woman was assigned to one of the few positions: officer of the court, officer of the police, or territorial councilor. All positions were held for two weeks only, and then the rosters were reset. The governing laws were simple: No murder unless in self-defense, no stealing no matter what, and no breaking agreements or "contracts." All grievances that didn't fall into any of those three major laws were brought before officers of the court, who mediated as necessary and strived to provide the fairest rulings possible, knowing an aggrieved person might one day be the judge in a case important to the current judge. Punishment for broken laws was simple: Guilty murderers received death (bullet or spearpoint to the brainstem); thieves received broken arms (that is, their dominant forearms had a dreaded appointment with Dr. James' hammer and chisel) and were compelled to return all stolen property and work off any debts accrued; rapists had both arms broken and usually dehydrated or starved to death from lack of outside mercy/intervention; citizens guilty of breaching contracts were compelled to fulfill their responsibilities to the contract or provide mutually agreed-upon restitution, and then receive a broken arm (dominant or non-dominant determined by the judge), unless the aggrieved, in any case, even the family members of murder victims, chose to show mercy.

Stone had everyone measure the size of the camps they'd created, and he used the average size to divide the ten-thousand acres into a grid that could include a camp and a small, completely necessary garden, and everyone who wanted to live on a square of the grid had to submit an application. This all happened right in front of everyone—an utterly transparent governance. The applications were chosen at random, and the process of actually organizing the new nation began.

Most people picked the plot closest to where they already were, but even those who had to move agreed that the temporary burden was worth being able to get around easier anyway, if they were really going to try to make the best of their existential shituation.

Dr. J chose the exact plot where our camp was already set up, and Miss Thompson was randomly chosen to govern, and Stephen Stone made her the territorial councilor, overseeing the organization and property rules of the still sparsely populated "district" where the Thompson camp was located.

The reason Dr. J picked the spot turned out to be a beneficial reason for everyone at Rushmore: Word had gotten around that anyone who needed a doctor should head for the tallest tree to the north.

A relative peace reigned for a quietish month after Stone's implementation of a rudimentary, volunteer government. The citizens of the dubious country of New America banded together to try to make the better parts of humanity's nature prevail, and it was working as well as Buster Tramp could have hoped, but in that month the northern hemisphere of the planet took a big turn away from the sun, and a CTR Team dispatched by the top brass of the Old American army was inserted into New America. With the return of the cold blasts of the South Dakota winter, the old powers found their opportunity to discredit and perhaps instantaneously destroy the emerging threat of the new nation.

The citizens of the entombed *Imperium In Imperio* of New America had thus far survived the fairer seasons, but while many of the recent emigrants had arrived prepared for the long haul, most of the political prisoners had been sent there with the clothes on their backs and were given a burlap blanket and a daily ration of sulfur-tasting water and hard black bread. None of them had had the luxury of knowing to purchase and bring gear for extremely cold temperatures, and everyone's food supplies were always running short, especially as more and more political prisoners arrived along with the fed-up emigrants, halving/splitting the bread rations, and a great agitation arose amongst the masses from the seeming death sentence of their inadequate provisions and their inability to leave the grounds in order to hunt for more food and furs, to survive.

Seeing himself as a conduit between New and Old America, Stephen Stone had chosen the plot of land closest to the easternmost tower, the one symbolically closest to Washington, D.C., and on a late November morning—Old America's Thanksgiving, amazingly enough—after the night of the season's first snowfall (fortunately late for South Dakota), huge numbers of people gathered in and around Stephen Stone's plot and rattled his tent until he emerged. And Stone took their communal agitation to that nearby tower, and he spoke to the guardsman.

"Soldier?" Stone asked.

"Yes, sir?" the guardsman responded. He was not rattled by the crowds because he knew of the kind of precision violence the drones above were capable of unleashing.

"I'm sure you can see," Stone said and gestured to the thin layer of snow on the ground, "the seasons have changed." He even gestured to the guardsman's own winter uniform. "And many of the people who live here will not survive unless we are given aid or are allowed to leave and return for the purposes of hunting."

The guardsman's face took on a sarcastic look of concern, and Stone interrupted the guard's response.

"I was hoping you could bring the situation to the notice of your superiors; I think we all deserve to know whether we're all just here to freeze and starve to death while the dead government watches it happen."

"We ain't dead, buddy," the guardsman, whose nametag said BILLINGS, said. "I still get paid, so something's still 'live."

"You're being paid?" Stone asked, legitimately curious—since Old America had gone defunct, the old hierarchy had been largely volunteering their time and living off of savings in a world that was suddenly dollar-friendly again, despite all the new rival currencies that had emerged in the economic void. Yet now, outside his new vast governmental knowledge, at least the military was still being funded? By whom?

"By whom?"

BILLINGS could see Stone was following some sort of mental lead, and he didn't want to do any more favors for these NLA assholes than he'd been ordered to, so he nipped Stone's curiosity in the bud.

"I get paid by your whore mother," the guardsman said.

Stephen Stone loved his mother's memory to tears, and he had to take a deep breath to calm himself.

Stone said, "Please take our question to your superior."

BILLINGS held up his hand like he was holding an old phone. "Ring, ring. Sir? Yes, does anybody up the chain of command give a shit about these traitorous asshole fucks? No? Nobody gives a rat's dick whether all these ass-clown losers starve or freeze to death? I agree! Thank you, Mr. President."

He hung up his fingers and said, "Sorry, friend."

In that moment, Stone saw all of his work, all of the truth he'd hoped to show the world, all the questions that he'd asked and found horrific answers to . . . it all amounted to one last question and one last horrific answer. He was perceptive enough to see almost everything that was coming, and after all that work, he snapped.

He cocked his arm back to strike the guardsman—one last desperate attempt at a minutely rattling strike from the innocent doomed good guy—when two bullets, one shot by the eastern tower's drone, one by the eastern tower's sniper, ripped through the air and separated Stone's right arm near the shoulder, and he staggered back, looked at the empty space where his arm used to be, looked around, with jets of blood spouting from the wound, picked up his right arm up with his left, looked at it incredulously, and passed out.

The crowd ran and scattered in fear, and the guardsman tied a tourniquet around the dextral stump that remained.

The Rage leader, a man whose real name was unknown to me but who called himself Zach de la Ciudadano, had been there, and he drove his truck like ass-fury to the doctor's camp, and Dr. James climbed aboard in haste upon being awakened and rode with Ciudadano to the tower, to Stephen Stone's unconscious body, which had BILLINGS' tourniquet already tied around the base of the bloody stump.

"Jesus, Zach. He needs a trauma surgeon; I'm an internist."

"Should I go get a carpenter then?" Zach asked and put the truck into park and hopped out.

"Even if I don't kill him trying to suture everything, he'll die of shock or an infection out here," Dr.

James said sadly to the windshield and stepped out of the truck and went over to the passed-out body.

BILLINGS watched them.

Stone—completely unconscious and sadly almost grinning—looked incongruously peaceful given his circumstances.

Zach said, "Ignorant bliss."

Dr. James didn't want to wake him up. Instead, he tried the churlish guardsman.

"This man needs a hospital and a proper surgeon."

BILLINGS replied, "That man is lucky to be 'live. Don't matter what he needs—he needs to stop raising his fists against 'Merican soldiers, is what he needs."

Dr. James' face went white. Either through vengeance or incompetence or Fate or stupidity, the NLAs had been sent or led to Rushmore in order to be culled. To be rid of. Those who question are a threat to those who want to rule. Was that it?

Whatever it was, winter had arrived.

Zach and Dr. James hefted Stone's body onto the bed of the truck and bounced back to the doctor's camp, where everyone was already awake and outside cooking breakfast after the commotion.

We ran to the truck when it arrived.

"What happened?" Miss T asked.

Dr. James hopped out and nodded in the direction he was headed: the bed of the truck. Candy had the youngest legs of all, and she read Dr. James and sprinted past him, but Dr. James caught her at the last moment and turned his attention to include me, too: "It's a little gory, but he's still alive."

He let us decide whether we wanted to look, and

we both scrambled up the back of the truck and looked.

"Oh, dear," said Candy, who started to get dizzy. "I don't think you'll like this, Leni."

Leni definitely decided to stay away after that.

We stared at the empty space where Stephen Stone's arm used to be, and we stared at that bloody stump. Then Zach and Dr. James pulled us down so the men could lay Stone on the clean blanket they'd just laid out.

Zach muttered to Dr. James while they were moving the body, "He don't feel *with us* anymore, Doc."

Dr. James agreed and thoroughly prodded and palpated Stephen Stone, and with each moment the doctor grew towards the bipolarity of fear and certainty: Stephen Stone, age forty-seven, was dead from either shock or a heart attack. Family records, discovered later, indicated a long history of early-onset heart disease.

But that didn't really matter to the damned NLAs. Zach drove around and informed everyone of what had happened, what the score was, and went on to the next camp to tell the same story. By early evening, a scene had developed at the Rage camp: There was talk of coordinated, retributive violence.

Once again, nearly everyone confined to the Rushmore camp gathered around, and with Stephen Stone gone, Zach de la Ciudadano had somehow become our *de facto* new spokesman: leader of the soon-dead.

President of the priceless dead cats.

Morituri nolumus mori.—
"We who are about to die don't want to."

"We gotta fight for our lives, right?" someone yelled from the crowd. "Let's go kill some of those fucking dicks!"

By the time Stone arrived and died I was fully recovered from my merciless flu, and in my recuperation from that sapping lingerer I'd taken to stalking the entire grounds of the camp, generally observing the great masses of dissidents, learning indirectly that very few people even there had lived a life like Candy's and mine. It made me feel estranged, and I kept away from them—not knowing what to say or how to even say it the way they would. They didn't talk anything like MJ, MT, or DrJ. I know I was big for my age, but I wasn't yet big like in the way that big adults often have where they tend to unwittingly become the objects of drunken people's bulletproof courage. People simply stayed out of my way, and I regarded them kindly enough that they didn't mind doing it.

Whether conscious of it or not, I did the same thing, in microcosmic form, at the impromptu gathering: I walked alone around the outside and observed the swollen scene at the Rage camp.

Candy Baby and Leni had arrived with Miss Thompson, and the three of them had located Dr. James, near Zach's truck, at the front of the gathering—because Dr. James felt like he should be there for Zach, who'd never even submitted an application to do any of the governing and was all of a sudden our new leader. As Zach paced the bed of his truck and considered the things being shouted at him, my family and Leni all put their arms around each other's waists and shoulders, to unify them in the swelling, moving crowd. Candy Baby and Leni were really close together, comfortably holding tight, feeling safe in each other's shared existence. They liked to stalk the camp as a pair, with three layers of protection: slung rifles, Candy's a weapon, Leni's a safetied empty threat Miss T forced her to carry on their walks; two, the freezing-cold aspects both girls were able to project into the world through their no-bullshit faces; and three, a nervous Miss Thompson often forced herself into their group, offering occasional adult wisdom and attempts at explanations for the incredibly human things they'd see. The two girls—the increasingly acne-ridden Candy, maturing, and the stone-silent Leni, who was as beautiful as she was deeply troubled—had become nearly inseparable. Despite our collectively miserable circumstances, I'd never seen Candy look so pleasantly copacetic, almost like she'd fit into some kind of long-sought symmetry.

Miss Thompson shouted to Zach, "An attack would be a waste of our own pain. The drones, Zach—tell the crowd what you told us."

"Emily's right," Zach announced. "Those things—" he looked up at the grid of drone-contrails in the sky and then looked hopeless. "Any attack we launched would be snuffed out before the wick were lit."

I could see it clearly, and I felt it myself: A psychological chill ripped through the crowd, and all dissent was snuffed and replaced by a big numb thought with no corners. *We were charged with death, and it was impossible to fight for our lives?*

A man chosen, if he has balls, or guts—clearheaded courage—will rise to an important moment, because an important person will fill the role necessary for the cogs of a greater process to continue, and Zach was somehow chosen, and he had the requisite clearheaded courage, but as a virulent individualist he loathed the idea of speaking for others, so instead he spoke the words he'd heard earlier in the day, at our camp, from the woman who'd just spoken up to him, and he combined his leadership position with her wisdom.

"But I don't even think about it that way. After all, what kind of wit do we show when we resort to violence? We show that there is no wit in our souls—

211

like those witless, tribal, devolutionary thugs up there—and that we are beasts throughout and deserve no better than a beast's slaughter. But if we survive with grit or die with grace, we will have shown that the very best of humanity could be found here and was allowed to perish because of the irrational fear and unholy corruption of the people who had the power to fix it. They kidnapped or led us into this trap, but the Jews were kidnapped and led into traps, and they were later given Israel. Would they trade all those lives to not have a homeland today? I honestly don't know. But this is our homeland right now, and it might be our tomb, but hardened grit, moral grace, and our pathetic epigraph have the potential to change the world.

"But if we launch an attack, we'll lose all that, and we'll be like everyone else.

"Those fools deserve our pity, not our hate."

It was a fine speech, but as I watched the crowd dissipate, it seemed like everyone left the Rage camp that night looking like they were hopelessly trying to kindle a very tiny candle in the cold black plains of stormy history.

Some people were muttering to themselves.

"Head of the Rage Against the Machine camp, and we're about to die because of The Machine, *and he calls for us to lie down and accept it with grace?* . . . What happened, Mommy? Mommy? . . . I don't care what *Rawhide* up there said; I ain't goin' down without a fight, no way—gonna be at least one dead soldier on accounna me if I'm 'onna die . . . As long as we got water and a little bit of food, and each other, we've got enough . . . I see it, what he was saying. He's right. I'm gonna throw up, but he's right . . . I knew we were dead when we got here; as soon as I saw that fuckin' mountain, I said . . . Gandhi got headlines in newspapers across the worl'; ain't nobody gonna see about us; we jus' raindrops."

I took a long way home through the dark and was the last to arrive at the camp, where everyone was warming themselves around the crackling and flickering firepit. Their expressions had gone from grim to a short relief at seeing I had returned, and then back to grim. After the short relief, but before the return to grimness, Candy Baby vented the family's frustration about my late arrival.

"Where have you been?" Candy asked with a scowling face. "We were worried *sick!*"

"I wanted to think."

Nobody replied, and I sat in the spot they'd left for me.

Nobody spoke but the fire, which chattered the same as usual—the sound was almost a relief.

"It has to be said, so I'm going to say it: Things might get ugly here, soon, as you can probably tell," Dr. James said, "and I think we need to have some sort of plan in place for when the top pops off this tragic mess."

"I just assumed we'd meet here," Candy said, and she turned to Leni. "Isn't that what I told you the other day?"

Leni nodded quickly and then turned away with terrible bashfulness while she and Candy petted the very relaxed, seemingly oblivious Tyger.

"OK, so we'll meet here," Dr. James said, "and if here is no good for whatever reason—"

"We'll all meet up at that awesome bomb-shelter in Curly," I said sarcastically.

"Yeah, or Daddy's cabin!" Candy added, playing along with my game for the distraction.

"If here is no good for whatever reason," Miss Thompson said. "Just survive first, however you have to—but do it!"

The crackling fire continued to flare and pop, and at least to me it felt like the freezing dark night all around us were not a night at all but rather some experimental black vacuum approaching absolute zero.

Naturam expellas furca, tamen usque recurret.—
"You may drive out nature with a pitchfork, yet she will still hurry back."

While the rest of the camps at the camp muttered and mumbled their way through another cold, starless night, the inserted CTR Team, which had set themselves up near the Rage camp, took advantage of the uncertain sentiment and enacted the first stage of the Action Plan they'd been sent to complete.

As soon as the last of the Ragers was asleep, the CTR Team silently crept into camp and killed them all with syringes of cyanide and changed into their clothes. They stacked all of the naked Rage-campers' bodies, including the great Zach's, in the tent the CTR Team had been using—turning it into a mass-grave body bag—and loaded the back of both Rage trucks full of speakers, rockets, the mass-grave tent, and other munitions. The nearby camps were too invested in the depths of their own mortal-existential swellings to notice the commotion at the Rage camp, and anyway there was always commotion at the Rage camp.

The commotion otherwise ended as the empty night endured, but when the first rays of gray light began to open the doors of the misty morning, the commotion suddenly also awakened and continued with the insanely loud blast of a recording, an electronic voice—unsettlingly foreign-sounding in the mute of the early day—that said, *"GIVE ME LIBERTY, OR GIVE ME DEATH."*

A bone-vibratingly-loud song exploded from the lead Rage truck's huge speaker system: the Rage Against the Machine classic "Freedom." The music thrummed through the minds and bodies of everyone shivering in the dawn's cold light—the song a revolutionary anti-anthem we'd all heard many times before coming from those trucks' speakers, but sounding somehow *different* in the eerie, early, perplexing morning that had suddenly been set in motion.

The commotion was back inside all of us—our eyes were open again.

"Jesus God, what is it today?" Dr. James asked inside the warm cocoon of his fully loaded hammock, awakening to the music like everyone else.

The wild music scrambled through everything. The shivering family, out of their warm cocoons (I had been awake and on the final shift of watch), jumped up and down in the cold to get their blood moving, to warm up, and suddenly we all saw both Rage trucks driving past, fully loaded with masked men and equipment, and all the men on the trucks were motioning for us to join them.

When the men in the trucks saw the confused looks on the faces of the waking Thompsons, they zoomed off to the next camp, in the hopes of stoking a very confusing, early-morning revolution.

"Suffice it to say that I have a bad feeling about this," Dr. James said. "Did that driver look like Zach to you?"

"All I saw were those masks," Miss Thompson said. "I don't know."

"Those masks were scary," Candy said, and Leni nodded, and Tyger scratched behind an ear with one of her hindpaws.

"'Day of the Dead' masks," Miss Thompson said to herself and all of us. "I don't like this at all."

"But why?" I asked—incredulous like everyone else. "Why, after what you and Zach said last night? What the hell?"

"I don't know," Dr. James said—we all had to speak with our stomachs to be heard over the din of the blaring music. "I'd say let's prepare for anything. Load up and be ready to go. Emily, do you know if there's anywhere we can go to be away from whatever might happen?"

"Anywhere's the same as anywhere else, from what I can tell."

"Kids," Dr. James said. "I want you to go into the woods and dig a hole we could all fit in."

"Like a grave?" Candy asked, and she asked with such emotion that even Tyger noticed her vibes and looked at Dr. James curiously.

"Like a foxhole," I said as reassuringly as I could. From seemingly the first words I ever read, I've preferred most of all to read about warfare. I announced to Candy and tried to reassure her with the confidence of my message, "It's our safest bet. We need a foxhole, and we need two feet of overhead coverage for falling debris, and if we have that we should be as gold as Midas' fingernails." (I borrowed a Candyism.)

"Sounds like a plan, General Patton," Dr. James said. "Now get to it!"

The music was so loud it became part of the atmosphere itself, and the Rage trucks kept up their holy helluva racket, summoning the attention of everyone in pretty much all of South Dakota—an air-cracking yawp in a morning otherwise maintaining its natural pace towards the day.

We kids all got shovels and makeshift digging implements and ran to the forest and quickly dug a deep foxhole for the whole family. We worked ourselves into a lather, digging hectically, driven by fear and orders and instinct.

"Good, good!" Dr. James came by, grabbed a shovel from Candy and said, "Candy, you and Leni go help Emily clean and load the rifles."

Dr. James went to work and tossed dragon-mouthfuls of dirt over his shoulders, determined to ready the family for whatever.

All of us kept up our fevered pace as the air grew brighter and yet more ominous, like as the air cleared of darkness the darkness injected itself into our feeling of impending doom. The women finished cleaning and loading the rifles and preparing the van and the camp for either a riflery dig-in or a hasty escape. The males dug the foxhole for the dig-in and covered it with the largest deadfall we could find—forget two feet; it must have been at least three or more before we were done: deadfall and mud and dirt overhead like a vault.

The ladies arrived at the foxhole and helped us drag more deadfall to the huge roof.

Everyone climbed into the foxhole and saw that we could all fit and had at least minimal protection from debris falling from above, and for a few seconds, before we all scrambled out, there was a moment when we were all in there together, afraid of what was to come, but still alive, and together.

Forgive me, forgive me, reader—I am crying. Let me cry. I can't think about our last moment together without crying.

I'll continue tomorrow.

Three words to damn the world: *Good people, hiding.*

Then we were all outside again, out of the family fox-hole, and Candy was looking at the trees above the van.

"Kids," Miss Thompson said, "James and I have to try to stop Zach and the others, or whoever that was. Stay here!"

She looked at her brother for reassurance—she herself was choking up out of intuitive fear.

"Stay here," Dr. James said, repeating his sister. "We'll be back as soon as we can."

The adults slung their rifles, and Dr. James grabbed his portable medi-kit, and our whole family faced each other on the verge of tears.

"I wanna go with you!" Candy erupted. "We wanna go with you!"

"Mom," I said, "please don't go. What can—I mean, what are you—?"

"Dante, my sweet boy," she said and wrapped me in her long loving arms, "we might be the only people who can get through to Zach. We might be the only people willing to try to stop there from being more bloodshed. We have to try. Your father didn't think he had to make a difference, but it didn't work. We have a chance right now, so we have to try: It's what he would have done if he were still with us. I know it."

I knew it, too.

She released me and embraced Candy and Leni, and we all said I Love You a million times, and Candy, as the adults were rapidly hustling towards the commotion, kept repeating, "Be careful! Be safe! I mean it!"

When the adults were gone, Candy said to me and Leni, "They better be careful."

I wrapped my arms around their shoulders and said, "C'mon, girls."

She and Leni went along with me—they were curious—and Candy asked, "To where?"

"I saw you looking up that tree," I said looking above the van. "I want to see what's happening, too. I'll boost you guys up."

"*Heeeeey, yeeeaaahhh!*—Does that sound good to you, Leni?" Candy asked in such a way that seemingly announced, "Of course it is, and we're already making our way up the tree."

They were both as light as baby animals, and soon unassisted (those little fawnlets were no match or help for my behemothness) I myself had lumbered on top of the van with them. The height of the huge van allowed us to easily reach a sturdy branch and start climbing the what-looked-like-an-aspen, which was leafed in the same way Mr. Justin had been coiffed: that is, flickering with brown and grey around the sides, and bald at the top. It was an easy climb for all three of us, even for timid Leni, and within two minutes we had reached the highest branches that could hold our weight, and we could see almost the whole camp.

I could see six of the eight towers, and I noticed

coldly and briefly that the sniper in the nearest tower was looking through his magnified scope and noticing us. Then he turned the scope towards where I turned to next: the still-rallying, music-blasting, revolution-fomenting Rage trucks.

"Do you see Mommy?" Candy asked. Lately she had been growing more formal in her relations with people—more mature—but obviously our plight and her fear must have driven her back to her older/younger habits, and she said "Mommy" rather than "her" or more appropriately "them."

Leni tapped Candy vigorously and pointed at the ground near a big blue tent: Miss T and Dr. James were headed in the same direction most people were headed—towards the Rage truck, which was rallying and wending its way down to the easternmost tower, where Stephen Stone had been shot.

We watched as the trucks fishtailed in the slushy mud and spun to remarkably orchestrated, symmetrical stops a hundred yards from the easternmost tower, where the song from the lead truck climaxed with five pulses of mortar being shot high into the sky and popping seemingly harmlessly way up in the air, like dud fireworks.

Four large men in the back of the second truck shouldered heavy launchers and shot rocket-propelled grenades into the tower, which exploded and was filled with the screams of men on fire whose bodies were no longer complete, who were looking at their own insides as their surroundings burned. And the tower filled with black smoke and tongues of fire, and I could hear the soldiers yelling in the tower nearest us in the tree: "What do you mean you've got nothing? Hit them! Hit them!" "There's nothing!" "How can there be—?"

A standard Peregrine is twenty feet long, eighteen feet wide, and contains two missiles, four tubes, and one-thousand rounds of depleted-uranium bullets, as well as a standard hydrogen-fuel cell, and is designed to fully ignite its munitions and fuel supply—and thus incinerate all its proprietary technology—if brought down by any means.

The first drone cometed from the sky and detonated near the base of the northernmost tower, right by us, and the shock- and heatwave smashed us invisibly, and the bright light from the explosion temporarily blinded the corner of my left eye, and we all screamed and started scrambling down the branches we'd just ascended.

The second drone came down while we were vertically halfway to the van, but it was farther away, and we only heard the tremendous explosion and briefly felt a breeze of its furious heat.

As if killing all the drones and creating an internal inferno at the tower weren't enough, the men in the Rage trucks then gunned down the eastern tower's guardsmen, placed two metaplastic charges on the tower's front legs, set off the explosives, and brought down the whole fucker.

Two arcs of light sang from the toes of the tower, and then it arched forward slowly, as if to bow, and then gravity drove it to the ground with ever greater speed until the head smacked into the frozen dirt and exploded in a non-explosive sense: came apart, and pieces rolled or scattered a small distance as they continued to burn.

There was no final announcement from either

of the Rage trucks. They merely regrouped, spun up spumes of slushy mud, and drove off past the corpse of the easternmost tower, into Old America.

As good or bad luck would have it, the third drone also hit a tower, and the tower was instantly incinerated. Those explosions shook the air as we landed on the roof of the van, and I scrambled off and caught Candy and Leni when they hopped into my arms, and we all ran to the foxhole in sheer, adrenaline-fueled fright.

The fifth drone exploded somewhere on the line between the foxhole and the easternmost tower, and immediately I felt a vile wave of nausea.

The only sounds in the foxhole were the sounds of our breathing and Candy saying, "Oh no, oh no, oh noooooo."

People outside were screaming on fire or screaming in panic or screaming in fright. We kids were in the dark under the double canopy of the forest and the foxhole. The fires flared and roared as people's vehicles and fuel reserves were caught in the witless aim of the unpowered drones that deadfell from the sky and burst into obliterating white-yellow halations of utter destructive force.

"I wanna *see*," Candy eventually said, unable to take it anymore. She started crawling out, despite Leni's nervous groping protests and my incredulous dead stare.

"Hell no, Candy!" I said when I realized she was serious.

"Dante, I'll *crawl back* in if I'm in *danger,* but I wanna *see* if they're *OK!"*

"We don't know where those things are falling!" I shouted.

"I want Mommy!" Candy Baby screamed, and she crawled out.

Leni and I looked at each other briefly, sighed, and started crawling out, too.

We had entered the foxhole with haste, seeking shelter from danger, and we emerged from the foxhole with caution, into a world on fire. Whole camps were orange with fire; people screamed and ran in panicked circles; the snipers in the remaining towers were seemingly firing at random, trying to bring order back to what had unraveled by using their hammer on every nail that announced itself, whether in triumph or for help; the sound was another din, the sight was Hellish, the smell was burnt, and the feel was panic-laden dread. Candy, Leni, and I monkey-crawled along the ground and used the van to shield ourselves from the debris that occasionally ripped through the air. Inside the van, Tyger was going absolutely insane barking like the barking would help.

"Where are they?" Candy cried. I could barely hear her over my fear. "Do you see them?!"

Leni and I shook our heads and kept looking.

I saw Candy Baby's mouth ask, "Dr. James?"

I looked and didn't recognize anyone. Nobody was heading towards us. Most people scurried in these chilling panicked circles, thoughtless, looking around and recognizing nothing. Some of the people were firing rifles and handguns up into the towers that were firing back at them with much more effectiveness, creating rivers of flesh blood in the frozen mud.

"C'MON, THEY MIGHT NEED OUR HELP!" Candy screamed as she herself panicked, and suddenly, from her crouch by the van, she burst into a sprint, into the shrapnel-storm of the exploding camp.

"CANDY!" I yelled, an otherwise wordless plea for her to stop and come back. But either she didn't hear or wasn't convinced of anything by my titular argument.

Then like a shadow Leni was gone and right on Candy's hip.

My own departure was much delayed by the fact that going out there seemed like it was more stupid than brave or helpful. I was afraid, too, though, and I also wanted my Mommy to be safe. Everyone I loved was in the war zone where I stood on the periphery, watching, and still I could not easily venture past where I'd already reached, which already seemed insanely dangerous, away from the foxhole we'd so urgently and appropriately dug and covered.

But everyone I loved was indeed out there, and I loved them more than I loved my safety, so when Candy looked back for the second time while she and Leni ran into the awful scene, I got up from my crouch and started making my way across the acrid battlefield.

And I started catching up with them.

The sixth drone crashed and vaporized a few moments later. The moments themselves vaporized as well. Or, at least, none of us has any exact memories of them. The drone volcano-splashed into the big blue tent, not far from Candy and Leni, and it blasted Leni into Candy, and Candy spun through the air as if she were made of hay.

There was nothing left of Leni. She absorbed most of the energy and heat from the explosion—a timid human shield vaporized instantaneously and gone like an angel without a whisper.

I saw it all and vomited.

Candy was knocked unconscious when her falling head slammed into the frozen mud, and from what I can recall I ran with my jumbled legs (after vomiting) to where she was laid out flat and not moving at all. I thought she was dead for sure, but she had a strong pulse, and I must have slung her over my shoulder in a way I'd seen Mr. Justin do once—I still can't piece together what I remember from what I've dreamt or told myself.

I have zero memories, dreamt or not, between picking her up and finding myself behind the wheel of the van. My more solid memories pick up as we are already in gear and driving along the outside of the camp (Dr. James had taught both me and Candy to drive before we left Sweet Bend), towards the nearest fallen tower, to ostensibly GTFO.

But soon I had to steer the van towards the inferno in the heart of the camp because a sniper's bullet had ripped through the roof and gone through the passenger-side door and would have hit Candy if she weren't laid out flat and unconscious in the back being thoroughly sniffed and licked by a repeatedly balance-shifting Tyger.

I saw a route through the inferno that would take me to the opening to the south, where one of the towers had exploded, but as I zoomed along—with surprising skill or luck given my newness to driving and the calamity of the scene I was navigating—I saw that I wasn't the only one who had the same idea, and a few other chopped vehicles were now racing through the same lanes of fire and trying to keep their tires from exploding.

The seventh drone's explosion flashed, blinked, in the side mirrors of the van, as I drove over the charred black ashes by the fallen tower and entered Old America again.

I drove until it was just us, until everyone else who escaped had already roared past faster than I was willing to go, and I pulled over jerkily when the camp's fires still flickered but were quite distant—the billowing smoke visible for miles and miles more.

I revived Candy. First I cleaned her burns and cuts as well as I could while she was still unconscious and wouldn't feel the pain, and then I smelling-salted her awake—and she woke up startled like most people do when coming out of an unnatural loss of consciousness, this time without the long inhalation.

She wanted to know what happened, where were we, where was everyone else.

I didn't have good answers for any of her questions.

"What *do* you remember, then?" she asked.

"I had just left the van, I was heading towards you, and there was an explosion—a drone, the big blue tent—"

"Nothing after that?" she asked.

A wag no.

I thought for a moment.

"Leni got hit," I said. "You both got hit, but Leni got it way worse, Candy."

I recalled that for a moment they were both there, running towards where they thought Miss Thompson and Dr. James might be, and then there was a wave of fire from my right. The wave smashed into Leni, and the wave passed, but Leni was gone, and Candy was high in the air.

"Did you try to help her?"

I didn't know how to answer that question—what could I have done?

"Did you?" Candy demanded.

"Candy, there was nothing left to help."

"What?" she asked incredulously.

"The fact that you're even alive . . . It was . . . like . . . the world's worst miracle."

Candy didn't say anything.

The news sank in, and she hated me. I could feel her hating me, and I just accepted it.

After a little bit, the news sank in further, and the hate receded slightly—replaced by emptiness.

A few more jalopies zoomed past us, and we both sat on the floor of the motionless van in a mutually stupid silence.

The mellow illumination through the passenger-side window was dark orange, and the set sun's diffracted afterlight glowed on Candy Baby's right profile. On the other side, my left profile was lowlighted dark silver by the cold eastern twilight's darkening grey whispers. The windshield ahead displayed a Salvador Daliesque narrative featuring the dying light of dark orange life being drained by a brown-red gash in the sky, which dripped its darkness into a fading purple bruise, which emptied into the crystal-black cemetery of the eastern night. Our white van raced down the road, straight into it, but we could never quite pierce into the art, which always remained on the other side of the glass, while behind the glass there was only the groan of the motor and the hum of the tires on the road and the dead silence between me and Candy Baby, our softly lit exteriors the magnificent inversion of the artless ugliness we felt inside as we made our pitiful escape, only to wait, to wait, to wait.

PART TWO

Bellum Omnium Contra Omnes—
"War Of All Against All"

Ubi amor, ibi dolor.—
"Where there is love, there is pain."

Six years. We didn't intend to wait six years, but when you're twelve and fifteen and all alone, you don't have much choice. You wait. You're not quite a person yet—you still need guidance. You need time to pass, to become physically and emotionally stronger.

Rather than guidance and strength, we received OmniViewing.

Miss Thompson, who loved the tangible feel of a book's verbal heartbeat, was radically opposed to the soullessness she saw in computers and OmniViewers, and she never permitted an OmniViewer inside of Biblio-Files. The computer, which she was always intimidated by, was at best, to her, a business necessity. Her culture didn't agree, though, and her store, if there were any luck to the timing, had died around the same time the country unraveled and the majority of the townspeople were forced to move on to look for work and food.

Candy and I took to the bomb-shelter's OVs readily. Here were global libraries of books and the spidering archives of websites, the deep annals of broadcast television and the entire history of film.

The bunker was stocked for the long wait, and looking back on it we must have undergone an arrested development down there, while we waited for Miss Thompson and/or Dr. James, while we OmniViewed and physically matured.

I entered at fifteen and left at twenty-one. Candy Baby entered at twelve and left at eighteen. I entered depressed and left a fanatical assassin. (I've heard it said that "Depression is rage turned inward"; in my case, over the course of six years, my rage turned outward.) Candy Baby entered devastated and left devastating. Frankly, we were never going to lead normal lives anyway.

Instead, we became mass-killers.

Eheu fugaces labuntur anni.

"This is actually it, Candy—wow," I said with as much enthusiasm as I could muster—I was certainly glad to be somewhere safe, but glad was too strong a word for the kind of internal void we both felt. The intention to relay the compliment to Candy was there—her memory and sense of direction were truly world-class—but my voice was dead flat from exhaustion and depression. I put the van in park and stepped out and manually opened the garage door and parked the van next to Kramer's dust-covered old dead Mustang. Candy hopped out before I pulled the van in and said flatly and tiredly, "Thanks, Big," and while I parked, she upended the fake boulder and started twisting open the circular door of the bomb shelter while Tyger urinated on the nearest corner of the Kramer house, her thin metal collar flashing and jingling with every step and movement in the red brakelight.

I had taught myself to use the powder-printer and was following a recipe from a cookbook I'd found, with Tyger tail-wagging hopefully at my feet—the Pink Floyd album "The Dark Side of the Moon" playing quietly in the background—when Candy Baby padded sleepily into the kitchen area. I said, "I took Tyger out and had a look around when I woke up—didn't see anything." Candy was still half-asleep and resisting waking up—putting off facing our fourth lives. "What'ch' cookin'?" she asked. I looked from the book on the counter to the bowl in my hands, back to the book, back to the bowl, and then at Candy. "The recipe says it's called 'Power Breakfast Nutrition Blasters.'" Candy heaved an I'm-now-fully-awake sigh and said, "I'm making something else. Turn up the music."

Poor Sylvia Thompson didn't have any fellow females around to talk to her and empathize with her when she ended her first menstrual cycle. The blood, which she'd been warned about—she'd had The Talk with Miss Thompson at the camp—arrived like an expected, unwanted surprise, and with it the sunrise of womanhood, and all poor Candy had around her to guide her into her life's day was her older brother, me, who was myself a wisdomless late bloomer whose face was one big pasty pore-splosion and whose mind contained nothing but trivia—no wisdom. Lately my voice had been sounding more equine than human. New abundances of hormones were elbowing for room via the chemistry of maturation in both of our bodies, and we went through that sometimes frankly gross metamorphosis alone with each other down in someone else's bomb shelter. Indeed, Candy and I were ushered through puberty by a fear of the outside world and more importantly by the mere hope of the return of a loving authority. And also by whatever knowledge we could gather from the shelter's fully loaded OmniViewers. In our fourth lives, we were back in yet another womb.

For the first year both of us were too depressed and despairing to do much of anything but eat food and watch for news of Miss T, Dr. J, or Saxon Rhysdale on the OV. If it wasn't the news, we found favorite comedies and dramas from the past and present, which helped us become somewhat better acquainted with the Old American culture our childhoods had mostly lacked. Candy Baby took the big bedroom, and while she did her OmniViewing with a personal viewer snuggled in the big bed with Tyger, I usually slept on the couch in the main room, glazed by the glowing gaze of the giant OV. Our minds pretty much temporarily emptied of our previous education; in fact we tried to forget everything but the basics of eating and breathing—

given the jagged edges of our short lives thus far—and our bodies bloated with the fat of complete, partially scared-petrified, partially teenage-lazy inaction. We were down in a rut, and every day we waited for Miss Thompson and/or Dr. James to come 'round and pull us out. But the rut remained, and the horizon, too, remained free of anything at all but the corpses of clouds ripped apart by crisscrossing security drones and all sorts of commercial and military aircraft.

Teenagers + severe psychic trauma + terrorized despair - responsibilities + hormonal maturation = human hibernation.

We slept despite our nightmares.

In Candy's recurring nightmare, she was swimming across a cold lake, leading the way for her family, whom she swore she could hear following her, but when her toes touched the gritty silt on the far side of the lake, by the trees, she stood and turned, and there was nobody there. The lake was a pane of glass, and a freezing wind began to blow and chill the heart of her bones. Then there was a nasty, sloppy, crunching sound coming from the forest, and she would wake up screaming.

Every morning, for more than a year.

In my recurring nightmare, the men who killed Mr. Justin were chained to the walls. I was in the middle of the room, and they were all very happy to see me, and even as the dream was beginning I was already screaming in fright. The prisoners were leaping at me, to pounce on me and bleed me and suffocate me to death with their throbbing weapons, and I could see that I was safe as long as I stayed exactly where I was, but that meant I couldn't leave the situation, either. The men would keep leaping at me, and the chains would snap them back by their necks and wrists and ankles, and they all wanted to fuck me dead, and I was just this crying, innocent, screaming little boy who didn't know what to do. Then a familiar grunt would catch my attention, and to my overwhelming horror I would see that one of the men leaping at me was Mr. Justin—he didn't recognize me; now his face and his whole being were the same as the others, with a corrupted heart full of love-murder—and when I saw him like that, not even recognizing me as anything but a body to dominate, I became so scared I started screaming again with such pitch and urgency that I would start to feel faint, which would drive all the men into an even more fervid lust, and the nightmare would start all over again during that scream.

Nearly every night, nearly every nap, for maybe the rest of my godfucked life.

Candy Baby found the key! On the top shelf of the big closet (she'd climbed up there out of extreme boredom), there was a funky-looking key that she immediately recognized as the most likely solution to the unsolved riddle of the giant metal door in the main room of the shelter—the obelisk that we would both occasionally, emptily stare at. "Big!" she yelled. "What?" I yelled in reply from the big couch. "I found it!" "What?" "The key!" I shot off the couch and jogged and jiggled to the master bedroom, where Candy was climbing down the metallic planes of the closet, her limbs and torso thinning out and getting all long as she aged. When she was on the ground, she held up the key and beamed with a big smile. "TH' KEEEYYYY!" she sang out, and I joined her, "TH' KEEEEYYYYY!" "Let's do it!" Candy Baby said, pumped her keyed-up fist, and headed towards the big door.

The locking mechanism glided like an angel at the key's frictionless insertion and twist, and the mechanical sound of a multitude of bolts unlocking simultaneously clicked through the room, and Candy Baby turned the handle and pulled the door, which seemed to be assisted by the subtle breezy pushing of the atmosphere in the area behind it. The door opened with a well-greased silence. And shortly we were armed and standing before the open door—with darkness there and nothing more. The light from the shelter's main room revealed the first few feet of what felt like a very long tunnel. It seemed to be breathing, but from a great distance. We looked at each other in confusion. Tyger paced before the doorway and growled at the yawning darkness.

Candy covered two big ponchos with chemlights, and she'd found a sort of pack-saddle for Tyger, which she also covered in chems, and I charged our headlamps and found a box full of spare batteries in the work area. After two previous, failed, solo excursions—one each—trying to reach the end of the tunnel, we decided we would dedicate a day to it and do it or die trying. The mystery of the open door was even stronger than when it was closed and locked and seemingly keyless and answerless. I wore a backpack full of food, water, batteries, and extra ammunition under my chemlight poncho. Meanwhile, Candy Baby carried both our rifles X-style across her back, over hers, and looked frankly badass in the dark like that. Together the three of us cast off quite a bit of light, and our headlamps were able to penetrate farther into the darkness. There were wooden beams serving as stabilizing frames every ten or so steps. The tunnel was wide enough for CB and me to walk side-by-side comfortably. When all three of us were completely in the tunnel, Tyger shot off about twenty feet ahead and disappeared into one of the walls. We ran up to where the dog had disappeared, and we saw a bigger-than-Tyger-sized opening in the wall, and we heard the sound of Tyger's claws on thin metal, ascending, then nothing. "Well, I didn't expect that," Candy said kneeling down to look into the opening. "I think I can see a little bit of light coming from in here." And then there was the clattering sound of claws on metal, descending, and Candy jumped out of the way when suddenly the opening was bright-green and full of dog. Candy said, "Big, I know what this is!" But I had already reached the same conclusion, and I said, "Tyger has her own bathroom." Candy said, "I love her but *Thank God*—I was getting pretty tired

240

of schlepping her. That's right, Tyger, I schlepped you good—but no more!" In better spirits upon our discovery, we continued into the void. As we walked, Tyger couldn't decide if she wanted to lead or follow and kept scurrying back and forth between us. The dirt all around us had been treated in some way, looked slick, like it had been glassed. And it felt smooth, too, but we didn't know what it was—glass didn't really make sense. Whatever it was, the tunnel felt solidly sturdy, but it was quite long and quite repetitious and seemingly endless.

It almost felt like the air had been knocked out of me when our headlights finally revealed a wall of dirt directly ahead. I had been so used to the ten-paced beams and the bottomless black well we were falling into laterally that the sight of a change in that two-hours'-driven repetition was startling, as in like vertigo-startling. At first it looked as though there had been a cave-in, but the closer we got to the wall I began to notice a series of rungs nailed into the last wooden frame, which I followed with my headlamped eyes up into a now vertical black well. Still no light at the end of the tunnel. "You found the key, your call," I said at the foot of the rungs. "You go first," Candy said. "I'll stay here with Tyger." It had been more than two hours, though, so first, Candy and I, in our fatness, had to rest for a little bit.

The rungs were sturdy and could handle my profound

mass. I looked up into the darkness and then at the next rung to be grabbed, and I started. I had braced myself for a mountainous climb, but it wasn't as bad as I'd thought it would be, because I relatively soon found myself up where "There's some sort of trap door," I yelled down to Candy. "Locked?" Candy yelled up. She was eventually answered by the sound of a trap door's squeaky creak open, but there was still no light. I could barely fit into the room above—very tight quarters. In front of me, after I closed the trap door again so I could stand on it in the cramped little area, I saw a handle on one of the walls, which I engaged, and the wall clicked open. I was in a sort of storage room somewhere. I'd walked in through a false panel in one of the wooden walls and now heard nothing but the muffled sounds of nature outside the building. I opened the trap door and yelled down the hole, "C'mon up," and I listened to the sound of Candy's ascent while I leaned against the wall and also listened for any human sounds besides the Sylvian approach. Tyger had barked a few times at first, but then nothing but Candy, who emerged through the open trap door carrying Tyger like a purse via Tyger's chemlight vest, saying, "I guess I wasn't done schlepping her after all." As Tyger sniffed from one corner to another, we investigated in the fluorescent green dark. There was one door, and neither of us had yet tried the knob. When all other areas had been investigated—the room mainly contained large boards of wood, paint, heavy hammers, and was not very large—we met at the door, and this time it was Candy's turn to lead the way. She turned the knob with ease, and we emerged in a smallish, faux-marble mausoleum that was lit dimly by sunlight streaming in through two narrow, glassless windows, or slits, in the walls. Sometimes the slits were the voices of birds, and sometimes they were the throat of the yowling wind, which whipped through the room and stirred the air and sometimes whistled through the gap between the doors at the front of the building in its escape. The front doors were brittle and wooden and chained closed from the outside—though I could've easily kicked them open if needed. Candy and I and Tyger looked through the tall slits in the wall and found we were in a cemetery on Curly's southern border. "What do you think this is all about?" Candy asked. "Looks like an alternate means of exit to me," I said. I added, in a mimesis of Mr. Justin, *"Safety is no accident."* Candy looked at me and smiled and then frowned, and said, *"Abundans cautela non nocet."* ("Abundant caution does no harm.") I smirked, and we turned and looked through the bright, breezy slits in the walls. There was nobody out there, and the clouds had been ripped to fractal shreds.

Candy and I were draped on two different ends of the luxurious couch beneath the big OV, and we wordlessly watched the handsome woman as she spoke into the screen: "Chilling footage ahead as we report that earlier today there was a bloody incident at an abandoned shopping mall in Minnesota, where a community of NLAs who'd taken refuge in the abandoned building were being forcibly driven out by a CTR Division sent there on the grounds of the former federal government's right of eminent domain. It's our understanding the soldiers were sent there on behalf of a program seeking to lay the groundwork of a gentrification in the war-torn suburb of Henley, with Henley fifteen years ago being the site of a bloody riot between the politically divided citizens of the town. Seeking to unify the country by healing the wound that opened when the Democrats and Republicans in the city went to war with each other, when each side blamed the other for the federal government's defaulting and plunging America and the world into an unprecedented global depression, unofficial DHS Secretary Frank Savage told *OV Rat News* that details about the actual incident today cannot be divulged in the interest of (former) national security, but these images were leaked to *InstaNews* several hours ago. They appear to have been taken by an amateur droner, and their validity has not been fully vetted, but if true they do confirm what one unnamed CTR agent reported candidly. Quote: 'It was a bloodbath. The NLAs laid a nasty trap. We had to level the mall.' Level them all, indeed. If you'd like to weigh in on the tragedy, simply enter the code and shout your thoughts at the OV, and if we like yours, we might play it at the end of the show and give you Twenty MegaCredits For Your Two Cents."

In omnibus requiem quaesivi, et nusquam inveni nisi in angulo cum libro.—
"Everywhere I have searched for peace and nowhere found it, except in a corner with a book."

Something happened to me: Endless propaganda and mindless entertainment no longer held my interest. Every day I grew more impatient and agitated. I was a fat, depressed, useless piece of shit, and it was starting to bother me. Every night Candy moaned with growing pains: She was rapidly thinning and elongating, and her face, too, was frankly awkward-looking at times, and she seemed to be in no hurry to unbury her head from the OV-entertainment sand. In a fortunate twist of fate, Howard Kramer had named his dogs Raven and

Tyger, and for the first time in the who-cares-how-long in the shelter, I found the candle of my interest in literature re-lighted, and I knew that a man who named his dogs Raven and Tyger would have stored some books on his apocalyptic OVs. And indeed he did: thousands of titles, hundreds of which I had never seen or heard of. Soon thereafter, every day I pulled a new record from the big wall and fed it to the needle, and I practically threw the arrow of my finger at random at the target of the library of titles on the OV. The first bull's-eye the arrow-finger hit was the title of a book I had never read before: *One Flew Over the Cuckoo's Nest,* by Ken Kesey. I clicked to the beginning, read the first line, and felt ice in my spine:

"They're out there."

"What are you doing?" Candy asked when she emerged from the bedroom to make something for lunch. I was on the couch as usual, in a concrete aquarium of Mr. Kramer's weird music as usual, but not watching any shows or playing any games—the OV was full of words; her brother was reading? What the heck? *"Randle P. McMurphy,"* I said distractedly in a low-wattage mimesis of Jack Nicholson, whom I knew had played McMurphy in the movie I'd forced myself not to watch yet. She asked, "Why're you *reading?"* I shrugged. "I just felt like it." "Why?" "Why the fuck do you do what you do, Candy?" I asked. Candy walked to the kitchen and muttered, "It didn't help *them."* I turned my face from the OV to Candy and said, "Don't be passive-aggressive, Candy: What do you have to say?" "Don't tell me how to live, dick!" "Candy—" "And what I *said* was that it didn't help *them,* our stupid *parents* or what*ever!* They both read like *idiots,* and they both ended up—" If she admitted it aloud, it would make it real, and neither of us could handle making it real at that point. "I know," I said. "I just remembered that they liked it, and I remember liking it, and right now it feels like . . . a way to . . . keep in touch? I don't know; I just got sick of the stupid OV crap. I wanted—" "*Dependable streams of beautiful words to drift the day upon?*" Candy asked in a mimesis that combined Jack Nicholson and Dennis Robert Justin. I chuckled. "Good one—yeah." Candy butterknife-slapped-together a simple bread-and-Peanut-Butter-AZN-Paste sandwich and returned to her room while I returned to Nurse Ratched's wretched pecking party in the mental institution. Before Candy closed the door, however, she turned around, stood in the doorway, and asked, "Big, do you ever get so mad sometimes that you want to cry, or, like, *punch* the whole world?"

It wasn't always dead-eyed grimness, but even when it wasn't it was only temporary. What I mean is that as a result of our spirit-deteriorating oblivion, Candy and I were occasionally forced to find or create oases and islands of real interpersonal fun for ourselves. To give one example of the few that still exist in my overfilled mind, picture Mr. Kramer's blaring music turning our half-lit bomb-shelter into a reverberating forest of rhythmic sound: "Born Under Punches (The Heat Goes On)" by Talking Heads. Thriving inside of that immortal atmosphere of musical joy, Candy and I were both flailing and intoxicated animals, dancing our white asses off. But it wasn't that sexy dry-hump dancing that I've seen on some OV videos and at Rushmore; rather it was like in those old movies where entire gangs of people would show off their toughness through exuberant-and-yet-threatening dance moves. Candy threw a set of moves at me that put me in my place, for a moment, but then I threw something at her that she couldn't even pretend she'd seen before, and she tried to recover, but—suddenly her face lost its competitive fun and turned serious, and she stood up perfectly straight, looking at the hole in the ceiling, puzzled. She pulled the needle from the album and ran and leapt into the air and scurried up the rungs to the door. I asked, "What's up, quitter?" From above she said, "I think I heard something!" Then I heard the strange something, too. Our predictable and torturous first thoughts: Could it be them finally?! I ran to below the hole in the ceiling and looked up as Candy spun the handle and opened the door, to see! A steady drumbeat of water fell from the black hole above, and then the hole turned white for a flash, then black again, and the air roared with tangible thunder. Candy, up at the lip of the vertical tunnel, watched the Curly night as the thunderstorm rained water, lightning, and bellowing sound down on the otherwise empty town, and from below, to me—as I clutched at nothing and fell further into the emptiness of our seemingly endless oblivion—it felt like maybe the arrhythmic flashes of lightning in the sky were an enigmatic Higher Power's attempt at trying to communicate something important to us, but at least in Morse code in English the flashes were just gibberish, and I quickly stopped trying to decipher the nonexistent message. Eventually Candy closed the door and slowly descended. But before she defeatedly dragged her feet to bed, she flexed her classic wit by putting on a different Talking Heads song to end the night: "This Must Be the Place (Naive Melody)."

Candy Baby was sixteen years old. From what I could remember, it was her birthday, and I had stayed up late the night before, baking her a birthday cake, and luckily she'd slept through Tyger practically biting the bedroom door in half before I let the dog out to join me where the smell of ingredients snowfell from the counter where I toiled. When CB awoke that morning and emerged into the main room, the lights came on, and I dropped the needle on a record, and "Birthday" by The Beatles filled the shelter with good birthday vibes. There was a chocolate cake on the table, too, with an icing tribute: "Happy SWEET 16, Candy Baby!" Rather than the giggling and gorging I had been expecting from her, Candy Baby looked at the cake, looked at me, looked at the cake again, and burst into tears. I went over to her, and she accepted my hug and hugged me with all her strength, and I interpreted it as the good kind of crying: It seemed to me that Candy, like all people, had needed to be reminded that she was loved and not merely tolerated. For me, and for almost anybody, to know Candy was to love her, but expressing that love was often difficult because of how vast that love felt, particularly given our long lives together. No tribute ever felt sufficient. And it turned out I had needed that tearful hug as much as Candy had needed to give it. Maybe, yes, that was it: She was crying because that big cake was what elder guardians and protectors were supposed to provide, not cowardly, surly, equally hormonal brothers. I had not intended that kind of end-of-chapter symbolism—had in fact just wanted to make Her Sweetness feel good for a little while because it just felt plain wrong to see Candy sad, and she'd been looking beyond sad and almost coldly gothic lately. But indeed the cake immediately and unintentionally came to symbolize something: We both had to accept that Miss Thompson and Dr. James were probably never coming for us, and this realization caused me to burst into tears, too. When our tears eventually abated, we broke the hug in laughter when a confused Tyger, eager for our attention, ended up yawning in a way that sounded like she'd said, *"Hrmm?"* Candy and I wiped the tears from our faces, and the new age, the New Dark Age, began, and Candy said, "Big Boy, it better be good, because I am going to HAMMER that whole cake down my gullet."

The New Dark Age continued that afternoon in the tunnel, after Candy's birthday party, where, having decided it was time to take the reins of my life, I began a daily hike/run with Tyger, to the mausoleum and back—ten miles, from what the OV maps showed of Curly. Almost immediately I noticed that my mood improved with movement. I was out of shape: I was the shape and had retained the athletic ability of a donut, and I was chock full of cake, so it was not a graceful run, and it was even aurally displeasing, but it was what seemed right to me. My teens would soon be over, and I was right at the age of most of the soldiers who've ever fought in most of America's wars. As I jogged, wheezing and jiggling, the steady onrush of the wooden brace-frames swam by and lulled me into deeper thought. In the current culture and socio-political volatility of America, under a protracted civil war full of spontaneous domestic battlegrounds, every citizen was a soldier, and I had to prepare if I wanted to survive, is how I saw it. I'd only worn the headlamp for light now that I knew the tunnel was free of surprises, but I'd put Tyger back in her glowing vest so I didn't accidentally kick her in the dark. The wooden frames jogged past us both. The Kramer provisions in the shelter would not last forever, and federal troops might return at any time. What were we going to do with our lives? Just as the tunnel's reliable rhythms perfectly matched my own, that repetition drove me to the central question of my birth as a citizen-soldier: "What am I going to do with my life?" "What am I going to do with my life?" "What am I going to do with my life?" The question and my breathing and my pace all fell into a rhythm, and I let my mind think without demanding an immediate answer. Some questions can take a long time, can drive a person crazy.

Candy Baby shot awake from a different nightmare— everywhere she went she fell off an unseen precipice and landed in another dream-consciousness where she walked a few steps and fell off an unseen precipice, &c.—and entered the day as surly as a wet cat. She put four claws across my face when she entered the main room and saw me on my way to the security door: "What the heck are we doing, Dante? What's the plan? Are we just going to *rot* here or what?" I closed the security door and turned off my headlamp and leaned against the wall in thought. "I've been wondering that myself, Can'." "I think I'm ready to leave," Candy said, and I said, "Yeah? Well then as you said, what's the plan? We leave here, we get picked up immediately by the cops or soldiers or mercenaries or citizen-soldiers, or we get killed by them or someone else?" Candy Baby was following her human instinct towards social interaction—towards a wider and more rewarding range of psychological transactions. "I want to get out there and have a life, too, Candy—trust me. I just feel like I'm not all that good at winging it, so I want to have a plan first." "Mr. Justin didn't have a plan," Candy said. "Of course he did, Candy—I'm sure he thought it all the way through first." "But he *didn't."* "How do you know?" "It's in his *diary*—he was *questioning* what he was doing right up until . . . ." I didn't say anything at first. Then I said, "That doesn't sound right." "You've *still* never read it?" I shook my head no—I'd still been afraid to, and also somewhere inside had felt like Mr. Justin would have shown me if he'd wanted me to read it. "You're crazy; you should read it. He . . . thought a lot of stuff." I didn't say anything for a while. While I thought about it, Candy went back into her bedroom and emerged with the notebook in her hands, which she flicked through the air with a tight spin, right at my face. I snatched it out of the air and hastily restored it to order, closed it properly and held it as if it were a fragile child. "Jesus, Candy!" "Read it, D—as one of Mr. Justin's children, I give you full permission. I think you'll see what I mean when I say that the old man didn't exactly know what he was doing when he decided to do it. And we gotta GTFO, bro, so think about that, too." I looked at the cover of the journal. "It's not . . . weird?" Candy thought about it and said, "Well . . . I've probably read it a million times, but I don't think anyone would publish it."

It was summer, and I ran the length of the tunnel and climbed the rungs and emerged in the mausoleum. In the spring I'd discovered that I could climb one of the window-slits to the rafters above, and standing on the rafters I could pop open the mausoleum's roof access, and once I was up there I'd strip to my skivvies and soak in the glorious sunlight while reading. This time I was reading Mr. Justin's last written words.

Legi, intellexi, et condemnavi.—
"I read, understood, and condemned."

DENNIS ROBERT JUSTIN— CAPUAN YEAR 12

Has it been twelve years here in Capua already? It has not! It has been one glorious day repeated!

(Those who wish to strip writing of exclamation points, I suppose, would too wish to snap Mayakovsky's spine, like a toothpick, and pitch the two pieces of him into a river.)

(And what about me, then? So many notebooks filled and flicked into the fire. Do I not love myself enough, or do others love themselves too much?)

#####

That is, one wretched day, and then one glorious day repeated, but I only add this note because the lone dissenting vote in my conscience will not allow me to forget all the things I've done that have sent my heart to its own depths, no matter how glorious my life has been otherwise.

#####

Omnia dicta fortiora si dicta Latina.—"Everything said

is stronger if said in Latin."

#####

In my nightmares my brain conjures memories of people from the old world who would tell me stories that were nothing but long self-compliments. I, like everyone else, have such self-praising stories, but I rather enjoy the quiet warmth they create in their golden internal silence. To give those stories away so easily almost feels like a desperate act of self-destruction—emptying the jar in the hopes of filling it. I mention it only because I realize now, in this unrefined cabin of occasionally painful retrospect, that I was guilty of this inglorious behavior myself this past April, in front of Emily, and I literally shudder now when I think about it, and I feel as though I don't want to forgive myself for it. Or at least not easily.

#####

I have no thoughts on a pile of mammalian entrails—bear, deer, eck setera: OFFAL!—because I never look at it. I think my revulsion at the sight is spawned by my revulsion at the thought of my own guts, my insides, what I'm made of so unromantically uncoiled and piled. When it comes to "cleaning" an animal, I am faster than Gandhi during Ramadan and Lent. (Oh, Dennis, you adorable little man, with your hidden guts.)

#####

"The right combination of words changes the world, makes a fortune, seduces the girl, unlocks the cryptic truth, and briefly shows us reassuring order in the complexity of reality. Pity that so few of us strive for the right combination and instead settle for the perfunctory. Pity more for we who strive for the right and so often miss; we do not 'land amongst the stars,' we thud amongst the furrow-brow'd and blank-eyed and sleep fitfully alone and morosely awaken to another chance to break our minds and hearts trying again." —Mohammad Wang

I light my votive candle tonight for every broken heart and mind in the world striving for the right combination of words. The philosophers, poets, comedians, journalists, and storytellers: When any one of them succeeds and creates valuable philosophical, artistic, and/or investigative truth, it is a potential boon to everyone else who will ever live.

#####

A Thought: All summer long the leaves in the trees throw black shadows on the ground, and then in autumn, as the unforgiving air cools, the regretful leaves themselves turn colorful and hurl themselves down where there are no longer any shadows.

#####

I have tried to give the children games, but I do miss American sports. Nevertheless although (and so but then) the children do not see them here in the forest, I do. I know I'm crazy, but to me, to see the trees reaching for the sun's rays . . . it's an endless jump ball, an eternal leap out of bounds for possession. A soaring eagle dives and meets a fluttering bat at sundown— interception! The insects go wild.

The children often ask me what I'm laughing at.

Speaking of which, just yesterday Candy finally cutely inquired (enquired? Look it up, old man! When you're not so sleepy, that is) as to what happened to the hair on top of my head. I told her it fell out when I was her age because I didn't clean up after myself.

Candy briefly went pale, but Big Boy was on to me, and my joke evinced a little chuckle out of that quiet giant.

#####

Am I myself just a cranky child who took his ball and went to live in his tree house? A decade in-country and I still worry about that sometimes—that the most derisive description is the truthful one. But can we have it both ways? Which is it? Children are often regarded as closer to God, and are constantly given praise for their ability to see through adulthood's phoniness, and so if it's true that I'm just a child, how is it that the ridicule should be pointed at the child for ultimately rejecting the whole mess as unacceptably off-putting? Can children help us to see ourselves, or are they incapable of wisdom? I refuse to accept that as usual it's both. I think evolution would probably have it be that children have an inborn knack for finding the best/wisest/most beneficial humans to gravitate towards, so I believe the former. Those who believe the latter will probably ultimately deride me as a cranky child sucking his thumb (at best) in his tree house. I have no problem with that, just as I hope that they ultimately really have no problem with me as a person, because I do not wish to harm anyone who does not wish to harm me. Which is another way in which I'm rather like a child.

I just didn't see any adults I wanted to gravitate towards—their whole scene was shit.

#####

Cuiusvis hominis est errare, nullius nisi insipientis in

255

errore perseverare.—"Anyone can err, but only the fool persists in his fault."

Some women won't let a good question die. Emily has stopped verbally asking, but her body language is constantly begging me—I can see it. And a few years ago Candy Baby started in on me, and she hasn't given up on the verbal nag quite yet, no matter how gruff I get. I've tried to live the answer, and let them figure it out, but they've asked me so many times that I feel like it might not even be them asking but Life or The Universe Itself wondering, or maybe something about my bearing is not that of a man who appears certain about the course of his life, and that's how they're trying to tell me that. Perhaps there is value that I put it into words, so I can see my own *ratio decidendi* ("reasoning for the decision") and judge it just like those two wish to. I don't think I'll ever have the courage to tell them, but here you go, Dennis. Like what you see?

I fled to the wilds when I saw that the alternative—the culture of my homeland—had become warped and dangerous. But I never seemed to be able to explain myself further until I removed myself from it entirely and was lucky enough to have my mind filled with the means of looking at and understanding what I had run away from. Even better, though, I discovered that I had run towards something: I had run towards REALITY.

In the decade after America and the Allies emerged victorious from the Second World War, there was a Baby Boom. American babies were boomed into a world where their motherland had just emerged victoriously on a global battlefield, but they were also born into a world under the constant threat of nuclear annihilation due to the intercontinental rivalry that had grown between the two victorious philosophies/ nation-states: capitalism & America, and communism

& Russia (meanwhile, the formula for the nukes themselves was born in fascist Germany, so go figure).

I've come to believe that in America the combination of being born into a newly matured hegemony (the victors of the world! the "best" of humanity!) but under the threat of instant annihilation from Russia led to the corruption of the American philosophy. Gone was the idea of the long goal—working hard over a lifetime towards betterment and stability—and it was replaced by a wave of unchecked confidence that whatever Americans did and said, seemingly no matter what, was for the betterment of America as well as all of humanity. And as I've said, the threat of instantaneous death made the long-term seem like a foolish thing to ever worry about. And with that unfortunate combination, the pernicious philosophy of the Baby Boomers was solidified: Live only for self-satisfaction in the moment—meaning do whatever you can get away with—because if it's good for me it's good for America and therefore it's automatically also good for the world and the ethically and morally superior choice.

I believe the above philosophy adds up to an attempt at "a birthright of enlightened hedonism," which is a contradiction. There is either hedonism or there is enlightenment, and from my perspective America accelerated its decay by believing its hedonism to be its enlightenment—by confidently leaping into the contradiction.

Ayn Rand once wrote something about how throughout history the more rational side always won the wars, so it's somewhat understandable that Americans felt that they had attained a sort of enlightenment—they had, after all, rid the world of Hitler and helped save the Jews from extinction, which were truly remarkable and honorable achievements. But life is infinitely dynamic, and today's rational champion will be tomorrow's reminiscent drunk unless he or she develops not only a respect for but a wisdom towards the fact that the game is always changing.

The Baby Boomers thought America had won the last game of all time, but the game kept going, and short-term enlightened hedonism largely prevailed in America while the world kept whirling.

Situational ethics reigned; usurious and pernicious, short-term, high-risk banking and business practices were said to be justified by the growth of an economy that had largely stopped actually creating value for or serving the interests of actual American citizens; the Military-Industrial Complex grew exponentially, the driving force behind a foreign-policy spear so savage it led to the joke, "I'm fed up, and I'd leave America, but I'm afraid I'd become a victim of America's foreign policy"; the Welfare State emerged, because with the value of long-term planning gone, many people perpetually needed, or thought they needed, government assistance in the right now. And in addition to that, the self-declared "Americans are always the wisest" concept led to a cultural intransigence where every individual parent and politician was incapable of acknowledging that he or she had culpability in creating a culture where the citizens demanded yet another contradiction: a free lunch. In the midst of all this wretchedness, when they weren't demanding the impossible, the Baby Boomers copulated and self-medicated so indulgently that venereal diseases became a legitimate and then fatal concern, and superbugs arose from the overmedication of impatient (unwise) patients.

I had relatives and knew many people who were Baby

Boomers. They were the kind of people who already know that your ideas are incorrect and frankly inscrutable. They were the kind of people who even when you're right they just stop and think for a second and then say they don't understand, and if they, the chosen born, can't understand it, then it must not be right, argument over, period, end of a sentence that never really began.

Those weren't conversations; I was only an audience that (not who) sometimes rudely voiced unwanted opinions from the void.

With the long future gone, the moment reigned, and nothing is more in the moment than the person experiencing the moment, and another wave overwhelmed American culture and the Baby Boomers: narcissism.

The only time any Baby Boomers ever heard anything I said was when they put my statement through a filter that searched for how the stated words would reflect on their ideas of themselves—not a reflection on the ideas themselves, but a reflection on how the ideas made them feel about themselves inside—and they reacted (not responded, but reacted) accordingly. Why did I run to the woods?

One of my favorite writers once put rather succinctly what I've been struggling to build towards: "America stopped being the best country on earth the moment it believed itself to be the best country on earth."

Consider all of America's trajectories on V-J Day in 1945, when the first Baby Boomer was conceived, and look at America's trajectories today, as the Baby Boomers hit their golden years: Nearly everything is on an unenlightened trajectory towards either chaos or slavery.

I stepped off the train, you could say. You could say I left town. Moved into the woods like one of those mail-bombing crazies. Mme. Rand, shouting up from Hell, might say I've shrugged, like the angel Emily once suggested to me here on Earth.

Indeed I shrug, but only at not being able to do anything.

What kind of effect would it have if I tried to wrestle the ocean? How could I win?

It would have no effect, I would never win, so I did what I could—I sought higher ground.

Odi profanum vulgus et arceo.—"I hate the unholy rabble and keep them away."

#####

The Brave Coward, or, Pathetically Brave

#####

The most crucially important statement of the second half of the twentieth century was declared in Dwight Eisenhower's final speech as President, and almost immediately the profound parting wisdom, FROM A MAN WHO'D DEFEATED THE NAZIS, was ignored by the very people his previous wisdom had saved.

A young man named Randall Sanders was arrested at an airport a long time ago for wearing a shirt that read, "R.I.P. United States of America, BORN July 4, 1776, DIED September 14, 2001." There were many people who immediately dismissed the man as an idiot for not only being wrong but getting the date wrong in his theoretical heresy, but the security forces at the airport weren't as quick to dismiss the, in their word, "threat," and during his trial Mr. Sanders went on to clarify that the fourteenth of the ninth month was "the date Congress passed the Authorization for the Use of Military Force Against Terrorists, which was a war against a military tactic, which was so [expletive] stupid it felt to me like all the brains in the nation must've been up in those towers when they came down, because three days later our government was full of brain-dead retards."

Although the man's freedom of speech was upheld by the Supreme Court, Randall Sanders was shot outside his house a few days after the verdict.

If Mr. Sanders were still alive, I think he and I might've enjoyed having a conversation, and I'd've liked to've talked to him about Pres. Gen. Eisenhower's speech, about how the late Mr. Sanders (among many others) had been raked over the coals because nobody had actually listened to that brilliant old bald bastard's parting wisdom.

#####

Entia non sunt multiplicanda praeter necessitatem.— "Entities must not be multiplied beyond necessity."

Reclining Here In My Cabin And Putting Together A List Of Things That Were Made Worse By The Baby Boomers (In No Particular Order, Just Riffing Here Because I'm Cold And Pissed):

-The Government: it was never great, but it became so corrupt that it fractured, and now Emily says all the world's major systems, whose reins they had their hands on, have collapsed;

-Boxing: the sport of sports in 1945 was turned into another highly corrupt embarrassment;

-The Sexual Act: with moderation it could have been a beautiful and permanent sexual revolution; now with every sexual encounter comes the risk of AIDS, hyperherpes, and supersyphilis; aka Hedonism Casts A Monstrous Shadow, You Assholes;

-The Economy: not only did the tumor of the Military-Industrial Complex tie our economy to wars it was disadvantageous to finish, but the banking executives, at the behest of the government, cannibalized the real-estate market and turned America into a nation with millions of empty homes and millions of homeless people, with a few banks not only owning huge amounts of foreclosed property but being subsidized for their troubles—receiving both the property and the profit; additionally, they fell for the global-capitalism trap that they were adequately warned about, and killed, almost as quickly as it could be done, every middle class in the world in the process; aka Hedonism Casts A Monstrous Shadow, You Assholes;

-Medical Care: insurance is a scam, and that's all anyone ever argued about when it came to American medicine—the coverage, not the care itself, which was above average but enormously wasteful financially, to absolutely everyone's detriment but the revolting insurance companies themselves, who eventually took their greed too far, to where doctors like James and thousands of others chose to destroy their professional names by renouncing all formally recognized medical affiliations and went into practicing medicine like old shamans, visiting villages and offering care for bartered payments of useful goods, because money wasn't worth anything anymore anyway;

-Money: they tried to cure a systemic cancer with end-less artificial blood transfusions, never considering the idea that the transfusions were only feeding the cancer that was killing everything else;

-American Liberty: The War on Drugs, perhaps the most embarrassing and gigantic failure in the history of American governance, and perhaps the biggest U-turn in the history of political philosophy, every one of its proponents should be lashed and feathered for being so contemptuously unAmerican;

-Social Security: scheduled to completely bankrupt the federal government right at the end of the Baby Boomers' lives, now the dead promise of a broken government, but the Boomers sail on from savings generated during a generation of global exploitation;

-Leadership: the last President of the United States who wasn't a corrupt sociopath was completely ignored by the public when he tried to warn them that things might not always be golden if they chose to look past certain American vulnerabilities. Nobody was interested in hearing about vulnerabilities, and the next time they heard about them, in the figure of Ross Perot, who was warning them about the global-capitalism trap, they turned him into the butt of every joke that year. Then our leaders received warnings about a pending Islamo-Fascist terrorist attack on U.S. soil, and the President went on vacation. When the Middle East–based attack happened, the President, a Baby Boomer, was reading to schoolchildren from a book called My Pet Goat.

Why did I leave for the woods?

#####

My Attempt At Fairness: Things The Baby Boomers Improved

-The Civil Rights Movement: Except here's my concern: Was anything really accomplished considering Emily says that people still argue about race constantly and there are still murders and beatings via racism? I would argue that yes, there has been a good amount of progress, but my counter to that counter would be to point out that individual liberty had been growing for hundreds of years before that, and while all races drink from the same water fountains now, Americans also gave up many of their civil rights in that time, too, like, say, the 4th Amendment. Nevertheless, America nominated, elected, and reelected a biracial President, so that's clear proof that there's been some progress, I guess. In short, Civil Rights Movement: Pretty Good. Current State Of Civil Rights: Pretty Bad. Tie goes to the Baby Boomers.

-The Internet—A Baby Boomer named Tim Berners-Lee invented the Internet, which even I have to admit has been a radical change in the world for the better for the most part. Kudos to him, as anything that's a threat to the seated powers has my vote, even though Berners-Lee and the Internet also unintentionally/completely destroyed any reasonable expectation of individual privacy and pretty much set fire to the news, music, and publishing industries.

-Corporate Profits—Hooray and golden days for the son-of-a-bitching crony-capitalists' legalized slavery through the manipulation of federal tax legislation, domestic pricing, and foreign wages. From the numbers, America's economy kept growing and growing, but the numbers represented a laughably small amount of people in the actual American economy.

#####

One last thought on those unenlightened fucks: The other day it occurred to me that in a way the Baby Boomers could generally be described as an entire generation stuck in the terrible twos—a petulant individuation combined with almost zero reality-based wisdom.

#####

Propter vitam vivendi perdere causas.—"To destroy the reasons for living for the sake of life."

#####

Big Boy looked like he wanted to cry again today. I wish it were easier with him, but I don't know how easy I can be without essentially ruining him by granting victory to his copious emotional turns. His sensitivity only seems to be growing. His emotions are oceans and plates big as the world. What am I doing wrong? Oversensitivity is a result of unhealthy levels of self-absorption—passing every glimmer of the universe through your unsatisfied ego. Such sensitivity is a blessing and a curse, if that's saying anything original. I wish I could see as much as he sees; I just wish for him to realize that he's a part of that glimmering world and not some sort of transcendent, disembodied, perfect judger of reality. Do I come across as self-absorbed; is that where he's learning it? You were put into the world, Big Boy. Yes, YOU are a wonderfully magnificent thing worth contemplating, but just imagine how great the universe must be if you were designed to be the subject, to live within the essentially infinite object. But don't pretend you're not part of the object, Big Boy—you're alive, and there's more to life than you. From the outside, my meditation and reflection may appear to be self-absorption to the children, might be where he's learned it and which Candy seems to have avoided completely, but then again I think she might have the opposite problem: She is always so worried about everything and everyone else she might run the risk of having a fundamental collapse of the self, at which point she would be vulnerable to any rhetorical wind that blew in her direction, and she would become easy prey to evil intentions (say what they might

265

about the overbearing nature of the ego, it is better to make decisions ourselves rather than automatically concede to anybody else's ego's request). It might be time to delve more deeply into meditation and prayer with them, religion and philosophy—I have stepped through those areas so delicately; I haven't wanted to color them at all if I could avoid it. I'll see what Emily thinks.

#####

"Write on fire!"
—M. Wang

#####

Big Boy attacked by a grizzly today—a tap on the shoulder from reality? Still too shaken to write it all right now. He did always want an older brother. Not much fun, was it, Big Boy? Some older brothers are worse.

Every day Candy continues a transition from being under my care to being one of my heroes.

Both of them . . . my heart consists of nothing but love.

#####

Sapere aude.—"Dare to be wise."

#####

It's over. We've been found. I don't know what found us today. It was as if the air itself had turned metallic and conscious and curious—a swarm of microscopic, translucent sleigh bubbles that were just all over the place. To me the only thing that's unambiguous right now is that it's over. We'll try to run. Maybe Emily or

James knows where to go next.

I read and reread Mr. Justin's notebook. And reread it again. I read and reread it until the sun burned my skin, and then I brought it back downstairs and headed down to the tunnel, to the shelter, to an important conversation with my sister, with an idea.

Hoc est bellum.— "This is war."

"Candy, no matter where we go or what we do, it's inevitable: We're going to end up in another federal detention facility. I know you want to go to that NLA compound outside Denver, but I just can't get behind the New Government movement lately. I'm sure you've seen the same reports I have. Without Stephen Stone, the NLAs largely just seem to stand for being *against* the Old Government, which is fine, because clearly the Old Government was a broken piece of shit, but I don't see the value in being a martyr for the cause of two and two *not being five*. And anyway, the local governments that allow NLAs in their borders just paint themselves with bull's-eyes, and the CTR Divisions come around and sweep everyone up like Passover. But I don't think they're being taken to another Rushmore this time—I guarantee it's either offshore or underground." I had rather thoroughly deflated Candy's ideas for where to go, but she did have one observation to make:

Regarding the underground detention facilities, she looked around and said, "Like this place." "Yeah—or dead underground." Candy didn't say anything else. "So here's my idea," I said and waited until I had Candy's attention before I continued. "Milton. Blank." Candy furrowed her tawny brows in confusion and searched her memory until she found the name, and her eyes went wide with the possible realization of what I was implying. "Big—! But how? The suburbs—" "Mr. Justin tried to stay out of the way, Can', but you read it in his journal, and we were there: They found him. They found us." Candy said, "Who's this 'they'?— Saxon said it was just that awful Blank guy." "Milton Blank is going to die, you believe your ass, Candy, but he's not the only one." She looked at the ground and then at me, and I held up Mr. Justin's journal. "They've done enough, Candy. It's time for them to go." "Wait— ?" "Yes. As many as I can. You said you wanted to get out of here; well I know where I'm going when I feel ready. You can come with me, and we can go to federal prison for trying to save America from herself, or you can leave whenever you want, without me, and take a chance on whatever life you can make out there. Syl', I really want you with me, but I'm not kidding: I'm going, and it's going to be a bloodbath." "Big, you've *lost your mind*—" Candy started to say, and I played my ace card: "GEORGE!" I shouted it so loud Candy went quiet. "Mr. Justin killed George, Candy, because George was a problem that couldn't be fixed. George was a danger to humanity, and Mr. Justin killed him." Candy was already ready to defend her Daddy, "How the heck do you know?" "'*One wretched day.*' It's right there," I said indicating the journal again. "But Mr. Justin said—" "I was there when you asked him, Can': All he said was that he helped George the best he knew how." There was a long silence while Candy ruminated. She leaned against the wall and continued staring at the ground for quite a while. Eventually she looked at me and said, "Mr. Justin and Miss Thompson and Dr. James all asked me to look after you . . . said that there are ways I could help protect you . . . but I'm not killing anyone, Dante." "That's fine. I just need your brain, Can'—I've got all the killing in the world inside me."

A few days into our now-conjoined training, while all three of us—brother, sister, and dog—were sucking air after a set of sprints in the tunnel, Candy exhaustedly and bemuso-ironically asked, "Why are we even doing this, anyway?" I had given the question too much thought to simply let it go to a rhetorical death, and I said, "Because of the Categorical Imperative." "What?" "Look it up."

Over time, and as our results visibly accumulated, our training turned from dedicated to pathological: We used half of the shelter's munitions stockpile while we practiced our rifle aim by shooting tombstones through the window-slits in the gunpowder-scarred mausoleum, going from aiming for tombstones to aiming for individually engraved letters, and then for certain parts of certain engraved letters; we looked up methodologies for training dogs and trained Tyger to recognize some new commands we could foresee being useful; we turned walks of the tunnel into jogs and then into hard runs; we found a simple set of weights and looked up workouts on the OV and trained with the weights until our bodies were ropes and knots of muscle; Mr. Justin had taught us the basics of self-defense, and through the basics the ability to see more advanced methods of combat, and we returned to that training: I toughened my hands by repeatedly and repeatedly and repeatedly punching the wooden side of a very sturdy crate (full of dried fruit) on a shelf in the pantry, while Candy didn't figure on doing any fighting, and thought the scar tissue on her sinistral hand from all the shooting-training she did had already stripped her hands of enough of their feminine delicacy. She didn't need the hands of a lumberjack; she was an unusually fast runner and planned on doing a lot of flighting if it came to that, because frankly I could handle all the fighting for us both. I had never been punched before, and I needed to see if I could take the pain of getting hit in a fight, but I was worried about unintentionally, reflexively destroying Candy if I let her hit me, so we decided to toughen me up by tying my hands behind my back and letting me learn how to dodge punches while Candy just WHALED on me—I could tell she had great fun with it—thereby somewhat doubly toughening both of her slightly padded (two taped dishrags) fists and my face. And O Doctor, she could bring some friggin' force when she tapped into that hate core Mr. Justin tried to teach us how to tap into when our lives are potentially on the line: that deepest part, your will to live, which can be manipulated into a glowing-blind, protective, adrenaline-fueled beast-rage. I learned I could take at least ten direct raw-muscled Candy Baby hits to the head and still have my wits to keep going, so we stopped because I was starting to feel nauseous and Candy was starting to enjoy herself a little too much.

We trained like we were about to invade a continent.

Scientia Vincere Tenebras—
"Conquering Darkness By Science"

We had one final test on the same day we launched the invasion. We knew the experiment would draw all the wrong kinds of attention, but our plan hinged on an untested theory, and we couldn't "go live" without knowing what would happen when we did it. So Candy Baby found the perfect place—a cul-de-sac of Curly houses across from a shopping center—and I kicked open the doors, and Candy Baby went to the creepy basements and set fire to a box of old magazines, a bookshelf, and a stack of papers: three houses in the sac thirty minutes later were one smoke-billowing inferno—surely a dazzling and smoky enough show in a federally shut-down town to attract the attention of a Peregrine. And soon enough we saw, from where we stood among the shelter's six transported running generators inside a closed-down, broken-into sporting-goods store five-hundred yards from the cul-de-inferno, a straight white streak in the sky turn into a question mark as it split from its course and headed towards Curly to launch an investigative nanotube. Candy and I watched in nervous terror as the drone approached silently. If Candy's theory was right, and if our math was correct, this was about to be one swizzle-stick of a show, and we would have to escape as quickly as we could. And if we were wrong, we were going to have to escape as quickly as we could, if we could at all. The drone came down directly towards us, and we watched its face get bigger and bigger, and then a little phallic doorway on the bottom opened and released a tube that popped apart and turned into the jingling, phosphorescent nano-mist we had seen before. The drone streaked directly over our heads, and Candy yelled, *"Now!"* and I threw the switch on the extraordinarily amplified MedicaMiraco, which, as Candy predicted, exploded like a bomb and ripped apart and set fire to all the generators and gave birth to a powerful electromagnetic pulse. We picked ourselves up off the floor and raced to the window and watched the phosphorescent nano-swarm as it fell to the ground like a calm drizzle of water, and when the air outside was back to normal we ran out of the partly burning store, to the parking lot, to see if we could spot the Peregrine doubling back. We were out on the pavement and looking back over the store's facade when the forest behind the store glowed orange, and the shock and sound of the explosion smashed us like an invisible tidal wave. After the shockwave and explosion, Candy and I looked at each other, and Candy leaped in the air and yelled *"IT WORKED!"* while I incredulously looked into the sky and said *"HOOOOOLY SHIT!"* Then we raced on stolen bicycles the seven miles back to the shelter, to where the packed and prepped and Tyger'd-up van was waiting and ready to go, and we escaped again.

It had been something like six years since the Rushmore tragedy. Candy was now eighteen years old, 5'5", 32-24-34, (approximately; I never asked her specifically,) one-hundred-twenty-one rockoid pounds (we had a scale), with a now-rounded-into-adulthood face: glabrous, pale skin, hazel eyes, her mouth a seemingly permanently empathetic pink pout, with a thin pale scar on her cheek from the explosion that killed Leni. I was twenty-one years old, 6'5", 44-36-40, (there was a tape measure,) two-hundred-forty rockoid pounds, with my admittedly cherublike face: I still wasn't growing much facial hair, so I easily kept clean-shaven and in my opinion facially appeared younger than young Candy—otherwise, physically, after all that training, I was All The Glory Of Man. But of particular worthiness of description as I piloted the puttering van onto the road out of Curly, towards Swanson Falls, were the two sets of the young would-be murderers' eyes—our eyes, Candy's and mine—which I could see faintly in the windshield's reflection. In that reflection our eyes were gleaming from the blue sky above and the dark road ahead, but in the center of those four points of softly reflected concentration, the eyes themselves had the deaths of empires in their purpose.

CTR Team 5 was led by Capt. Perry Heimler, a chewed-up piece of metal who'd served six tours of duty for the former United States of America as a warrior with the Army Rangers. At the onset of the civil unrest, when most soldiers returned home to protect their families and property, some soldiers, the few in Special Forces with no wives or children, opted to continue fighting while being subsidized by the AARBB—an organization with more than one-trillion dollars in savings and that was still holding out in the primitive new economy, and an organization that was seeking, at all costs, to restore and maintain the general and cultural infrastructure of the Old United States of America, to return things to the *status quo antebellum*. Heimler was thirty-eight and had been raised by Boomers and felt in their debt, so he enlisted in the controversial branch of Homeland Security and was able to convince a few of his old soldiers and respected associates to join him in the fight for both profit and America.

CTR Gunner First Class Hector Mass (a surname Americanization given to the family by a hasty customs agent in too much of a xenophobic hurry to write out the full name of Masaleñejo), was a thirty-year-old career soldier who had never married or owned a house or car of his own. *Nomen est omen*—"The name is a sign"; he was a large, muscle-heavy Mexican-American who was truthfully much more into the profit than the cause: His family, still living terribly in the hollow husk of a Mexico that was also shredded by its own domestic insurgencies, desperately needed the money and loot he was sending them from the American fronts the Team fought in. He had a fat face and almost no lips, and the gash of his mouth was always, as Heimler once described it, "frowning from the inside." Aptly named and aptly titled, he was a first-class shooter, and his expertise with firearms made him indispensable to Heimler, who was well aware that Mass lacked a certain exuberance for the cause of restoring America to its former Baby Booming hegemony.

Intelligence Officer Constance "Connie" Caliente was a thirty-five-year-old intelligence operative with experience in many of America's former international war fronts: She'd held positions with the CIA and NSA before all investigative government agencies were moved under the umbrella of Homeland Security after the first collapse. A mix of Italian and Spanish, she had the sort of face and skin that could simultaneously pass for Italian, Spanish, French, Jewish, Arabic, Persian, Greek, and pretty much Miss Armenia. She had a Masters in Linguistics (age twenty-one, U. Chicago) and Foreign Policy (age twenty-three, Harvard Kennedy) and was fluent in nine languages. Through the course of her tradecraft she'd learned she was bisexual, but more importantly she had worked with Heimler overseas. She was swarthy, tallish, thin, and contained the sort of overall beauty that penetrated and fractured most men's intelligence (there are even psychological studies that have proved such a thing really happens), which obviously was beneficial for her job, as she was not interested in men's intelligence but in their secrets. She already had a man. And before that a woman.

The final member of the CTRT5 foursome was a thirty-six-year-old Research and Reconnaissance Specialist named John Shade. "The Shade," as he was called, was, as they say, the last of a dying breed. Formerly the work of R&R had been carried out by usually eight soldiers with existential balls bigger than Poseidon's rage, who'd creep into the night or the bush and probe as far as they could into the enemy's lines, to gather information on troop placements and weaknesses, exposing themselves to potential ten-thousand-to-eight ratios of killing power—in short, literally the most dangerous job on Earth. But since the overwhelming advent of Drone Warfare, the work of R&R warriors had fallen to extreme specialization, but it was a specialization that Heimler needed: Drones could gather objective data, but the Powers That Be still needed human ears for human, non-recorded data-gathering. Such specialized work was highly profitable for people like The Shade and Connie, and CTR Team 5 had been the highest bidder for those pricey services. The Shade's intelligence never fractured from the sight of a beautiful woman or an ugly injustice: He was The Shade, and he was nothing but ears and secrets. He and Connie Caliente were lovers who both viewed marriage as hopelessly atavistic. The Shade was the one of the most ordinary- and normal-looking guys you could imagine. There was not one thing that could be pinned down as unique about his appearance other than the fact that if you looked at him long enough you realized that he looked like dozens of different people you'd known or seen in your life. Any man would be drawn to Connie's rare combination of brains and beauty, but although many women were drawn to the even-keeled, almost protective neutrality of The Shade's personality—he was, after all, tall, approachably handsome, and most importantly not even seeming really to be real, just an idealized fantasy of Manhood for women to project their favorite attributes on—none was so drawn to him as Connie, who was almost obsessively pulled, emotionally and physically, towards his impenetrable mysteries and infrequent but intense personal revelations.

Together the four of them had been the newest iteration of CTRT5 for the past six months, the majority of which had been spent on a mission that had spiraled out of control and was soon to be completed or aborted in favor of something possibly more important.

Coincidentally, The Shade was balls-deep in a university coed when the orders to withdraw came down the line through his earpiece. The young woman below him was the daughter of the president of the university, and she had an extremely tight, hot, wet vagina that made The Shade release his liquid essence faster than he'd ever released it with a woman before, even with Connie. Her name was Bridget, and now the name Bridget was virtually engraved on his distinguished member: Bridget—The Champion, And Don't Tell Connie.

She was a clinger, and she'd fallen for "Professor" Shade hard like the diamonds she was already seeing on her fingers and around her neck and in the little pearl moons of her adorable earlobes—she felt like it was a certainty that he would give her everything she ever wanted now that she had given him everything of herself.

They coitus-uncoiled breathlessly, and Bridget O'Brien snaked her arms and legs around The Shade's body snuggle-style while he stared at the ceiling and tried to figure out the fastest way to get the information out of her now that this connection had been made.

"Do you love me, John?" Bridget asked. She surprised herself, as she didn't intend for that to be what she first said, but it was just that she'd suddenly found herself starved to hear an aural signature to finalize and underscore the lovemaking act.

The Shade brilliantly feigned a deep, personal joy. He leaned up on his elbow and, with his free hand, touched Bridget with one of those affectionate face/neck embraces where the hand is on the side of the neck and the thumb comes up right by the pulse near the ear, and the woman is filled with an intimate thrill. "If you'd asked me what I were thinking about just now, I would have said that I was wondering if it's possible that this is the best moment of my entire life."

Bridget smiled and grinded her tingling love-button into The Shade's bare hip, but she was not completely satisfied. "So, yes? You love me?"

The Shade knew exactly how to play this. He was almost home. He started with a joke.

"Are you trying to get me to go down on you again or something?"

She laughed and faux-pushed him away, finger-tips to his chest.

He took the fingertips into his own and said, "Why, of *course* I love you. Bridget, Snugglepussy; can't you see that it's always been love, from that very first moment? I *love* you."

Oh, yes—her womanly spirit was having its own sort of orgasm, a fulfilling echo of the physical ones from moments ago. She was worthy of being loved by this amazing man and could feel it all throughout herself. She leaned back again like he'd leaned back satisfied before—temporarily and yet completely soul-sated.

"Good," she said, raising her head back up from the pillow, "because I love you so much it turns me into an animal sometimes."

He leaned over and kissed her deeply.

Intelligence Officer Connie Caliente, piloting CTRT5's Peregrine, watched and listened electronically with the rest of the Team at the top of the Drake Hall tower. She knew what The Shade needed, and she knew how to deliver a message, so she deployed a missile that burst above Bridget O'Brien's off-campus house with such a loud explosion as to make young Bridget scream in fright.

"They broke through! They broke through! We're going to die!" She was trembling with fear.

The Shade looked her in the eyes and said, "I have to get you to your family—where are they?"

Bridget didn't even hesitate. She loved this man, and he would soon be a part of that family, and she could tell John about her father's location if she could tell anyone, and she did.

"There's a secret chamber under Ellsworth Hall. It's from the—"

With a balled-up fist, The Shade knocked Bridget O'Brien out cold.

He started getting dressed and said, "You guys hear that?"

"Affirm," Perry Heimler said over the intercom. "Phoning it in now. We'll meet you at the river for exfil."

"Right-right."

Capt. Heimler got on the intercom with his superior officer, who had the amazing name and title—*nomen est omen*—of Gen. Graham Warmaker, or at least with Warmaker's aide-de-camp, Pvt. Jeffery Kennedy, and said, "Kennedy, you there? Heimler here."

A chill ran through Pvt. Kennedy, but he was so used to his job he just continued automatically, and he clicked into the intercom and said, "Heimler there, Kennedy here—go."

"We've got root-good info here says O'Brien is in a bunker below Ellsworth Hall. Copy?"

"Kennedy copy. But sir, are you sure, sure, sure?"

"First, second, third, the answers are all the same."

Kennedy clicked into the intercom and said, "Kennedy copy. Steady one." Then he walked across the hall, into the War Room, and wordlessly summoned Warmaker from the throng of officers and aides cluttered around the map of the campus—wordlessly because Kennedy's face was already telling a story Warmaker wanted to hear.

When they were alone in the hall, Kennedy said, "We finally heard from Heimler, sir—he said they have root-good information that President O'Brien is holed up in a bunker beneath Ellsworth Hall."

"Heimler?" Warmaker asked. "This just happened?"

"Yes, sir—surfaced and reassigned to Dweezil, off to somewhere near Rushmore, from what I gathered."

"Well I'm surprised as a horse's wife to hear they're alive. The good news is that if what they reported is true, we're not going to be here much longer, either. Have CTR Teams 1 and 2 full-drop Ellsworth Hall. This campaign should be over pretty quick if

Heimler really found the snake's head."

The river stank and was cold. In the summer it had been wide, warm, sluggish, and lakelike, but now in autumn it had shrunk to nothing more than a malodorous, freezing, industrialized pane of sewage-black.

The Shade waited on its banks and watched an attack drone rocket several blasts of fireworks down at the ground. A building in silhouette from the fire crumbled into itself from its base, and when it was a flat inferno another attack drone dropped another volley of missiles and churned the building's rubble into a sort of sandy-liquid-fire-tornado.

Then three additional, different-looking drones screamed onto the scene, and a ravenous dronefight took place over the campus. The three arriving, busted-looking-but-operational drones must have been part of the student-army's stockpile, and their pilots were top-notch. The Shade watched impressed, and the whole spectacle was enough to ease the rapid exfil of the rest of the Team, whom The Shade saw walking towards him with their necks craned to watch the dogfight.

"I'm glad we're getting out of here," said Hector Mass. "These little shits give me the heebie-jeebies—they ain't afraid of nothing."

"Remind you of someone?" Heimler asked ball-breakingly.

"No, Cap'—I'm scared of everything," Mass said. "It's why I shoot so good."

The Shade looked around and didn't see Connie. But then, yes: She turned away from the campus and her face was illumined by the screen of her small MOV, which she was looking at with her best listening face, and when she turned off the MOV to address the men who were anticipating her report on their next mission, the grotesque glow of the screen's light was replaced by the far more endearing illumination cast by the fire from the burning campus and the moonlight bouncing off the oily river.

The Swanson Falls Medical Center was formerly the Swanson Falls Elementary School. It became a medical center when the town made the transition the same year the federal government collapsed. When the government dissolved, so too did the majority of hospitals, and now the nearest operational hospital (the old one had federally mandated Do Not Enter warnings on every entryway) was five-hundred miles away. Seeking assured medical help for their ailments and protection from the feral hordes of people and animals that resulted after the collapse, the predominantly wealthy, retired citizens of Swanson Falls pooled most of their money together and financed the metamorphosis of the local police force, turning it into a well-regulated, community militia, and they also offered a contract to a group of unemployed doctors and nurses to convert the already-closed-down elementary school into a new hospital.

When Candy and I arrived on the outskirts of Swanson Falls, after a long and painstakingly secure trip, the town was surrounded by militia checkpoints. And sure enough we followed a shady road into town and found ourselves on the unfriendly end of a pair of rifles by a shack, with a nervous-looking fellow holding a clipboard and waving us towards him, where I rolled the van to a slow stop.

"Names?"

"Dante Thompson."

"Sylvia Thompson."

The man looked at us closer.

"Married or siblings?"

"Adopted siblings."

"He was adopted; I was chosen."

The man humorlessly wrote a lot of stuff down on his clipboard.

"IDs?"

"Stolen in a robbery."

After a bunch more writing, he looked up from the clipboard and asked, "What'ch' doin' here?"

"Looking for work."

"Oh'y'?"

"Yes, sir."

"What kin'a work?"

"Our uncle, this was his van . . . he was apprenticing us to be road doctors, so we know our way a little bit around medicine."

"We can hunt, too. If you give this guy a twenty-two and march him a thousand paces, he could still wing a squirrel's testicle—and you pick which one."

"We're both capable farmers, as well."

More writing.

"No guns allowed in town. You got guns in there?"

"Of course."

"No guns. Hand 'em over."

"Sir, we need someplace to live, so we'll hand them over, but what if I want to go outside of town someday and go hunting in these fine forests? Will I be allowed to use my rifle?"

"We get the gun, you get a receipt, we got an armory. Good-good?"

"Yes, sir."

One of the riflemen came over and joined the first guy in their search of the exterior of the van. Top and bottom and all sides. More information was recorded.

"Please step out of the vehicle."

While Tyger took a leak and the clipboarder

282

rooted around inside the van, the rifleman tapped the barrel of his gun against the brown cross and asked, "What's this about? I seen 'em red and blue before, but not brown."

"Our uncle was a strange guy."

"He was very Christian—said the brown represented the mud from which humanity was given life, and that he was only capable of brown-cross help, not red or blue like Our Savior's blood, which was divine."

"What happened to'm?" the curious man with the clipboard asked as he emerged with our stockpile of ammunition.

"He died at Rushmore."

The air filled with ugly vibes from the men at the checkpoint.

"He was uh NLA?"

We could sense that these men, like most, did not favor NLAs, so Candy said:

"God, no."

"No, he was just helping."

"He was that kind of guy, Christ-like, you know, he, like—"

"He saw the NLAs as, like, lepers—like they needed his help."

"Like I said, he was a real weirdo."

The checkpoint officer asked, "And you? NLAs?"

"Americans, sir."

"Ain't no America anymore."

I could tell the man didn't mean that—that it was some sort of test—and so I pointed at my own chest, at my beating heart, and said, "Yes, there is, sir."

The clipboarder's eyes scoured my face for the truth. Then he put out his hand in greeting and said, "Name's Jim Benson. Welcome to Swanson Falls, y'all—God bless 'Merica."

Rapidly responding to our experiment and escape, three drones R&R saturation-bombed the town of Curly and a wide radius beyond. The town, like all towns by that point, had been R&R bombed before, but never with this quantity, and this time the quantity was able to wriggle enough into some of the airholes outside the tunnel, and into the trap door in the mausoleum, and into the gap under the fake boulder to alert Connie Caliente and CTRT5 to certain areas where they should start their investigation.

It was morning, and the Team was gathered outside of the Roader that they'd driven into Curly from the nearby base at Northshaw. They'd crossed the country and town through the silver mist of the young day and stopped outside of the locked mausoleum as the whispy, ghastly haze was starting to be burned off by brightening sunlight.

Hector Mass fired a bullet through the small lock chaining the mausoleum's wooden doors shut.

"The R-bots found an air pocket behind a wall in the back," Connie said, reading from her MOV and then showing them all on the map provided. "See?"

"Shade, you and Hector check it out while Connie and I go to the Kramer house," Heimler said.

He was behind the wheel before the two could assent, and then Connie slammed the passenger door, too, and the Roader whisked off in an unusual quiet given the beastly vehicle's size and firepower.

Mass turned from the Roader and The Shade was gone, already inside. He stepped into the darkness of the building and looked at the names on the faux-marble walls. The Shade still wasn't in sight.

"John?"

The Shade briefly whistled his location, in the hallway in the back, and Mass headed back there and found The Shade on his knee, picking the lock, which soon clicked.

Based on Connie's map, they quickly found the fake wall, and The Shade, a lifelong fan of mechanical riddles, quickly figured out how the mechanism worked. The wall opened, and Mass pulled up the trap door on the ground behind it, and they both looked down into the pitch-black abyss.

They pulled their oculars into place and turned on the night vision.

When they reached the bottom of the rungs, their NV oculars—even the ocular on Mass's rifle's powerful scope—couldn't penetrate the farthest darkness, which as we know was miles away.

They'd been told to check it out, so they started hiking in.

After they'd hiked for a while in silence and darkness, Hector Mass snickered and said, "I bet you love it down here, Shade."

Perry and Connie had a much easier time on their hands. The Roader brought them to the property, and soon they were both braced behind the hollowed-out boulder, fingertips into the soil.

Heimler said, "One, two, three!"

They both put all their strength into moving the boulder, and instead of the fight they were expecting from mass and gravity, the thing flew open so fast it hit the far end of its pivot and slammed back down, breaking Heimler's left pinky toe.

"SWEET FUCK!" he roared into the air from the pain.

Mass and Shade got along fine in that both didn't say much and didn't want much said. But that dark and that quiet were augers into both of them, and it brought out a discussion.

"Connie upset?"

"Nah—she loves when I fuck rich hot college chicks."

"But she knows that's just, like—"

"Sometimes you know one thing and feel something else."

"*Sheeeit.* All the time. You actually love that O'Brien girl?"

There was a hesitation.

"Nah," The Shade said. "She wasn't anybody."

"*Sheeiiit.* How do you fake it, then? I can't fake it and get away with it—women can always smell my bullshit."

"I don't know, man—I guess if there's people like you, there's people like me."

They hiked a few steps in silence before Mass concluded, "That's fucked."

The Shade did one of those acknowledgements of humor that consists of a smirk and a brief push of air through the nose.

"What'cha gon' do about Connie?"

"She'll get over it," The Shade said. "It's like my girl Joni said, 'Laughing and crying, you know it's the same release.'"

"Joni, huh?" Mass asked, impressed. "Did you get her before Connie?"

That seemed to conclude their talk for now.

Erik Montana was the head of the Swanson Falls Militia, and his breath smelled like the rotting colon of summer roadkill, and maybe he knew it. The air in front of my face pulsed with waves of fresh air and decaying flesh as Montana leaned his head up close to mine while I aimed the barrel of my rifle at the distant paper target, and the pulses of Montana's bad breath placed a significant, noxious obstacle in the way of my instructed mission: making an accurate kill-shot from five-hundred yards.

I squeezed the trigger.

Ten minutes later, the same breath was again in my face, only this time the revolting cloud was punctuated by the words: "And it is my duty and honor to welcome you, Pvt. Dante Marcus Thompson, to the Swanson Falls Defense Force."

We shook hands and turned to the handful of other militiamen who witnessed the ceremony, who all mildly applauded. Afterwards, I chit-chat-met the other men, and the crowd dispersed, but Montana was still there.

"Let's have a talk, son."

"Yes, sir."

"Pvt. Thompson, what're your *goals?*"

"Sir?"

"What do you want to *do* with your life? Where are you *going,* in the grander sense?"

"I can be honest, sir?"

"I expect it, Thompson."

But I didn't know what to say. I obviously couldn't tell Montana the full truth, and I started to panic, bad, sweating cold. I tried to hide it by looking at the ground.

"A fine answer, son," Montana said. "An ephebe in my outfit ain't *got* no goals—the only *goals* he's got are my orders."

"Yes, sir."

Montana paced the room in thought.

"You said you and your sister drove up in that brown-cross medi-van?"

My orders were wise from Montana's perspective and serendipitous from mine: In the event of an attack on the town, I would be the "St. Mary's Overlook"— occupying the bell tower of the St. Mary's church with a big nasty sniper's rifle from the armory; in normal times, I would be a medical assistant at the overcrowded hospital, simultaneously also serving as hospital security.

Montana, evidently, had been quite impressed with me. Or perhaps even the wealthy, securitized suburbs were starting to decay in the stagnant waters of the nation's crippling socio-economic morass, and there was a great, growing need for people with certain skills and energies.

Perry Heimler was the first down the ladder into the shelter. He followed the light from his headlamp down to the floor, and from there he limped over to what he presumed were the light switches, but when he engaged them there was no response.

"Great."

From above, Connie said, "Good-good?"

"Bring an extra light if you've got one in that bag."

It was a few moments before the quiet sounds of Connie's descent reverberated through the room. During that time, Heimler looked around but didn't spot anything strange. When Connie dropped to the bottom, she said, "No lights?"

"No power."

"Yeesh—so how do you want to split up our search?"

"I'll take the doors, you take this room."

Heimler didn't want Connie, in her mental state, being near anything that might remind her of her problems with The Shade's undercover endeavors— like a bed.

"Yes, sir."

From the first bedroom, Heimler brought Connie an OV, which she ran, along with the giant OV, through DataMine. While all of that compiled, she searched the rest of the room and found nothing useful other than noticing that all the weights and tools bore signs of usage—nicks and smudges, fingerprints and discoloration.

Frustrated by the fact that Connie wasn't finding anything useful either, Heimler'd already searched the smaller bedroom and the bathroom—he'd found nothing but the OVs—when he entered the only room left: the "master bedroom." Also nothing—wait, an OV that he walked out to Connie. She was still distracted by her own problems, and she didn't even say anything when he handed it to her, and he walked back to the bedroom in an even surlier mood.

He slammed the closet door open with force to alleviate some of his frustration—he wasn't proud of it, but it was also meant to be a passive-aggressive reminder to his touchy Intelligence Officer to get her stupid head back in the game—and cause-and-effect reigned: Heimler's mighty throw of the door swung the door to the far apex of its turn, and it smacked into the metal stopper with a loud clang.

"Yikes—you all right?" Connie asked from the main room.

Heimler didn't say anything. He was about to slam the door shut when something caught his eye: On the top shelf of the closet, hanging over the lip, was the white tip of a paper iceberg. From how cleaned-up the rest of the shelter had been, Heimler knew an out-of-place sheet of paper was worth climbing up to and grabbing, so he put his good foot on the first shelf and braced himself with his right hand and reached up and grabbed the paper with his left.

"Captain Heimler?" Connie called from the other room.

"Got a note here."

A personal note is the sort of thing that catalyzes the interest of an Intelligence Officer, and instantaneously she was in the room, at his side, helping him down.

He held the note up, and their two headlamps turned the page into a white glowing rectangle of light.

The handwriting was cursive, tiny, neat, and feminine.

Dear Mr. Kramer Or Any Kramers Who Find This Note,

My brother and I lived in your shelter for six-and-a-half years, after our guardians were killed by a falling drone at Rushmore (or imprisoned in the aftermath—we still don't know what happened for sure, but it's been long enough that we've had to bury all our parents in our hearts because some kinds of hope will only drive a person crazy, as we bet you know). We ate your food and used your soap and powder and toothpaste; we ruined all six power generators during one of our stupid experiments at the end of our stay, and generally we behaved like selfish, scared pigs. For all of that, you have both our eternal apologies and our undying gratitude. We have no money—we have nothing to offer you for repayment. We just hope you know that we've decided to leave, to DO SOMETHING about the fact that you ended up wherever you ended up and we ended up here. My hope, which my brother calls dubious, is that you can look at our upcoming endeavors as our repayment. Our acts of revenge will be acts of retribution on behalf of you and ourselves and all of those in humanity who've been wronged by those who will taste the teeth of our indelicate wrath.

You'll be happy, surprised, and/or relieved to know that it was Tyger who led us here. She was being chased by coy-wolves, and we killed the coys, and she loved us after that, and we loved her already.

It's funny in the not-funny way to me, now that I think about it, that we're about to do the same thing again, this time to the coys who chased you and us into these cages.

Bless you and be well and thank you forever,

Sylvia & Dante

"Jesus Christ," Heimler said.

"Whoever these people are, they've cracked," Connie said.

"I'll say," Heimler said.

It didn't take long for Connie to run the terms Sylvia, Dante, and Rushmore through DataMine before the name Emily Thompson came up, and while she did that research Heimler did some research of his own: He took off his boot and sock and looked at his thumb-sized pinky toe.

"OK, Captain Heimler, you ready to hear this?"

Heimler looked up from his foot and said, "Go."

The reader already knows our story; CTRT5 got their first glimpses.

After she finished reading the parts of our DHS bio-docs that weren't classified, she added, "I guess it's not hard to see why they cracked. Their bios are enumerated nightmares, and that's only what we're allowed to see. I mean it makes you wonder what else could have happened—"

"I guess that's why the DHS sent us here with rockets up our asses."

"Well, the DHS *is* responsible for the deaths of the only people in the world who ever loved or looked after these kids, and five days ago the same kids somehow took down a Peregrine: There are plenty of reasons why the DHS sent us."

"And I'm saying I agree, Connie—so let's figure it out. What're they up to?"

"We can do some satellite traces and see if they pick up the kids leaving here—doubt it'll work, but it's worth a shot. And otherwise we've got their OVs."

"Then let's go see if DataMine's finished."

"This place is creepy," said Hector Mass passing through another wooden frame.

"Yeah."

"How much—"

"This is boring. I'm going to run it."

The Shade, an effortless runner, started jogging into the abyss.

"Psh. Enjoy yourself, Shade," Mass pretty much

said to himself. "Ain't fuckin' runnin' unless I have to."

"Can you believe this?" Connie asked. "I mean—"
"These people—" Heimler said. "These kids . . . ."
"This is like three different PhDs' worth of reading material—and they searched for, found, and read it all without raising any DHS flags?"
"This—" Heimler said, looking at the list of titles of books, textbooks, games, documentaries, dramas, comedies, &c.
"Either Sylvia or Dante or both have . . . brains like . . . they're living *Anarchist's Cookbook*s."
"Is this Japanese poetry?"
"Jesus—you name it."
"The Free Education movement once again cracks a whip against the powers that formed it out of greed and laziness. Now we've got a generation of freaks with the means."
"And we gave them the motive."
The mood shifted.
"Connie, I've tolerated it from you once already, and that's my fault, so just know now that if you ever say anything like that again, you're off the Team. *Off.* I don't give two kitten-whiskers about your family ties when it comes to our mission. Ours is but to do and die, Officer Caliente—not to question how we got here!"
"You're right, Captain; I just said it to help us understand, to, like, accurately frame . . . the whole buffalo. I mean one of these kids downloaded everything from advanced textbooks on Underwater Demolition to tons of episodes of an old cartoon called *Squawky Talker*—I think everything, including a significant role the government plays in their motive, matters, if we're going to track them down."

Heimler looked like he wasn't listening. "Captain Heimler?"

Heimler came out of his thoughts. "Hm?"

"Hello? You there?"

"Why was the note on the top shelf?" Heimler wondered aloud. "It's a semi-apologetic letter to a potentially revenant family, but it's behind two closed doors and nine feet off the ground. Why?"

Heimler stood from the big couch and walked to the master bedroom. Connie wasn't following, either mentally or physically, so she just watched.

"Bingo."

Heimler felt like maybe they were starting to make some headway, because that's when The Shade, panting, started knocking on the large, locked metal door from the other side.

"Where's Mass?"

The Shade, heaving for air after his long run, nodded back towards the yawning darkness. When he finally caught his breath, he said, "Captain, permission to step outside and have a word with Connie—just until Mass catches up."

"Granted, but make it quick, and get your damn heads back into it—we still have a long way to go before this A.P. is complete."

The Shade and Connie climbed the ladder up to the top, by the garage, and Perry Heimler paced the dark shelter in thought. It was on his fifteenth lap that he noticed the punched-smooth façade of the crate in the pantry. The wood around the edges was still rough, but a one-foot square in the middle was flattened down from blows, including one I was particularly proud of, which left an indent of my fist right in the center.

Heimler balled his fist and put it into the indentation, which was a polo field compared to the suburban lawn of his own fist.

"It's a goddam shame they're not on our side."

There were no useful leads at the sporting-goods store, which had burned down completely, and the air scanners didn't pick up any unusual traces of anything in the atmosphere there or at the burned houses, so CTR Team 5 got in their Roader and sped off to a small town called Miners Lament, north, on the only lead they had left.

A woman is a human first before she's a lady, even if some people choose not to see it that way. When someone makes an unwanted advance on a lady, she seeks a brave knight to save her; when someone makes an unwanted advance on a *woman,* even a woman as young as eighteen-year-old Sylvia Thompson, the woman has two options: a call for the authorities, or a risked attempt at self-defense.

Enter Lawrence Peter Gallfly: a Baby Boomer living at 235 N. Stoneridge St., perhaps the epitome of his generation. Gallfly's skin was white paste, and he seemed to puff paranoia and hatred into the air as he sat there, eyes raking his field of view, like the rest of them, worshipping every glowing inch of a wall-sized OV—The Beloved, Immortal, Chattering Cyclops. He, (Gallfly,) older, ethical, still seeking to do right in the world, somehow, from his couch, almost never turned away from the Local, National & Global News Reports, which trumpeted their ideas into him and which he magnified and breathed out himself, at the indifferent walls. *"It's pissin' me off,"* is what he often said. He was unsatisfied with how his life had turned out, as if that were a new phenomenon. He'd felt entitled to a great life, and he'd had a relatively safe life, but he was unsatisfied with the quality of it—he wanted more and better—for, my father would argue, Gallfly had lived his life in a revolting and narcissistic ignorance that could only produce such a stubborn hollowness.

Mr. Justin and I might be wrong, but Lawrence Gallfly was a cranky old fuck, and he wasn't the only one. Even the nice ones were only nice on the outside— it seemed.

Author's Break: There were some legitimately good ones. I think Mr. Justin might have been able to make some friends out there if his family life hadn't've gone so thoroughly to the dogs. Hell, Hank Jaggar turned out to be one of my favorite non-Thompsons I've ever known, and I feel relatively certain he and Mr. Justin would have been friends if they'd ever met.

But from Boomer-loaded Swanson Falls really all I can think of are three: Dr. Cohen, a woman named Eileen, and her husband, Manuel. They were all good people, and our father would've liked them, too. I think the reader will eventually see why Candy and I liked Dr. Cohen, but the only "good" stories I have about Eileen and Manuel are that on two separate, unrelated occasions, I caught them off-guard with a medication delivery, and when I walked in, I swear both of them looked about as depressed as anyone I've ever seen. They looked like Mr. Justin looked sometimes.

What made Lawrence Gallfly a contemptible old fuck, besides his aforementioned shallow life and Golden Years spent grunting impotently at the OV, was the fact that he was the type of person who thought his advanced age and medical ailments afforded him the authority to get away with making unwanted advances on young women. Can you blame a fool for making one final misguided stab at happiness at the tail end of a lifetime of such immediate thrusts towards self-gratification?

Well, Candy did.

"Sylvia . . . my Sylvia Divine . . . c'mere a second—I seem to be having some trouble here."

Gallfly labored for breath in those pauses.

Candy rolled her eyes, dropped the bag of medicine on the dish-cluttered kitchen table, and stepped into the foul-smelling living room haunted by Gallfly's belching and farting paste of humanity.

"My oxy tank ain't workin' right—*it's pissin' me off.*"

The only reason Candy even entertained the notion of going over there was because she always liked solving problems, but she felt a bad vibe right away and kind of split her mind into two parts—one part Fixing Mode, the other part Physical Defense Mode—and made her way to the tank by walking between Gallfly and the OV, which, Candy being in the way of the screen, momentarily annoyed Gallfly.

"Did you change the settings on these valves?"

Candy was leaning over the tank, looking at the readings upside-down from over the top due to the way Gallfly had positioned everything, and he had his opportunity: He reached up and pulled the awkward-positioned Candy Baby onto his lap and began working his hands over her clothes and trying to work them under, to her bare skin, where her treasures were.

The instant she realized the moment was serious and not a horrible attempt at humor, she grabbed the wrist of his right arm with her left hand, took the crook of the same arm's elbow with her right hand, and pushed down while she brought her bony knee up and snapped Gallfly's forearm like firewood.

Gallfly, bursting into sudden-bone-pain, threw Candy off of his lap and held up his right arm, and a little less than half of it was dangling grotesquely and uselessly.

"YOU BROKE MY ARM, YOU BITCH! YOU STUPID BITCH!"

He probably said more, but Candy walked out the door and got into the van and had a small heart/panic attack. She felt an overwhelming, nausea-inducing wave of adrenaline and emotion. Wave after wave, in fact. But each time less powerful, less far up the shore.

Within a few minutes she was on the van's new MOV.

"Dispatch, this is Sylvia in White One."

"Go ahead, White One."

"Lawrence Gallfly has a broken arm and needs a doctor."

A few days later, after the brief hearing, Candy Baby passed Erik Montana's Bad Breath Shooting Challenge and became another member of the Swanson Falls Defense Force. From that day forward, when deliveries were required, I would be sent to men like Lawrence Gallfly, who constantly eyed me ruefully, and Candy

Baby would be sent to the widows and spinsters, who spun endless melodramas about disrespectful children and nonexistent grandchildren in the former case and wallowed like pigs in their own undaunted self-obsession in the latter.

O Homines Ad Servitutem Paratos— "Men Fit To Be Slaves"

-Unus Multorum ("One Of Many"), Widower: John Abraham Slauson, b. 1950, 234 Beech Rd., bedridden, a weekly dosage of Dormira commercial opium, administered by drip for pain after a diabetic foot amputation. His house's walls were crowded with lifelike crucifixes. Slauson was not demented, but he never acknowledged my presence in any civilized way—nothing beyond an annoyed grunt. Mr. Slauson watched the OV and reliably snarled, "Every since they put that godawful comm'nist niggry in office . . . Every since they put that tar-black niggry *coon* in the Good Lord Jesus's American White House! . . . Ought've sent all the niggrys back when we could—niggry'd up the whole Jesus-lovin' country!"

-Unus Multorum, Widow: Patricia Emily Fillingsmore, b. 1948, 112 Foxtail Rd., diabetic, a Dulcinea insulin delivery, to be used as directed. "Oh, Sylvia, it's you—please come in, dear. How are you? Wonderful. Is that—? Yes? Well, before you go, won't you have some

tea with me? It's a blend I discovered with my eldest son when I visited him in Santa Barbara! He was working construction on a new housing development there. Please sit. Sylvia, I'll be *insulted* if you don't join a grieving old widow for a sit 'n' a sip for just a bit of your day. That's a girl. You're very kind, child—unlike my children. My eldest son . . . I tried to keep him in line. I gave him and his brother every inch of my soul. And what did they do? They've never done anything! I gave and gave, and I think I gave too much, maybe. I gave them too much of me. Now, can you believe it? they depend on me—their poor mother. They say it's the economy, but I know it's the econo-*me* they mean. M-E. I've made life too good for them—their sacrificing mother wrung her heart out for their benefit. Now? They're downstairs. They both live down there ever since Gary's firm dried up—it's very nice for them, though. It used to be . . . Harold's office. And an exercise room. But Sylvia, I'm *happy* to have them down there now. I'm *fortunate* . . . I'm *blessed* to have them nearby, you know, because— But look at me blathering about my kids. Are you enjoying your tea? I found it with my son Gary years ago, and wouldn't you know it the same kind of tea was mentioned by the handsome young eulogist at the funeral on Sunday, so afterwards I went to the— No, I didn't know the deceased, but he seemed very loved; it was quite beautiful to see everyone there. I just felt . . . what's the word? Shoot. Well I'll just say that if my being there helped in any way, I'm glad to have gone, because going there always helps *me* lately, and the people all seem very rewarded to have me there. Oh, yes—every Saturday and Sunday. Sylvia, I'm *happy* to do it."

-Unus Multorum, Bachelor: Melvin Thomas McGuinn, b. 1955, 502 Lily St., broken leg, Oxycordal for pain as needed. "Oh, it'sth you, Sthylvia—I'm stho happy it'sth you and not that nasthty mean old homophobic *beastht*

they sthent lastht time; why I almostht wasth afraid for my life! Oh but I sthupposthe there will alwaysth be bigotsth. Alwaysth bigotsth. Very sthad. But look at you, you darling little thing, you. Tell me: How ARE you? Well isthn't that justht beautiful to hear on a cold morning like thisth? And look at you wearing that sthkinny old jacket!—child, in thisth weather you bestht button up to your neck: The doctortsth in thisth town are quacksth down to their green feathersth. You catchth a cold you catchth your death here, misthy— and I ain't lyin'! I sthee you like my dollsth—don't worry! Everyone lovesth them: They're my little loving darlingsth. Aren't they justht *to die?* Delishth on a dishth? They're my sthweet pretty little babiesth, and I sthay let the fuddy old Christhtiansth have dollsth on the wall of their sthexy mutilated sthavior. That might be love to them, but my gorgeousth dollsth are my love. What? No! Ha, ha, ha! Sthilly Sthylvia! They are NOT lined up to look at me; thisth isth justht my favorite sthpot in the housthe. It killsth me that you went there, darling, but no, that'sth not why. I sthwear—that'sth hilariousth, though!"

-*Unus Multorum,* Widow: Betsy Elizabeth Hollings-Felix, b. 1957, 211 Spruce Woods Dr., atomized Ventinol for chronic asthma. "So let's see, that was the year suicide surpassed traffic accidents as the leading cause of death in America, and I remember because . . . well, I'm too old to hide in shame anymore, and my grief is just a healthy pain now: You see, one of the suicides that very year—ooh, look out for Petey under your legs; he's feeling awfully social this afternoon, isn't he?—anyway, one of the suicides that year was my son, Alex. Petey, *scram*—I've got company! And then my husband shot himself a month later. Hm? I just . . . I don't know; I got through it. Why, good *morning,* Princess Victoria—so very glad you could join us today. Sylvia, I tell you that cat would sleep through her entire life if you gave her the choice. Anyway, like I was saying, how do you get through anything? You just do. And Mortimer helped. He was Alex's. He was the only one left. *O-kay*, Your Highness, I'll get your food in a minute—*sheesh!* But yes, little Mortie was a darling, handsome old tabby. I poured all my love into him when my men were gone. . . . Now I have all these wonderful treasures with me, and—*Wesley!* Claws off the drapes, mister! Don't make me get the stick!—anyway, what I was trying to say was that they help me cope with . . . how things turned out. And I'm the only reason they're still alive—they're very, very lucky to have me around, and I love them very much."

-*Unus Multorum* Couples: Philip Andrew Baker, b. 1949, and Jane Anne (Collier) Baker, b. 1950, 1179 Manta Blvd., He: syrettes of Phenotyl for diabetes; She: Ripresitol pills for clinical depression: "The Candyman's here, honey!" "Hello, Dante! Getting bigger, I see!" "Big as a cow's house, this one!" "Big as a barn!" "Strong as a roof beam, too, I bet!" "And here shepherding pills. Son, why aren't you out there fixing things for this country?" "What?" "Oh, dear. That's terrible." "That really happened? I thought that was just in a movie." "Well then, I understand, son, I quite understand." "Good God, Pip, that boy of ours is graceful as a tank on those stairs." "Michael—" "Hey, nice lab coat, *Incredible Hulk;* this guy from the hospital or something?" "It's Dante from the hospital, dear—with our medicine, and he's also on security for the town." "Dante, this is our son Michael." "What's up, Dante? My parents giving you shit?" "Ha, yeah, I'm *visiting.* Nah, man—I live here now." "Michael does OVs!" "That's not what you call it, Janey!" "They're not OVs?" "Jane— Pardon my wife, Dante—those pills are a blessing, but I swear they make her . . ." "Nutty as an acorn." "Hey!" "Sorry about them, Dante—what can you do about your parents?"

-Unus Multorum, Widow: Marcia Marie McCloud, b. 1955, 221 Joshua Blvd., Ripresitol pills for clinical depression. "Sylvia, I've been meaning to ask: Are you on any social media? I looked for you on all my favorites and didn't find anything. Yes, an old woman like me can enjoy her time on the OV! In case you've been looking for me, I'm on *TalkLaugh* and *OV Wisdom,* and I'm on *SeeViewer* and *SpinTracts*—you can find all these accounts if you search using my Life License, by the way—anyway, I'm also on *DOCTOR BIGGLES, MyTown, This Life, Me/My,* and *ChickenBeaks*—that place is hilarious. And I tend to troll *MeWorthy.* And of course *RothReport* and *NewsRods.* And sometimes I'll even shout at *OV Rat News.* I'm not afraid to admit I like *NewsRods,* by the way. It's just as good as the other news, only with a little something extra, you know? No offense if you're offended. Sylvia, how old are you, anyway—nine? *Eighteen* and you're not on ANY social media? What do you do with your free time? . . . Oh, I'm sorry, Sylvia; I don't mean to laugh at you, but BOOKS? No, I guess it just seems like that's a waste of your life. We needed books back when . . . Sylvia, we can talk to the entire world now! The entire *world* can hear everything we have to say! It's all happening on your OV! And you're reading books! It's called progress, child—you might want to look into it. You must not have received much of an education. Home-schooled? There you go; no wonder. I guess I'll just say I think you could benefit a lot from listening to everything I have to say—you might learn something."

-Unus Multorum Couples: Holly Marie (Mayhew) Simpson, b. 1952, and Marvin Montgomery Simpson, b. 1949, 5871 Main St., Apt. 5, He and she: various medications for heart, kidney, and blood disorders. "Praise Jesus, he's here!" "The pizza?" "No, Monty! That big ol' boy from the hospital is here with our

rattlesnake—hear that rattle? Hyup, hyup—used to be poison, now it's medicine you hear that rattle." "Praise Jesus." "Say, Dante, boy, I've been thinkin' about what you asked me last time, and I keep comin' back to the same thing: I think this civil war has the potential to be a great thing. Heck, if I was young enough I'd be out there *fightin' for Jesus!*" "Oh, Monty, there you go again." "Well it's true!" "Yeah well I can't argue with him, Dante, 'cause I think he's right! We got all these folks out there so obsessed with theyselves and willing to kill for it; well you know what, if they gonna kill you, you gotta kill them first. What's the use of Jesus if there ain't nobody spreading His word? He said to turn a cheek, but we've been turning our cheek all our lives, and look at us!" "This ain't a retirement!" "Cowering here! Why, there's a world to be won!" "Humanity at stake." "Casey's at the bat!" "We've let the Jews and A-rabs and A-theists have the reins for too long, and look at what we got!" "If there's blood to be shed, I hope it's all shed for Jesus." "You said it, sweetie." "Praise Jesus."

This is me back in the cement oblivion of this oblivious Island, reflecting.

You see, Mr. Justin struggled with it, and so did I: confirmation bias—the temptation of admitting that maybe my understanding of things was cooked and flawed.

Everywhere Mr. Justin looked, before he shrugged and moved to his camp, he saw guilty Baby Boomers and cultural devolution. And that's what I saw, too, when I started to see the pattern he laid out in that journal.

But if you want to find a pattern, you will. Mr.

Justin used to always say that to us, to warn us against projecting our own thoughts onto a universe that is run by its own ideas, independently of ours. He said the brain could turn any man into a fool if it only ever looked for what it wanted to see.

So what of my beloved Categorical Imperative, then? I recall a few nights where I looked up every refutation of it that I could find, but my confirmation was only further entrenched (enbiased) by how incredibly unswayed I was by all the others' attempts. Nevertheless, in that research I discovered that there's a chance my understanding of the concept itself is either flawed or cutting-edge, as my version of it allows for moral value to be based on the individual ego's choices in the existential myriorama of human experience rather than on what Kant seems to have interpreted to be the universe's massive and simple requirements. He says not to treat anyone as a means to an end, and then he treats all of humanity as the means to the end of whatever the universe demands! I say we sit in the seat of consciousness for a reason, a personal reason, and we must strive for harmony with the universe, but certainly not be its doting bitch.

My proverbial wheels kept spinning, looking for better traction.

Did I just *want* to see what Mr. Justin and Candy and I considered to be the Baby Boomers' vast self-involvement, -entitlement, and -esteem overdoses? (Furthermore, did they ever ask themselves any questions this categorically imperative? We've all made calamitous decisions, but how many of *them* shredded their souls and smashed the ruins together looking for one spark of wisdom?)

My entire time at Swanson Falls was a combination of anxieties over being caught before, during, or after the savage crimes I was increasingly worried I didn't even have the conviction to commit. Was I just suffering from a delusional confirmation bias?

I puked a lot.

I exercised even more.

Luckily people never knew the real me.

Mr. Justin always minded, and he'd tried to train me not to, but *they'd* forced me to mind.

I had an agenda. I struggled to find certainty in its virtues, and yet it also felt like the greater dishonor would be to let the Boomers get away with what they'd done to my parents, to me, to my sister, and to this once-better place.

I may have suffered from a confirmation bias. If I did, I still do. The Boomers described *supra* ("above") were just examples. If you look at the list of the dead, you will see their spiritual brothers and sisters in decay.

If I have a confirmation bias, the clinchers were either Candy Baby or Milton W. Blank.

Incepto ne desistam.—
"May I not shrink from my purpose."

When I realized I was really struggling with my will to go through with our plan, I brought up my concerns to Candy one night when she stopped by my dirty room at the hotel. I told her I thought that considering how well we'd blended in, we could probably ride this out for a while.

She slapped me as hard as she could and asked me, "You would *join them?*"

She left without saying anything else, disgusted.

The gymnasium of the school-turned-hospital was a dimly lit, grim place referred to colloquially by the hospital staff as the Terminal Towers, for in order to accommodate the swollen numbers of terminally ill patients in the aging suburb a local contracting firm had converted the gym into what almost looked like the sleeping area of the world's largest tour bus: row after row of stacked individual bed areas, fifteen high, each with adjustable mattresses and personal OVs, with all medical information being fed into an OV in the teaching-lounge-turned-nurses' station, where any terminal-patient health emergencies set off an annoying alarm that always set the staff into motion.

Candy Baby, fully armed, was stalking the corridors of the Terminal Towers as part of her security rounds. In her all-black SFDF security uniform, with her hair tucked into her helmet, and her collar up, she was an androgynous source of serious potential firepower. In their uniforms, all members of the security force, besides individual height and width, looked the same—it was an intended effect.

The doctors and nurses were always supposed to close the drapes on the individual units after riding the lift and visiting the patients. And the patients closed the drapes when the staff forgot—the vain diseased and dying were ashamed of the way they looked as the process of death unraveled.

As she walked the corridors, Candy heard many mumbled prayers, clenched weeping sounds, incontinent flatulence. Everything in the Towers sounded so sad to her—even just the sound of someone quietly watching something ordinary made her sad when she walked by.

It was a process she wasn't used to—all the deaths in her life had been sudden as Hell.

She found it disgraceful, tragic, and somehow

obscene. Morose? There was something very wrong in there, but she didn't know what.

Her MOV, which she'd forgotten to turn down, burst with a voice, "SYLVIA, STATION WHITE ONE FOR DOCTOR TRANSPORT."

Candy quickly lowered the volume and replied. "Good-good, Annie. Address?"

"2215 Deep Woods Drive. Patient: Milton Walter Blank reporting symptoms of an M.I.—meet Dr. Cohen by Bay One ASAP."

The retired and cloistered Milton W. Blank had surfaced—and Candy knew she couldn't let him die still holding onto his secrets, without paying any sort of moral bill.

As calmly as she could, she said, "Good-good," and then she broke into a dead sprint to the van.

Most of Swanson Falls was a fungible pattern of "Mini-McMansions" that were erected in the late '90s and early '00s—before the Baby Boomers collapsed the real-estate market. The streets of Swanson Falls were gridded, and the plots of property were evenly divided. But not everywhere. At the far north end of town, near the falls themselves, there was a cul-de-sac of full-scale mansions, which Candy and I didn't even know about until Candy drove Dr. Cohen up the nearly hidden dirt road that led to them. The mansions stood in the forest, by the river, near the falls, and they were large, dark, and looked like an unnatural, gothic imposition. The forest was one thing, and these spiky "houses" were something quite foreign—gargoyles creating corners in a piece of landscape art.

Candy seemed to be accelerating the closer she got to Blank's gargoyle, to the point that she noticed

Dr. Cohen's hands clench into nervous fists.

But she stopped the van rapidly without skidding the tires, and both medical attaches bolted out of the vehicle and towards the panicked, overweight woman flapping her flabby flipper-arms in the doorway.

"Hurry! Hurry!" the woman blubbered. "The kitchen! Straight back!"

The inside of the house was as dark as the shadowy forest outside, but there was a rectangle of light at the back of the otherwise deep-hued, huge foyer, and Candy followed Dr. Cohen's surprisingly fast waddle to the body on the floor, with his back leaning against the cabinets, his face pinched in pain, his hands clenched to his chest.

"Help me, doc! Help me!" the frail old man pleaded. "This is it—this is it! It *hurts!* Oh, God, I'm dying. Oh, *God!*"

"Are you helping him?!" the wheezing wife asked as she finally reached the kitchen. "He still looks *sick!*"

Leaning over Blank, checking the patient's pulse, Dr. Cohen said, "Sylvia—"

Candy knew what that meant, and she turned to the woman and said, "Ma'am, the doctor is tending to him—please go to the other room and give us the space we need to do our jobs."

"Why—I'm just trying to help! You're not helping him! What are you doing? He's dying! Help him!"

Mrs. Paula Jane (Sneed) Blank was much bigger than Candy Baby, and the big fat old woman tried to push the little Security Nurse away so she could really get right up into the doctor's face with her rapidly devolving mind-state, in order to spur him to a quicker cure and better care, but Candy and I had rather extensively trained for moments like this—or at least kind of like this.

There are pressure points on the body that if properly manipulated by outside contact can quickly render someone unconscious, and you can bet your bottom dollar that that was a physical language Candy—the innocent, who left all the brutal people-killing to her violent-hearted brother, me—had become fluent in while training for the mission.

Within three seconds of the woman's attempt to push Candy out of the way, the disagreeable woman was unconscious and being guided safely to the ground, braced by the petite-but-powerful teenager.

"Need anything?" she asked Dr. Cohen, who looked up, saw the woman on the ground, and said, "Yes, a SterileBurst from the van—we have to stent him here, right now. Drag her to the foyer and cuff her to that ugly statue so she doesn't come charging in during the procedure."

Dr. Cohen was speaking into his MOV while Candy drove them back to the hospital. "Patient Milton Walter Blank: acute arterial occlusion, blue on arrival, proceeded with routine PCI, intrascaffolded with SmartStents. Flow back to ninety-eight effective. Note: patient deceased for two minutes during procedure, revived with Chalker's CPR. Breathing and biocounts stable now. Traditional post-surgical follow-ups recommended. Given medication history, ten p.o. daily of Rystorcia. Incident Report: Patient's wife was dolorous and tried to assault Security Nurse Sylvia Thompson, who rendered the woman immobilized—How did you do that, Sylvia?" He kept recording as Candy said flatly, "Pressure points." Dr. Cohen, one of the only good Boomers, and a very good doctor, chuckled and said into the MOV, "Rendered the woman unconscious using pressure points."

Candy had barely heard the old doctor's question, and her quiet, flat reply was wrought from the fact that most of her brain's conscious processes were poring over a brand-new memory.

Candy was in the foyer checking on the moaning, unconscious, handcuffed Paula Blank when Dr. Cohen emerged from the sterilized kitchen and said, "OK, then, that's done. Be a dear and clean up my equipment in there while I bring this one back to the world and tell her what happened. The patient is up and should be talking—he needs to be on his way to health."

"Sure," Candy said and nervously walked back into the kitchen, where Milton Blank was looking at a pool of his own blood on the ground, from the surgery. Then he looked up at Candy.

"You the nurse?" he asked, his breath wheezing but his skin already much more normally colored than when she'd arrived.

"Nurse and security, yes," Candy said, almost shivering from fear of being discovered.

"What's your name?"

". . . Sylvia."

"Sylvia . . . Sylvia . . . ."

She wasn't just going to stand there and let him remember, so she began to clean up noisily.

"Is there any chance you know who I am, was, Sylvia?"

Candy's heart pounded in her chest. "I'm sorry—I don't follow."

"Milton Blank. Do you know that name? You remember who I was?"

The doctor's equipment was packed into the kit-bag, but her hands, holding the bag, couldn't feel anything anymore. She trembled, but besides that she no longer had a physical body: Her entire physical existence was fear.

"I'm afraid not," she said.

She sprayed the bloody tiles on the floor with a cleaning solution and got on her shaky hands and knees and wiped up the blood while Blank looked down at her with scorn and spoke.

"Of course not. I tried to save this goddam country, is who I am, was, and here I am, dying like any old *dog*—a national hero, a man who did his best for the land that he loved, and for what? For a generation of kids who just threw it all away—with no respect for the people who actually tried to give them the best world they could."

She had so many things she wanted to say, but her fear was the fear of being caught before she and I could give the Blanks our full reply, so as she finished wiping up the floor she said, "There's always hope, Mr. Blank—maybe instead of throwing it away we just let someone else have it for too long."

That unusual response cleared Blank's head, and he emerged from the depths of his indulgent woe-is-me. For a moment he smirked, and then the clouds returned, and his brows furrowed, and he looked at Candy and said, "Do I know you?"

"Yes," Candy said, eyeing the room to be sure that she was done and facing Blank: "I'm the Security Nurse, and I'm leaving. Goodbye, Mr. Blank—I'm sure I'll see you again."

The specific memory in Candy's mind was the way Milton Blank stared at her intensely—scouring his memory and her face as she left.

Her stomach filled with knots when she realized that she and I now had less than two days to complete our mission and escape Swanson Falls.

Damnatio Memoriae— "Damnation Of Memory," or "People Who Are Pretended Never To Have Existed"

The Northshaw District 5 Federal Detention Facility in Miners Lament was a former federal penitentiary and unofficially still was. The max.-capacity and -security prison was the darling of the former federal government and currently housed the majority of the former republic's most dangerous male criminals and political threats.

After the Rushmore fiasco, the former feds swept into the burnt, shrapnel-torn camp and arrested any surviving NLAs and sent them to the Northshaw 5.

Perry Heimler and Connie Caliente sat in a square grey room that had one table, two chairs, and a thickly grated, frosted window. In the hallway they heard the clack of footsteps and the jingle of chains, and the door's knob was turned forcefully. The door flew open, and Warden James Kilpatrick ('58, Motherfucking Boomer) loped into the room and called behind himself, "Two more chairs."

He said to Heimler, "You say the DHS wanted him—well, here's your God-damned traitor."

The jingling sounds reached the doorway, which was darkened by something in a prisoner's uniform. It was not a man, but it was not an animal. Perhaps it was a man's soul in gnarled cloth?

Face and arms pale as moonlight, the withering skeleton serving as a pathetic clothes hanger that was

313

holding up a vile fabric of inflamed and suppurating sores—not a single thread of muscle between skin and bone. The eyes bulbous, blue, and uncomprehending, the face otherwise covered by a rat's nest of a pale-blond, -grey beard, the long hairs omnidirectional, the skin so white it looked blue and pink where the veins glowed through. The smell was the smell of waste and decay.

A guard brought in two more folding chairs and left, and Kilpatrick motioned for the prisoner to take a seat, but the prisoner just looked at the warden and then continued looking around the room, seemingly blown away by everything it was possible to see in there.

Kilpatrick again gestured for the prisoner to take a seat, but the prisoner didn't notice it among the billions of other phenomena he was ecstatically enjoying taking in.

"Prisoner, *take a seat!*"

The warden took the prisoner by the neck and led him to the chair and shoved him down. Connie and Heimler watched with pity as the brutalized man just accepted the treatment and went with it.

"This is Rhysdale?" Heimler asked. "This *thing* doesn't look anything like the man in the photo on file."

"He's been a very stubborn guest," the warden said. "We've had to teach him some manners."

"By incrementally killing him?" Connie asked, unable to restrain her disgust.

"Captain Heimler, would you be so kind as to keep your little pug from yapping?"

Heimler put his arm across Connie's way, pulling rank, to bar her eruption.

"Warden Kilpatrick, may we have a few moments alone with this man?"

"Absolutely . . . not."

It descended into a battle of eye contact, and

anywhere else in the world Capt. Perry Heimler would have been able to impose his will and get his way, but not at Northshaw 5. So Heimler grinded his teeth momentarily and said, *"Fine."*

He turned towards Rhysdale, who was staring at Officer Caliente like he'd just discovered Religion, and asked Rhysdale's face a question.

"Are you Saxon Neal Rhysdale, born January fourth, nineteen-eighty-five?"

The former M. Sgt. was utterly euphoric to see such a pretty sight up close and in real life. *Look at that woman's beautiful face. Whatever they're saying must be for her benefit. I'm here to help her, and she wants me to help her, and she's so pretty.*

"ANSWER THE QUESTION!" Kilpatrick roared and slammed his fist on the table, which shook Rhysdale's reverie, and the prisoner shrank back a little bit—into his seat and himself.

"Can you at least just confirm for me that you're Saxon Rhysdale? I have some questions for you about Dante and Sylvia Thompson. You remember them?"

Rhysdale looked at Heimler and appeared as though he really wanted to tell him the truth, but he simply couldn't form any words at the moment—this was all too new. Who were these people? Where'd that woman go? There she was!

"PRISONER!"

He felt himself being choked, but as long as whoever was choking him didn't cover Rhysdale's eyes, it didn't matter really. He could die looking at that pretty lady's concerned face—it'd be a pleasure.

But then the choking was gone, and the two men were yelling, and the woman seemed even more concerned. She was even pretty when she was worried. Look at her lower lip! He had to say something! Say something!

His throat made a groan. The woman noticed! She called the attention of the men, and she looked at him again and encouraged him to speak.

He wanted to tell her he loved her. It was the only thing there was to say. She had brought him out of that hole in the mine—she was literally an angel; she must have been—and he was desperate to thank her for bringing him to what must be Heaven. In profound gratitude, he dug deep inside himself and bellowed the song that sang in his heart.

"Down go the Blanks!"

All the faces were looking at him with the same look, even the angel's.

Heimler asked, "What?"

"More of this nonsense again?" the warden asked. "I warned you this man is insane."

"Down go the Blanks!"

"What's that mean, warden?"

"Down go the Blanks!"

"It doesn't mean anything—it's just what he says," the warden said and again put his hands on the prisoner. "Silence! Answer the man!" he shouted and shook Rhysdale until the wretched bag of bones stopped howling his slogan.

The warden said disgustedly, "Guard!—take him back."

The stinking, crying, resisting pile of death was escorted out of the room by a dead-eyed guard, with the desperate prisoner pleading wordlessly to his angel for help—who only watched him get dragged back to Hell.

The warden looked at Heimler and Caliente and momentarily dropped all the pretense and shrillness from his voice and demeanor. "It's all he says anymore—like he's touched," the warden said. "He just screams it into the darkness:

"'Down go the blanks.'"

After that, CTRT5's leads on us Thompsons went dry, and they spent two months following Heimler's guesses until the Swanson Falls Defense Force finally updated their rolls and submitted them to the DHS after a special request from DHS Secretary Frank Savage, and DataMine immediately scooped up two important names.

Mr. Justin's camp was nearing the weather-shredded end of its first decay, and all day long above them helicopters had roared back and forth while CTRT5 investigated the area for the second time. While they were digging through the remains of the remains, Heimler and Caliente's MOVs chirped to life, alerting them both to the fact that the DM dweebs had located the two siblings on the rolls of a suburban defense force a fifteen-hour drive away.

Heimler said to Connie, "Too far—is there a flight?"

Connie checked her MOV for flights and said, "Domestic air has been suspended, and all our planes are taking troops and trucks to Chicago."

"Christ," Heimler said. "What about all these helicopters?

Connie checked.

"Savage is using them all for his big—"

"Right . . . Right," Heimler said. "Must be why Dweezil is being such a prick about this—can't risk anything."

"Definitely," Connie said. "Which means we've got to get going right now. I'll go tell John and Hector."

Quo Amplius Eo Amplius—
"Something More Beyond Plenty"

Milton W. Blank awoke in the middle of the night. As he rose out of his deep sleep, he felt like he was remembering something, and the memory drew him into the world, but as he came awake he couldn't remember what it was. And then he heard a groan, and he remembered it was a groan he was remembering, and his eyes opened wide and he looked around.

At the foot of the bed his wife was moaning unconsciously, tied to one of the metal chairs from the kitchen.

Then he noticed that his own hands were also bound and tied tight to the steel bedpost.

He tried to scream for help, but his mouth was taped shut.

"Good morning, sunshine," Candy Baby said. "Remember me?"

Blank looked at her in fear and confusion, then vague recognition, then real fear.

"You had a hunch, huh?" Candy said. "Thought so. That's why we're here already. Just as you were starting to feel better finally—too bad."

I stepped out of the shadows and towered over the desiccated parasite that (not who) shivered in terror. I said, "We need to have a talk, old man, and here's the rules: You scream for help, the tape goes back on, and I go lose my virginity inside your fat wife, and then I kill her, and then I kill you."

"It'll just be a talk," Candy said. "We just want to hear your side of it."

Throughout most of that, Blank's chest rose and

318

fell rapidly—his body was otherwise tensely rigid from his panic—but Candy always had a real nice way with people, and ultimately Blank believed her as much as he believed me.

"OK, here we go," Candy said and approached the shivering old man's head while I held a handgun to Paula Blank's brain stem.

The layers of duct tape came off with an audible ripping sound, and Blank moaned briefly.

"I do remember you from before my procedure, miss, but I can't quite remember why," Blank said. "It's right there, but I don't have it. I am afraid of you; I know that much."

"You'll figure it out soon enough," I said.

"Mr. Blank, do you remember an American named Dennis Robert Justin?"

In his long career, Milton Blank had overseen the operational logistics of more than seven-thousand Action Plans, so that name too was a vague piece of trivia that didn't quite rise to the surface.

"We've seen your medical records, Mr. Blank—we know you don't have dementia."

"I'm trying, miss—it's fuzzy. It's been a . . . long life."

"How about Project Velvet Waves—is that also fuzzy?"

It was not. Milton Blank's memory of Project Velvet Waves rose ugly and putrescent to the surface, and consequently his face drained of what little color that had remained.

"You two, you were there on the river, on that boat!"

Candy said, "Hey, look at that, B—he remembers killing our father."

"That wasn't my fault!" Blank said. "Do you know what kind of *pressure* we were under to—"

But rudely I didn't let him finish that sentence. I walked over and held a pillow over Blank's face and snapped the old man's left thumb. The pillow absorbed most of the pain-howl.

Candy walked over and jammed a local anesthetic into the thumb's nerves, and the shrieking stopped.

"There's another rule," I hissed. "You're only allowed to talk when answering our questions. That's a rule I just made up just now because I had to, because I see that you have a lot of things to say that don't matter to me."

Blank looked to Candy for help. "I can only help with the pain, Milton—you think anybody in the world could stop that animal over there? I'm just trying to keep this from being too gruesome for you and Paula—we just want information."

"Are you ready, or would you like me to give your wife the old wake-up thumb?"

"What information?"

"Tell us about Velvet Waves—every word of it."

The sweaty Blank, as well as he could, tried to explain the decision-making and the process behind the dreadful incident. Rather than blaming himself, he repeatedly bemoaned "the times."

"So my father and that National Guard team were just a means to an end—some failed experiment? Some disastrously hubris-driven *experimentum crucis?*"

"Young man, I've already admitted to you that they weren't honorable times—"

I leaned in close and grated the words into his ear: "Old man, the *times* were dishonorable because the *leaders* were dishonorable."

"How do you make it?" Candy asked.

It looked like it was a relief for Blank to look away from me. He said to Candy, "I can't tell you that."

"If you can't tell us that," I said, moving to the foot of the bed, "can you watch your wife bleed to death?"

"What? No, no, no, no—son, if I tell you . . . ."

"We'd have the ability to kill people? Mr. Blank, I assure you that we already do."

I unsheathed my knife, grabbed the ethered-unconscious Paula Blank's head and exposed her neck, where I glinted the knife-moonlight's reflection across the old man's face.

"Jesus, please no, please, Jesus, no, please!"

"We want information, Mr. Blank—we have a broader view in mind than mere vengeance, and clearly we love innocent people more than you do. But who's innocent anymore? We seek that kind of knowledge. Today, we'd like to see the key that unlocked our father's mind. The sandbag that dropped his final curtain. You can understand that, right?"

"What will you do with it?"

"Nothing worse than what you did with it."

"Mr. Blank, your wife has three seconds to live: Three. Two."

"Atomized MDMA, Devil's Breath, Doxologica, and dried astras foraker. That's Velvet Waves."

Candy and I, both hardcore shelter-students of chemistry, looked at each other and simultaneously said, "Oh, shit."

I don't know what quantities of each," Blank said. "You'd have to ask the lab coats."

We were nearly certain Blank hadn't lied to us, because at least my understanding of the chemicals mentioned had the potential to produce the results that killed Mr. Justin. MDMA for the existential plea-sure, Devil's Breath to temporarily cut off conscious movement, a shit-ton of Doxologica to spike empathy all the way up to love, and dried astras foraker as a wild goddam catalyst.

Candy sat down at the desk out of Blank's sight and began assembling a vial of her best guess at a makeshift Velvet Waves using the vast *materia medica* she'd incrementally collected from the hospital and medi-van in order to extract whatever exact ingredients would be needed when it came to gametime—right now.

"What about Rushmore?" I asked. "My sister and I have done six years of research, and we've never seen a single report that actually matched what we saw before we escaped."

Fearing that we knew more than we'd let on, and that maybe somehow honesty would save the bound Blanks' lives, the old man described the CTR false-flag attack—Operation Jolly Roger—and its intended and successful effect of undermining the small bit of NLA/New Government progress produced by Stephen Stone's speeches and leadership and ideas.

"You stopped it because it was *working?*" Candy asked derisively from the corner, nearly betraying her role as Good Cop.

"Two psychopathic teenagers couldn't be expected to understand the compl—"

Kablammo—the oldest man I've ever punched in the face.

"I'm real smart," I said in an intentionally stupid-sounding way. "Explainz it to me big brayns, dawktuh."

Despite his circumstances, Blank gave me a look before he spoke.

"Don't you see how it would have been the *death of America?* We gave you traitors that useless land because we wanted to show you all to be helpless fools, but that dead idiot Tramp and that treasonous Stone started making it work, and the growing numbers of people willfully entering that Freedom Zone made us look ineffective, evil even, and I certainly couldn't sit around while the greatest nation in the world was undermined by some ignorant anarchist sideshow!"

I lost my temper again and did the old pillow-muffled finger-break. Left index. Blank shrieked into the downy feathers for a while before Candy grew too annoyed and came over and numbed him and then returned to the light from the desk lamp in the corner where she was working—the desk looked like a little laboratory.

I said, "A whole generation and nothing but vanity, narcissism, and cowardice—all the way to the grave. How truly pathetic. Or is it 'piteous'?"

"Both," Candy chimed in from the corner.

"It is both," I agreed.

"You kids don't know what you're talking about; you don't know what you're doing!"

"Well then you'd think you and I would get along better considering we have so much in common."

"Finished," Candy announced from the corner.

Phase One was almost complete.

"Excellent."

Candy grabbed two gas masks from a large black canvas bag in the corner and tossed one to me.

Then, to make the moment real horrorshow for the doomed Boomer, I dramatically brandished a hypodermic needle that was brimming with a clear liquid.

"You know what this is, Milt'?"

Blank just looked at me, the shadowy mountain holding a needle.

"This is enough magic juice to turn Mrs. Blank over there into the hormonal equivalent of Mr. Blank for about a day."

I expertly plunged the hormones into Paula's neckblood. She still didn't awaken, so I put my hand over her mouth and noogied her sternum painfully until she shot awake, and she screamed into my palm, and I grated some words into her ear, *Be quiet or you're dead.*

Some women know a good threat when they hear one.

"What's happening here, Miltie?" Paula asked after I felt her calm down a little and let her go.

"Just a little friendly Q and A, Mrs. Blank," Candy said. "My brother has a few questions for you."

"Miltie, are you OK?"

"He's a peach," I said. "Right, Miltie?"

Milton nodded slowly, with a tear down his cheek, and said, "I love you, dear."

"What's happening, Miltie? Why do I feel so strange? Have I been drugged?"

Slap—big slap. The only woman I've ever slapped. Silence.

"Paula Sneed Blank, seventy-five percent of your husband's savings didn't come from his salary and is nearly impossible to trace. Did you ever ask poor old Miltie where the money was coming from?"

For a moment Paula Blank could have been our old picture-dictionary's entry for "Guilt."

"Your husband was a corrupt bureaucratic monster, and you never took a moment to ask yourself if you should stay with him?"

"I did ask myself," the woman said sadly. "But I loved him. I love him."

"And we loved our family, bitch," Candy said. "This is done. Masks on."

"What's happening?"

"I love you, honey."

"What's happening, dear?"

I put on my mask and hurled Candy's prepared vial against the wall, and the air puffed with mist.

When both Blanks were finally and grotesquely blue in the face and dead throughout, Candy and I went downstairs, outside, under the glassy night sky, and hugged each other and cried silently with rage and hate and mourning, until the tides of emotion were a gift—a fuel to burn, to finish what had only just begun.

The shortest distance between two points is a straight line as the crow flies, and the shortest distance between two points for CTR Team 5 was a jaggedly straight line as the Roader goes.

The Shade was the sort of driver who could bring an engine to orgasm—he drove the Roader as hard as that militarized engine could take it, and CTR Team 5 sped towards Swanson Falls at one-hundred-forty miles per hour on a direct path from Mr. Justin's old camp.

Even past a hundred in a Roader the world feels normal after a few moments.

The seating arrangements over the course of the day's drive: The Shade was behind the wheel the whole time, Hector Mass was up top manning the .75 caliber, Perry Heimler was asleep in the back, next to a console occupied by Connie Caliente, who was trying to use various DHS channels to contact the Swanson Falls Defense Force.

Without prior contact, they could try a white-flag arrival, but they'd still be at risk of coming under fire by the entire town's defensive shield if they were mistakenly viewed as a false-flag technical, and besides the unannounced, unhelpful first impression, even the best Roader could only handle so much attacking force. Swanson Falls had an armory like few others in the former America, and Connie started to grow worried when repeated attempts failed to yield a response from the militia's HQ.

"What's going on out there?" Connie asked herself.

"What do the drones show?" Heimler said in a sleepy tone.

"Typical suburb last time I checked, but no time like the present for another look."

An interesting story spreads like wildfire—and consequently by midmorning three-quarters of the Swanson Falls Defense Force had gathered around the Blank property, each hoping to see if he or she could get a look at the possibly apocryphal scene being described around town as some kind of macabre double-suicide or -murder.

In the Roader, Caliente said, "Wow, look at all those trucks and soldiers at that one house."

"Whose property is it?" Heimler asked.

Connie shuffled through the town's DigiRecords and went pale: "Milton Blank." She frowned and said, "Captain Heimler, d—"

"'*Down go the Blanks,*'" Heimler said with enraged frustration. "Jesus Christ—how the fuck did we miss that?"

"Captain Heimler, I'm seeing the property right now, and it looks like maybe the Blanks really did go down," said Connie. "It's swarming with members of the SFDF."

"You'd better be wrong, for all our sakes," said Heimler, who angled his head towards the front of the Roader. "Shade, how long?"

The Shade looked back and shook his head no, meaning: Even though they were taking advantage of the Roader's All-Terrains and cutting across the plains of a defunct farm and keeping away from the trap-laden roads, which were all but useless for travel anymore (Candy and I had painstakingly taken the back roads from Curly to Swanson Falls after we came upon a wall of guns one day and I almost flipped the van), they still had quite a long distance to go.

All day on the drive the sun bloomed and rose and

now was falling.

CTR Team 5 was well ahead of schedule, but they wouldn't arrive at Swanson Falls until nighttime, and by nighttime the whole suburb was a hellish scene.

Many men's sexual drives are catalyzed largely by visuals, and if OVs were good for anything they were good for providing horny viewers with literally millions upon millions of pornographic pictures and movies, and consequently I had fallen into the same sexually self-stroked abyss as many men from my cloistered and nearly hopeless generation.

OV pornography didn't offer Candy the same pressure-relief system, and consequently the first time Candy saw Dr. Jonathan Gold, OBGYN, whatever machinations that power a woman's internal sexual desires—and considering how I eventually lost my virginity, those machinations remain a complete mystery to me—went into a sort of warm overdrive, and she stood there in reverie, vacillating between a powerful physical need and the anxiety that comes with that kind of vulnerability. Desperately hot and cold at the same time.

It's what makes us all mutes when we first see a person we desire in a way that has the momentum of billions of years of life behind it. It can be overwhelming.

Many times we try to acclimate ourselves to the person by attempting to linger in their physical presence while under other pretenses. *Oh, you're in the Break Room, Dr. Gold? Why, I was just passing through here on my rounds. What a coincidence.* That was a talk Candy had solely in her head while taking her sweet time checking the Break Room for any possible terrorist activity, once almost saying something to the coffee-brewing doctor, but then stopping when the doctor turned towards her.

Sometimes the person doesn't notice; sometimes the person notices and doesn't want to have noticed and so pretends to remain oblivious; and sometimes the person notices and wants to have noticed and seductively corners the young quiet girl late at night in the break room and says, "I thought I might introduce myself."

Given the odds of her ending up back in a federal prison, Candy Baby wasn't interested in taking things slowly once she knew that the doctor liked her like she liked him. She made that obvious, and the good doctor—thirty-four years old and given verbal permission to do "whatever" he wanted with the thin, blonde, kind, strong, beautiful eighteen-year-old woman—was only too happy to oblige.

They obliged each other quite often after that.

And in the afternoon the day after the Blank interrogation, Candy Baby, who was fulfilling a part of the plan as well as trying to empty her head of the gruesome memories of the sexuo-suffocating deaths of Milton and Paula Blank, rocked the doc's world with an extra spicy lust.

This time, after all, would be their last.

Candy Baby found that she loved Jonathan Gold but didn't ultimately love him eternally—he was a phenomenally handsome, talented doctor, with no personality.

But he more or less inspired her passion, and she certainly inspired his, and afterwards, in his office, Candy asked him if he wouldn't mind leaving first— she was still on her security rounds and didn't want to raise suspicions with them leaving at the same time.

She kissed him goodbye, and when he was gone Candy finished getting dressed, grabbed the backpack she'd stashed under the desk, used Gold's stolen key to open the cabinet containing Swanson

Falls' MedicaMiraco, and replaced the real one with a lookalike she'd made using a 3D printer. When the real MM was in her backpack, and the office was returned to normal, she backed through the door and bumped into Dr. Cohen, who looked at her confusedly, and she said with much too much rapidity, "Good evening, Dr. Cohen, I thought I heard a sound coming from Dr. Gold's office."

Dr. Cohen was too busy to care, but he was also a witty, observant old man, and he said, "Yes, there have been some unusual sounds coming from that office lately."

He looked at her and smirked, and she smiled her best attempt at a smile of the ignorant.

The doctor had already moved on.

As casually as she could, she hiked the backpack back to the van, where she switched that one out with an identical backpack that had a 4x4-inch brick of armed MetaPlastic (once you were in the Defense Force, access to the armory was a surprising snap). By that point her hands were shaking from fear, but there was also a bit of violent, vengeful hatred within her, just like in me. You see, there were people she and I and our father hated, who were to blame for so much death and injustice, and she was going to shine a light, is how she got through it, she said.

She entered the elementary school and turned towards the Terminal Towers, and immediately she was noticed and addressed by Mrs. Laramie Cromwell, Chief Nurse. "Hiya, Candy—protectin' or schleppin'?"

Candy was lucky it was Mrs. Cromwell—both women had always gotten along affably—and Candy was able to say honestly, "Today, unfortunately, it's both."

"Oh, you poor thing, but I hear ya—these days, if we can work, they work us to our bones."

"You said it."

"Well, have a day, darling."

"You too, Laramie—and hey," Candy said.

"Yes?"

"For the next few hours, keep all staff away from the Towers; Erik is having me clear out the corridors again for training."

Mrs. Cromwell rolled her eyes and said, "To our *bones*, Sylvia."

Iugulare Mortuos— "To Cut The Throat Of Corpses"

Candy's heavy SFDF boots thudded on the gym floor and echoed in the rafters. Walking through the second set of doors, into the gym itself, was an excursion into The Stench Of Death. The ventilators did their best, but that smell could pierce crystal.

The gym was quiet as usual. The doped conversational mutterings from the patients and the crackly monologues from the blasted OV headphones produced a soft white noise between the bootsteps on the ground and their echoes in the rafters.

Four rows up, ten rows deep, the empty, white-sheeted gurney was still there. Candy quickly climbed seven vertical rows of that tower and pulled the curtain open. Just as tonight's first backpack was pulled from under an absent doctor's desk, the second, fully armed backpack was placed on top of an absent patient's sheets—in what we'd both independently calculated to be the bomb's money-spot.

Candy had thought about doing it so much, and had trained for it so often, that when she actually did it a lot of the experience's freshness was already worn off, and she just did it—started the bomb's timer. With the bomb armed and counting down, she zipped the backpack closed and pinned a piece of paper to the outside. She read the paper, and a clear tap of mourning's marrow hit the page. The paper read:

"Elizabeth Marie Franklin has something she would like to say."

SFDF Security Nurse Sylvia Thompson descended the tower and ran to the main doors, which she locked from the inside and barred shut, and then ran to the emergency exit, where she disabled the alarm, exited, ran to the van, and drove towards the Skarnoff farm while her eyes watched the Swanson Falls Elementary School Gymnasium/Terminal Towers as it stood there, in the golden light of day, in the last moments of its existence.

BOOM.

I had finished my delivery rounds early, and I was up in the tower at St. Mary's. Given the brightness of the afternoon, the light from the explosion was largely unnoticeable, but the sound shook windows for miles.

From my elevated viewpoint, I watched the Swanson Falls Gym change from normal to a brief flash of light and then a cloud of grey smoke and debris, followed several seconds later by a sonic boom that I literally felt pass through me, and after the sound passed, all the land down beneath the tower was sporadically dotted with the high-pitched squeals of car and house alarms.

I descended the tower with a paintbrush and a hunting knife, with Tyger at my side.

Omnibus locis fit caedes.—
"Let there be slaughter everywhere."

I knocked on the front door at 221 Abel Dr., the first house on my map.

Dressed in my reassuring Swanson Falls Defense Force uniform, I enquired as to the occupants' safety and explained to them that yes, there had been an explosion and that I was tasked with going around to make sure the townspeople's OVs were functioning properly, to receive any necessary emergency messages from Mayor Blackwater or SFDF Capt. Montana. When they allowed me inside, Tyger emerged from the shadows and took my place at the door, under orders to Speak if the house were approached by anyone, and I stepped inside and quickly opened the Boomer homeowners' necks like animals.

I cut the woman first, and the man turned and looked confused, and I stabbed into his neck, too. I was strong enough to catch them both as they fell, and I held them by their feet while the blood drained out on the carpet, keeping as much of the blood away from myself as I could, and nobody made a peep I was so strong and quick. Then I dabbed the whiskers of the paintbrush into the blood and wrote on the mirror in the nearest bathroom: "I."

The plan was working.

The deaths mounted.

I didn't revel in it—maybe in the same way the old soldiers in the old wars didn't revel in it, at least from what I've read. I was killing an enemy that (not who) needed to be put out of existence—forthwith. I'd killed animals, and the Boomers never really developed into full humans. Additionally, people have no moral qualms when harmful bacteria are eradicated, so to me it really wasn't much different from things I'd done before—not at the time, to bitter old death-hearted me. Like Mr. Justin said, if you do something enough, it starts to feel ordinary. I'd killed deer and rabbits and birds and bacteria. I'd slaughtered the fake preacher and puked but didn't feel guilty for it over time. The Boomer old cowards had done worse: They'd destroyed a culture, crippled a nation, enabled the deaths of Mr. Justin and Miss Thompson and Dr. James and tens of thousands of real American soldiers, all out of mass laziness and greed, delusion, guilt, weakness, cowardice, entitlement, intolerance, fear, and stagnant political infighting.

There was no glory in it. *Death to the enemy,* like always, was all it was.

After I emerged in the backyard of the first house and used the snow to wipe the worst of the blood off my black SFDF uniform, I went to the second house, told them about the explosion, was invited inside, and wrote "AM" on the bathroom mirror nearest the bodies.

Most houses took no more than two minutes I was so good and prepared.

There were a few times that I heard footsteps on the basement stairs, and sometimes outside the house, on my way to the next, I heard the wails of the aged children who'd come up and found the blood and bodies and the bloody bootprints leading to the message-bearing mirror. The Boomers' children all called for help on their OVs, but an entire wing of the hospital had just exploded, and it would be a long time before there would be any open lines to the Defense Force, to let them know there was even a problem.

A few times Tyger barked twice, and I heard the jingling of her collar as she rocketed to the back of the house, per training, and met me back there, and we watched from the bushes while a Defense Force truck drove by slowly and announced to the neighborhood, "STAY IN YOUR HOMES. ALL IS WELL. STAY IN YOUR HOMES. ALL IS WELL."

Candy Baby was a disturbingly effective tactician.

I went back into the house and wrote a word on the nearest bathroom mirror: "THE."

Then I snowed off the blood again and made my way to the next house.

"KHAN."

The blood sprayed and flowed and made that heavy hissing sloppy sound. Lots of bodies. More and more bloody words on the windows to the self. More screams. Calls for help.

Most of the time it was rote, steelminded, cardiovascular work that I'd never even wanted to do—which I tried to address in my message. In fact, only once was there any joy in it.

And such a confusingly perverse joy.

And maybe the love of my life—which should tell you something.

Audentes fortuna iuvat.—
"Fortune favors the bold."

The elderly husband at 505 Dawn St.—the Sybil residence—was old and grizzled and scowling. His wife was hunched and slim and trembling, and they both went dead without a sound, and they were light to hold and drained easily, and I was just coming out of the bathroom when I saw the Sybils' daughter—Edna-Jane—standing there, over their bodies, looking at the bloody agent of the Security Force, me, and pointing an illegal 3D revolver at my chest.

"I knew it," the woman said. "I felt it down there."

"   . . . "

"You did it?"

I continued just looking at her, ready to dive out of the way the moment she cocked back the hammer, but she stayed her hands and asked another question, *"Why?"*

"   . . . "

"You're a murderer," Edna-Jane said, realizing the implications of each word as she said it.

I said what I could, which I thought would only make sense to me: *"Actus me invito factus non est meus actus."*

It seemed to fluster the woman. I started moving towards her, slowly.

"Whose act is it, then?" she asked. She ignored my confused look and waited for an answer. Edna-Jane either knew Latin or had memorized old gems like I did in teenage boredom. I decided to be more specific, in our native tongue.

"They killed my father. They killed my mother. They killed any chance I ever had of doing anything with my life but killing them. This isn't where I want to be; it's where I've been brought."

"Astra inclinant; sed non obligant." ("The stars incline us; they do not bind us.")

I mildly chuckled. Clever girl, this one. I replied, *"Audemus jura nostra defendere."* ("We dare to defend our rights.") And I added, *"Minatur innocentibus qui parcit nocentibus."* ("He threatens the innocent who spares the guilty.")

Edna-Jane looked at her parents and then at me and flashed her Latin wit one last time: *"Felix qui potuit rerum cognoscere causas."* ("Happy is he who can discover the causes of things.")

I took the verbal hit, and she saw it, but she grew too cocky and let her guard down.

In our interplay she hadn't noticed that I had come within striking distance, and my right hand shot out and knocked the gun out of hers and grabbed her wrist, and the woman's physical wattage surged into a strong fight, trying to regain control of the situation. But I was a big strong murderer, and to me in that moment her squirming resistance required token energy to overcome, but I felt like I could also feel something like that she actually *wanted* to be overcome. She grunted, "Let me go, you sick bastard," and she wrestled her torso and hips against my body, which was wrapped over her to keep her in control. I had only seen this happen in dramatic and pornographic movies on the OV, but here it was happening: The lithe, struggling young woman's gyrations were starting to give me, her subduer, something of a hissingly powerful erection, and the woman could feel it in her struggles, and she said, "Oh, no! Don't you dare! You *murderer!* You *sick fuck!*" But she was thrusting against me even harder, rubbing her backside up and down the mean shaft in my pants and gripping at my arms in a way that was more sexually demanding than an attempt at escape, and she grunted and said, "Don't. You. Dare." She squirmed and struggled and grinded, and finally she let out a groan and said, "Ohhh, *fuuuuuck meeeee!*" And I couldn't stop myself, and the young lady wasn't really trying to stop me. I ripped off her house dress and yanked her underwear to the floor and let the monster out and rammed myself inside, to the hilt, and she growled with delight, and I supercharged the pistons of the God Engine, and she grunted and thrust herself into my thrusts, and almost immediately I was having way too much fun to contain myself in the greatest place on Earth, and I blasted every bit of my essence deep inside her while she dug her fingernails into my legs and moaned and sighed, *"Oh! You dirty, sick bastard . . . ."*

I let her go and slumped next to her on the ground, and the air in front of my face glinted for a moment before I threw my arms up, towards the glint, and felt my face being sliced by my own knife. Immediately the gash was hot, and I wrestled the knife from her and knocked her out by smashing the back of her head against the floor.

That's how I lost my virginity: I consensually raped some insane, encaged genius-woman, who then immediately tried to kill me, in the middle of a domestic invasion.

The dishonorable times continued.

Eventually, after hastily suturing and bandaging my face-cut and cleaning off all the blood, I emerged outside, Tyger sniffed my crotch briefly, and I walked on air to the next house.

The Terminal Towers explosion happened near the southern edge of town. I worked my way from the northern edge to the south, in the opposite direction of the expanding dragnet. And after several hours of house-to-house slaughter—if you want more details, do it yourself—I reached the point where my trajectory and the dragnet's would meet, and Tyger, outside the Monroe McMansion, started barking like we'd reached the end of days.

Once again, Candy's tactics were astounding— there was a giant oak tree accessible through a balcony on the second floor of the Monroe house. With the windows out front flashing white, blue, and red, I called a command to Tyger through the door before opening it. "Tyger, *bag*." The door opened, the dog shot into the room and sniffed out the location of my backpack and scurried into the open flap. "Good girl. Now *quiet.*"

I could feel Tyger breathing on my neck as I ascended the stairs. I left a trail of bloody bootprints up to the balcony of the master bedroom, where there was one final splotch of blood left on the railing as I leapt to the branch that I had only faith but not proof could hold me.

Oak trees are beasts of strength, and my dog-supplemented weight barely registered in the branch's bend, and I, the black-clad man in the tree, pulled myself up and walked and swung across the tree's length, to the other side of the fence, over the street. While up in the tree, hidden in the branches, I watched the SFDF dragnet slowly pass by. Then I descended the branches like a ladder until I did a hang-drop to the ground, where I left more indicative bloody bootprints in the middle of the street.

I walked to a tree lawn and followed its snowy length until I saw that once again my boots didn't leave any blood anymore, and then I felt safe to follow the plan's course and headed back towards the hospital in the hollow of the dragnet.

I still had half of my very long message to write on the mirrors.

I still had an overpopulation to cull, and I headed to the next house.

Thinking globally, acting locally.

By that point, Candy had driven the van the long way around the Skarnoff property and parked it behind the old barn—safe there because the old man didn't have the strength to come out to the barn anymore—could only look out the window, but couldn't see behind the barn from the house—and his aides wouldn't be back until tomorrow afternoon.

Throughout the day, Candy had taken her time in saddling Skarnoff's two old horses—Kloppy and Her Majesty—in preparation for the escape.

Once the horses were saddled, Candy went to work on the back of the van—prepping the power system for our makeshift EMP, which, so far, didn't look like it would be necessary, but Candy proceeded anyway because many of history's great thinkers agreed with the wisdom of caution. (An abundance of which, as we know, does no harm.)

And anyway she was relieved to have something to keep her mind from worrying about me and the dangers wrought by my murderous deeds, and frankly also worrying about if she'd ever be able to forgive herself for what we were doing.

Candy Baby didn't like to kill—the only people she ever killed were the Blanks and those terminal patients who were dead anyway—but she also knew what it meant to enable. She wished she had a better idea, but still the only idea she had was to try to protect her brother, me, during his, my, pugnacious, quixotic bent. Plus, she felt a quiet pride over having done something retributive in Leni's damned memory.

She felt it was better to busy herself with the technical intricacies of the improvised EMP—she could do that other thinking later, probably in prison or after she was dead herself.

She started on the wiring in the golden air of early evening and worked into the night, just as I continued my own work, and when night fell she toiled in the muted green illumination of some chemlights while the wind skirled around the weather-gnarled edges of the old barn.

Well into dark, as she was finishing, which was also around when she expected me and Tyger to arrive tromping through the woods by the barn, Candy was chilled frozen by the sight of headlights and a search-light turning off Beech Rd. and down the Skarnoff farm's long driveway.

For hours and hours the windshield of the Roader presented The Shade with nothing but the rotting face of a stagnant continent—devoid of human newness, where following the local roads or going offroad just showed the same repeated story of nature reclaiming where the wave of the old prosperity had broken and turned back.

Swanson Falls made for such a great, safe neighborhood for Boomers to retire in because it was nearly self-sufficient. There was a freshwater lake as well as a salt mine nearby, the dirt was arable, the forest that remained was original growth and kept the winds in check and was the home of small wild animals that could be hunted if food became too scarce in some continuingly ugly future.

Most of America's suburbs showed up like the fallout zone of a cultural-nuclear blast in the heart of her major cities, but Swanson Falls had been a standalone, organized community designed by one of the few suburban developers to ever actually apply wisdom and empathetic insight to its civic designs. Rather than relying on the culture offered by a decaying city, Swanson Falls, practically in the middle of nowhere, was designed to provide its own, and the idea would have worked had the Boomers not all settled there before the real-estate market collapsed. Consequently the town square was empty and the businesses around it were mostly closed, because the lazy and aging Boomers couldn't be bothered to stop shouting angrily at their OVs to head outside and live amongst humanity. Usually, the town square was a depressing, empty place—a little fractal of the empty world outside the occupied homes.

The Roader ripped across the plains that fed into Swanson Falls. Night was falling, and The Shade was starting to go a little loopy from the monotony of the sights (fading though they were) dragging along in front of him, and then he was sure he was loopy because he blinked for a second and suddenly a point on the horizon was flashing with blue and red and bright white lights.

"The hell is that?" Hector Mass called from the gun pit.

"I'm pretty sure that's Swanson Falls, guys," Connie said from the console. "But I'm still not getting through to them."

"It looks like it's as bad as we thought," Heimler

said. "Shade, take it in easy to the guard shack, but Mass?!"

"Yeah."

"They fire on us, you take 'em out—we don't have the luxury of time; the kids might already be on their way out of that mess."

A few times one of their children answered the door, only they weren't children anymore. One time, to give an example of how it went when that sort of thing happened, it was a forty-two-year-old man who answered the door, and he was pissed.

The door opened and the man said, "What?"

"Who's at the door?" an elderly female voice called from inside.

"Some dick from the DF!" the man shouted. "Just a sec; I'll get rid of him."

"Hello, sir; I'm Dante from the Defense Force, and I've been dispatched to make sure this household's OV is working."

"Yeah, sure, we were just watching it," the man said and slammed the door.

I knocked again.

"What?"

"I've been dispatched to verify with my own eyes that the emergency channel is working, as I'm sure you've heard about the explosion earlier."

"Yeah—is that why come the blood?"

". . . Yes."

"You was there?"

"Sir, I have many more houses to get to. May I step inside for a moment?"

I held up a real-looking proclamation from the Defense Force "legally" permitting this temporary intrusion.

"You got exactly one moment, buddy."

One moment was all it took—the man started heading to the living room, and I slid out a blackjack from up my sleeve and brainstemmed the man and caught his unconscious descent and laid him in a chair by the door.

"What's going on back there?" said the same voice from before.

The living room was essentially a hospice: There were two hospital beds lying parallel to each other, facing a big, blaring OV showing the local-news coverage of the hospital explosion, and each bed held a frail old patient who scowled at the world and then looked afraid of the glinting knife and the big man in the black-and-bloody uniform advancing.

First the wife, this time, then the intubated husband, as quickly as possible. The knife entered the neck and slipped to the other side, and the blood pumped out in impressive arcs and then glubbed while the Boomers gargled goodbye. The bodies were tipped from the beds, and the grey carpet pooled and soaked with blood to match the bloodstains on the walls.

Before I left, the nearest bathroom mirror read: "KHANS."

Tyger watched as I cleaned myself, and we moved on to the next house.

"AS."

The next house.

"ENEMIES."

I had read a book about the Columbine shooting, about how sometimes people on a killing spree get a sort of murder-fatigue and find that they prefer the terrorizing to the killing.

But was this a killing spree or an act of war? I never felt that fatigue—just the same stoic feeling of doing a job that needed to be done by someone with courage and nothing the fuck to lose. Lots of people afterwards called it terrorism, but isn't every act of war an act of terrorism? The War on Terror was a war against acts of war, then.

In that light, RIP Randall Sanders—you saw the truth and they killed you for saying it out loud.

Randall Socrates.

No, it was not a killing spree—by definition a spree is an unrestrained indulgence. There was plenty of restraint in Swanson Falls. We could've killed lots more people if we'd wanted.

It was war—a smart war, a precise war.

And it was fashionable at the time.

The Second Civil War was raging, with sides split between those who wanted the Old America and those who wanted a New—whatever that meant. The Old had subverted itself through corruption, and the New had been calamitously undermined through the Old's false-flag attack on Rushmore and its own inability to offer anything but contrarian objectives.

It all amounted to the fact that we the sad Thompson siblings had found the hill we were willing to die on.

I was tempted to make a comparison to America's first Civil War, to talk about famous/infamous hills that Union or Confederate soldiers had died fighting for, but to this day I have mixed feelings about that war, and I don't know how to compare it to ours. Of course President Lincoln was morally correct in taking a stand against slavery, but can't his federal trumping of states' rights have been one of the key moments in American history that led to not only the vast powers of the bloated, eventually collapsing federal government (having taken those powers from the state governments) but also the start of the transition from the President being "Chief Executive" to being "Chief Executive And Lawmaker"? In short, Elected King?

The hill Candy and I were willing to die on was the hill we were storming, full of the people who continued to elect kings and pat themselves on the back about their great advancements in civil rights while industrially ensnaring every third-world economy on the planet, while technologically spying on their innocent brothers and sisters and overfilling their nation's prisons and penitentiaries, while forever granting ever more powers to a federal King-government that launched at least a dozen "police actions" in different countries, led its own and the world's economies over a cliff, kidnapped and vaporized our mother and uncle, and brutally murdered one of the few real heroes who ever lived.

It was the hill we were willing to die on because it was the hill we knew we would die on whether we fought back or not.

Houses and more houses. More bodies and words and muffled cries of shock from basement-dwellers who should've never been living there anyway and who were now homeowners because of me—something that would last longer than their grief over the death of their irrationally selfish, cowardly, narcissistic (statistically speaking), government- and culture-destroying parents.

I gashed necks all the way down Beech Rd. and finished my mirror message, and the Swanson Falls bloodbath itself, at 234 Beech Rd., the street and house closest to the woods that led to the Skarnoff farm.

My final confirmed kill for the night was widower John Abraham Slauson, who almost looked like he'd already expected me to show up one night and finish his misery. By the end, given the late hour for the elderly, I was picking backdoor locks to get in and killing the Boomers in their sleep, as many were too old or medically withered to be able to answer my phony knocks anyway. So when I showed up silently in the crucifix-laden Slauson living room, the old man happened to be awake, and he watched me with utter hate.

"I knew it," the footless old man said from his bed. "Already knew no young Christians left in the world, and now it's Satan come to get me. Black and red, I know the devil. You here to tempt me? No? You ain't got *nothing* for me, so come kill me, Satan—I'm ready for where I'm going. I'm comin' to you, Jesus."

"Old man," I said, "why hasn't it ever occurred to you that you don't get to decide who the real Christians are? Even schoolchildren know that that decision is your God's, and I think your invisible God would be offended that you consider your limited intelligence and perspective up to the task of wisely discerning the transcendent value of other people's lives lived in the moral and ethical morass of the human experience."

"What? You don't know what the damn hell you're talking about—all I heard was a bunch of big words from a psycho that don't got no substance in the real world. You're here to kill me, which means you think you know morality like God yerself, so who—"

"I do not pretend to be acting or thinking on your invisible God's behalf. Perhaps, by merely being human, I am doing what your invisible God wants me to do— designed me to do, so make your peace, Old Loser."

346

"I *cain't* make no peace while I got some blood-soaked murder-man in my bedroom, *Satan* himself telling me what it means to be a proper Chri—"

The man made a brief series of indescribable sounds before I tipped his frail old body headfirst towards the floor, and the blood rushed out and soaked into the carpet.

The final bathroom mirror said, "GRASP?"

Tyger barked twice and circled around to the back of the house, where she met me at the back door, and we both peeked around the corner and saw a state-of-the-art Roader hauling ass down Beech Rd., towards the rendezvous farm.

"Shit, Tyger, we gotta move."

Man and dog entered the black forest behind the Slauson house.

"Captain Heimler, this whole city is FUBAR—what do you want me to do?" The Shade asked as he drove past a platoon of SFDF soldiers who all shot at the Roader thinking it had something to do with the explosion. Rifle bullets couldn't pierce the Roader's plating, but if the SFDF got serious, their armory had a few weapons that could, so CTRT5 had to do something fast.

"We've gotta incapacitate the city. Connie, where can we set up an HQ? We need to override the SFDF drone and drop the entire IncaTube payload."

"John, there's a farm I'm highlighting on your MOV—plenty of space to set up the dish, and no SFDF anywhere in sight. But speaking of which, they might be thinking the same thing about those IncaTubes," Connie said, "so I'd advise everybody to get your masks on ASAP."

"Yes, ma'am," Heimler said curtly.

My eyes took a few minutes to adjust to the blackness of the forest floor at night, where even most of the starlight was blotted out. From the sound of things, Tyger was navigating herself through it just fine, but half-blind and surging with adrenaline I had plenty of troubles—fallen trunks and branches, like the grasping arms of *rigor-mortis'd* bodies trying to drag me down with them where they'd died. There were five-hundred yards of this forest to get through, and it got to feeling like an MMA battle.

I kicked and stepped over deadfall and was slapped and jabbed and kicked by branches in the near-total dark. Human eyes were built to adjust for survival, and they adjusted enough to do the job but not enough that I wasn't bleeding, bruised, and bullied. Nevertheless, I could eventually see where my feet were landing, and one after another that's all it takes to bring a man to a clearing—a clearing that I still couldn't see.

The rustle of dead leaves thoroughly agitated by animals chased by the frightening sounds of Tyger's hungry or playful sprinting approach provided the only sounds in the immediate area around me in the dark. I could still hear the sirens of various emergency vehicles screaming in the streets behind me, but ahead I heard nothing, and because it was dark, and because I was completely paranoid, I began to think I wasn't following a straight-enough trajectory through the forest. I might be circling lost and losing time—Candy might be in SFDF custody!

I picked up the pace and took a harder beating because of it, but I kept up the breathless and painful pace anyway because I could feel neither the breath nor the pain—only the panic.

Never in my life did I think I'd ever be so relieved to hear the somewhat distant sound of a horse's protesting whinny.

I followed the sound as if it were visible, like an audible beacon. I followed it until I reached a clearing where my sister was feeding the horses and reining them to a post outside the barn, saying to the whinnying Her Majesty, "Shhhh! Quiet there, sweet girl."

"Candy."

"Captain Montana, we have authorization from—"

"Listen, lady, we've got a five-alarm shitstorm on our hands here, and I need my goddam drone, so fuck off!"

"Captain Montana, this is CTR Team 5 Captain Perry Heimler—the people we're after are the people who stirred up this shitstorm. Like it or not, I'm having Officer Caliente commandeer the Swanson Falls drone under AP #5221, and I promise you that when our job is done your job will be a whole lot easier."

"Where the hell did you people come from?"

"Thank you, Captain Montana—we'll be in touch. Over, over."

Perry Heimler called up to the front of the Roader: "Shade, ETA?"

The Roader blasted through a wooden fence and into the farm's pasture, where the mechanical behemoth was brake-stomped to a skidding, cinematic stop.

"Ahora."

The farm was calm and quiet, and the members of CTRT5 felt safe pulling off their gas masks now that they were away from the town's dangerous commotion.

The doors of the Roader opened, and everyone piled out on wobbly, road-weary legs.

"No rest for the wicked-hunters," said Heimler— one of his catchphrases. "Shade, you and Mass open the dish over there while Connie and I ready the terminal and the battery."

Under a sky now bright with twinkling stars, The Shade and Mass hucked the drone-dish over to the clearing and anchored the base. While Mass pivoted the stem of the dish and unlocked its arms for their unfolding, The Shade happened to glance over towards the barn and saw something that caught his attention.

"Shade, what the hell, man? I'm doing this myself here."

The Shade ran to the Roader and put on his helmet, pulled down the optics, and turned on the binocular effect.

"Oh, *shit.*"

"What the hell, Shade?"

"Connie, the kids escaped Jolly Roger in James Thompson's white medi-van, right?"

"What?"

"We're looking for a white van?"

"Why?"

"Connie!"

Connie said, "Yes! Why?"

"I think they're here."

"What?" Heimler asked.

"Captain Heimler, I think at least their van is

parked behind that barn. Come over here and take a look."

The moment I had whisper-said *"Candy"* was a few moments after the Roader had brightly and boldly entered the Skarnoff property, tore ass down the driveway, and blasted through the wooden fence, which meant that upon my arrival we had to quickly convert a relieved hug into a dash into the darkness of the old barn, where we were joined by Tyger.

We all watched the Roader and its occupants through slits in the decaying walls.

Tyger whined.

"Tyger."

"What are they doing?"

"Setting up something."

"We should get out of here right now—while they're distracted."

We headed towards the van and consequently didn't notice, at the time, that John Shade had taken an obvious interest in the area of the barn.

"Candy, you stay here with Tyger and the horses— it only takes one of us to do this, and if either of us deserves to die tonight, it's me."

"OK," Candy said readily, which made me chuckle darkly.

"This better work," I said and got into the van.

We didn't say goodbye because we couldn't.

We just flat-out couldn't.

Once I was behind the wheel, I took a deep breath. The way I saw it, I had about a one-in-ten chance of surviving this. But it was like Candy had once said: "When you've got nothing, they've got everything to lose."

I turned over the engine, and the Swanson Falls drone roared overhead.

"Perfect," I said.

I meant it.

"The van is moving!" The Shade called out and ran to the Roader and got in. "Mass, give me metal support—I'm going after them."

Hector Mass was only too happy to scurry back up into the gun nest and get this thing over with.

"Connie, you set here?" Heimler asked.

"Yeah, I'm good—go!"

Heimler got in, and the Roader roared off towards the pale van chugging across the pasture.

What happened next was balletic warfare—the final masterstroke of Candy's plan.

The van couldn't outrun the Roader, and certainly not the drone, and definitely not any rockets launched by the drone. The van was doomed, and I was possibly doomed as well. That .75 could kill a skyscraper, and a real part of me felt like I was driving directly into my death.

Dis aliter visum.—
"It seemed otherwise to the gods."

Heimler ordered Mass to take out a tire rather than take out the whole van, which the Roader's .75 was more than capable of. And indeed, boom went the barrel and bang went the van's aft passenger-side tire—and not just the tire but the tire, wheel, and axle—and the van did a three-sixty Earth-skid that threw violent quakes at everything inside it, and I was lucky the old bitch didn't tip over in the spin. When the van finally rocked to a rest, I now had the additional worry that the explosive quaking had disturbed the painstaking wiring-work Candy had done in the dark.

I'd find out soon enough.

The van's sudden spinning skid forced to The Shade to stomp the brakes again because already the Roader was gaining way too much ground on the already-skidding van, and when The Shade stomped, the brakes clamped, and the Roader skidded wildly on the icy horse-dirt and came to a rocking stop. Still too close for comfort as they'd left their gas masks God-knew-where, The Shade threw the Roader into reverse without looking back, and the back of the vehicle cracked right into the trunk of an original-growth oak tree.

"Christ, Shade!"

"My bad, Cap'—the hell's a tree doing in the middle of a horse field?"

"Hit them with the light, you idiot!"

The Roader threw a spotlight on the hopeless van. Over an intercom, Perry Heimler announced, "Prepare for IncaTubing—don't resist; you'll be fine; the effect is temporary."

The drone completed its turn and grew thin as its face—its two glowing red eyes—headed directly towards me. At the same time, The Shade turned the wheel, to get the Roader away from both the tree and the van—to avoid being IncaTubed by the Peregrine—and was turning the wheel and putting the Roader into drive while I was remembering all those movies I'd seen on the big OV in the shelter, where the heroes, facing the horrible brunt of the advancing army, had to wait, wait, hold . . . HOLD . . . HOLD!

NOW!

I folded as much of my giant body as I could into the area below the steering wheel and in front of the seat, slammed one hand down on the accelerator of the in-park, running van, and flipped the switch on the console by my other hand. All the power from the engine and the stolen generators in the van combined and surged into the MedicaMiraco that Candy had stolen from Dr. Gold's office, and another huge EMP was born, grew, killed the electronics in the van, then the Roader, then the IncaTube rocket's guidance system, then the drone, and the MM exploded just after it unleashed all its amplified electromagnetic power.

The interior of the van burst into flames—an inferno that was making that demon-whisper sound that fire makes when it's really going—and I desperately grabbed for the door handle, turned it, and rammed my shoulder into the night.

The cool dew of the grass was one of the great momentary pleasures of my life, to be honest—that sweet peaceful feeling of frozen spears of horsegrass coolly kissing the back of my neck—but I was pulled out of my pleasant moment in the dewy pasture by the awesome sight of the powerless drone gliding overhead on a steady downward trajectory.

The air above me stirred in the sudden void produced by the departed drone, and five-hundred yards past my feet the fucker hit the ground, and the liquid-hydrogen fuel tank was punctured by its own rupturing sides, and a familiar white explosion filled the night sky with its blinding light. The heat wave from the explosion arrived a few moments later, and it swept over me on the ground after I'd rolled away from the van and tried to keep rolling but was startled by the power of the explosion—how disconcertingly nearby it had happened. I never really felt the heat wave for my shock.

Then there were two fires on the pasture: a giant circular post-explosion smoldering ruin, and the fully engulfed van.

I waited for another round from the Roader, but nothing happened.

I stood uncertainly and found that I could walk— if I could walk, I could run, and I hobble-ran to the barn, turning back occasionally to look at the Roader as it sat there with a menacing impotence.

Candy's presumption had been correct after all.

When the improvised EMP took out the Roader's electronics, the operating system's protocols, recognizing a system-wide problem, completely locked all of the vehicle's operations—including those that made the door latches grab and release. There was one door that allowed for manual override, but it was at the back of the Roader, barely two inches from the tree. Despite Heimler's loud and repeated, explicit instructions to The Shade, the other doors just weren't going to open until a Swanson technician could come replace all the fried electronics.

Consequently, Heimler and his men were locked in, and Connie was locked out. And with Connie's handgun trapped in the truck, they were all helpless to watch me run across the field to the barn.

"Where's he going?"

"Do you think the girl is still in the van?"

"If she is, she's a crisp."

"This is fucking ridiculous—Shade! Try it again!"

A dry clicking sound.

"Captain, right now this whole fucker is D-U-N."

Connie tapped at the window nearest Heimler. The window and armor were bullet- and soundproof, though, so all they could do was pantomime to each other.

Their pantomimed conversation amounted to:

Connie: "You guys OK?"

Heimler: "Yes. But we're trapped."

Connie: "Did you see Dante Thompson head towards the barn?"

Heimler: "Yes. Go follow him."

Connie: "Hell no."

Candy figured the Roader would be shut down, but she also figured the men would be able to file out of the back and possibly launch an attack on me/the van after the EMP, so she'd had my SFDF sniper rifle trained on Connie and the now-impotent Roader the whole time.

I reached the barn and said, "What happened?

356

Why weren't they shooting?"

"Looks like they're stuck and can't get out."

"Holy shit, really? What about that woman, then?"

"She just has a dead MOV."

"Should we—?"

"No."

She must have felt that her simple no wasn't enough to convince me, so she finished her argument.

She said, "Inspector Javert."

Heimler's eyes went wide, and Connie turned to see what he was looking at: A dark-brown pair of heavily saddled and packed-up horses trotted into the darkness between the two fires in the pasture. On the back of one horse rode a large, black-clad male, undoubtedly Dante Thompson, me, and on the back of the other was a black-clad petite blonde, undoubtedly his nongenetic, adopted sister, Sylvia. We were also draped in our old coy-wolf pelts to block the winter winds.

Candy and I looked over at the Roader as we trotted our horses into the night, and when we saw Connie by the side of the vehicle watching us, we waved respectfully.

Connie's MOV was fried, and it was ten hours before they were finally able to reset the electronics and open the doors of the Roader. Swanson Falls didn't have any machinery that could move a fully loaded Roader, and the cantankerous old Skarnoff—a beloved friend to Mayor Blackwater—refused to let anyone cut down his sentimentally treasured tree, but eventually the resourceful Officer Caliente was able to convince some locals to chop it down anyway while the SFDF was out investigating the bloody homes. Nevertheless, thanks to either luck or incompetence, the chopped tree ended up tipping directly on top of the Roader when it came down, and it took several more hours to dismantle the tree piece by piece. Six hours into the wait, inside the Roader, Hector Mass had bad stomach trouble and nowhere to go, and so he went where he was. Diarrhea. A tshitnami of it gathered in his underwear and slowly flowed down the back and insides of his legs, already slightly cooled and foreign-feeling by the knees, and then dripping wetly off the pant-leg with a tocking sound as it hit the metal hatch at the base of the Roader's gun nest. The smell from the lingering diarrhea eventually made Mass puke, and by the end of the wait the hatch was a filled toilet that was dripping brown tears into the dark yellow pool of Heimler and The Shade's urine at the bottom of the Roader, in the area below, where Heimler and The Shade watched the nauseating drip of piss and shit and chyme for hours.

Ten hours of smelly waiting, then a long, screaming argument with Erik Montana about the fate of the Swanson Falls drone—Montana was eventually convinced of the truth of all their claims—and four hours of cleaning and resetting equipment before CTRT5 could even begin their investigation, with the SFDF's full support, in the pursuit of the siblings—me and Candy—who came to be known as "The Khans."

These pages already know most of the important details of the night, and over the course of two weeks of investigation, CTRT5 eventually discovered most of those same details, including the sequential order of all the killings and thus all the words I had written on the mirrors.

The note turned out to be of particular interest to anyone who read it—a glimpse into the mind of this mad, mad madman.

Mind-numbed and on the run, Candy and I didn't say much to each other for two days—not much beyond Candy saying things like, "Did you hear something?" and me saying things like, "Let's stop for now"—and thankfully the unusual sound of eight large hooves astride filled the conversational void with a sort of audible equivalent to the simple entertainment of watching tongues of flame lick and consume wooden logs in a firepit. The hooves clopped, plopped, clacked, pocked, and thumped as the giant horses carried us mind- and body-numbed siblings north, towards the massive Watterson Forest.

The silence was the silence of a sweet-sick feeling. We had done it, but what had we done? I felt the heights of triumph and the depths of guilt simultaneously, and my outward silence was wrought by the deafening roar of that moral, internal crossfire hurricane. Candy Baby later said she felt a different kind of triumph and a different kind of guilt. Her triumph was that her tactical plan had worked almost perfectly, like pretty much couldn't have gone better besides the post-coital vagina carved into my face, and Candy's guilt was the guilt of not having had to kill anyone who wasn't days away from death anyway—unlike me, whom she loved, whose hands were soaked in mortal blood.

Frankly at the time we both had a lot of processing to do before any words would even feel close to having a useful enough meaning towards explaining a shred of a goddam thing we felt and thought about what we'd done.

On the second day, our out-of-shape riding-legs ached terribly, and yet we pushed the horses as hard as the horses could go, and all five of us (two humans, two horses, and Tyger in a baby sling under Candy's coy-pelt) traveled within the ether of a domineering obsession that drove us all into a blissful monothought: *the physical pain, the physical pain, the physical pain.*

Halfway through the day, it started to rain, and the rain turned into sleet, turned into snow, and though our discomfort increased, that was fine, especially because sixteen hours of the two horses' easily trackable hoofprints quietly disappeared under the gleaming accumulation of soft unique white frozen raindrops.

A few hours later, shivering, we arrived at the edge of the fabled Watterson Forest—known to the locals as the Green Wave. We unpacked the horses and sent them away rather than butchered them for the meat because we were packed with enough AZN-Paste (courtesy of the SFDF) to keep us alive until the spring, and then we heavy-packed ourselves with the cargo the horses had carried.

And walked between the trees, and looked for the forest.

Two weeks after the Swanson Falls massacre, Connie Caliente knocked at a wooden door and was let inside by a confused, unshaven, pajama-wearing man. Connie stepped inside and hugged the man hello. "Seth!"

"Connie . . . hello . . . uh?"

"It's been forever! How ARE you?"

Seth Roth was still standing by the door, and Connie didn't want to enter his place ahead of him.

"Hi . . . uh . . . Connie—what are you doing here?"

"You haven't changed a bit, Seth," she said affably and entered anyway and went to the kitchen and fixed herself a glass of ice water. "You get to the point faster than a straight line."

She emerged from the kitchen and jingled the glass. "You mind?"

"Of course not—I'm just . . . is anyone else with you? I'd rather this not be pleasant if it's about to be unpleasant."

"Oh, jeez—I'm sorry," Connie said blushing, "I didn't know you'd heard that's what I do." And then she said, "But of course you'd know—you're pretty much *the* frickin' media. No, no, I'm here alone, or, that is, John is outside waiting, 'cause actually we need your help."

"I'm an independent news writer—how much money do you think I can donate towards high-level national mercenary security that I don't believe in?"

"Wow, you're being rude, Seth," Connie said smartly. "We need help from your *brain,* not your stupid wallet."

Seth Roth looked at Connie for the truth, saw past all the new defenses she'd learned in her training, to her childhood core, and saw that the truth was there.

"Sorry, Con'—I just never expected to see you again unless—" (His statement almost ended: "—things in America kept deteriorating to the point that an Action Plan called for the death or imprisonment of all independent news media.")

"Yeah, well, I understand. Sorry to barge in like this, but we just came from a pretty bad scene—"

"Where?"

"I promise you'll get all I'm allowed to tell."

" . . . "

"And the people we're after, who are responsible for the incident, these people left us a note."

" . . . "

"*And* some of the language in the note reminded me of the kind of stuff I remember you being interested in back in school."

The man was intrigued. He grinned.

"And to think my mother said my World History major was useless."

That seemed to break the ice finally.

Roth added, "Con', do you read my website?"

Caliente hesitated before answering, ". . . Yes."

"You hesitated, which means either you're lying, and you've never read it, or you have read it, and you realized that I wasn't just going to cave because of our old friendship."

Connie laughed because that was such classic Seth Roth thinking—and spot-on.

"I'll assume it's the latter, and here's what else I'll assume: You want me to see this note and write about the incident. That's the win-win? I get to break a big story and you get a viral manhunt?"

"I swear to God, Seth—*bees* must seem lazy to you."

Seth Roth's friendship with Connie Caliente was over, but a good newsman never turns down a lead.

He asked, shields down, "So what happened?"

"He's still a good man, folks!" Connie beamed and then turned a more Seth Roth–approvingly informational: "OK, anyway, you know that big securitized suburb—Swanson Falls?"

"Sure—I remember when they built it."

"There was a bloodbath there two weeks ago. The jammers have blocked national access to the local reports, so you'd be the first to report it, and trust me, Seth—I do value our old friendship, and I swear this story will help you more than you think."

"Connie," Roth said slowly, "tell me about this bloodbath."

To the best of her understanding, Connie told Roth what happened—about the explosion, the dead Blanks and Boomers, the improvised EMP, the horseback getaway.

"And at every victim's house there was a single word painted in blood on the mirror of the bathroom closest to the bodies. At the end of the investigation, each of those individual words added up to a note from the killers."

Connie pulled out a photocopy of Capt. Heimler's transcription of the note from the mirrors, unfolded it, and handed it to Roth, who'd been silent in that way where a person just soaks up everything passively, for contemplation later. But the letter drove him towards Connie's prompt, and he took the note from her with a heavy hand.

The note read:

I AM THE KHAN AND REPRESENTATIVE OF THE HEAVENLY KING—THE ONE GIVEN POWER OVER THE EARTH TO RAISE UP THOSE WHO LISTEN AND CAST DOWN THOSE WHO DO NOT. I WONDER, O YOU DOOMED, BOOMED BABIES, WHY IT IS THAT YOU HAVE FORCED MY ARMIES TO CONDUCT THESE GRUESOME MACHINATIONS THAT YOU HAVE MANIFESTLY EARNED AND SHOULD HAVE LONG AGO ENACTED UPON YOURSELVES OUT OF SHAME AND ATONEMENT. I AM AWARE THAT YOU WERE A WEALTHY AND POWERFUL PEOPLE, THAT YOU HAD UNDER YOU MANY SOLDIERS AND IMPLEMENTS OF WAR, THAT YOU HELD THE REINS OF A GLOBAL SUPERPOWER; HENCE IT IS DIFFICULT FOR YOU TO SUBMIT TO ME THROUGH YOUR OWN VOLITION—AND YET IT WOULD BE BETTER FOR YOU, AND HEALTHIER, WERE YOU TO SUBMIT WILLINGLY, FOR THE HASTENED DECAY YOUR LEADERSHIP MANIFESTED HAS LEFT YOU PATHETICALLY VULNERABLE DESPITE YOUR INFINITE STATE OF SECURITY. FURTHERMORE, IT IS A MORTAL SIN HOW YOU HAVE THRUST YOUR RAVENOUS GREED OUT INTO THE UNPREPARED WORLD, ALL TO SERVE AN AGENDA LASTING THE EXACT LENGTH OF YOUR IRRATIONALLY SELFISH LIVES. YOU HAVE FINANCED THE LEGAL AND CULTURAL PERSECUTION OF THE NLAS—OUR UNFORTUNATE SPIRITUAL BRETHREN, WHOM YOU UNWITTINGLY CREATED THROUGH YOUR OWN CALAMITOUS DECISIONMAKING. YOU SCOWL WITH JEALOUSY AT OUR GENERATIONS' LIVING HOPES AND IN DERISION TOWARDS THE VAST DISAPPOINTMENTS YOU YOURSELVES HAVE PROJECTED ONTO US FROM WITHIN YOUR OWN FAILED SOULS, AND SO WE ORDER THAT YOU NO LONGER HOLD US BACK FROM TRYING TO REBUILD THE ASHEN KINGDOM YOU

YOURSELVES IGNITED THROUGH YOUR SELF-INDULGENT FANTASIES, AND DO NOT HAVE THE NLAS NOR WE KHANS AS ENEMIES, FOR OUR CAUSE IS OUR BIRTHRIGHT, AND YOUR BIRTHRIGHT IS EXPIRED. MORS TUA, VITA MEA. MY SISTER AND I ARE THE FIRST ENABLERS OF A JUSTICE THAT HAS ROOTS THAT TRACE BACK TO YOUR BIRTH—A JUSTICE THAT YOU CANNOT ESCAPE, YOU WHO LIVED CHAINED TO MEDICATIONS IN YOUR CHEAP SUBURBAN CASTLES. HOW WILL YOU EVADE OUR GRASP?

"Holy fucking shit, Con'."

"Yeah, so do you see why I came to you?"

"OK—wow, right, anyway, what I can say right off is that whoever wrote this has studied some history. This verbiage seems like it's based on a boilerplate of the sort of letters ancient generals used to send to their enemies before launching their invasion. Like a sort of bellicose advance diplomacy—sort of, like, 'here's why you've already justified my righteous invasion.'"

Connie let him continue, but Roth's thoughts started turning to questions.

"All the dead were Baby Boomers? These siblings declared war on a dying generation?"

"Off the record, they killed more than eight-hundred people in a matter of twelve hours, brought down a Peregrine, and temporarily incapacitated our Team, Seth—and they got away. We need your help more than just reporting the story. Do you see anything in there that suggests where they might be headed next?"

Roth took his time and read the note again and

shook his head. "Sorry."

Connie rose to leave.

"You think they're just crazies—these people? What should I say about their past?"

"That's why we're going as far as coming to people like you for help—we don't know. There are almost no records of these kids beyond the fact that their guardians must have died at Rushmore."

"'Must have'?"

"The full Rushmore story is still classified even to us—and there's something else in their file that's even more obscure and Top Secret, something we only recently discovered that had to do with Milton Blank, who I told you about—so we're up the creek and paddleless on a melting glacier in sharky waters, Seth."

"So what should I say, then?"

"I'd stick with what you know, which is what I've told you."

"And my source?"

"My Team and I are in full support of this story—in fact, we're hoping if our names are out there the Khans might come after us. It'll be easier to catch them that way."

"Connie," Roth said after he read from her that she was about to leave. "If you ask me, and you have, people don't set out on horseback bound for civilization."

She opened the door.

"But maybe that's what they want you to think," he added cutely.

Connie gave Seth one of her old Connie faces, and she said, "I'll send you the details and some statements for your story. Nice seeing you again, Seth—sorry it had to be on a pile of dead bodies."

Connie was gone, and Seth replied to her bouncing shadow on the hallway wall, "That part was inevitable."

The *RothReport* story about the massacre at Swanson Falls, validated by CTRT5, was read by a quarter-million people within the first hour of its posting. It had all the elements the people vacantly staring into their OVs thirsted for: real-life murder, terrorism, detonations, declarations of war written in blood by enigmatic, wanted siblings, three pictures of hot people (two surprisingly sexy SFDF ID photos of a blue-eyed beauty and a cherubic stranger, as well as an equally alluring photo of the Hellenic Connie Caliente, with her flinty cohorts in the background), a cash reward for information regarding, and finally the actual content of a creepy note that called to arms perhaps the most heretofore undiscussed split in the splintered husk of America.

Within a week, there were copy cats, and the story grew larger, and the DHS cash reward for information regarding added zeroes, and the manhunt expanded. But the manhunt itself started to split with intentions: Some people still believed in the dollar, in the old country, and wanted the cash, and some had given up entirely on the former America and were instead seeking out me and my sister in the hopes that we could all try to do what the letter mentioned—rebuild the broken idea. They wanted to embrace us for finally finding our nation and culture's true common enemy.

That part—the part where the letter actually started to inspire the younger generations to turn against the Boomers—was something Connie and Heimler had not anticipated.

Nevertheless, it happened, and the message grew,

and there were more copy cats—nothing on the scale of what Candy and I had done, but enough that some savvy Boomers started to sleep with their precious guns under their pillows at night.

Most of the copy cats left notes—and the notes indicated something revoltingly troubling that Candy and I had not foreseen.

But we didn't hear about the copy cats for weeks.

The Watterson Forest comprised approximately one-hundred-thousand acres of (former) federally protected, temperate woodland, due west of Mr. Justin's old campgrounds on the Blunt. And this forest, too, had a river run through it—the trout- and steelhead-filled Hobbs.

Candy's plan involved us horsing and hoofing it there for three primary reasons: one, to hide from the technocentric authorities in an atmosphere where we had prior knowledge of how to survive, two, because we had read of a possibly friendly community of fellow survivalists inhabiting the vast woodlands, and three, because a possibly friendly community in a giant woodland would probably make body-heat-scanning drone-passes pretty much useless given the large numbers of human-sized things giving off human-like heat down in the gigantic forest, and unless the DHS decided to carpet-bomb the fucker with growingly expensive R&R tubes, the forest had the chance of being a mighty-fine stack of hay to hide under and try to survive in while we planned our next move.

We set up a temporary shelter that first night—something that would work while we daily hiked out deeper into the forest looking for the just-right spot.

In five days of hiking we saw some decent spots but no other people, nor even any signs of other people, so we relaxed our security a bit—or, that is, I fell back asleep when Candy tapped me for my turn on watch.

On the sixth morning, in the dark grey light of pre-sunrise, Candy and I were awakened simultaneously by the loud sound of a man's raspy voice:

"Green Wave newcomers, you are surrounded by riflemen—be you friend, or be you foe?"

CB awoke and looked at me both scared and terribly disappointed. I felt ashamed for being so lazy and stupid.

The voice outside: *"I repeat: Be you friend, or be you foe?"*

Candy looked curious and quietly asked me, "Who would say foe?"

"What was that?" the man outside asked. *"Speak up, or those words were your last."*

"I asked my brother who, given our circumstances, would say foe."

Candy thought she heard someone behind us chuckle.

The first voice said, *"Those who say friend are making a promise to be a friend—that's a fool me once, shame on you thing, yes?—but those who evade it have something to hide."*

CB said to me, "Good answer."

"What?" asked the man.

"I said good answer to my brother."

I called out, *"Sorry, riflemen—sometimes when my sister gets spooked she acts weirdly casual. The fact is that we heard there were good survivalist people here, and we were raised by a good survivalist, so if that's what you are then we're already family."*

369

The man outside said something.

"What?" asked Candy.

"I was saying good answer to the others," the man said more clearly.

The silence of the morning amplified the clicking sounds of rifles being put back on safety.

We emerged into the cold morning and met the man who'd interviewed us awake and the others he'd brought with him. The Watterson leader was a grizzled old woodsman named Hank Jaggar—without question the best Boomer Candy or I ever had the rare pleasure of knowing.

Erica Jenkins could make almost anything edible. She lived in a shelter with her husband, Hatchet, who was an Eagle Scout and talented at just about everything involving forestry and survivalism. They had a child, a cute chubby two-year-old named Panda, whom Candy had taken to looking after while Erica cooked for the quad.

A quad was a collection of four self-built shelters established around a large self-built firepit, to allow for a personal space as well as a set of neighbors with whom to be conveniently social and take some of the pain out of the Green Wave's oftentimes rugged, isolated existence.

The Jenkins family lived in the large shelter Hatchet had built for his family, Candy Baby lived in a shelter she designed herself and gratefully received help building from me and the charmed Jenkins family, and I lived in a shelter based on Candy Baby's design (I'd had my own design initially, but Candy's turned out to be way better). Both the Jenkins and Thompsons were new to the Green Wave, so the last spot for a campground in our quad was still just untouched forest. For now, it was two families in three shelters.

Candy was bouncing little Panda in her arms and talking to Erica, who was tending the stew pot. This was one afternoon about a month or so after our arrival.

"Mr. Jaggar said we were free to set up wherever we wanted if we didn't want to live in the quads, but it seemed so obvious for us stay around other people. Has anyone come here and lived alone?"

"We haven't been here that long, so I bet Hank would be able to say more, but I've only heard of two people like that—two young men. One arrived a few days after us, and the other a couple weeks ago. But they both . . . ."

"They both what?"

Erica could see that little Panda was distracted—looking at something deeper into the forest—and not wanting to say any of the associated words in her daughter's hearing, Erica pantomimed to Candy the act of firing a bullet through her own brain.

"Oh," Candy said.

"I think that's why they came here to begin with, though."

"Right. So I guess it's not like they lied when they answered friend not foe."

"Yeah, they didn't lie—they were friends to us; they were just foes to themselves, which I suppose is a tricky thing to admit to."

"Yeah . . . *fellows de se.*"

Candy fell deep into a thought.

"You think you'll ever feel comfortable enough to tell me where you keep going in your head?"

"That depends; do you want to talk about why you guys ended up here?"

"Hm, I guess you're right—not many good things to say about how anybody ended up here."

"Maybe that's really what everyone in the quads has in common."

"What's that?"

"We're here because we're from somewhere way worse."

The patterned-yet-chaotic sounds of the forest filled the conversational gap.

"You know," Erica said, "I think that would be depressing if this place weren't so . . . interesting."

A crashing, grunting, branch-snapping flurry of sounds came from the west, and all three ladies turned towards it. What they saw gave them a momentary startle: Hatchet and me hunched and bracing against the sprawled attack of a gigantic twelve-point buck.

But after a moment the women realized the buck was dead and that we were dragging its carcass towards our quad's cleaning table on the Hobbs. Tyger ran around me and Hatchet and the carcass, scanning the perimeter for unfriendly or edible smells. Occasionally she ran to me and jumped at me and pawed into my legs and leaped higher, seemingly just to catch the air. While the dog circled and leapt, we grunted and dragged.

"Atta boy, Hatch!" Erica hollered to her husband. "Work those buns, you stud!"

Hatchet pulled the rope, letting his body weight do most of the work, and once the deer's hind legs were high enough off the ground, I jammed the locking mechanism into place, and Hatchet said, "You drain, I skin, you quarter, we split?"

"Good deal."

"Need a knife?"

"Nah—I'm a teeth guy."

I walked over and kneeled down and leaned in, but then I unsheathed my cleaned, sharpened hunting knife and said, "Just kiddin'."

Hatchet was mildly amused, but his amusement turned into intrigue when he saw that I sort of kind of lost myself for a moment.

"Dante, you OK?"

"What? Yeah, sorry."

"Want me to do it?"

I tried to reassure Hatchet, but it came out too intensely: *"I got it."*

The knife went in and came out with a savage, expert quickness—precision violence. The blood flowed.

"I've drained so many animals in my life, Hatch'— I've just seen a lot of blood, is all."

"If it bothers you, dude, I can take care of it next time."

"No, it's fine—just kind of got lost for a second. I don't mind it at all."

We split the tasks and split the buck, and Hatchet had just graciously given me the pelt (even though it was he who'd done all of the sophisticated hunting-work, tracking, and coordinating) when Hank Jaggar came hustling up.

"Hatch', Dante, we've got some more newcomers. Store that meat and get your rifles."

"Watterson newcomers, you are surrounded by rifle-men—be you friend, or be you foe?"

A sleepy-sounding *"Hm?"* was issued from the

tent, and Hank Jaggar repeated himself loudly.

Then a voice from within the tent said, "Baby, wake up—there's people outside!"

"Mmm?"

"I'm not going to repeat myself!"

"Friends! Friends! Who are you? We have no-where else to go!"

They were a desperate couple—both runaways, it looked like, at least to me.

I didn't know what John Shade looked like, and I'd only seen Connie Caliente from a distance in the deep dark.

Connie had dyed her hair dirty blonde and was just a master at looking like someone else, so I didn't even get a whiff of recognition when I saw her, and The Shade just looked like himself, which was everybody. To me, they were complete strangers.

Candy and I never got to learn much about their cover-personalities because when they emerged from the tent in the pale light of dawn, they met and greeted Hank Jaggar with warmth, like finding their real grandfather, but when their new grandfather introduced them to me, their faces went pale.

"What? What is it?"

"Do you know who this is?" the male, "Paul," asked.

"Who? Dante?"

The haggard couple both turned to each other in shocked confirmation.

"What in the world is going on here?" Jaggar asked.

The newcomers seemed too stunned to explain, so the old man turned to me.

What looked like a sudden misery on my face be-came a hopeless acceptance.

Seventy-six people lived in the Green Wave—or at least lived in the camp quads.

The "newcomers"—Connie and The Shade, "Daphne" and "Paul"—had clung to Hank Jaggar as closely as they could. They did such a good job playing the part of scared/intimidated newcomers that neither Candy nor I ever got any impression that they were CTR agents who'd figured out where we'd gone, and right up to Jaggar's big meeting they played their roles perfectly—pretending to trust Jaggar while also pretending to be half-frightened about what kind of collection of people this could be.

The whole matter set Hank Jaggar's concerned brain into overdrive, and Hank put on a look that people followed out of curiosity.

His *de facto* leadership faced its first political challenge—namely, this unfolding mystery that had already so shaken the giant young Dante Thompson.

Within an hour, everyone from the quads who could feasibly attend that day had gathered in the clearing where community meetings usually took place, and curious murmurs filled the crowded clearing until Hank Jaggar stepped up onto the smooth stump of a dead arboreal giant and looked over the quieting crowd.

He had an OV in his hand, and the OV still had some power—its batteries still had some rechargeable snap. His face bore a look of, like, moral determination, a look that also appeared to be an attempt at making his sober, conscious, hard-fought morality infectious in the crowd. He was determined to deal with this situation wisely, and he hoped that somehow wisdom could be willed into himself and his fellow men.

"Ladies and gentlemen, we have a situation before us that requires a great amount of clear thinking, and I hope we can conduct this discussion with that in mind. I will not allow emotions to trump a deeper truth here, so anyone who starts feeling emotional had better also start feeling reticent, because the path to truth involves not getting off on the first emotional exit, OK?"

"The hell's going on, Hank?" an older fisherman from another quad asked.

"Until now, whatever past we had behind us was kept there, but this morning some information was brought to my attention that puts . . . things into a perspective we need to think about."

The crowd shifted and muttered uneasily. Candy, Tyger, and I were at the back of the crowd, ready to run if things took a turn for the riotous.

"I will not yet disclose who it is, but some members of our community are currently being sought by a nationally funded CTR Team, and you all know the kind of resources they have available, even in the decay."

"*Yeah?* What the Hell did they *do?*" a male fisherman asked plainly—he and Jaggar must have been friends. "If it's even true."

"Before we get to that, do we really care what anybody has done before they got here, as long as they don't break our rule while they're here?"

(The only rule in Jaggar's corner of the Green Wave: "Don't do anything to anyone that you wouldn't want everyone else to be able to do to you," which Candy and I both quickly identified as a folksy rendering of Kant's Categorical Imperative, the punishment for which was the only punishment the community could offer: banishment.)

"I mean," Jaggar continued, "aren't we all getting away from the past? Haven't we given up on that world anyway—so wouldn't a crime there, to us, be, like, a *good* thing?"

"Fuck that, Hank—what if they're murderers?"

"Before today, our last arrivals were the Thompsons five weeks ago, and the Jenkins before that—at least ten weeks amongst any potential psychopaths and nothing untoward happened to any of us."

"What about them two suicides not long back?" another voice called out.

"Trust me," Hank Jaggar said. "Those two incidents have nothing to do with this."

"I don't care what they did, Hank, but I don't want no drones around here. We got somethin' good here, and I don't want it gone on account of some bad folks using our good community to hide in. Ain't that a violation of our rule?"

"I don't know—let's think about that."

"What the heck did they *do?* We see you got that OV, so let's have it, Hank!"

Jaggar seemed to notice the OV again, in his hand. "Right, OK, well, I suppose it's worth knowing." He powered on the OV, which was already set to an article written two days previously on *WireFlash:* "The headline says, 'Swanson Falls Copy Cats Strike Corn City':

"'Two retired Corn City residents, Samuel and Gloria Smith, 84 and 83 respectively, of Peach Tree St., were killed last night by an unidentified group of assailants. The Smiths were executed in such a fashion as to lead the Corn City Militia's chief detective to believe the homicides were part of a copy-cat trend that has been striking many parts of the former nation after the horrific Swanson Falls slayings.

"'The throats were cut, and there was writing on the mirror,' Detective Drew Bukowski admitted after much prompting. 'There were different sizes of footprints in blood on the floor, and there are several known packs of kids who roam Corn City's streets at night, so rest assured, we're going to find who did this. Listen, folks, if the war is here, we'll show the war the door. Corn City just wants peace and prosperity back here in the heartland—justice and peace, all of it.'

"Justice, peace, and prosperity. Noble goals for a dwindling town rattled by yet another new fear.

"'I thought we raised our kids better than this,' said one Corn City mother who wished to remain unidentified. 'Why ain't nothing ever going right anymore? Why ain't they tryin' to fix the broke things instead?'

"The perpetrators must not have fully read the official *RothReport* write-up of the Swanson massacre, because the nearest mirror was filled with a multi-worded message: 'IT'S OUR TURN TO DO WHAT WE WANT.'"

(When Jaggar read that part of the article, Candy and I looked at each other and saw that both of our faces had drained of color.)

"It's an eight-word mantra that has become an OV meme, with many kids being put on CTR watch lists for ramping up generational rhetoric and signing their statements with that declaration."

Candy Baby said to me, "Oh, my God—we have to go, Beebs."

I said flatly, numbing myself to the hollowing knowledge, "I know."

"Baby Boomer Phillip McGuinty was asked of his opinion of the recent developments. 'These kids don't have Jesus, is what it is. They don't got Jesus, so we got guns. Yeah, sure, we Baby Boomers weren't perfect, but we respected our elders. We did our best, and we did a damn good job. It's not our fault kids today ain't got Jesus or a heart. I got my gun, is what I got, for any kids that want to come after me and blame me for the rotten world: I got something for *you*.'

"The Swanson Falls slayings took place December fifth in the new, highly securitized suburb formerly known for being one of the best neighborhoods in America to live in. On that night, some people"—Jaggar skipped over our names and changed "a pair of siblings named Dante and Sylvia Thompson (pictured)" to "some people"—"murdered more than eight-hundred Baby Boomers, blew up a hospital, crashed a security drone, assassinated former DHS Secretary Milton W. Blank and his wife, and left a belligerent three-hundred-twenty-five-word note in blood on the mirrors of the dead's homes, one word, one mirror, one home at a time. The note was a warning to the Baby Boomer generation that the youth were fomenting an overdue revolution against the former America's elders.

"The two are still at-large, and CTR Team 5, led by Captain Perry Heimler, is offering ten-million DHS dollars for any information on their whereabouts.

"'When I first heard the story about them folks in Swanson Falls, I thought it was pure horse apples,' said Detective Bukowski. 'But here we are—these are crazy, crazy times, I guess, even here.'

"If there's one silver lining to the last month of tragedy, it's that lately, and possibly, given the quotation below, in response to the suburban attack, there have been new talks amongst former government officials about reconstituting the former federal government, with many of America's warlords having been rounded up and both sides of the political aisle finally seeking a compromise in the hopes of restoring law and order to a nation that has been hit as hard as any in the world by the global economic downturn.

"Said real-estate mogul, former Senator, current DHS Secretary, and leading champion of the rebirth of the nation, Frank Savage, 'For years we've allowed infighting to distract us, and we've been forced to try to get by on our own, but time and practice have again taught us the immortal lesson: United we stand, divided we fall. Just as we've allowed the Swanson Falls killers and all our other intergenerational skirmishes to divide us, it's time for all Americans to unite against that kind of pure evil and end this inhuman conflict once and for all. Indeed America has a powerful enemy: herself. How do we make her good again? Through Virtue, Justice, and Compromise.'

"For now, at least in Corn City, there is less evidence of federal Virtue, Justice, and Compromise than there is of innocent dead Baby Boomers."

There was a voidish silence in the clearing when Jaggar finished, as when a speeding train has passed.

"Just so we're clear, Hank, you're saying the Swanson Falls, like, *assassins,* are here among us? I don't see any packs of homicidal teens, but I haven't seen everything there is to see in these trees."

"Yeah, Duke—the assassins."

Hank Jaggar looked young for his age, and in fact he was one of the youngest of the Baby Boomers. He admitted as much to the crowd; he was born in 1961.

"I don't know if they knew I'm a Baby Boomer, but I don't think they'd come after me even if they just found out—if they're here, they're one of us. And besides, it sounds like I'd already be dead if I were their enemy."

"But Hank, the droones, 'ey? What're we goona do aboot the CTR droones, 'ey?"

"We have no reason to believe the CTR Team knows they're here; if they did know, don't you think we'd have been buzzed by now? The newcomers who showed me this have been following the story like, they say, most of the nation has, so if that information were out there, they'd know."

"Why are they here, then?"

"Who, the newcomers or the Swanson Falls killers? Either way, it's the same as why you're here. You don't load up for the Green Wave unless you're looking for something that's not out there anymore."

The crowd murmured.

"So what's it going to be, then? Did they break our rule or not?"

Hank Jaggar had been avoiding that question, but it was time to face it. The clearing again went quiet as they awaited his pronouncement.

In that quiet, I cleared my voice and said, "Don't worry about it, Mr. Jaggar."

With big eyes the crowd all watched us walk up and join Hank on the big stump.

"What are you doing, Dante?"

I addressed the crowd instead.

"It was us, and we're leaving."

The crowd murmured, with a frosting of agitation.

Puzzled, Hank Jaggar asked, "What?"

"Mr. Jaggar, my sister and I would like to thank you and the Green Wave community for being so fair to us in our stay here."

Candy Baby said, "What those kids did in Corn City—what they wrote . . . Our actions have been terribly misunderstood, Mr. Jaggar, and we need to try to clarify them, if we can."

"How you going to do that, blow up a college?" someone said from the safe anonymity of the crowd.

I turned to Hank Jaggar and offered my hand. "Be well, Hank."

"We haven't said you kids have to leave yet—hell, why do you think I'm here if I loved my generation so much? I see your hearts, kids, and I see that they're good hearts. It's a messed-up world led us all here, I know."

"Hank, if there's really a God, it must be insanely frustrating for God to watch the ways men twist the

Bible's words to suit their laziest wishes. I'm not saying my brother or I am godlike, but something important we've done has been misunderstood, and we still have the ability to try to clarify our intentions."

"Or maybe we never understood it ourselves."

"Whatever it is, we need to try to fix it if we can."

"What are you all saying? We can't hear you," someone shouted from the growingly agitated crowd.

Hank Jaggar was a good man, and we received a nice psychological stroke from the minor note of sadness in his voice when he said to the crowd, "They're leaving."

Most people ruminatively accepted the news—quiet murmurs—but one woman from the back shouted, "Good riddance!"

I pulled apart my shelter and stacked the wood for the Jenkins' use. Candy Baby left her shelter standing, and for the first time the Jenkins ever saw, she held Tyger by a leash.

She approached the Jenkins family, who were wordlessly, confusedly, sadly watching us pack up to leave. We ourselves had been silent, too. Only the forest spoke, and it didn't say much.

At the sound of my shelter crashing to the ground, Candy walked across the quad, to the Jenkins family, who were standing in their own quad, which placed them amongst the general looky-lou smattering of people who'd gathered to witness our hopeless emigration, and said to Erica, "I think—where we're going, or probably
. . . ."

Little Panda waddled over to the leashed Tyger and played with her, and Tyger, tethered, played back mildly, but also eyed Candy.

Candy looked up from the little scene and towards Erica and held forward the human's end of the leash, unable to actually say the words.

"Sure, honey—sure, Candy, we've got her," Erica said. "She'll be happy here."

Candy nodded, and Erica wiped the tears from her own eyes.

Candy cry-smiled in thanks at the couple, then she kneeled down, to Tyger's wise old face and Panda's ignorantly joyful little chubby one, and she asked the Chubster, "You like Tyger, Panda?"

Panda had just learned what a thumbs-up was, and she thumbs-upped and said, "Ya!"

"Good," said Sylvia. She put her head to Tyger's and kissed her fur and hugged her neck and said to the little girl, "She's a good old dog . . . make sure she always knows you love her."

"O'kuh, Sylwya."

Candy had to walk away without saying anything else or she would have died of love and sadness and despair—of being too full of life's painful inflations, seeing too much through Tolstoy's holes in this existence, which show us something greater.

She hadn't planned on it, but once she took that first step away she just wanted to keep going, so she walked over to her packs and started piling herself with her gear. I could see that she wanted out, so I hurried and finished stacking the wood and jogged over to the Jenkinses and said to Hatch, "I bequeath you my stacks, or give them to whoever needs them. Be well, old man."

"Be well, young man."

"Thank you for everything, Erica."

She said nothing but inclined her head in a sad nod, and I bowed to them both.

I kneeled down and ran my big fingers over Tyger's ears and neck and body, the speedy old bitch.

I kissed her on her cheek, and she tried to lick my

face, and I told her I loved her.

Then I understood why Candy wanted to leave, and I walked away and rapidly packed myself up as she had.

Aut viam inveniam aut faciam.—
"I will either find a way or make one."

Hank Jaggar escorted us out to where he and some of the others had first found us.

"Do you kids even have a plan?"

" . . . "

"You're just going out there, what, to be arrested, tried, hanged? You went through all that trouble, and now you're just going to turn yourselves in?"

Candy and I were both dazed and trying to figure that shit out ourselves—we just knew we had to go.

"We thought we would be able to lay low here before we struck again, but we didn't realize that we would become so intertwined with such great people and inevitably put all of you in CTR danger. And now those new people arriving and recognizing us? It's only a matter of time—"

"I think we thought the ideas were contained in the people, Mr. Jaggar," Candy said. "But the ideas have spread from those people to others, and we need to figure . . . ."

Her mind lapsed back into the concern itself before she could finish stating what exactly the concern was.

"You're both stumbling around trying to figure out what you're trying to say, and now you're planning on walking out and frickin' *improvising* a solution?"

"Aut viam inveniam aut faciam," I said. Hank had never memorized any Latin phrases—he must have used to have a career and a life to live, before his generation ruined everything.

To clarify I said, "Hank, our father hid from them, and he didn't even do anything wrong, but they found him eventually, and they killed him right in front of us. And then they killed our mother and friends. You think, whether we're here or not, they won't eventually come to this place and kill or imprison everyone here, too? We'd thought we were onto something with what we did, but it turns out that our actions appear to have instead inspired the reelection of old patterns in new people."

Candy said, "Sometimes . . . like . . . a sacrifice . . . is necessary."

"Seems to be necessary—praise Jesus," I said.

"We thought it was the Blanks and the Boomers, but maybe it's us. Maybe we're the sacrifice."

"Thank you for everything, Mr. Jaggar."

Candy Baby hugged the unreceptively incredulous Hank Jaggar and then slowly crunched down the snowy path, towards the opening we first arrived through. Then Hank, catching up to the moment, offered me a somewhat stunned handshake, and I backed away uncomfortably. Rather than addressing that, I said, "Hank, I figured they couldn't all be bad, and I didn't know all that many . . . Anyway, *you* are a good man, sir, and my sister and I are both proud to have lived in your amazing community, however briefly." Then I looked around for a moment, and the nagging thought completed itself, and I said, "I bet he would have liked you—it's sad."

Mr. Jaggar wasn't following much of what we were giving him, given everything he was being given at once, but he wanted to understand as much as he could. He asked, as I was already walking away, "Who would have liked me; what's sad, son?"

"Our father," I said over my shoulder.
I stopped and turned to him.
"And . . . shit . . . pretty much everything."
We both weakly waved goodbye.

Morituri nolumus mori.

The forest thinned out and became a large grove, which gave way to dead flat farmland. We marched with lead legs, with no soul put into the effort—just dread. We were carried forward by dread. By the feeling of Fate. By sheer will. By the grace of a cold, distant Godless God.

"Big barn," I said. "Let's go rest there and think—I don't feel right."

Candy Baby came out of her thoughts and slightly changed direction, towards the barn.

What are we going to do? How can we clarify our message appropriately, or should we just turn ourselves in? Would the CTR Team even arrest us, or would they feel the greater good would be served by an easily explained battlefield execution? Was that it? Were we about to die? What could we do or say to get the genie to finally do what's best for once?

The field was white with snow but not so deep that our walk was made any more miserable than it already was. The extremely bright whiteness hurt my eyes, but I didn't mind; the purity of the whiteness was a pretty distraction. Winter is an ending, and all endings are inherently beginnings. The whiteness I saw:

Was it whitewashing the old cycle or providing stored fuel for the new?

The wind was a cold swirling whore, and the sun was just much too bright—the piled snow's reflective whiteness drove straight into my brain.

The supersonic rifle slug drove straight through Candy's shoulder, and she spun around and fell, fountaining blood throughout her bodily spin. *"Ow!"*

Another bullet whipped past my head—I could hear the zip and feel the breeze of it—and I dropped to my hands and knees.

"Have I been shot? They got me? Who got me? Have I been shot?" Candy asked me and the bright blue sky.

"Yeah, Can'—you've been shot."

"Why? We were just walking!"

A rifle slug tagged my left hand, right through, a quarter-stigmata. The blood gushed and pooled and mixed with Candy's in the snow.

"FUCK!" I shouted, from the growing cold throb. The eye of my left palm was just a hurricane of pain. How was Candy not screaming?

"They're going to kill us here! They'll never know! They'll never hear what we meant! Can you run? You've got to run! Run, Dante! We're a threat! We really found a pressure point! Run!"

Then we both heard the mild, throaty sounds of the Roader, which emerged from behind the farmhouse itself, where Hector Mass was scurrying into the truck from the house, where one of the second-floor windows was wide open on the coldest day of the year.

The Roader spun up a rooster-tail of snow as its tires spun out, chunked through the snow and ice, bit into frozen earth, and drove the truck forward, towards the growing red island of blood.

I put my arms around Candy, put my head next to hers, and said, "I love you, Candy."

Candy didn't say anything. I pulled back and

saw that she was silently crying at me, hopelessly and despairingly bawling. And through that look I felt all the love there was to feel in the world pouring from that anguished, tortured, wordless face.

I stood and said, "I'll see you soon. It isn't over yet, sister; you're stronger than they are!"

I dropped everything but my rifle and booked to the woods.

One, two, three NOW! One, two NOW! One, two, three, four NOW! One NOW! One, two, three NOW!

I changed direction with every now as the Roader pumped devastating round after devastating round into the crumbling forest. Single rounds felled entire trees, and I zigzagged with a warrior's determination to survive, to regroup, to find a way to win what appeared to be an inevitably unwinnable war.

The rounds felled trees and kicked up floating castles of snow and earth, but none of them met anyone named me, and soon even the scope in Hector Mass's artillery nest lost my large frame in the multitude of trees to the northeast.

The Roader stopped, and Heimler arrested Candy Baby at the same time John Shade and Connie Caliente emerged from the forest with their Sigs drawn. They'd headed towards the whumping of the Roader's terrible cannon.

When they emerged, they saw that there was only one person receiving medical treatment by the Roader. The Shade did one of those hawk-whistle sounds some people can do, and Heimler looked up and saw the other two members of his Team coming towards him and hand-signaling, "Mission success?"

He replied negatively, and the two members

reverse-traced my blood all the way to the crimson island in the open field.

"What the fuck happened, Hector?" Connie asked truculently. "I thought you could shoot. Or do you not know the difference between one person and two people? Between a leg and a shoulder?"

"Connie, give it a goddam rest," Heimler said.

Connie looked to The Shade for emotional support in her vulnerable moment, but she caught The Shade staring at Candy Baby's face instead, and her emotions exploded.

"GOD!" she screamed and huffed off to be alone.

There was a void of silence in her wake, and after a few moments Hector Mass said honestly, "Rogue winds or something, Shade—I don't know. I never missed a shot since I was ten. I don't know, man; between that old man's tree and these winds, Fate must be on these kids' side or something."

Candy, pretending the morphine had knocked her unconscious, had to bite her cheek to keep from guffawing at the idea of Fate being on any Thompson's side.

"Yeah, well, Fate also left us a bloody trail in the snow," Heimler said, butting in. "Let's take the girl somewhere safe and figure out how we plan on bringing in the boy."

The winter sun quickly leaned back to the horizon and drained the day of light and color as it traveled to places it apparently preferred for now, until the night sky filled with that glowing purple air over the snow. In that time, I found a safe spot and entrenched and braced for whatever may come.

"No fucking way I'm letting you go alone, Shade," Heimler said in the desk lamp–lit basement of the farmhouse. "That kid is stronger and might be smarter than you, and it just doesn't make sense for you to go alone."

"Do you know anyone who can stalk quiet as I can, Cap'? Do you think Mass will be an asset to me in those trees? Do you think Connie knows how to cover silent terrain?"

"Connie's great in the—"

"Respectfully, Captain, Connie knows people, but nobody else on this Team could get into that forest and get close to that kid but me. General Dweezil isn't going to authorize randomly firing R&Rs and Incas into that forest in the hopes of getting lucky, and we have a blood trail to follow anyway."

"John—"

"This is what I do, Cap'. Trust me . . . I got it under control: I've got a line on how this fucker thinks."

The Shade stressed the words to punctuate the unspoken point that he'd been correct after all—the Thompson-Khans had horsed two days north to the relatively familiar confines of the Green Wave while the rest of the nation looked in their bathroom mirrors—and he pointed his words at everyone on the Team in response to the looks he was getting for his tactically necessary brutal honesty.

Heimler considered The Shade's arguments, looked at Connie and Mass for counterarguments, received from them nothing but pissed-off looks at The Shade, and finally said, "Fine, *White Feather.* Go get him before dawn, before he comes after us."

The Shade, now a snow leopard, stalked silently across the forest floor in the grey-purple air of pre-dawn, but everything he saw was electric green through his night-scope ocular. The bloodstains in the snow showed up as much darker streaks, obviously, than the pure white snow around them, and watching the streaming trickles as he hiked almost felt like he were a data-drone following a long river from miles above.

He crept steadily through the forest and didn't exactly fret over the occasional noises he or the environment would make—clustered trees have a disquieting way of diffracting and killing sound. What he sweated, though, was what he'd just found: a trap.

Fortunately in his ocular the bootlace stood out profoundly over the brightness of the snow, and The Shade followed the design of the trap from the bootlace to a dead-drop snare—a heavy rock dangling over a fine black powder and a few grainy pebbles—which appeared as though it would be nothing more than an audible warning for the setter.

The Shade silently stepped over the bootlace and continued following the dark river of blood from miles and miles above.

He became so transfixed with the consciousness-shift he'd noticed from the techno-periscopic effects of his night-vision ocular that he almost set off the second, deadlier trap: another bootlace was attached to a vine that was tied to a heavy, spiky, dry piece of deadwood, which, if unleashed, would've swung in a long gravity-fast arc following the same trajectory as the trail of blood—the log affixed to the straps of my big rifle case.

It looked to The Shade like the first trap had been set up to put him into a panic, the second to take advantage of the panic with an unseen, decisive blow.

He was correct.

But The Shade knew the rule of threes, and he discarded the paradigm-shift nonsense of his vision and stoked his vigilance as the light in his ocular grew more and more vibrant.

Outside the forest, the sun had risen, and the light and color were returning to the air in front of his face.

The Shade stopped and took off his helmet and let his eyes adjust to the subtle light of the early morning. He looked down and saw the deep, dark crimson of my blood in the snow. The sight of the blood in natural light reminded The Shade of the stakes of his forest creep, and he hunched lower to the ground and continued forward, helmet back on but *sans* night-vision—to where the blood became only dots, to a clearing.

The clearing was silent, and clearly The Shade was near Dante Thompson because the snow of the clearing was trampled and retrampled by big boot tracks. The far end of the clearing held a sizable lake of blood, where the young man, I, must have addressed the wound to his, my, hand, for there was no trail of blood leading away.

The Shade walked the perimeter of the clearing and looked for any prints headed deeper into the woods. There were none. There was the path we had both followed in, there were enough bootprints for there to have been a dance party, and there was nowhere else Dante Thompson could have gone.

The clearing contained two juniper shrubs—one bigger and fuller than the other—and that's where The Shade turned his attention. He walked towards the larger one, and as he looked closer he could see that its base was just a little too human-shaped. He was so convinced that he opted to bypass his helmet's body-heat ocular.

Instead, The Shade withdrew his Sig and spoke to the shrubbery.

"I finally broke my woman, Dante. She's totally

mine now—I own her. Last night I got her to film me while I fucked your sister in her hot little asshole." He crunched a slow path around the big juniper. "Do you know why I fucked her shitbox rather than her dirtbox? 'Cause there's a giant hairy bush on that girl, son—she's got some nasty vag' action when you come to it." He chuckled to himself. "But, Dante, that ass was a palace. You ever had it? You aren't *blood* siblings, right? A *lot* of years in that bomb shelter together ... I guess what I mean is that when the pubes are long like that it burns my dick if I stick it in the pink. You ever notice that? You ever fuck anyone besides raping Edna-Jane Sybil, Dante? Anyway, doesn't that stupid mute whore sister of yours know what century it is? Long pubes like that?" The Shade chuffed to himself. "Actually, never mind. I read your file: You guys aren't even from this *millenium,* huh? Raised by NLA freaks. By fuckin' losers. Some dead hermit creep and some Rushmore whore? You ever seen that video? *Jaysus* it looked like she could fuck a lot better than your little bitchster. My girl and I were unimpressed. We might tape over it and try again tonight."

The Shade braced himself to shoot, aimed the gun at the juniper, and asked, "Want to watch?"

A dog barked.

The Shade turned and saw a brown-black blur— *the me-smelling Tyger!*—rip across the clearing and leap. Then The Shade felt the dog's savage bite on his left forearm and dropped to his knees and wrestled with the deeply serious old mutt.

Four things then happened in extremely rapid succession: The Shade pulled the trigger, Tyger yelped horribly, Tyger died, and I launched my attack.

For a moment The Shade must have thought that perhaps a tree had silently fallen on him? But then he realized he was under yet another physical attack, and all the normal gears of his training fell into place.

The gears and training, however, were useless,

because I was two-hundred-forty pounds of uncommon fury, and I quickly pinned The Shade to the ground, chest down, and took the man's arms, one at a time, with my good hand, and folded them over his back until both shoulders came out of the sockets and both humeri cracked in half. The pain was so great that The Shade let out two squeals of helpless agony that were diffracted by the trees.

I ground my knee into his back and said, "Tell me where she is, or you die badly."

The Shade didn't even bother squirming—he just stared into the ground in shock and tried to catch his agonizing breath.

I chucked a handful of snow into The Shade's face and repeated myself. "Tell me where she is, or you die badly."

"What's die badly?"

I grabbed the lower-broken portion of his right arm and flopped it around so that the two halves of the broken humerus clacked together audibly, and another screaming squeal was born, followed by watery vomit.

"I was coming up here," The Shade said, laboring for breath, "to escort you back to where she is."

"Bullshit," I said.

The Shade turned to look at his assailant and saw a big shrub bearing my mud-camouflaged face.

He'd been threatening the wrong juniper.

"If you were sent here to escort me, why would you come up here planting seeds in my head that would harvest your blood?"

"Aikido—I thought you'd be easier to take down if you went berserker."

"I'm a big man."

"I've taken down bigger than you—big men have big weaknesses."

"Indeed. But broken arms are bigger weaknesses."

The Shade looked at his arms and then at the ground. "Indeed."

I picked up his Sig and took my knee off his back—*"Don't move"*—and went over to Tyger's cooling corpse.

"This dog had a brother that was also killed by fucks like you. We loved this dog. You killed Tyger."

"He started it," The Shade said.

"She."

The Shade had already played his one card, and he was upset that the finished game was ongoing. "Look, you can either kill me, or I can take you to your sister, or I can die here of shock. Which will it be?"

"'What's it going to be then, eh?'"

"What?"

"What's your name, guy? Besides The AARBB's Little Bitch."

" . . . "

" . . . "

"John."

"John, where's my sister?"

"She's where I can bring you if you make me some splints for my arms."

I decided to deploy a tactic Mr. Justin used to use—probe-guessing and reading body language for the truth.

"She's nearby?"

The Shade's face went blank, and to me he looked like the sort of guy who'd try to throw me off if I were on the right track.

"Jesus, she's in the barn, of course," I said and watched The Shade's face go so empty he might as well have said yes. But I played along a little further. "Or is it the house?"

The Shade's broken arms really took him out of his game, and he tried to make it look like the house mention had really hit home, but the effect was terribly melodramatic. Definitely the barn. I bet that shooter's in the house. He's next.

"John what?"

"   . . .   "
"   . . .   "
". . . Shade."
"John Shade?"
"Yeah."
"Not anymore."
The Shade bled to death. The air was full of sun-light.

Though the sky was squintingly vibrant, the earth was frozen, and I had miles to go before I slept. Instead of trying to bury Tyger in the frozen ground, I built a large bonfire and incinerated her poor noble body in its heart, and I let The Shade's rapidly cooling corpse attend the ceremony with something like what Miss Thompson might've darkly referred to as Irish Respect, which is the deep respect the Irish give to the dead. Doubly so if already dead themselves, presumably.

I heaped piles and piles of deadfall on the chest-high pyre, at the base of which was Tyger, and after it was ignited I threw armloads of green fir branches on the orange-glowing, snapping logs, and a thick column of smoke started rising into the sky. A warning to the rest of CTRT5.

Then I prepped my rifle, re-prepped my ghillie suit, and headed back to the clearing, towards the farmhouse.

A cold wind sliced through the leafless trees and received soft shushes from the evergreens.

Audi, vide, tace.—
"Hear, see, be silent."

Over the course of four hours, the juniper shrub emerged from the trees at the edge of the clearing. What had started as the misty grey of early morning had bloomed into a bright blue afternoon—the sky a pulsing bright, bright, *bright* blue, and no clouds whatsoever, and bitterly cold: all the heat in the area seemingly being pulled up into that white hole in the otherwise empty sky.

The Shade's MOV announced, in Perry Heimler's voice: "Oh-twelve, Shade, what's your ten? You seeing that smoke?"

I stopped microcrawling and listened. At the same time, I peered through the scope on my rifle and watched the rifle barrel pointed out the open upstairs bedroom window of the farmhouse.

"Shade? Are you with him?"

" . . . "

"What's your ten, Shade?"

" . . . "

"Shade!"

The house was yellow, and the icy windows were framed in white. I watched the barrel.

"Think I got something, Cap'."

"What?"

"I don't quite know, to be honest—think I just see something that might be worth checking out."

"Mass, we don't have time for your stupid shit; I've had enough waiting—we're doing this my way. Blue Tango, Blue Tango. Blue Tango is a go."

The rifle barrel hadn't moved whatsoever. It was pointed at an empty spot in the clearing and was what—paralyzed? What could it see?

The Roader's engine growled to life, and the carnivorous vehicle jetted from its spot by the barn

397

and across the clearing. It followed my and The Shade's tracks into the Watterson Forest. And as the Roader passed between me—the unmoving juniper-ghillie—and the horse stable, the sun and the angle of the windows on the truck threw a burst of sunlight across my eyes.

Between that point and the point when Heimler used the driver's targeting system on the .75 to take out the first tree in his way, I was temporarily blinded and had to fight the urge to make the sudden move of dropping my head and trying to rapidly blink the blindness away. Instead of that, I just closed my eyes and let myself be blind for a little while—Mr. Justin had known that my sensitivity could lead to flights of panic, and he'd worked with me as much as he could to teach me ways to slow my psychic dives, relax, and take the time to find the great commonalities between myself and this existence.

When I opened my eyes, the blindness had abated slightly, but I was still seeing a flash of light by the stables. A smaller flash, though.

Circular.

SHIT!

I urgently rolled my juniper-ghillied body, aimed my rifle until an angle was lined up with the circle, SWAG'd a distance and wind bearing, and executed.

Two shots were fired across the bright clearing.

I'm writing this—I won.

Hector Mass is dead.

I immediately stood and high-knee snow-sprinted across the clearing, to the barn. I didn't check on the other shooter—Mass—because either he was dead or not, and I'd find out soon enough, but I had to get to Candy before that Roader returned.

I made it all the way to the bales of hay by the door when I stopped. I caught my breath and listened for sounds coming from the barn. I looked through my scope at the house, and the propped rifle was still aiming at the empty spot in the field.

Heimler had closed the barn door behind him when he got in the Roader and shot into the forest, and at the time I didn't know exactly how many people comprised the CTR Team that had been sent after us, so I wasn't willing to risk barging in quite yet. Instead, I entered the barn through sound.

I shouted over the bales of hay, *"Cuh-CAW! Cuh-CAW!"*

I listened. All I heard was the sound of the wind and the distant, occasionally whumping, chainsaw-like grind of the Roader's progress in the forest: Some roars can't entirely be diffracted by the meditating trees.

And the sound was getting closer: The Roader was returning.

I called out again, *"Cuh-CAW! Cuh-CAW!"*

I listened for absolutely any sorts of sounds coming from the barn.

Nothing.

I realized, and said aloud, "Oh, shit—she's in the house!"

And just as I rose to dash for the yellow farmhouse, Connie Caliente sneaked up, shot a military-grade Taser into my neck, and electrocuted me into submission.

Past submission.

Unconscious.

Charta Pardonationis Se Defendendo—
"A Paper Of Pardon To The Outlaw"

I awoke screaming, "LET HIM GO!" and my shocked rise to consciousness found itself halted painfully—handcuffed by my wrists and ankles to a stainless-steel table, my sinistral hand-hole flaring in pain from all the sudden movements.

The first thing I recognized when I accepted the reality of the situation I'd awoken into was the red cyclopean eye of a recording video camera. Then my sight fell beyond the camera and read some words spray-stenciled on the far white wall: HEARTLAND FEDERAL DETENTION FACILITY.

Seated in front of me—next to the camera—were three people: a disgusted woman, a tired-looking soldier, and a middle-aged man in a snappy suit. Something was moving in my periphery, so I turned in that direction and saw the exiting back of someone—a woman?—I never saw again. The first thing I heard in my return from the fog of my deep sedation was the unseen person's voice from the hall, feminine, saying something like, "Anytime."

"Annnd he's back," the middle-aged man said to me. "Dante Thompson, my name is Frank Savage, and I'm here representing the Justice Department of the Theoretical New United States of America."

" . . . "

"My colleagues here are CTR Information Officer Connie Caliente ("Daphne" from the forest, now full of loathing) and CTR Team 5 Captain Perry Heimler (the tired-looking soldier). They are the ones who arrested you, and they will be handling the application of the course of action agreed upon today. Mr. Thompson, do you have any questions about anything you've been told so far?"

My brain was still trying to catch up with the moment, so everything Savage said reached my ears after a two-second lag. Once I was a bit keener and had looked around and more properly oriented myself with the menacingly insipid interview room, I made a brief, passive-aggressive point of rattling the chains of my handcuffs—left hand bandaged big time—before saying:

"Where's Candy?"

"What?"

I looked at the people and then looked at the table.

"Sylvia—my sister."

"Your sister is being held at a detention facility like this one—she has agreed to our deal."

"Already?"

"You don't know the deal yet."

" . . . "

The woman loathed me. The soldier was just deeply tired, it looked like.

"What are your concessions?"

"I'm sorry?"

"A deal from a theoretical government is a contract written by a fetus, not a promise in writing from a dead old man, so if I'm being offered any deal other than a bullet to the brain stem, then it's because I'm needed for, what, political reasons? Which means my sister was right: We hit a nerve. And a generationally divided United States is not a states united. So again I ask: If the civil war is over, what are the concessions?"

"You're a sharp kid," Savage said. "Here's the deal: You've murdered hundreds of innocent people and two federal agents, but if you show up and sign the peace accord with the rest of America's ideological representatives, you'll be given the same clemency as everyone else who signs it."

I didn't say anything; some people start talking while they process, but not I.

"Forgive and forget?" I finally asked cynically.

"For the greater good—yes."

"There's an awful lot of hate in people's hearts these days, Mr. Savage—you think witnessing an accord will douse that kind of fire?"

"Even anarchists want peace, Dante—we have a real opportunity here; we're *making* a real opportunity here."

"What's peace to the fox is war to the hens," I said. "So what kind of peace are we talking about—the peace of respecting or the peace of obeying?"

Frank Savage started to dislike me, it looked like.

"You want to talk about obeying versus respecting, Mr. Khan?"

"They were never going to respect us. They morally crippled the world and turned their scorn towards us, and others, and whatever was convenient except the truth, and now the disease has fucking spread. So I sign an accord, and the most irrationally selfish and narcissistic generation in the history of humanity and their self-entitled mutant offspring will suddenly achieve enlightenment? They'll shut their mouths and beg us to forgive them for turning the beacon of the world into a crack pipe?"

"I don't know if you're being intentionally obtuse or playing an angle or what, but Dante the rebirth of the United States is inevitable—if we don't have you at the conference, we'll have Sylvia, and if we didn't have her, we'd hire lookalikes and then have them die in 'unfortunate' accidents after signing the accord. You're being given a very clear offer right now: Hop on the train of events, Dante, or kiss Anna Karenina hello and goodbye."

I smirked. I muttered to myself a line I'd once heard on an old Bill Hicks comedy album: *"We've got ourselves a reader."*

I looked up from my thoughts.

"Who really coordinated this peace conference?" I asked. "Who's leading this quixotic shit?"

"You're looking at him, Mr. Thompson."

"Well then lay it all on me if you want me to agree."

"There's no time, Dante—there are tremendously important international machinations in place that require a united American response. Now that we have you and your sister, we've apprehended nearly all of the nation's rebel leaders. The rest of the extant CTR Teams have been given top priority to apprehend the rest, because we're going to need everyone's help."

"You've got lots of problems, Mr. Savage, but I only have one, as far as I can tell."

"Dante, you yourself know what happened! The country inflated and then was punctured by something blunt, deflated, and crashed into the rest of the world. With the crash came the blame and acrimony that turned belligerent in response to the corruption that fed itself blind. It all desperately needs to be fixed."

"And how do you propose to fix it?"

"Through a pact. United We Stand, Divided We Fall. That's what the pact will be called, which we'll all sign. What it stands for is the idea that everyone has been wronged, and there have been crimes committed and deaths submitted for all the myriad causes that I've endeavored to bring together, to bury the proverbial hatchet, to have everyone find it in their hearts to accept that all the innocent and guilty dead from the past are from here forward to serve as an ongoing reminder that on the day the pact was signed, all of America's divided factions came together to find the commonalities of, as you said, human respect, in the hopes of the betterment of all people."

"What kind of government?"

"After we sign the accord, we begin structuring

the new government, and we will work on it for as long as it takes, with feedback from every group."

"How could that ever work?"

"I'll make it work, Dante—trust me. When history needs people, people rise. You rose; you forced the Boomers to take a critical look at themselves and their world—you planted a seed. Now I'm trying to plant another one."

I suddenly and somewhat inexplicably remembered/realized something. I turned to Connie.

"You were lovers with the man I killed in the woods?"

Her loathing was a form of mourning, I realized.

The tired soldier grew angry. "Don't talk to her."

"He said he buggered my sister while you videotaped it."

Connie was oddly ruminative for a moment. She closed her eyes, opened them, and then slapped me across the face as forcefully as she could. Right hand. Very strong woman. Not as strong as Candy.

It took me a moment to recover. "He said he broke you. He didn't even need to say it, because I didn't give a shit, but he seemed to really enjoy the idea that he'd, quote, finally broken his woman. I didn't want to believe he . . . but you, Officer Caliente, you look broken."

I turned back to Frank Savage. "So OK, maybe Sylvia and I represent the Generationalists, or whatever catchword we're being called, but who did you get to represent all African-Americans? American Catholics? American women? How did you draw the line?"

"Dante, consider the fact that I've been working on these questions for nearly twenty years. At the conference, you're going to be escorted by Captain Heimler here, just like all of the other warlords will have CTR escorts. Once the agreement to form a new nation is signed, and the government has been structured, you and Sylvia will be free like everyone else—and if we do it right, I believe a better era will begin."

Two days later, Intelligence Officer Connie Caliente came to my cell in the Heartland FDF, and we had an all-night talk. Why? I had information she needed to know before she made an important decision, and she had information I wanted. We both *quid pro quo'd* each other dry, and I've already integrated everything I learned from our conversation into the rest of this story.

A day later I was informed that she'd resigned from CTRT5.

I won again.

It was once said, "God is not a second-rate novelist."

Where was the peace ceremony being held?

Frank Savage owned a real-estate firm that had commissioned the construction of a massive resort on a river in the Titan Mountains nearly two decades ago.

The Hidden Woods comprised a three-hundred-room modern-rustic hotel, a big jing-jangling casino, an absolutely abyssal indoor/outdoor swimming pool, eighteen holes of golf, ten-thousand acres of forestry (with hiking, biking, and snowmobiling trails carved throughout—and let's not forget the fishin' in that dark Blunt River), as well as a five-hundred-seat theater for films and live performances.

Those were the grounds, and for the event pretty much everything man-made had been covered with those three American colors. So many banners and streamers and bright signs that from a good enough distance the grounds looked like a snowy-white, fir-dotted forest that surrounded a towering metropolis of red, white, and blue flowers.

But the closer the helicopter flew, the more I could see that it was all the same signs and streamers and banners I'd seen thousands of times before on the OV. Some of the others in the helicopter said, *"Ooh!"* and *"Aah!"* but I hadn't been raised to worship those colors, so they were just trivia, and anyway I was thinking about the little bend in the river I'd seen a few minutes ago.

We flew closer and could see the news vans with flowering satellite dishes and cameramen in heavy parkas filming the grounds and the people and the helicoptery.

Our helicopter landed on the pad farthest from the door where the man with the white gloves was motioning all the new arrivals inside. When the helicopter door opened, I hopped out and started heading for the white-gloved door, and Capt. Heimler hustled to catch up and grabbed me by the arm.

Above us, the helicopter's rotors produced a deafening whumping, and I, being grabbed, stiffened, looked squarely into Perry Heimler's eyes, and said, "DON'T. TOUCH. ME."

A solid soldier knows a valid threat. He put his hand down and put his other hand on the holster of his Sig, to convey his own valid threat.

I shot a responding look at Heimler that said, "All your bullets are little bitches compared to what I am."

I walked to the walkway, away from the helipads, towards the white-gloved door, followed by Heimler—a composition of motivational opposites: Me looking at everything except Heimler, and Heimler watching only me.

When we were far enough away from the whumping of the engines, I stopped looking around, turned to

Heimler, and asked again, "Where's my sister?"

Heimler said, "As far as I know, she's on schedule to arrive just like everyone else."

"When?"

"I really don't know—I just know that my superior has been reporting that everything so far is on schedule."

I turned and continued.

The man at the door—in the white gloves, motioning and smiling—said, "It's through here—you'll see."

At the far end of the impressive room was the stage. All the seats in front of the stage had been removed, and dozens of the attendees were in small, uncomfortable pockets of standing conversation—some of them, and it was usually obvious who, had CTR escorts huddled nearby: fellow warlords and spillers of blood. The room was filled with that unintelligible sound produced by the layered conversations of hundreds of people simultaneously, which I've always found unnerving.

I chased a ghost and was chased by ghosts: I chased the ghost of my sister, whom I couldn't seem to find amongst the gathered, and I was chased by the ghost of that eerie sound, of those uncomfortable words announced over the noise of the collective chattering itself.

Most of the circles were interviews between Frank Savage's chosen American leaders and members of the extant national press.

At the front of the room, on the stage, a sign said, "Conference Will Begin at Noon." A clock next to the sign said, "11:25."

I stalked the theater and circled it and kept watching all the doors for any sign of Candy. Many of the other leaders seemed to recognize me, but none of them said anything to me, perhaps due to the look of sister-finding intent on my face or the fact that some of them were horrified and/or agitated Baby Boomers themselves. Too many, in fact, for my tastes, but at that point seeing my sister was all I was really worried about. I'd return my attention to the pernicious Baby Boomers when it came time for us to argue for our country's fate.

More men arrived. A few women arrived, too. No Candy. The only other person around my or Candy's age was a female being interviewed by someone from *NewsWire,* but the girl didn't look very friendly, and her CTR escort was no joke.

The clock said, "11:51."

A tall female reporter being hovered over by a cameraman, stopped me and said, "Dante Thompson, *The Khan,* I'm Alicia Vernalstorm from *OV Rat News.* I see that nobody else has had the guts to talk to you. Frankly, we'd heard rumors you'd be here, but we're all quite shocked to see you in person. In fact, one leader said he's completely terrified of you. Talk about that."

I furrowed my eyebrows and looked at the woman and asked, *"What?"*

I moved on and returned to the door where the greeter with the white gloves had been, and I walked back out to the heliport, in the bright cold, where the wind whipped but no helicopters hovered. The helipads were full of motionless and parked machines. There was space for one more, but the sky was empty but for the miles-up drones.

When I turned back inside I noticed that my escort hadn't followed me out, and when I reentered the confusion of the conversation-resounding theater, my spine was encased in ice: I saw Heimler standing by the door with his finger to his earpiece, face looking deeply concerned.

When Capt. Heimler felt my approaching rage,

he sobered and addressed me and said, "Your sister's helicopter sustained a mechanical malfunction."

I no longer had any blood. Or anything at all. Inside.

Heimler saw my despair and let me stew in it before he pulled me out of the casket: "It landed—just had a problem and landed in a field. From what I hear everyone's fine and relieved and already mainly just annoyed. Some vans are on their way to pick them up at a nearby toll road and bring them here."

"Are they going to delay the ceremony?"

"No—it's too late: the network orchestration is on a schedule, so the vans will carry a broadcast of Savage's speech for your sister and the others in transit. They'll be here soon as possible."

My worries were momentarily forgotten due to the squealing of a freshly-turned-on microphone.

The ceremony was beginning, and unlike everyone else I didn't move any closer to the stage. I stood there by the door; I wanted to be right there the moment she arrived.

"United We Stand, Divided We Fall. Haven't we learned that already? Weren't we previously warned by our forefathers? So what happened? We were divided, and we fell. How did we fall? That's what we've spent the past ten years, twenty years, fifty years arguing about, thereby self-fulfilling the doomed prophecy. But then, the initial prophecy may have been correct, for there was guilt, and all of us were guilty. Ladies and gentlemen, no matter what political philosophy you believe in, the basic social contract requires a united agreement for each of us to fulfill our end of the bargain and to respect the other person's end as well. After we no longer agreed as to what that social contract stood for—when our own definition was the only one we recognized—we were divided. Today, here, right now, we begin the authoring of a new social contract. Through technology man has changed the world, but those technological advances have also served as crutches for mankind to get away with not having to change our individual selves for the better. Technology has grown, the comforts and pleasures of life have improved, but has human morality? Character? Our psychological quality of life? Have we leaned harder on advancing our technology and comforts because improving our ethics and morality required the more difficult work? Well, we have seen what happens when our understanding of morality is muddled—our decisions lose their wisdom, our trajectory lowers. To improve our relations with each other, we need to be able to see the humanity in each other. From right to left, anarchy to democracy, all systems of fair government, all open societies, they all require everyone therein to be able to recognize one another's basic humanity. Adolf Hitler did not recognize the basic humanity of the disabled and those with certain ethnic backgrounds, and the world's revulsion towards his ghastly actions is an indirect but clear statement that every independent individual in the world, no matter what race, sex, or cognitive ability, has a certain inherent baseline equality of rights given and owed, and we must all respect those rights or risk becoming a divided people once again, and lose our way. So what are those rights? Are they still the same as at our former nation's founding? Life, Liberty, and the Pursuit of Happiness? How shall we define those terms in our times? Gathered here today are the best and worst of humanity. In each of us is the best and worst of humanity, and I've gathered all of you here in order to try to see if the old adage is true about a small gathering of people changing the world. Here we have pious men and political theorists, and we also have regional warlords, NLAs, Liberals, Conservatives, Unified New Governmentists like myself—we all bear responsibility for what America has become, and we all must take responsibility in building her back up. If anyone here makes you sick, that's good—we must find common ground with those who make us sick. We must find common ground with everyone and build the world from a solid foundation, or we're all doomed. United, we can begin; divided, the end just continues.

"Today, the attendees here have all agreed to sign an accord vowing to end, as far as they and their causes are concerned, all violent or persecuting actions against any other existent groups or individuals, so that we might all begin on a Page One that comes after a prologue of billions of years of forward-moving evolution.

"Today, to put it boldly, is the conception of a better tomorrow!"

The attendees responded with a sustained applause, and eventually Savage had to motion for it to die down, and then he pulled out a sheet of paper and said, "OK, let's get started."

He read from the paper: "Speakers for the AARBB, Stephen Toadvine and Stephanie Tends, please step forward."

A polite round of applause after the two signed the accord and were embraced, arms around their shoulders, by Frank Savage, for the bright lights and flashes of press photography.

The signing was beginning, and still the doors behind me remained closed as tombs. I was turning to shout at Heimler when I saw a light at the other side of the room. Several security staff stepped in from an unseen door, followed by men and women in formal-wear, like the other attendees—one, two, four people. But no Candy!

"Speaker for the Automotive Industry: Arthur Ramicott."

I started walking along the side to the door where the new arrivals were emerging.

Applause for Arthur Ramicott.

I scanned the new attendees and then re-scanned the ones I'd seen before. More names were read, people arrived, but Candy did not!

"Heimler, where the FUCK is my sister?!"

Heimler gave me the one-second finger while he talked into his MOV. "Yeah—OK," he said and addressed me: "Your sister had a medical emergency—her wound reopened from the impact of the hard landing. She's being driven to a nearby emergency center to get new stitches."

I started heading for the helipad and said, "Then tell one of those fuckers to get ready to put a bird in the air."

"I can't. You have to be here, Dante—she's in good hands."

"How the fuck do I know what kind of hands she's in? Do you even have her? Did she escape or something?"

Somehow Frank Savage had already arrived at, "Speakers for the Generationalists: Dante and Sylvia Thompson."

There was no applause at the reading of the names; rather, the room emptied of other interests. Everyone stopped chattering and looked around to find the Khans.

"You have to go up there, Mr. Thompson."

"Not without my sister."

"Please, Dante—this is bigger than the two of you."

Frank Savage squinted and found me at the back

of the room—without Sylvia.

"Dante, I see you there."

The crowd chuckled nervously.

You know when you feel something so deep it's not only in your bones but it's in the marrow's marrow, at the spearpoint of experience, being continuously regenerated?

I felt sick. It was a goddam farce. I'd been fooled. Candy was dead? Candy had escaped? Would I ever know? I'd sign their farcical accord and suffer the aforementioned unfortunate accident. Like my sister already had. They'd already gotten rid of her.

How did Frank Savage get all his money in a time when nearly everyone with money was corrupt? He was corrupt!

It had been perfectly packaged: the description of a new tomorrow, sanctioned by the hens and yet authored by the same old foxes. The ruse was beginning anew. The lessons hadn't been learned; the lesson learned had been to make it look as though the lessons were finally learned!

I knew it.

Omnia mutantur, nihil interit.—
"Everything changes, nothing perishes."

A Little Fable
by Franz Kafka

"Alas," said the mouse, "the whole world is growing smaller every day. At the beginning it was so big that I was afraid, I kept running and running, and I was glad when I saw walls far away to the right and left, but these long walls have narrowed so quickly that I am in the last chamber already, and there in the corner stands the trap that I must run into."

"You only need to change your direction," said the cat, and ate it up.

Iustitia Omnibus— "Justice For All"

For a moment I was dead again because I thought my sister was dead again, but it soon occurred to me that there was just as good a chance that she'd already realized it was a farce and had escaped while she could, so I didn't stay dead because I still had that hope. But I couldn't escape. I was there, I was being called forward, and I knew I had to walk to the stage, escorted by my CTR chaperone—a biological pair of handcuffs. I would sign the accord with my good hand, and I knew what would happen then, and I let it happen because that would be my last act as a free man, as a man who still had the ability to act for himself, as a doomed little mouse who needed only to change his direction.

I walked to the stage, and Heimler followed me cautiously. People watched rapt.

Frank Savage said, "Where's Sylvia?" and I replied woodenly, "I'm told her helicopter sustained mechanical trouble, and she's been sent to an emergency center to have her wounds readdressed."

Frank Savage lied, "Oh, that's terrible news—I'm so sorry, Dante; I'll have them send you to where she is right after this."

I swallowed hard and said, "I'll bet you will."

Frank Savage looked undressed in the face, and I stared at him, to intimidate him, to rattle him, and without saying anything else I took the ceremonial pen from his hand and wrote where I was pointed and waited by the document for Savage's startle-delayed, photographic embrace around my stiffening shoulders.

Dennis Robert Justin was the only man who ever touched me with affection. I loved my father-figure with an immense and fearful love, and sometimes, when I was very young, Mr. Justin would gather me up in his arms, and all the fear in the world would temporarily be gone, and I would exist securely in the comforting cocoon of the genuine affection given by my caring, powerful guardian.

I was in the pubescent fog of a late-blooming fifteen when I was double-traumatized by the half-powered dosage of Velvet Waves and the horror of seeing my father-figure fall in love with and rape a company of other men and be raped by a company of other men.

I knew what would happen when New Boss, Same As The Old Boss Frank Savage tried to put his arm around me.

The National Guardsmen had touched me and briefly felt my nuclear-reactive fury. The fake preacher had touched me, and I'd gone blind with psychic rage and killed him and would have killed him twice if I could've.

Just the contact of subduing The Shade was enough to drive me to break both of the man's arms before a second thought could occur. And The Shade ended up dead, too, but that was his fault.

I knew what would happen, and just before Savage reached up, to drape his arm and pose for the picture, I closed my eyes and thought about what I'd written, and thought about where I was, *sans* Candy, and waited for my own performance.

My last decision as a free man was to give in to the part of myself that I couldn't control, especially with my sweet sister no longer around to keep me in check.

Frank Savage's hand reached my shoulder, and the show began.

What I inscrutably scribbled on the accord:
 "Fool Me Once"

Quem deus vult perdere, dementat prius.— "Whom the gods would destroy, they first make insane."

I erupted into a psychopathic rage and took my right hand and squeeze-crushed, knotted, crumpled Frank Savage's windpipe with all of my strength. Then he fell back and I followed him down and I felt my body being hit by something, but only vaguely, and the security forces must have started Tasing me, but I couldn't feel it, but it somehow registered that I could see that Frank Savage was feeling the effects of the Tasings—his eyes kept bugging at the same sustained intervals at which I seemed to be hearing a faint humming sound.

Somehow the Tasing wasn't working—given the importance of the people in attendance, IncaTubing wasn't an option—so the security officers started to pile on top of me and pull me off of Frank Savage, but the great numbers of them groaning and pulling at me reached into the depths of my unique psycho-reflexive fury and sent me into an even more determined attack against them all. I elbowed faces and tried to break arms and broke arms and spun out of headlocks and kicked in half anything not moving fast enough. The few token women in attendance were on the outside screaming for help, for me to stop. The same goes for the more fay, corrupt M-I-C scum who were also screaming for everyone to *"STOP IT!"* I saw another face, and smashed it with my knee. A hand gripped for my own face and I ended up with two bloody severed fingers in my mouth.

Fifteen, sixteen members of the security force. Each had to contain one part of this unrepentant dynamo of hate and fury, and I, the big psychotic animal, battled in rage until, evidently, I hyperventilated and passed out.

Quam bene vivas referre, non quam diu.— "It is how well you live that matters, not how long."

I awoke here.

As for the extent of my duration on this island so far, the rarely and yet unpredictably changing climate means that my only reliable time-signature comes in the form of Muciferous Facility Guard FRANKS's cobbled boots: They were relatively new when I got here, then they wore down, and he had them resoled, and now they're worn down again. Two years? Does it really matter?

Here I am now. All those supernovas, all those trillions of years, all those memories of other people's lives and mine, and then today, blink, here again. I awoke in my cell here on The Island, with the others who've never been allowed back in the reconfigured states.

The United Sham of America.

What is the new nation? What happened to the world outside? The outside world doesn't reach us here outside the world. I don't know. I can only say what I would have said had the New Constitutional Convention been anything other than a reestablishment of the same old order, with a glossy new avatar for everyone to congratulate themselves over.

It kills me that Frank Savage was so on the right track with his questions and thoughts. But indeed, it's by being near the right track that people can be led in a subtly and yet exponentially more calamitous direction.

In a direction conductors like Savage can take advantage of.

I saw it.

Ars longa, vita brevis.—
"Art is long, life is short."

If we really were to have the discussion Savage claimed to want to open, if I were ever allowed to clarify the cryptic promises made in my letter and state what I really believed, I might say that I believe in an old earth: I believe the earth and the stars, the whole universe is profoundly old, as old as I've read in textbooks. I don't know how or why, but I can see and feel the deep age in everything, even new things. I believe that in a lifetime battered by trauma and sadness, no matter how much I've cried or refused to cry, the old universe never bent to hear my whispered woes or wipe my eyes: It kept humming its own transcendent song. Thus I believe we only control as much of the universe as our physiology allows, and we must strive to understand and refine the exact limits of that control, and to not demand more than reality and our accumulated knowledge can provide, nor more than our moral weaknesses can handle. I believe the old world will exist when I'm gone, but that this old universe may end one day, too. I believe that those who believe the world only exists in their minds are setting the foundation for sociopathic behavior, solipsistic homicides, and unreasonable, downright dangerous projections onto an inevitably disappointing (and perhaps scapegoat-creating) past, present, and future.

I believe that the living individual is the subject within the object of this ancient existence. I believe that while I am a living being amongst living beings in a shared objective existence, the simplest rule for governing the moral/ethical behavior between living beings is the aforementioned Categorical Imperative. "Act only according to that maxim whereby you can, at the same time, will that it should become a universal law." In other words, we shouldn't do anything to anyone else that we wouldn't want everyone else to do to us. Like Hank Jaggar's lone rule in the Green Wave. And at the same time we should be doing the things we would want others to do.

I believe we should spend our lives finding truth. We should be creating and aggregating beauty. We should be improving ways of fulfilling human needs for the sake of the game itself—fiduciary profit being a corollary benefit at best.

America's governing philosophy used to be a schizophrenic argument between those who believed in the Platonic morality of men serving each other and those who believed in the Aristotelian morality of man serving himself. The names of the political parties representing those ideas have changed over time, but the governing philosophies remained the same, and the contrasting premises placed America's legislation on a divided foundation. As time passed, the divisions were entrenched until neither could even find it in themselves to respect the other side.

They blamed each other for the decay, and indeed they were right, for they were both to blame.

I believe that there are fewer dichotomies in life than we think. I believe it's possible to live a life for the self as well as for others. I believe there is a startling beauty in the symmetry between the greatness of who I am and the greatness of the rest of the living world; the vastness of my internal existence and the vastness of the ancient universe. Each must be remembered and respected, for without an I, a person is a slave, and without a you, a person is a monster.

I believe America's Founding Fathers built the government they built for a reason, and I believe the Baby Boomers and their ilk ruined the harmony of the three branches when they allowed the Executive and the Legislative branches to merge into one horrible office that consequently led the nation into a collapse.

And I believe all those Presidential assassinations that happened next were a reaction against the merging of the office rather than actions against the individual men and women who held the position. After all, if you put all of the ruling powers onto one person's shoulders, a full-scale revolution is always one bullet away. Much too tempting and stupid and lazy.

What Would The Baby Boomers Do? OK, Now Let's Do The Exact Opposite.

I believe American leaders and thinkers should have actually *applied* the Founding Fathers' wisdom rather than just quoted it.

Of humanity I believe only in individuals, because there are only individuals. All racial arguments are atavistic: There are no races. Political structures have dissolved: There are no governments. A bloodline is just a genetic link, and where you like to put your privates is not the sum of who you are: There are only individuals—*Homo sapiens* who fundamentally exist.

(For the record, one of the shrinks here, before I lost my patience with all their incredible nonsense, informed me that I'm not homophobic, which I always thought, but instead suffer from a particularly malevolent form of "andro-aphenphosmphobia"—fear of being touched by men. So that settles that.)

I believe Candy is alive somewhere and happyish, wise and safe—I believe I have to believe that or I'll kill myself. (*Dum vita est, spes est.*—"While there is life, there is hope.")

I believe all of these things have become clear as I've gone over this story and looked at everything that happened, and consequently I'm disturbed to find in retrospect that I've violated my beloved Categorical Imperative many times in my life. Thus I believe I've earned my sentence despite the fact that I've learned from the radical errors of my ways:

No matter how sour my heart has turned, raw violence is an inhuman answer. The Baby Boomers were lifelong philistines and users of humanity, wretched swine whose leadership enabled my guardians' murder and the complete collapse of a once-great nation, but I didn't solve anything by killing their desiccated old bodies, because the Boomers' terrible *ideas* have spread to the younger generations, and it's the ideas themselves Candy and I should have been going after, for to mark out all the wrong answers in bloody red ink is not to provide a solution: One must stand *for* something. One must *live* one's solutions. I see that now.

And anyway those wise old doomed Latin fucks already said it, knew it, and Mr. Justin lived it until he died from it: *Malo periculosam libertatem quam quietum seritium.*—"I prefer liberty with danger to peace with slavery."

In retrospect, perhaps in a different life Candy and I could have tried to end the Second Civil War not through terror and death but through the defeat of the ideas that produced the divided, irrationally selfish culture. We should have written a book first—something beautiful and transcendent and entertaining, to form a glorious positive out of all this wretched pain.

But then again, people's reading habits shrink as their narcissism, self-complacency, and mindless entertainment options grow, so who in America would have ever read it?

About The Author

Daniel Donatelli was born in Cleveland, Ohio, in 1981. He was an all-state baseball player in 2000, and he wrote the first draft of his first novel on winter break during his freshman year at Ohio University, where he made the baseball team and quit on the same day, having decided to defenestrate himself through the window of youthful athleticism and into the long fatal plummet of deep literature. He graduated from OU in 2004, moved to Los Angeles, made a bunch of money doing corporate QA garbage, and in 2010 he moved back to Ohio and co-founded H.H.B. Publishing, LLC, and released his first two novels. Mr. Donatelli is an unabashed bibliophile, and he currently lives in his thoughts.

About The Author's Other Books

Jibba And Jibba consists of two darkly humorous novellas, each featuring a lovably angst-ridden, existentially disquieted Jibba narrator. Buy it!

Music Made By Bears is a beautifully written, radical offering on the altar of philosophical/spiritual fiction. Buy it!

Oh, Title! is an oftentimes humorous, thoroughly thought-provoking collection of essays, stories, and more. Buy it!

For more information, visit www.hhbpublishing.com.

CPSIA information can be obtained at www.ICGtesting.com
Printed in the USA
LVOW06s1606260214

375274LV00001B/111/P

9 781937 648152